Relativity

e. k. Deutsch

A very special thank you and a middle finger to Covid 19.
You sequestered me in the country, removed me from my life as
playwright/director/producer in Manhattan, and gave me time and space
to find out if I could write a novel. Fifty-one chapters later,
I got my answer. I think I'm hooked.

I also want to thank my husband, Art, for his patience, humor
and encouragement, and for my indefatigable and brilliant
sister/editor, Linda Wolf. Most amazing humans.

Oracle
PUBLISHING

Oracle Publishing
Virgil, NY 13045

Publisher: Oracle Publishing

Printed in the United States of America
First Edition: February 2025

ISBN Paperback: 978-0-9895552-2-7

Library of Congress Control Number: 2024917400

Cover artwork: iStockphoto LP

Contents

Foreword

A family reunion in a country setting. A middle-aged, sheltered housewife. Her sighting of multiple UFOs that changed her life. All of this is true, including the book's epilogue, which features the actual word-by-word transcript of my appearance on a national UFO-based radio show.

The rest, an apocalyptic tale of challenges brought about by impending global collapse and destruction – well, that's fiction. At least so far.

In the dreaded "logline" every writer needs to have in their back pocket when asked, "So, what's your story about?" (also referred to as "the elevator pitch"), my answer is, "It's Scarlett O'Hara for the 21st Century. A pampered housewife finds her power during a global apocalypse."

That's pretty much it, in the proverbial nutshell.

To coax you to open to page 1, you will find love, family conflict and cohesiveness, a sexy love triangle, murder, autocrats and rebels, UFOs, civil unrest and breakdown, cannibalism, and yes, a satisfying ending pointing to the inevitable sequel.

I hope you enjoy the ride.

e. k. Deutsch
Virgil, NY
February 7, 2025

Chapter One

Meteor

Another body floated into the hot white light, and another, and another. Emma felt herself rise along with them – she reached to touch them, to hold them back, but a force much stronger than her desperate grasping held her in an iron forcefield. Below, more bodies rose, silently and inexorably, as a giant fireball exploded into the Earth, burning and crackling. Its flames rushed at supersonic speed across the landscape. She entered the light, felt it sear to her marrow and beyond, to her very soul. She became white light, suffused within and without.

Is this death? Where are Earl, and Jed? What have I become? Scream, Emma, can you scream? I'm trying, my mouth is opening, my chest is trying to inflate, my voice is caught in my throat – what will become of me?

She shook violently back and forth in the searing brightness…*what, what?*

"Honey, honey, wake up. C'mon honey, it's a dream, it's a dream." Earl gently stroked her face and rocked her back and forth as she gasped and shuddered. "Another one of your bad dreams. C'mon now, baby, are you awake?" Emma nodded slowly as she blinked into the room.

"Oh God," she whispered, eyes wide. "It was horrible. Everything was on fire, the Earth was burning, we were rising from the flames into this hot light, so many of us, and I couldn't find you. I couldn't find Jed."

"Darling, do you ever have nice dreams? I can't count how many times I've heard you scream and moan in your sleep."

"I'm sorry my dreams don't meet with your approval, sir. Since they come from the unconscious, I seriously doubt they can be legislated, even by someone as compelling as yourself."

Earl sighed. Emma was, indeed, awake.

"No, come on, I just don't like to see you suffer." He kissed her tenderly. She softened, as always, under his musky thrall.

"It was one of those dreams. Technicolor, every detail retained after regaining full consciousness. You know what that means."

"So, we're all going to burn up and fly into embers? Maybe it's your reunion. You're leaving today. You know how worked up you get before these things."

"No, if past is prologue, this dream is going to happen, but I have no idea how or when." She sighed and flopped backwards on the bed. "You don't know what it's like being this way. I've been having these since I can remember, and there's nothing I can do to hold them back."

Earl held her face. "You could just possibly be wrong, honey. Maybe you'll be at a campfire at the reunion roasting marshmallows, and you'll get too close to the flame. And maybe I married a witch."

Emma put her hands on his. "That you did. How do you think I bagged you, oh Playboy of the Western World?"

"It was those baby blues, and these," He smiled and tickled her full, round breasts. "And this." He tickled her crotch.

She screamed with laughter, jumped out of bed, opened heavy blackout shades to reveal a bright, sunny morning, and ran into the bathroom. "It's time to get up, you've got to get ready for work, and I've got to get out of here. You know I can't drive later in the day. I keep threatening to fall asleep at the wheel."

He lay back in bed and rested his head on his outstretched arms as soft tendrils of sunlight played on his body – his long, lanky body that extended the length of their king-sized bed. His dark, hooded eyes opened and closed slowly, like a sleepy cat, and Emma wanted nothing more than to jump on him. But the Family Reunion beckoned, Earl's heart condition precluded excitement, and the dream hovered. She wanted to purge it from her memory, and vainly hoped it would fade into oblivion, but she knew dreams like that could linger for days, sometimes forever.

The sacred hush of their mountain cabin beckoned her as she packed. It was so different from the incessant hum of their New Jersey suburb, where the Manhattan skyline was visible from several neighborhood vantage points – an imposing landmark during Emma's neighborhood walks in the suburban hills, sometimes colored by fog or smog, or rising in brilliant bas relief on clear days.

Whenever her car approached the George Washington Bridge and the skyline loomed into view, Emma softly whispered, "There's my girl." She had loved the brash city in all its colors and moods from the first day of her arrival in the early 1970s, fresh from Upstate New York, determined to make her mark as a journalist.

Then came September 11, 2001, when Emma and open-mouthed neighbors stood at the Highcrest Avenue skyline vantage point and gaped at smoking towers that looked like giant upright stogies, until they fell. A wiry, gravel-voiced man stepped from his white Chevy truck, stared at the smoking ruins and intoned, "Probably that Bin Laden fella."

Who the devil is that?

Shortly after 9-11, Emma and Earl bought their cabin in the tiny hamlet of Corinth in Upstate New York ski country. They called it their "Hit the Fan Hideout" in case the world teetered on the edge again, which Emma periodically warned was going to be a harsh reality sooner rather than later. Even skeptic Earl learned over the decades to take his wife's intuitions seriously. They figured terrorists wouldn't bother with their remote little hideaway tucked in the pines, and dirty bomb fallout from Manhattan couldn't possibly reach that far.

These days their purchase was bearing sad fruit, because in this summer of 2017, international news along with disturbing, prescient technicolor dreams threatened to seep into Emma's peaceful, circumscribed life.

Charismatic, crude new President Armand Cain was raising hell in Washington and beyond with his racist, isolationist America First propaganda. Protest marches burgeoned across the country, some violent, between Cain followers and anti-Fascist groups. Signs with his slogan "Strong AF" dotted local lawns like malevolent mushrooms, and Emma couldn't go anywhere without seeing his rabid followers sporting red baseball caps, emblazoned with his motto.

Emma's answer was to eschew the evening news while she prepared dinner for Earl. Her classical NYC radio station would have to do, but over time even their brief top-of-the-hour newscasts proved troubling. The national, even global unrest peeked around the edges of her life like a persistent ghost.

"It's all they talk about on Facebook anymore," she complained to Earl. "What do they expect me to do about it?" Things would settle down; she was sure of it.

They always do.

Her three-hour ride through the Catskills and beyond filled her with happiness, for even though she missed Earl, she cherished her private times on the mountain. Emma's mountain was magic, pure and simple. From the moment she stepped into the alpine air, her lungs billowed and her heart soared. Swallows swooped overhead, the nearby peak with its furrows of ski slopes was green and lush, and everywhere was blessed silence.

"I'm here...I missed you," she whispered to the quiet cabin. Everything was blessedly the same, no dark corners, no ghosts. Emma required neatness and efficiency, but always with a warm and welcoming esthetic. Tasteful prints brightened the plain white walls of the cabin, the warm brown sofa was softened by woolen afghans and quaint, colorful throw pillows, and in the center of the living space, the fireplace mantle was dotted with family photos in wrought-iron frames.

Emma made the bed with fresh sheets, unpacked her things and headed to Egan's, the small grocery store several miles away in the town of Haddonville. She sighed as she forced herself to acknowledge her delicious solo reverie had to be broken periodically over the next four days to accommodate her family's yearly summer homage to their checkered, chaotic and colorful lives together. "Probably at least 25 people this year," Emma muttered as she tossed her empty suitcase into the bedroom closet. "And most of them chatty." *I won't think about that now. Tonight is mine.*

Egan's was packed with the usual cast of characters – pale, harried mothers with pasty, strident children and screaming babies that leaned dangerously out of rickety grocery carts, dark circles under their eyes.

Bored teenagers skulked down grocery aisles holding giant bottles of soda and family-sized bags of chips.

Bronze, sun-wizened farmers and construction workers chatted quietly with each other as they looked around furtively with that odd waxen glaze in their eyes that reminded Emma of the human lumps that slept in puddles of urine outside Manhattan's Pennsylvania Station. When these suffering specters lifted their heads weakly to stare without comprehension at passersby, their eyes had the same bleached, rheumy stare. *What is that? Is it from too much suffering, too many whips and scorns, or just exposure?*

She did not feel like one of Egan's denizens; to her they were a different species. She felt even more out of place lately, since a large portion of vehicles in Egan's parking lot sported bumper stickers praising the new president, and Emma knew Subarus were considered "liberal cars." The looks she got these days seemed dark and menacing somehow, but maybe she was imagining things. Maybe.

Back at the cabin after nightfall, she unloaded her groceries from the trunk and marveled at the gibbous, glowing moon and the staggering array of stars with no ambient light from nearby towns to muffle their brightness. As she walked down the narrow, soft macadam path she heard a sizzling sound in the sky over the mountain in front of her, and looked up to see a blazing orange, red and yellow ball hurtle toward the mountain. Just before it made contact, the ball crackled gently, abruptly fizzled, then terminated into a curlicue of orange vapor just above the horizon.

Fireworks?

She waited for the boom that accompanies such pyrotechnics. Nothing, just crickets and the friendly blink of fireflies along her path. *Hmmmm.* She stopped mid-step to think.

A meteor. She had just seen a meteor. Not the kind she was used to on her forays into her suburban backyard at just the right time of night or early morning to see predicted meteor showers, those tiny white dashes in the night sky. This was a meteor with what Emma called "Kazatz." Kahonees. This blazing bruiser of molten rock demanded full attention as

5

it performed its cosmic Kamikaze ritual over the silent, hushed mountain. She smiled, and felt her body relax.

Maybe that was what I saw in my dream, amplified exponentially. A burning fireball, a feeling I can't escape, something I can't control. Good. I'll take it.

Chapter Two

Mountain Man

Her mid-morning ride from Corinth to the reunion at Spring Glen was a scenic loop-de-loop of slalom-like curving and dipping country roads and sprawling vistas of hill, mountain, valley, lake and sky. Around each new bend were fresh paint-worthy scenes of shady lemonade porches that fronted well-kept vintage farmhouses, tail-swatting clusters of black and white cows, woolly clumps of grazing sheep and the ubiquitous cornfields. Most of the stalks were the requisite "knee-high by the fourth of July" and then some, since it was mid-July.

Emma's Sunday-artist eyes drank in the scenery, and as she analyzed colors hidden in the shade of a crumbling barn or the light of passing clouds, she composed a running commentary on her internal and external world.

The descent from the wilds of Corinth along Route 44 culminated in a steep yawning slope parallel to Cutler Lake below. Hurtling down that hill never failed to catch Emma's breath – she felt at any moment her car might fly into the air as sailboats skidded along the huge blue lake's surface, and seagulls fluttered overhead. On the prosaic plains of Troyville, New York, past worn-out bars and funky shops catering to kids from the local Community College, Emma felt the town was a giant, unkempt dorm room. Cozy, if you don't mind the clutter and dirt in the corners. She almost couldn't believe she grew up in that town – it had been over 35 years since she packed up and sought her fortune in Manhattan.

Once past the infamous Troyville "Octopus," a tangled conglomeration of route intersections, flood control bridges and confusing traffic signs, Emma climbed Route 91 along Victory Street, the very street she and her sister Lynn walked over and over as children on their way to Westside Elementary School. The houses were all still the same; even the sidewalks had the same rakish tilt from winter heave and thaw and encroaching tree roots.

A gentler slope greeted Emma at the end of 91 as Lake Macanaw came into view, along with the B&Bs and wineries that dotted its perimeter. Spring Glen was at the southern mouth of the lake, and had a decidedly less collegiate feel than Troyville. Tourists, NASCAR diehards and hardscrabble down-and-outers were more its style. But the star of Spring Glen was something Emma longed for all year, something that made all the family drama and consternation worthwhile.

The Gorge Walk.

Spring Glen State Park was a tourist magnet, but managed over many decades to keep its lofty wildness and pristine beauty. As a gesture to the public, it had rustic campgrounds and a very large, clean swimming pool just inside its entrance, along with a huge, flat rectangular lawn that terminated in a massive stone multi-purpose pavilion at its far end. A short road connected Glen Rest Lodge to the upper entrance of the park, which was the main, and perhaps only, reason Lodge patrons forgave the musty, run-down rooms, abandoned tennis court full of torn cement and wild grasses, and the Lodge pool condemned by the State. Not to mention the Lodge restaurant that still considered "almondine" the height of haute cuisine. All this paled against the majesty and wonder of The Gorge Walk.

Emma sighed, pulled into the crunchy gravel of the Glen Rest parking lot, and looked for signs of her family's tenancy. She dreaded the prospect of walking the gauntlet of family hellos before she would be free and on her own in the wilds of the Glen. The bright spot was her son Jed, 23, fresh from his job promotion to Senior Copywriter in Manhattan. She saw so little of Jed these days; he had turned into a man when Emma wasn't looking. She knew his cabin number, and knocked on his door, but there was no answer. She had no choice but to head for The Party House.

She picked her way up a rocky, hilly connecting road past tiny cabins where laconic, beer-bellied men and their careworn women saved their pennies for brief respite on Adirondack chairs, the strong summer sun on their weary faces and bodies softened by the blessed shade of towering spruce trees.

Rising where the first hill leveled off, in all its dreadful prominence, appeared...The Party House – a large log cabin rented every summer by Emma's sister Carol, her husband, Joe, and their five boys. Buttressed by a ramshackle assortment of ad hoc underpinnings, including what looked like a jack on top of several cement blocks, the Party House threatened to roll off its moorings onto the lawn, and every year it remained inexplicably rooted to its spot under spreading pines. There were usually several family members perched on the large, round logs ringing the open front porch, but not now. It was empty but for mosquitoes and circling bees. Emma sighed gratefully. All she wanted was to briefly connect with Jed, then make a beeline for the Gorge Walk.

Husky male shouts issued from the top of the hill behind The Party House, and Emma smiled as she recognized Jed's distinctive "Hah!" following a loud horseshoe clang of metal against metal. As she rounded the path to the hilltop she stopped for a moment and watched Jed and his cousin Aaron, best pals since babyhood, continue their brotherly bonding and competition as young men. They looked like brothers, both broad-shouldered and muscular, with shocks of straight short brown hair and full beards. Jed was slimmer and quicker than Aaron, with lightning reflexes and a sharp, feral look that missed nothing. Aaron was careful, shy and ponderous, but nonetheless doggedly determined to win.

"Hey," said Emma softly. Jed and Aaron turned, and Jed ran to Emma with his hands held out to his sides. His palms were black with dirt from the old horseshoes, and he smiled apologetically as he hugged Emma "no-hands" style.

"Hi Mom. We invented a new horseshoe game."

Emma laughed. "I don't know the old one."

Jed smiled and replied, "Neither do we." He proceeded to breathlessly recite the rules he and Aaron concocted that involved a complicated series of points depending on what part of the post the horseshoe hit, or in what section of the pit it landed.

Emma shook her head, "As long as you understand it. Everything OK?" Jed and Aaron nodded impatiently, eager to resume the game. "I'll see you for dinner, OK honey? I'm going to walk the Gorge."

"Yep!" Jed chirped over his shoulder as he and Aaron headed for the pit. "Love you, Mom!"

"Love you too," Emma replied. Even now breaking away from Jed was hard. She loved to watch him, she never tired of it, but Jed hated being fussed over.

Relieved she hadn't encountered more family members to slow her down, Emma scurried toward the road to the park entrance. She felt like she was headed for a clandestine rendezvous, and her heart raced with excitement. A group of Amish girls played volleyball on the large flat lawn in front of the park's stone pavilion. A tour bus was parked along the side of the road, probably theirs. The girls wore the requisite "plain" dresses and bonnets, and their tanned feet were shoeless and sturdy. Emma felt momentarily uncomfortable in her yoga pants and camisole top, and marched quickly past the girls, who gave her a passing look or two.

"Heck, I still look good," she muttered under her breath. "Or maybe they're wondering why that old hag has the nerve to wear something so skimpy." Emma was 55, but could pass for a woman in her 40s with the right lighting and a full complement of sleep. As the years wore on, this became more and more difficult and time-consuming. Size 6 was her limit, and nothing over 130 pounds. She thrived on exercise, discipline and a healthy, unrefined diet, but little puffs were appearing under her eyes, puffs that didn't disappear during the day, and when she pursed her lips a series of crevices appeared.

Hell, I'm 55, I'm entitled. She stared oxidation in the face and eschewed suction, injections or the dreaded plastic surgeon's knife. She had been a babe in her prime and was blessed with an ample bosom, small waist and large, round accommodating bottom that still managed to get a rise out of gentlemen of a certain age. Her hair was still blonde with natural streaks of shiny silver and white, and her big, round eyes were bright blue. She wasn't going to go gentle into that good night, not without a good fight.

She shook out of her reverie and brightened when she saw the familiar arrowed sign, "To Gorge Trail" and scampered down a series of narrow stone steps to the first blessed landmark, a small lily pond at the beginning of the South Rim Trail, Emma's favorite. The guttural twang of bullfrogs greeted her from the pond, and she turned left to the opening of the South Rim.

Most tourists followed lower trails that flanked the swirling eddies of the rivers, falls and watering holes of the gorge, flanked by majestic cliffs dotted with precarious trees that clung for their lives to the vertical rock walls. Emma loved her path less taken that rose steeply through tall pine forests on the soft, silent trail made from decades of composted pine needles. Sunlight dappled through the trees. Emma heard the rushing water below, and knew she would run into almost no one on the path.

Heaven. She smiled broadly and started climbing, stopping here and there to marvel over an unfamiliar, exotic wildflower or listen to the sound branches made when they rubbed together in the wind. Her breath quickened as the climb intensified, she knew she had a long way to go before she reached the top of the cliff line where the trail leveled off. She was grateful for her years of biking, walking suburban hills and weight work. Her thighs and heart were strong, and although she was panting and drenched in sweat, she continued to march up the steep incline.

After a few miles the trail began to level, and Emma's pace accelerated. She wanted to go deeply into the woods where she could feel her boundaries loosen and forget where she began and the forest left off. *Thoreauville, that's where I belong.* She needed it more than breath; she had waited a long time for this special taste of freedom.

She imagined herself as her favorite daydream, Emma Kaplan...Mountain Woman. No Evian and hanky for Mountain Woman, and no carefully coifed blonde hair. Mountain Woman drinks straight from the stream thanks to forest savvy and cast-iron innards, and her long, wiry gray/white hair is full and flows in the wind as she walks, no, glides through the forest. Her bow and arrows are casually slung over her shoulder, and a thick knife is sheathed at her ankle. Mountain Woman fears nothing and no one. Emma held this dream like a beacon in front of her as she bounded down the trail to the next important landmark, the Norfolk Southern train trestle.

The trestle appeared at a sunny trail opening, and the trail continued beneath the overpass flanked by imposing No Trespassing signs on either side. Emma, Mountain Woman always assumed this meant no trespassing on the train tracks. It certainly couldn't apply to the trail, even though on the far side of the overpass the trail was barely visible underneath grasses and weeds, and trees on either side of the disappearing trail bowed toward each other like wedding procession archways. Emma pushed on, wading through tall thicket until the trail resumed ahead of her away from the sun, where grasses and weeds didn't have enough light for a toehold.

A rustling sound on Emma's right side startled her. She imagined a bear or perhaps a frightened deer, and to her shock, out of the tall grasses popped a bona fide Mountain Man. He was tall. By Emma's fevered estimation he must have been at least 7 feet tall, and painfully thin, with a long, dusty dark brown beard that ended in a point near the bottom of his ribcage. His clothing was a series of dark, torn tatters, and his waist-length thick brown hair was matted and tangled. His eyes were pale, almost white, *those homeless eyes again*, Emma thought frantically, but they weren't dull and torpid, they were flared and terrified, like a trapped animal.

This wild, startled Mountain Man stood motionless in front of Emma for a few seconds, mumbled unintelligibly, then darted past her, deeper into the thicket beyond the trestle. When she looked desperately around to track his path, he seemed to have vanished - all she could hear was faint rustling in the woods.

She ran briefly back toward the trestle, stopped, looked furtively behind her and mumbled, "Emma, you schmuck. Don't turn your back on him for God's sake." She imagined this tall, scrawny, probably horribly smelly Mountain Man jumping on her and having his twisted Mountain Man way with her, his muddy Rasta-hair bobbing stiffly as he ignored Emma's screams. She burst through the underbrush, scrambled under the trestle, eyes wide, and ignored the welts rising on her arms from sharp branches.

Emma, Mountain Woman was rapidly morphing into Emma, Warrior Maiden with a generous dollop of Emma, I Almost Peed My Pants. She walked quickly and defensively, as she glanced periodically behind her for signs of approaching danger. As she walked, she shouted, "I hope you're

12

not too attached to your balls, because if you come near me, you're going to be in a world of pain!" All that answered her brazen declaration were the sounds of birds, locusts and the wind.

Emma raced along the rest of the trail until she ran into a timorous-looking couple with two leashed rescue greyhounds. She resisted the impulse to talk to them or ask if they saw a tall, skinny, crazy guy on the path. All she wanted now was to get back to her family members, who were looking better by the minute.

Chapter Three

The Famn Damily Dinner

The Dinner, an ironclad tradition of the Shaw family, was winding down, and it was picture time. Every year Bonnie and Richard Shaw footed the tab for their ever-growing clan, every year Bonnie enlisted the one overburdened waitress assigned to the room to take a group picture, and every year the family had to squeeze together just a little tighter to fit into the shot, courtesy of active spousal loins and new significant others.

Magically, Richard, Bonnie and their progeny always managed to be smack in the middle of the picture, their various satellites instinctively knew where they belonged in the family solar system. Emma felt Jed's arm around her shoulder as they posed twice, "just in case," and she cherished the rarity of this show of affection. Jed was quick to say, "I love you," after each phone call or visit, but to feel him close was rare and precious.

After the picture Richard struggled to his feet and grabbed the handles of his "horse," a walker with a built-in seat that went everywhere with him. As he began to maneuver slowly and painfully toward the party room exit door Bonnie whispered to Emma, "He's tired," and many members of the party watched him inch doggedly forward. He looked straight ahead, and may as well have been alone in the room, so deeply entombed was he in his own private world of pain, frustration and regret.

Several family members chirped, "Thank you for dinner, Grandpa," "Love you," and "Sleep tight." Richard raised one hand in a brief staccato salute without breaking gaze, and disappeared through the doorway as Bonnie and Emma exchanged knowing looks.

Bonnie said softly, "He's not doing very well."

Emma replied briskly. "He's 82, Ma. He's entitled."

"Well, so am I," Bonnie puffed proudly. Her round, soft, almost lineless face and short, plump, sturdy body gave no clue to her octogenarian status, her pale blue eyes still bright and full of interest.

"You'll live forever, Mom. I'm convinced." Emma replied, Bonnie smiled and shook her head, then grew pensive when the waitress presented her with the check.

"Here we go." she whispered, and put on her glasses to look at the bill. Emma looked over her shoulder and was shocked at the tab, $718.00, until she tried to divide it by 25, and figured with drinks it wasn't that bad.

The group slowly disbanded, but not before Emma related her Mountain Man story to sisters Lynn and Carol and Carol's husband Joe. Carol and Joe had been living off the grid for years, and Emma silently reminded herself not to denigrate the Mountain Man's long matted beard and likely lack of teeth, since Joe's teeth were long gone, he often forgot to put in his dentures, and his long, fuzzy red-brown beard put ZZ Top to shame.

Carol's body was riddled with rheumatoid arthritis, and she inched painfully in and out of car seats and chairs, letting out a huge sigh when she settled onto her next perch, then held court with smiles, jokes and stories.

Joe chuckled as Emma related her tale, and said, "You shouldn't be out alone. You're going to get killed, you know."

Emma bristled. "Why? Why should that be? What is this, Iran? Should I wear a freaking burka, hide in my house and be afraid to inflame men's loins?"

Joe grinned knowingly and said gently, "It's the way it is, Emma, you can't change it."

"Watch me. I'm thinking about self-defense classes and learning to shoot. I refuse to be intimidated by *men*. Even if our current president is a sexist pussy-grabbing creep." Joe shook his head and closed his mouth.

"OK Joe, Emma..." Carol sighed as she stood slowly, assisted by her cane. "Time to say goodnight." Lynn helped Carol out of the restaurant as Joe followed.

Emma plopped wearily onto the front seat of the Subaru, turned on the ignition and looked bleakly at the digital clock above the dashboard. 9:31. She slowly navigated the crackling gravel driveway in the dark, around RVs and souped-up Chevys and past the noisy restaurant with its bar going full tilt. The moon was a sliver away from full, the sky was clear and full of stars, and Emma was finally *alone*.

Chapter Four

Strange Lights, Strange Night

As Emma turned from a lakeside road onto Route 79, she felt light and clean, and immersed herself in the comforting darkness as warm summer night air wafted through her slightly open car windows. Thankfully she knew the way – she often got lost in the dark as her mind hummed and whirred. Without landmarks she was a hyperactive mole tunneling in the darkness. At the top of a long ascent where Route 91 commenced to the right and Route 79 continued straight ahead, she noticed a large light low in the sky. It was glowing in shades of gold, yellow, and yellow white, and looked oddly like a giant golden disco ball.

I wonder if there's a playing field there. Or maybe it's one of those lights on power lines to keep planes away, but it's so big....what the heck is that?

Her curiosity and need for answers eclipsed any other considerations, and she decided to remain straight ahead on Route 79. She was drawn in an almost trancelike state to the strange object. She pulled off the road at the closest open vantage point and got out, but left the engine running.

There it was, suspended, totally silent and totally still.

She stared, transfixed and disbelieving, as the ball glowed benignly. It seemed about 3 telephone pole lengths high in the air, maybe 50 feet away and appeared to be around five feet in circumference or larger. There were no strings or supports of any kind keeping it there, and it hovered unwaveringly. A minute passed, maybe more, as Emma stood in awe and the orb remained benignly stationary. The glowing light began to pulse as the ball glided gently and soundlessly to the right toward Route 91. It picked up speed, and as it accelerated its pulsing quickened.

Emma shook herself out of her shocked reverie and exclaimed, "Jesus Christ, Jesus Christ, UFO, fucking UFO!!" She jumped excitedly into the car and turned around so quickly her tires screeched, and gravel and clouds of dust flew into the air as she barreled onto Route 91. She continued to exclaim loudly as she fumbled for her cell phone, feverishly followed the speeding ball down the dark country road, and frantically dialed Jed's number. No answer, just a phone message. She searched hysterically for Lynn's speed dial and pushed the link. Lynn answered cheerily and Emma shrieked, "UFO!! UFO!!! Get Jed! GET JED!!!"

"What???" screamed Lynn. "Where are you? What's going on?"

"Is Jed there?" screamed Emma. "GET JED!!" Emma could hear Lynn yelling urgently for Jed in the background and heard other voices join in excitedly.

Jed got onto the phone and breathlessly asked, "Mom? Are you serious? Where are you? Is it coming for you?"

"No, I'm following it, I'm on Route 91."

"Where on 91? Mom? Where?"

"I don't know for God's sake..." Emma's voice trailed off as she saw the ball ascend rapidly into the sky and join two other balls of light. She stopped her car and got out, still holding the phone.

She could hear Jed yelling, "Mom! Mom! What's going on?" but she couldn't speak.

In the distance she saw four more balls form strange elliptical patterns in the sky, like stars gone mad, and along the horizon line in front of her, a large low-flying ball hurtled toward her. "Eight UFO's, for God's sake, EIGHT fucking UFO's, I can't believe it. Oh, it's coming right at me, I've got to go!" Emma yelled into the phone as she jumped back in the car and sped down the road. "Crap! I hope they don't take me on board. I don't want any fucking PROBES for God's sake." Her heart was pounding, her forehead was sweaty, and she felt lightheaded. This was no dream, no fantasy.

Emma Kaplan, UFO Woman. Holy shit.

"Mom! Mom...listen to me, where are you?"

"I don't know, I can't read the road signs, I don't have my glasses on...just a min...oh shit!" Emma swerved as a deer loomed in the road ahead of her and gazed in mild surprise at her racing car before it jumped into the brush at the side of the road.

"Christ, I just missed a fucking deer. This is NUTS!" Emma squinted as she tried to see the name of an upcoming street sign. A station wagon screeched rapidly out of a driveway several yards ahead, then screeched back in just as quickly. Emma wondered if they were seeing the same thing and didn't know which end was up either. It seemed the entire countryside had gone insane.

She slowed slightly and squinted to read the sign as she tried to keep tabs on the meandering orbs, "Rachel Carson Way, it says Rachel Carson Way!" she screamed. "But I'm not staying here."

"Mom, we're in the car, we're coming to meet you," Jed yelled.

"You are? Well, that's nice, but I'm not waiting for you, I'm following them. It looks like they're headed toward Troyville. Look up, where are you? Do you see them?" She could hear loud baritone shouts. "Who's in the car with you?"

"Doug and Chris and Aunt Lynn," Jed replied huskily. "Mom, we see them. Holy shit. Ho-ly shit."

"You do?" Emma was elated. "They're something, aren't they?" Amid all this craziness, Emma was grateful to be sharing this mind-blowing experience with her son.

The phone transmission was breaking up, and Emma shouted urgently, "I'm losing your signal, I'm going into Troyville. I'll call you when I stop somewhere we can meet." She did her best to drive in a straight line down the dark road as she followed the lights that seemed for all the world like fireflies playing with each other among the stars. *This is crazy*, Emma thought, and she could feel her perceptions of her world and its boundaries expand, brighten, and grow crystal clear as she watched the dancing orbs.

She began to lose sight of the objects as the approaching ambient lights of Troyville impeded her view of the firmament, and she pulled off Route 44 into the parking lot of the Troyville High School playing field. So many years ago, Emma used to sneak into a nearby lot during history or math class and get high with her boyfriend Skipper Lewis. Sometimes they walked to the nearby falls and made out under a tree, and here she was, looking for UFOs and feeling so...different all of a sudden, like she had awakened from a long, foggy dream.

19

Her phone rang. It was Jed, and she gave him her coordinates. While she waited for her sister and the boys she left her car lights on and leaned against the car so she could crane her neck and see the sky without getting a cramp. Her neck was beginning to mutiny after over an hour starting at the sky. She saw the lights very high among the stars, almost disappearing out of sight, and below them she saw two parallel lights in gold and red tones blink very quickly and race across the sky.

She smiled without knowing why, almost like she was watching old friends. Two runners puffed by, and she pointed skyward, gestured for them to look, but they stared at her blankly and kept running.

Jed and the group approached in Lynn's van, pulled quickly into the parking lot next to the Subaru and screeched to a stop. The boys piled out of the van and exclaimed over each other, "Holy crap, it's amazing...where are they...do you see them...man oh man I can't believe it…" They all looked heavenward and grew silent. Nothing. Occasionally they thought they saw something, but it always turned out to be a plane with its signature red, white and blue blinking lights. Lynn was weary and cold, her small-boned little body wrapped in a fleece blanket with fringed edges. She wandered away from the group and peered upward. Emma thought she looked like a tiny homeless woman.

"Tell me what you saw," said Emma urgently.

Doug replied, "We saw three lights going around each other, irregular, you know. They looked like stars."

"I know," said Emma. "You didn't see any others?"

Doug shook his head. "No. Only three."

Chris nodded, "I saw the same thing. I know they weren't planes; I don't know what they were." Jed was quiet.

Doug looked at him and said, "Jed saw a ship."

"What?" exclaimed Emma.

Jed was pensive, and said slowly, "I was looking through the moonroof of the van, and I saw three lights against a giant dark triangular thing in the sky. It was huge. It blocked out the stars." Jed looked thoughtful, and a little frightened. Everyone was silent as they tried to process the information. A ship. What the hell. A giant ship?

Lynn yawned and said wearily, "I've got to go back. I think we're done. You OK, honey?" she hugged Emma warmly. "Why don't you come back with us? I don't think you should be alone tonight after all this."

"Are you kidding?" exclaimed Emma. "I'm fine!"

"You sounded so scared on the phone," Lynn replied solicitously.

Emma laughed. "Scared? No way! I was excited! I'm thrilled! I saw eight freaking UFOs tonight! I just hope I can sleep." She smiled beatifically.

Lynn watched her fondly and shook her head. "Fearless. Tarzana on the vine, that's my sister. Better you than me."

Emma kissed Lynn's cheek with great affection and replied, "That remains to be seen."

Lynn smiled weakly, "All I know is I'm going to try and forget all about this as soon as I can. I've got enough to worry about without alien invasions."

Emma sobered. "That's true, you do...sleep tight." Lynn was newly widowed, finding her sea legs in a solo world where, in addition to intense mourning, all responsibilities and worries fell on her.

Doug stood with his back plastered against the van, looking upward, as Chris opened the front passenger door for Lynn and she climbed in wearily, gently shut the door and waved weakly at Emma. Jed hugged Emma and said, "It's no big deal, really. People see these things all the time. Night Mom, see you tomorrow, love you."

Emma mumbled distractedly, "Love you too," watched Jed climb into the side door and stood silently in the parking lot as her sister and the boys drove away. *No big deal?* she thought. *No big deal? Well, it's a big deal to me.* The eight objects in the sky had opened a giant can of cosmic worms in Emma's life, and she was about to go fishing.

Chapter Five

Questions

When she arrived at the cabin, Emma knew it was late, but she had to call Earl. Earl usually tottered off to bed at 9:30, read mystery novels until after 10, and slept deeply until morning. It was 11:30, and Earl answered the phone in a clear, accusatory tone. "So, *there* you are."

Emma sighed impatiently and replied urgently, "I don't want to discuss your conjugal paranoia right now, clearly projection on your part, but that's for another time. Honey, you won't believe what happened to me tonight."

"Whatever it was, you weren't answering your phone."

"I couldn't answer my phone, I was in the middle of freaking nowhere being dive-bombed by UFOs! And you know I can't get service when I'm in the boonies. I barely get service from Spring Glen."

Earl's voice softened a little. "Honey, what are you talking about? UFOs? Little green men? Did they ask you for a date?" Earl. Jokes. Absolutely everything.

"Yes," Emma replied with a stifled giggle. "They want to have my babies, listen, I really truly saw eight UFOs tonight on the way back from the dinner, one of them up really close. I'm so psyched, freaked out and...I don't know what all at once. And Jed, Chris, Doug and Lynn saw them too. Well, three of them. Oh honey, I wish you were here. I don't want to sleep, I'm running on pure adrenaline, I can't believe it."

"Are you sure they were UFOs?" He asked with a yawn. "Maybe they were...you know, whaddyacallems, weather balloons." His voice trailed off sleepily. He was used to Emma's hyperbole, and now that he knew she wasn't bedding down a yahoo, he wanted to go to sleep. After 18 years of marriage Emma knew any further conversation would likely end in a hearty snore.

"I'll tell you all about it when I see you tomorrow, now go to sleep, honey bunny. Can't wait to give you a big kiss. Nighty night." She made loud smooching noises into the phone.

"Nightie," Earl smooched weakly back.

"Sleep well honey. Tell your girlfriends to vamoose before I get there." No response. She set the wireless back in its cradle, went to the picture window in the living room and looked at the moon.

I'm so lucky she thought. *A loving albeit way too charming husband, great house, country retreat, successful son and...eight UFOs.* She never felt closer to the Universe than she did at that moment.

"Weather balloons indeed," she sniffed.

The next morning Emma bade a tactile farewell to her mountain aerie and reprised her ride to Spring Glen to put yet another Reunion in the rearview, and to pick up Jed, who was probably as done with Reunion culture as she was.

She reveled in these long car trips back to civilization with her son, even though he spent the first few hours blasting music from his iPod to educate his mother on the latest musical trends – a regular routine since Middle School. Eventually he softened his independent stance enough to share confidences and fill Emma in on the latest family dirt from the younger generation.

She did her best to be receptive and not offer advice, a hard lesson almost learned since she liked to push the envelope, but Jed would have none of it. He revealed his inner life when he was ready, and not before, and woe to anyone who questioned a Jed Campbell opinion, rather, a Jed Campbell fact.

Jed's father Owen, Emma's first husband, was a painfully handsome, hard-edged man who sequestered his soft, sensitive core inside a defensive perimeter worthy of a war-hardened Medieval castle, and Jed followed suit. Emma was never sure if nature, nurture or both were involved, but there it was.

Jed was beautiful, with dark-fringed green eyes, heroic dark brows, straight light brown hair, an aquiline nose, full lips, straight white teeth and the Campbell bone structure that made even street-smart Manhattan girls giggle self-consciously.

Emma often imagined the Jed of the Future, softened by the inevitable whips and scorns of time. Maybe he'd finally released his internal drawbridge across his crocodile-infested Moat of Infinite Protection, at least on weekends or with a highly trustworthy consort.

His smile was genuine, and his eyes sparkled as they did when he was too young to know what waited for him outside his mother's smiles and welcoming arms. Maybe that Lamborghini engine inside of him, that skittish, high-strung nostril-flaring racehorse had settled and mellowed into a deep, rich hum, a joyful OM of peace and contented industry. Mothers always hope. Mothers with active imaginations hope in Technicolor.

She steered the Subaru off the gravel road onto a small hill next to Jed's tiny cabin, stepped onto the handkerchief-sized deck and knocked on the door. No answer. She picked her way down the uneven roadway, still muddy and rippled with gullies from recent downpours, until she reached the ramshackle Party House. The worn screen door percussed softly when closed, too tired to slam, and Emma blinked at the quiet darkness inside the cabin.

"Hi, Aunt Emma," droned a husky, exhausted voice. Emma could just make out her nephew Timmy "Bruiser" Morrisey's prone body on the couch.

"Hey man, what's up? Hung over?"

"Nah," replied Bruiser with a smile, instantly cheery. "I'm not used to food like that. At home I eat raw pretty much."

"Raw......meat?" Emma asked slyly.

Bruiser sat up slowly and chuckled. "Yeah, you know us hicks from the sticks. Raw squirrel, 'possum, you name it. No...I'm eating salads, fruit, you know. The good stuff."

Emma's heart softened, and she replied gently, "That's great, honey, it really is. I'm proud of you." Bruiser beamed. "Seen Jed?" she asked.

"Yeah, he and Aaron are playing tennis." He pointed to the hill behind the cabin.

"Thanks," Emma responded as she headed for the screen door.

"Pretty cool about the UFOs," Bruiser remarked. "We see a lot of them around the trailer." Emma stopped in her tracks, incredulous.

"Really?"

Bruiser answered casually, "Oh sure. A lot of people see them around here. It's because of the lake."

"What, they like to go fishing?" Emma quipped nervously.

"No," Bruiser smiled knowingly, "Lake Macanaw is one of the deepest lakes around, so they probably have a base at the bottom or something. People see them go in and out of the water all the time."

She sat openmouthed on a ratty wicker chair next to the door. "Are you serious? Has it been on the news? Why haven't I heard about this?"

"Ask the government. Newspapers and cops aren't allowed to talk about it. They call folks who see them crackpots, or say UFOs are weather balloons. It's like this all over the world."

Emma was galvanized. "Well, I'm going to talk about it, to anyone who'll listen." Bruiser scuffed to Emma and patted her shoulder.

"Good luck with that, Aunt Emma." He ambled to the kitchen, took a ripe banana from the top of a mountain of fruit on the crowded sideboard, peeled it and ate thoughtfully. "Let me know what happens."

Emma stood resolutely, "Oh, I will, you can count on that." Bruiser smiled and nodded. She could imagine what he was thinking – Aunt Emma on the warpath, this should be fun.

Emma strode up the hill to the broken-down cement wasteland that once passed as a tennis court at Glen Rest. Aaron and Jed were still at it, this time they'd concocted a convoluted tennis game predicated on avoiding the cement stalagmites on the grassy, dirty abandoned court.

"Hi Mom!" Jed said brightly, in between lightning jabs and expletives.

"Hi honey…. ready to go any time soon? You know I can't drive too late in the day, I fall asleep." Jed stopped and regarded Emma with thinly veiled perplexity.

"Mom. I'm going to be with you. I can drive. Why don't you walk the gorge again or something."

It was Emma's turn for the Evil Eye. "Because…it's time to go. You have work tomorrow and I'd like to get home before midnight, since I'm driving you all the way to Brooklyn then back to Jersey. Unless you'd like to take another plane back home." Emma knew, with Jed, practicality wins.

Jed's shoulders slumped. "OK, but we need to finish this game."

"Fine, I'll be making the rounds – don't be long, please," and Emma picked her way down the steep hill and set her shoulders for the long goodbyes.

After the requisite hugs, kisses and final group picture were accomplished, Jed and Emma were on the road. Emma steered down the steep, rocky driveway past the Party House amid a loud, smiling chorus of "Bye!!!" and enthusiastically waving arms from the relative-choked porch. Emma smiled and chuckled.

"What?" asked Jed with a smile.

"I wonder if they'll wave when one of us is lowered into the ground." Jed grinned as he plugged his iPod into the car's sound system.

After two hours of Indie music instruction from Jed and promises from Emma to download the Fragrant Sewer Rats, or whatever their name was, the conversation turned to UFOs. "Jed, I think I should call the local police and the newspaper, and report this."

Jed shook his head, "You can try. I bet they won't do anything."

"Why? Isn't this news? Don't they care what's going on in their own front yard?" Emma exclaimed.

"Mom, Aaron says they reported what they saw around the trailer to the cops and the papers, and nothing happened. But you know the Morrisseys – they believe 9/11 was a government conspiracy, Jesus is coming back in a flaming chariot, and all that. Who's going to believe them?"

"Exactly my point," Emma replied emphatically. "Maybe they'll take me seriously."

"Maybe," Jed replied without conviction, then smiled. "But it was pretty great anyway. Something to tell your grandchildren."

"Remember to give me some when you get around to it," Emma countered.

As plaintive music from the Plutonian Buttwads oozed from the Subaru's aged speakers, Emma planned her campaign.

Chapter Six

Talking to a Wall

Back home, Emma had phone calls to make. Important UFO phone calls. She was sure Spring Glen authorities would be interested in her experience. Her first call; the Spring Glen Police Department.

"Dispatch," said a toneless, robotic voice.

"Hi. My name is Emma Kaplan, um, two days ago I was on Route 79 in Rutland outside Spring Glen, and well, I saw something strange in the sky. A round orange orb, a UFO. I'd like to report it…."

The voice broke in dully, "We don't handle reports like that. You can try the local paper." Click.

This stunning lack of interest shocked Emma, and she resolutely dialed the Spring Glen Gazette, certain they'd jump on her story and want every detail.

"Editorial," said a slightly more animated voice.

"Hi. This is Emma Kaplan, I was in Spring Glen a few nights ago and saw what I'm sure was a UFO in Rutland on Route 79…"

"I'm sorry, Ms. Kaplan, we don't handle this subject, but you can go online and report it to the UFO community."

Emma sputtered, "But…I've heard there have been many sightings around the lake; why isn't this news? I'm a journalist, and if multiple reports come in about unusual phenomena, it's worth investigating, isn't it?"

There was a pause on the end of the phone. "Not to us, I'm sorry. Good luck to you. Have a good day." Click.

Boy oh boy. Emma sat back in her office chair, dumbfounded. She googled 'UFO orb sightings,' and was flabbergasted to find thousands of reports from across the world, including videos of yellow, orange and red orbs just like hers. Were they ever on the evening news? No. In the paper? No.

Emma was officially on the hunt.

She found the National UFO Reporting Center and filled out their online reporting form, which joined hundreds of other sightings reported in just the last few months

She knew what she saw. She knew it was real.

She called Lynn to commiserate, and was surprised to find Lynn had been googling orb sightings too, and shared Emma's frustrations. "They're everywhere, you know?" Lynn exclaimed. "I can't believe no one's interested." Lynn confided that her son Chris and his wife stood underneath a hovering UFO a few years ago in Illinois until it sped away after a few minutes without a sound. The two shrugged their shoulders, got back in their car, went home and didn't give it much more thought.

"What?" Emma exclaimed. "You're kidding!"

"Nope. They figure it's part of the landscape, and they know better than to make a big deal out of it. People who do get mocked. A lot. Better to let it go, Emma."

"Looks like I have no choice," Emma replied glumly.

While Emma picked peas in the garden she periodically glanced up at the gray-blue overcast sky, half hoping to see a shiny disk, an orb, anything. When she took out the garbage at dusk, she stood at the bottom of the driveway, scanned the sky again, and felt it taunt her.

"I know you're there, you little fuckers," she accused the riotous sunset. "Show yourselves." Her sighting had changed her, not only because of its otherworldliness, but also because it felt, in some strange way, normal. Right. She shared an odd connection with the glowing ball – it communed with her, and she wanted more. She yearned like a wolf howling at the moon, hoping to draw it down to her, to walk on it and finally, finally connect with something greater than herself and her comings and goings, chores and routines.

I'm not going to give up. I'm going to keep telling my story to anyone who will listen.

Chapter Seven

Through the Looking Glass

"Spit," Charlene said from behind her white medical mask, her bright blue eyes crinkled in a smile as she raised Emma's chair up and pushed the overhead lamp out of the way. Emma drank diluted mouthwash from a tiny paper cup and spit dutifully into the sink as running water spiraled around its edge. She frowned ruefully as bits of blood mingled with the blue mixture and swirled down the drain. "Not to worry," Charlene assured her. "I was in there pretty hard."

Emma held her jaw as if she had been punched and quipped, "Yeah, you got me all right."

Charlene whispered, "I know someone you need to talk to." She looked around furtively, nodded when she was assured Emma's dentist, Dr. Pullman, was out of earshot, and pulled her chair even closer to Emma. Her eyes above her mask were full of worry. "You know, about your flying thingies."

Emma had been coming to Dr. Pullman for decades, and she and Char often huddled in between tooth scrapings and rotating brush heads loaded with minty pumice-laden dentifrice. Over time they became fast dental chair confidantes with built-in 6-month updates.

In the early years it was the usual talk about husbands, children, dieting – Char's nemesis – and morphed over the years into Char's whispered warnings about the coming Apocalypse. She had a truck ready to go, loaded with supplies, and was at the ready to gather her mother and daughter and hightail it to their cabin deep in the Adirondack Mountains.

Emma had good-naturedly humored Char, and accepted her fringy beliefs as the imaginings of someone who watched too much of what she now called "Government TV." USA News, the media mouthpiece of the blustery new "president," promulgated his wild conspiracy theories about a Deep Dark State high up in the Intelligence Community that was out to get him and other True Believers.

Emma believed that in time his followers would grow weary of his circus barker bloviating, and return to their slow underground simmer of resentment at being The Forgotten White People in an ever-browning nation. Emma wanted to think about him and his burgeoning cult as little as possible. He set her teeth on edge, and his rabid followers made her uneasy.

But now, Emma felt a deeper sense of kinship with Char, and a grudging acceptance that maybe, just maybe she and her right-wing consorts might be onto something.

"Who should I talk to?" Emma whispered. "A UFO expert?"

Charlene removed her mask and brought her face close to Emma's. "No. A psychic. She's the one who told me about the coming changes. Emma, she's been right so far about everything. She knew about my mother's diabetes, and my daughter's boyfriend. I never told her anything. She says something awful and deadly is coming, and we need to be ready to go in a jiffy. She can probably tell you what those orb things are, and what they want."

"What's her name?" Emma asked grimly, as her fireball dream reached around the edges of the bright, sterile room.

"Lily Fortas," Char whispered, looking around furtively. "Here, I'll give you her email." She opened a nearby cabinet, took out her pocketbook and fished around in her wallet. "Oh, I've got her card. You can have it – I have her on speed dial."

Emma looked at the card and blurted, "Ocala, Florida? I'm not planning to go to Florida anytime soon."

"Oh, she does phone readings all the time," said Char. "She's really amazing, you should try her."

Emma pocketed the card. "Thanks. I will."

Char giggled, "You lead a very interesting life."

True. And getting more interesting by the day.

That night Emma engaged in what she called "reality testing" about her sighting and the events of the last few days as she turned Lily Fortas's card over and over in her hand. *Maybe it was a Japanese lantern, maybe a bunch of people released them, and that's what I saw floating in the sky. Maybe.*

She shook her head. *Yeah, sure. A pulsing, strobing Japanese lantern that traveled faster than my car and rose into the sky in the blink of an eye. Sure. Turbo Asian lantern on meth.*

"I saw them. They were real," she whispered to the walls. And now everything felt so small in comparison, and so strange. *But this Fortas dame. Is she for real?*

After several emails and texts pinning down Lily and Emma's respective schedules, a time was set for a Skype session in between Lily's Krav Maga class and Emma's dinner prep.

"She seems like a real ditz," Emma recounted to a bemused Earl over breakfast the next morning. "I didn't need all those texts about her Shih Tzu's diabetes, her meth-addicted son Cal who came to Jesus and lives in the wilds of Upstate New York, or her neighbor's illegal piñata business. There aren't professional standards for psychics, and she damn well made sure she got her PayPal payment in advance. What a racket. This better be good." Earl nodded good-naturedly as he bent over his scrambled eggs and toast. Char was looking more and more like a chump to Emma by the minute.

That afternoon Emma signed onto Skype and fiddled with the light over her monitor. "I don't really look like that, do I?" she fretted, as she saw an old, double-chinned woman looking desultorily back at her. "It's got to be the lighting." A few adjustments and she looked suitably middle-aged and glowing. "O.K. Four o'clock, time to make the call."

She squinted at Lily's number on her card, since she was too vain to wear her glasses for this encounter.

Lily picked up on the third ring, but the screen was black. "Emma, is that you?" she queried in a high-pitched, quavering voice.

"I can't see you," Emma replied, talking too loudly, as if maybe the camera would work if she yelled at it.

"Oh, dear. This happens to me all the time….just a minute," and a series of scratching, rumbling sounds came over the monitor. "Sometimes if I jiggle it….," a loud percussion, then, voila, Lily Fortas in all her psychic glory came into view.

"Wow," Emma said. "I guess hitting cranky machinery still works." Lily was silent. *Oh great, no sense of humor. This could be brutal.*

Lily was a lanky, pale, careworn older woman with high cheekbones and long, wavy bottle brown hair with gray roots. Her eyes were heavy-lidded and sunken. She was dressed in a flowing white tunic, her neck was ringed by an imposing turquoise choker, and large flowering tropical plants surrounded her. She looked appraisingly at Emma for several seconds, then slowly intoned, "You need to be ready. You're not ready."

"O…K… um… Ready for what?"

"For the changes. They're coming, and you need to be ready. You are going to go on a long, difficult journey – you, and your family. You must know how to survive the changes. You have been avoiding dealing with something you know in your heart to be true."

Wow. So much for small talk. I guess since I already paid her she isn't going to charge me by the minute like those online psychic scammers. "What kind of changes are we talking about? I mean, Char told me you said she needed to be ready to get out of town in a big hurry. Because of these changes?"

Lily closed her eyes and began to sway sideways, and a faint hum issued from her closed lips. "I'm going into my room, my special place, down the stairs, one, two, three, four, five, six, seven, eight, nine, ten, eleven, twelve….all will be revealed to me in this place…" She began to breathe heavily and put her hands on her sternum. "Oh, oh" she moaned. "Oh no….."

"Um. May I speak? Ask you questions?"

Lily held out an outstretched palm to quiet her. She continued intoning, "The ethers, the ethers are a Universal Ocean of information, of vibration, I swim in the ethers, I pull pictures, sounds, smells, truths, the future and the past from the ethers." Lily's eyes startled open and Emma jumped in her seat.

"What do you see?"

"What did *you* see?" Lily replied. "You saw something very unusual, you saw the Sky Scouts. They changed everything for you. They've been watching you from the beginning."

This was getting way too real for Emma. She didn't tell Lily anything about her sightings in the emails, she just said she wanted a reading and was a friend of Char's. *Char must have told her. She must have.*

"No, she didn't," replied Lily coolly, and she regarded Emma calmly.

Emma's jaw dropped open and her eyes widened. *Damn, she's better at this than I am.*

Lily continued, "In my room, I see and hear all. I am a Sky Woman, they are in me. They have been part of humanity for thousands of years, and we are their sacred experiment. I can hear your thoughts." Emma never felt so naked, so exposed in her life, and her heart was pounding. "You are afraid," Lily said gently. "You should be. You are going to be challenged in ways you never dreamed. I see change, death and transformation all around you."

Emma felt dizzy, and colorful streamers flowed back and forth before her eyes. "I think I'm going to faint," she said weakly.

Lily spoke firmly, "No. No, you will not. You are going to join me in the ethers. I am going to show you what is coming. Close your eyes. Have trust in me. Fate has brought you here for a reason. Close your eyes, and breathe deeply. I will send you the images."

Emma felt herself swirl downward, spiraling into a dark space in which her body floated.

Lily's voice echoed inside her head, "You are in a safe, timeless place, here with me in the ethers. The images are coming...." The space became filled with bright light. Even behind Emma's closed eyes the light was blinding, and her body was overwhelmed with heat.

"What is this? Is it God?" Emma whispered.

"No," said Lily quietly. "It is the source of Life, and of Death. It has given, and soon it will begin to take away. Life as we have known it will disappear, and in its place only the strong, brave and well-prepared will survive. You will be one of these, if you begin now. The Sky Scouts were there to warn you, and others."

"Sky Scouts…you mean the orbs?"

"Yes, you have been with them twice before this."

"No. I only saw that other vehicle, the huge one, in the '80s. There was no other time."

Lily's voice grew tender. "Yes, the night on Long Island. You were pregnant, and the neighborhood was full of what you remember as firecrackers and bright, bright lights. You do remember that."

"Yes," Emma said slowly. "Yes, but…"

Lily interrupted gently, "What is your next memory? The next day?"

Emma recounted, "I was bleeding, I went to the hospital in Southampton, they did a sonogram but there was no baby. They thought it was in my tubes, they used a scope through my navel. But there was nothing there."

Lily said slowly, "It will surprise you to know that you never went to the hospital. This is an implanted memory. They took you that night, they removed the child from you, it is a hybrid. You are a hybrid. Your bloodline has been implanted with DNA from the Sky People. Remember during your pregnancy with your son, when you left your body? That was not a dream."

Emma was reeling. "It seemed so real, but, no, no…too fantastic," she recalled dreamily. "I woke up suddenly in the middle of the night, I was hovering over two sleeping people, and I realized it was Owen and me. Then I took off, very fast, over an ocean as the sun was setting. A golden ball of light was next to me, it talked to me. Oh my god, the ball of light, it looked just like…," Emma grew silent, stunned.

Lily said gently, "Just like your recent orb experience. It said, 'You worry too much. No need to worry. You're going to have an Angel baby.' And you had to get back, back to the growing baby in your womb, the precious Sky Baby. It was not pleasant coming back into the body, was it?"

"No," Emma recalled. "When I was out, there was this amazing music, a chorus of voices so beautiful, more beautiful than anything down here. After I smashed into my body I heard the tiniest little bit of that music, like someone trying to tell me it was real. But, how can you possibly know all this?"

35

Lily began to hum, and said in a singsong, "Past, Present and Future, all happenings live in the ethers. They surround all in a membrane. I have learned to dial into the frequencies of people, of places and civilizations. I am going to give you something for your journey, advice for the road you are about to take. Learn all you can about living life without water coming from the tap, without grocery stores, or electric lights, or cars."

Lily took a slow breath and continued, "Read all you can, do not listen to naysayers. You are not mad, I am not mad. We are Hybrid Sky People, there are many like us, beacons into the future of a planet hanging in the balance. You have felt different all your life, you are one of us, and we are the future of the Earth World. What mankind does from this moment forth will determine its continued existence, or its extinction. You must be ready."

Emma knew Lily was right. In addition to her prescient dreams, from early childhood she knew what people were thinking, and who was going to call her on the phone a few seconds before the phone rang. She knew The Orange Menace was going to win the election, even as those around her scoffed at the idea, but she had a lasting vision of him taking the Oath of Office the February before he was elected.

She protected herself by keeping these gifts secret from all but her most trusted intimates, and after she confided her "gift" to Earl during their courtship he joked, "Better keep that under your hat, or the men in white coats will come for you."

For a brief time in her 30's she became a paid psychic, clandestinely working from home, but grew weary of clients who only wanted to hear what they wanted to hear. Emma figured she was just a sensitive, an odd duck, and resolved to accept daily prescient intrusions as part of her natural landscape, and nothing more. But a "hybrid?" A lot to digest.

And her missing baby, spirited away by otherworldly beings? Her already permeable sense of 3-D earthly reality was melting around and through her.

Lily's voice broke through Emma's reverie. "I bring you a gift of the Guardians, who have been with you from the beginning. They will help you transition out of the ethers. I am here if you need me. Peace be with you on your journey."

The monitor went dark. Emma felt herself being pulled out of the darkness by unseen hands, a giant flaming ball approached her menacingly, then her body was lifted up, up into a bright, peaceful place, then gently lowered back into her office, into Third Dimensional time and place. She nestled softly on the couch by her office window, the couch she had lounged on countless times as she read, and pondered, and wondered. It was dark, two hours had passed, and a sliver of moon peeked from behind the giant cottonwood tree outside her office window. Emma heard the garage door open. Earl was home, and dinner hadn't been started.

"Pizza," she whispered. "This is a good night to order pizza."

Chapter Eight

Lights in the Sky

Late summer arrived, three weeks after Emma's sighting. Sweltering days alternated with crisp mornings, a deep blue autumn sky and plants riddled with munching insect holes that made Emma's perennial garden look like a shooting range. Twenty years ago Emma brought her houseplants indoors by the middle of September, but these days she waited until late October and even early November before overnight temperatures dipped reliably into the low 40's.

Emma quietly and methodically planned their eventual exit to the cabin, thanks to Lily Fortas's warnings. Her time in the arms of the Guardians both haunted and comforted her as she steamrolled ahead in survival mode. She bought a small trailer and stored it in the garage, and had a hitch installed on the Subaru.

She purchased piles of books on survival after the apocalypse, be it nuclear, political, economic, or biological. She was surprised to find not all authors were hardened, battle-tough marines or crackpot conspiracy theorists. Some were self-reliant old and new hippies, farm wives and displaced urbanites embracing life off the grid.

At dusk in late summer Emma ventured into the garden to collect Italian parsley from her herb bed for the final touch in a massive pot of "Churkey Soup" she was preparing for tonight's dinner and beyond. She used frozen chicken carcasses from Sunday night roast chicken dinners, and her Thanksgiving turkey carcass still laden with juicy tidbits of meat, fat and dressing that held a place of honor in her jam-packed basement freezer. When she had several carcasses she hauled out the stockpot, roughly chopped onions, celery, garlic, shallots and carrots, added bay leaves and fresh herbs, covered it all with a combination of chicken stock and water, threw in liberal pinches of salt and cracked pepper, and simmered the brew for hours.

The concoction was rich and redolent after its day-long simmer, and was ready for frozen chunks of "Chicken 4 Soup" that had been waiting in the freezer for months in large Ziploc bags for its moment in the cauldron. Emma strained all the solid bits out of the broth and skimmed the top several times to remove fat.

She sautéed another round of onions, garlic, carrots, celery and shallots, cut finely this time and cooked tenderly in olive oil, poured in the broth and added green beans, chickpeas, kidney beans and brown rice pasta. Finally, the chicken was added at the very end to avoid overcooking.

As she knelt by the herb garden to cut parsley in the approaching darkness, she marveled at the sliver of new moon rising over the tall pines and oaks of the backyard. She stopped short to stare at the northern horizon, which pulsed with swirls of colored light. It looked like Jimi Hendrix, Jim Morrison and Janis Joplin were giving a celestial concert replete with light effects. Emma hurried inside, turned on the television, and rinsed and roughly chopped the parsley.

"The Northern Lights are moving South, more at eleven," teased Emma's favorite news station.

"Good Lord, what would cause *that*?" Emma mused as she stirred in the parsley and placed a loaf of artisan bread to warm in the oven. "Honey!" she yelled out for Earl. "Come look at the sky!"

"I'm on the throne," he yelled back.

"Well, it's really something," Emma replied. "I hope it's still there when you're done."

Earl emerged wiping his hands on a towel and Emma hurried him to the northeast-facing window in the living room. "Look!" she exclaimed as she pointed at the swirling multi-colored lights.

"Whoa," Earl said softly. He took Emma's hand and they walked outside to stare at it. Their neighbors were doing the same up and down the cul-de-sac. Nature was putting on a fireworks show, but the air felt unsettled and electrically charged, very different from the lighthearted festivity of fireworks. Emma felt goosebumps rise on her forearms. She knew from her daily encounters with the unexplainable that goosebumps meant, "Pay attention, this is important, this is real."

"Something's wrong," she said darkly.

Earl hugged her and laughed. "Oh honey. It's beautiful. Probably something to do with climate change. Let's eat."

Emma startled. "Oh God, the bread, it's probably fossilized by now!"

Earl groaned. Bread was, for him, the very staff of life.

As Earl desultorily dunked his parched bread in his soup, Emma ate her dinner on a tray in front of the TV and scoured the Internet on her laptop for information on the strange light display. "They say it's Northern Lights, but they've never been this far South before," she reported to her glum husband. "It could be a precursor to something called a Coronal Mass Ejection." She giggled. "Sounds kinda porn-y." Earl grunted. Emma read on.

"OK, this is from NOAA…'Coronal Mass Ejections (CMEs) are large expulsions of plasma and magnetic field from the Sun's corona. They can eject billions of tons of coronal material and carry an embedded magnetic field (frozen in flux) that is stronger than the background solar wind interplanetary magnetic field (IMF) in strength. CMEs travel outward from the Sun at speeds ranging from slower than 250 kilometers per second (km/s) to as fast as near 3000 km/s. The fastest Earth-directed CMEs can reach our planet in as little as 15-18 hours. Slower CMEs can take several days to arrive. They expand in size as they propagate away from the Sun and larger CMEs can reach a size comprising nearly a quarter of the space between Earth and the Sun by the time it reaches our planet." Emma looked up at Earl, her eyes wide. "Holy crap. Are we going to get fried?"

Earl intoned, "Keep reading. I'm sure this isn't the first time."

Emma turned accusingly to him drooped over his bowl. "Honey, I know food is very important to you, and bread is now the love of your life, since your heart beats like an out-of-control jazz band, and Dr. Brodsky and your crappy veins forbid sexual congress, damn their hide. Can you *please* at least try to develop a little interest in something outside your alimentary canal? This is unprecedented. I've got a really, really bad feeling about this. Something horrific is going to happen."

Earl looked at her dryly and muttered, "A low blow my dear… and I shall try to be serious."

"Sorry honey…But do you really think I'm being hyperbolic? Overdramatic? Can we not go there right now, please? This is scaring me. You should know by now my Spidey sense is never wrong."

Earl softened at Emma's troubled face. "Yes, yes. Darling, you're scrunching. Your face will freeze like that." He sat next to Emma on the couch and put his arms around her. "I'm going to have to tickle you…"

"No!" Emma laughed. I'll spill the soup! Come on honey, don't!" She stood up and ran away from Earl's teasing arms and wiggling fingers, and he was too tired and too old to chase her. He picked up her laptop and continued reading.

"CMEs travelling faster than the background solar wind speed can generate a shock wave. These shock waves can accelerate charged particles ahead of them – causing increased radiation storm potential or intensity."

He put down the laptop. "Honey, it says these happen all the time, sometimes there's a little disruption in transmissions, it's no big deal. Come on, finish your dinner, I promise I won't tickle you. The bad thing that's going to happen is when you least expect it, I'm going to tickle you until you pee your pants."

Emma did not feel comforted. "The sun emissions may have happened before, but that," she pointed to the Eastern horizon, "has never, ever happened before, not in my lifetime."

"I'm going to bed," Earl replied resignedly. "I'm assuming you're not."

Emma typed furiously on her laptop. "You assume correctly."

Chapter Nine

Attack From Above

At Washington, D. C.'s NOAA Headquarters at 3 a.m., Day One of the unprecedented auroras, the graveyard shift tracked weather patterns, played hacky sack with a small stuffed effigy of the current joke of a POTUS, and ordered fast food from Grub Hub.

"Hahah! Epic *Fail*!" exulted Hannah O'Malley, fledgling Assistant Federal Coordinator of Meteorology, as she tossed her curly chestnut mane streaked with purple and took another bite of her burrito.

Evan Holdset, Deputy Assistant Administrator for the National Weather Service glumly picked the battered POTUS sack off the floor. "You cheated." He sulked.

"It was a bank shot Evan. It's allowed," Hannah crowed.

"In Hannah O'Malley world maybe," Evan replied darkly.

Computing and Communications Liaison Stuart Candler swiveled his chair away from his monitor and interrupted the feud. "You guys, you better look at this."

"What?" taunted Hannah, "Did widdle Stewie find a teeny weeny wahm fwont?"

Stuart blanched and continued, "Those auroras in the Mid-Atlantic, they're getting stronger. The magnetic readings are off the charts."

Hannah sighed and rolled her eyes. "It's plasma Stewie. Perhaps you've heard of it. We know there are active sunspots, and we've been expecting a moderate to major mass ejection storm for weeks. Just like we had in January, and last summer. No biggie. A couple of satellites will get the hiccups, a bunch of suburban TVs will show lines and static for a few days."

Stuart typed busily and pointed accusingly at his monitor. "Does *that* look like business as usual to you?"

Hannah and Evan stared at the screen for a few moments, then Evan said slowly, "What. The fuck. Is *that*?"

Stuart pulled real-time satellite images of solar activity heading toward Earth that showed a giant, expanding magnetic solar wave 10 times the size of Earth heading for Russia. "And we're next. There's another one right behind it. It's growing exponentially, it's a fucking solar tsunami."

"That's impossible," Hannah said in disbelief. "It's never happened before. There's got to be a mistake."

Evan sat in his swivel chair and muttered, "Time to believe our lying eyes. We are so fucked."

Hannah rushed to her monitor and began typing furiously. "We've got to warn them."

"Who?" asked Stuart.

"*Everyone!*" Hannah bellowed. "It's going to hit us in less than one hour!" She chatters excitedly, "I don't get it, yesterday it looked like garden variety solar activity. We've got to call the assho...president. The grid is going to fry unless everyone hooked up to electric power freaking unhooks!"

Stuart hurriedly pulled up the White House hotline phone from a desk drawer and put the call on speaker.

"White House," answered a crisp female voice.

"This is Hannah O'Malley at NOAA Meteorology. We have an urgent situation; the president must be informed."

"I'll patch you through to his Chief of Staff," the switchboard operator said calmly.

"Oh Christ on a stick," Hannah muttered, "We don't have time for this."

Seamus Kelly stirred in the dark bedroom as his phone pulsed insistently and vibrated off his night table onto the floor. He sleepily fished for it, put on his glasses and widened his eyes at the call number. "Kelly," he said as quietly and officiously as his semi-conscious state would allow.

"Emergency call from NOAA, transferring now..."

Hannah's breathless voice spilled into the receiver, "Sir, this is Hannah O'Malley at NOAA, we have a situation..."

Seamus interrupted, sotto voce, "We can't do anything about a hurricane until it's almost up our asses, climate change is debatable, and it's fucking 3:15 a.m. This better be really, really good, since you're calling on the 'Wake the POTUS' line."

"Sir, you've probably been briefed about the sunspots, the solar storm on the way?"

"Yessss," Seamus hissed quietly. "It's no big deal. Not worth a press release. Why are you wasting my time? Call me in the morning, the much later morning...good night."

He moved to hang up, Hannah screamed "It's growing – we don't know how or why. There are massive waves of solar magnetic storms heading for Russia and the Middle East, they're going to hit there…." She checked her watch "Now! Then Europe, then…we're next."

Seamus sat back against the headboard with a thud, which woke his wife and sleeping dog. They startled and stared at him as he demanded, "What does this mean?"

"It means we have to get as many power grids as possible offline immediately. We're going to lose power in huge areas of the globe, Russia first, then the Middle East, then it will keep heading west. There are at least two more solar waves behind this one. Anything actively running on electrical power – cars, planes, houses, computers, servers, power plants, anything – is going to fry, not to mention the great majority of satellites. Their circuitry will be rendered useless, it may take weeks, months, maybe longer to replace all the satellites and transformers and get us back online. Only offline systems will survive. Sir, we only have an hour, maybe less…"

Simultaneously multiple phones rang at NOAA, and Seamus's phone beeped furiously with new message alerts. He sunk his head into his hands. "Looks like you're not the only ones who figured this out." He stared at his rapidly burgeoning alerts. "Listen, I've gotta answer this from the Head of Joint Chiefs. Get the word out, everywhere!"

Hannah blanched and stared at her phone. "Jesus, I've got to call my sister Liza, I've got to call my mother, and my brother. Shit, Liza's in Manhattan, it's going to be a zoo in an hour. She's got to get out!" She began frantically dialing and screamed at Evan and Stuart, who began dialing their cellphones in a panic. "We've got to get on the Emergency Alert system, NOW!!"

Her voice lowered as she murmured into her phone "Dude, you've gotta get out of there. Seriously. Something's coming, grids are going to be fried, the city's going to be nuts. No! Don't start the car yet, wait until the first wave is over, until tomorrow morning. I'll call you if satellites aren't fried. Tell Mom and Colin to hang tight in DC, I'll bring them here when it's safe. You're what? You've got to be kidding. Are you keeping it? Jesus, your timing is impeccable. I'm sorry, I'm sorry, I love you sis. Never forget that."

She hung up and yelled, "C'mon, let's roll!"

Chapter Ten

Harsh New Realities

Emma haunted the Internet and TV news the rest of the night and into the early morning as pundits predicted massive solar storms, and Evangelical leaders warned of approaching Armageddon. She fell asleep against her will on the couch, and woke a few hours later with a strained neck and drool dripping down her face. *God, it's so quiet. Why is it so quiet?...But, what's that...that engine sound?"* And then she realized.

Her neighbors' portable generators were on. The recent violent hurricanes caused a run on portable and whole-house generators in the neighborhood, and after Hurricane Sandy the buzzing of generators dominated the cul de sac for over two weeks.

Before Emma fell asleep she turned off power to the house and put their whole-house generator on hold. She knew when the solar mass hit the generator would automatically turn on in 12 seconds after sensing no power, then its internal workings would probably fry. She was loath to flip all the switches until she knew it was safe, but she also dreaded losing power for additional hours to the refrigerators and extra freezer.

"It's probably OK, isn't it?" she muttered to herself as she stood in front of the power boxes in the garage. "The neighbors' generators are working. Do it," she said resolutely, and flipped the switches. Basement and garage lights flicked on, and the garage sump pump's light glowed green. "Good," she said shakily. "So far so good."

The television was working, the wi-fi was on, but she couldn't get the Internet on her phone. She checked the refrigerators and the freezer. All were working courtesy of the generator. What was happening out there? She was able to get a few fuzzy, static-filled local stations on television as harried reporters spoke urgently about vast power outages due to intense coronal mass ejections. Large portions of the grid all along the East Coast were fried, cars were stopped in their tracks, people were trapped in elevators and on subways, traffic lights were out, and looting had begun in inner cities. A few wavy, semi-garbled accounts were coming in from reporters able to transmit from their locations, and panic was clear on all their faces.

Emma felt dizzy, queasy and her heart was skipping beats. She ran to the bedroom to wake Earl and stopped abruptly to watch his peaceful face. *What is going to happen to us, to him? Maybe this is the last time he'll have a peaceful night's sleep.* She shook him gently. He smiled lazily and reached for her. She sat next to him and stroked his forehead. "Honey, we have a problem."

He chuckled and said, "I hope it's not bread-related."

Emma's eyes filled with tears. "No," she choked softly.

Earl's eyes widened. "Honey, what is it?"

"The coronal mass ejections. The East Coast is basically shut down, I can't get a signal on my phone, and except for a few news and radio stations, TV is out. Fried. I saw it on a little local station we can still get. No one knows how long it will last, or how bad it is. Our generator will only keep running as long as the natural gas supply holds out, and my research indicates the stockpile could give out in as little as two weeks."

Earl sat up, galvanized. "But we can get propane, right? We have that conversion thing."

"Unless you took a night class in energy engineering, forget it. Propane supplies will run out anyway, and it won't take long. People are stuck all over the place; we are in seriously deep shit. Grocery stores are going to run out of food, hospitals will run out of emergency power. This isn't going to be fixed anytime soon. Honey, we've got to get out of here and go to the cabin."

Earl sat back, shocked. "No, I'm sure it can be fixed."

"Maybe not for weeks. It's not going to be safe here. People will get desperate, and please don't tell me I'm being overdramatic. I've been getting ready for this for months. Lily said the changes were coming, and they're here! We've got to *go*! You *have* to listen to me."

She grabbed his arms and looked at him imploringly, but he slumped back on the bed, color drained from his face. He looked like a beaten-down old man. He disengaged from Emma, stood up slowly, and

47

distractedly opened his closet door to pull out his suitcase. Emma's heart broke watching him. He was such a creature of habit; transitions were hard for him.

She wanted to ease him slowly into retiring to the cabin, but this came at him like an ice-water plunge. She knew Earl was most likely not going to fare well without his precious creature comforts, not to mention all the heart medications that would eventually run out, and the doctors he visited every week or more.

She spoke gently, "Honey, we don't have to go this minute. We still have power, and it will take a little time before things really start to go south. Take a shower, have breakfast, we'll make plans. I've got to try and reach Jed. We still have landlines. Those wires are buried, so maybe they're still working."

Earl stood close to Emma and held her, they looked into each other's eyes for a long moment and hugged tenderly. They sensed deep in their bones these quiet, peaceful moments would soon be in very short supply. Earl, of course, made light of it. He waltzed Emma slowly around the room and sang, "The party's over," in her ear.

Emma couldn't help but laugh briefly, then pulled away from Earl and scolded, "You've got to take this seriously. I mean it."

Earl smiled and shook his head, "I predict it will be over in a few weeks, and we'll be back here, unscathed, in our own little paradise again." *God, will he ever get serious?*

The landline rang. It was Jed.

"Mom! Mom, are you OK?"

"Yes honey, our generator is working, we're fine for now."

"You've got to leave, right now."

"I know, so do you. Can you get here? Is your car working? We have to go to the mountains. I'm serious."

Earl yelled in the background, "Worrywarts, the two of you, worrywarts," as he pawed through his closet deciding what to pack.

"I know, the city's going to be crazy, really soon. Yes, the trailer is in the garage, I'm going to pack and get it out." Emma was profoundly thankful her son had the same prescience and long-range thinking that fueled her Always Be Prepared stance in life, unlike her often infuriatingly lighthearted, thick-skinned husband.

"And I'm going to bring Liza." His new girlfriend.

"Oh," Emma replied. "OK. But what about her family?"

Jed hesitated. "Mom, we're in love, and….she's pregnant."

Emma startled. "Oh? Oh! Oh my goodness. Is she, do you, are you going to…."

Jed interrupted, "We're keeping the baby Mom."

Emma hesitated, then replied quickly, "This is not the optimum time, but we'll make it work. Just get here in a hurry, please! You've got to get out of there, and I need you to help me hook up and load the trailer."

Emma Kaplan, Emergency Earth Mother.

Chapter Eleven

The Gathering Storm

Emma's sleep-deprived, grainy eyes scanned the folded paper stuffed in their mailbox. "Emergency Cul-de-Sac Meeting, 8 p.m., Don Melnik's garage." It was mid-morning, three days after the first mega solar coronal mass ejection. Most of the grids across the globe were down, and solar storms kept coming in smaller waves, like cosmic aftershocks. The sky was pale orange with green streaks. It looked to Emma like a melting orange Technicolor creamsicle, and colors pulsed in circular eddies day and night. Distant sirens blared from the highway as Emma stood next to the mailbox and prayed for an end to the waking nightmare.

Their generator was still blasting, but no one knew how much longer natural gas reserves would hold out. Some neighbors' generators ran on propane, more and more stories were coming out about propane supplies running low or being held hostage by armed sentries. Some generators had gone silent. Grocery stores were almost empty, the supply chain was close to non-existent, water pressure was dwindling, and families began using buckets of water from their swimming pools to flush the toilets. Planes couldn't fly, interference from solar waves and the frying of most satellites produced sparse radio and TV transmissions full of static and largely inaudible, and the Internet was completely down.

Emma lay awake night after night as questions and worries whirled through her head. Earl slept courtesy of sleeping pills, and Jed and Liza played video games in the basement guest room. *We're not going to hold out here much longer, but how safe is it out there? Can we get to the cabin? Has it already been taken over?* Emma, Earl, Jed and Liza had been packing their cars and the trailer attached to Emma's Subaru for days as Emma struggled to process their next steps. *Don will know*, she thought.

Former Marine Don Melnik lived in a fortress at the top of the cul-de-sac, in between the modest split-level of a local police chief and the palatial manse of a disgraced Mafia boss who recently returned from a stint in Federal prison. It was rumored the Mob palace had been sold to an Asian gynecologist to pay the boss's legal debts and help him make a new start in Florida, but black limos were still parked outside his four-car-garage. "I wonder if he'll be there tonight," mused Emma. "How does one converse with a member of the Mob?" She chuckled and caught herself. "C'mon Emma, gangster etiquette should be the last thing on your mind."

She stopped on her way up the driveway to watch Earl struggle with more gallons of water than anyone should carry as he staggered to the trailer now hooked up to Emma's Subaru. "I'm sure glad we bought that trailer," Emma said to Earl triumphantly. "Everyone thought I was nuts when I told them it was for the Big Getaway when everything goes south. Aren't you glad you married a hippie-dippie intuitive Girl Scout?"

Even Emma was beginning to tire of the I Told You Sos. They seemed superfluous in the face of the massive, life-threatening problem she struggled to wrap her arms around. There was no response from Earl to her pronouncements as he huffed and puffed and sweat dampened his shirt, dripping from his face like water. "Earl!" she shouted.

Exhausted, harried Earl turned toward her and shouted back, "WHAT?"

"Put those down, you're going to hurt your back!" Emma hurried up the driveway to help him as he began to drop gallon after gallon of her carefully preserved water onto the concrete floor of the driveway. One of the plastic bottles split, and rivulets of water seeped down the driveway and settled into cracks in the macadam. "Honey," she crooned as Earl leaned against the trailer and wiped his profusely sweating forehead with his shirt. "You need to rest. Let me do it." Earl nodded and shuffled into the house like a man in a trance.

This is not going to be good, Emma worried. City-boy, devil-may-care woman magnet Earl was a lover, not a warrior. Emma knew the lion's share of toting and slaving was, as usual, up to her. *I should have thought twice when Earl said in the early days he wished he lived in a horizontal world. For God's sake, he even pees sitting down.* This was all right in the civilized world, where he crowed about hiring people to do the heavy dirty work Emma couldn't, but what about this threatening new world? How would he cope? Could Emma keep him alive?

She thought back to a sunny summer day around the pool. Earl and his son Doug lounged in chaises under a giant umbrella as Emma scurried back and forth, tended to the pool and the garden, and brought cold drinks. Earl pointed to her and exulted, "Wind her up and watch her go!"

"We'll see how far I can go now. We'll soon see," Emma muttered to herself. *Could she hold up? What was going to happen to them?*

Jed and Liza, up until at least 3 a.m. with video games and junk food, were sacked out on the basement guest bed, Jed's German Shepherd Buddy and Liza's miniature poodle Shatzi at their feet. *Future lunch, Buddy,* Emma thought grimly as she passed them and walked up the basement stairs to the kitchen. She wondered if anyone knew how bad this was going to get.

Lily Fortas knew. Emma wondered if she could reach her now. So far only landlines were working with any reliability, since most satellites and cell towers were fried to a golden crisp, and none of her family members used landlines anymore, except Emma and Jed. *I wonder if Char got out,* Emma thought. She could see Char and her daughter in their truck, hightailing it to the hinterlands. Carol had assured Emma on their midnight phone call just before everything shut down that Bonnie and Richard had their plans in place for an exodus to Carol and Joe's compound in Zion, and Emma's solar plexus ached thinking of Richard and his walking "horse" and Bonnie's careful, gingerly little steps.

"Don't worry" Carol assured Emma. "We're going to get them out of there as soon as it's safe, we're ready for this. The boys are all here, and Lynn says she's on her way. Just you guys stay safe. And come to us in Zion if you're in danger, we'll take care of you."

"Godspeed Char, thank you for the heads up, and God, who or whatever you are, if you're listening, take care of my family," Emma whispered as she scouted every room to determine what to take, and what to leave behind.

Almost all television stations were black save a few small cable stations able to shut down in time, but even their transmissions were wavy, and sound traveled in and out. Harried local anchor people working way above their pay grade were flummoxed about how to talk cogently about apocalypse after years of covering chili cook-offs, Rotary Club meeting schedules and local weather patterns.

The Information Age had come to a dark, silent standstill, but not before one wavy transmission captured Emma's attention a few days earlier. A local TV station, WMNX out of Newark, NJ, featured a grainy video shown by a breathless reporter of swarms of orbs over Washington, D.C., major airports, and nuclear facilities. "We don't know what they are, or why they're here," she reported breathlessly from outside Newark Airport. "Our military can't intercept them, since nothing is flying during the solar storm, but it has caused a lot of speculation about whether they caused this disaster. Some wonder if they're a secret advanced technology from a rival superpower. At Newark Airport, this is Stephanie Schmidt, WMNX News."

As she spoke, a blurry video showed dozens of orbs flying in formation over the Pentagon, then blinking out one by one in the darkness. "Lily, it looks like you were right," Emma whispered to the sky, and every night she scanned the firmament for flying orbs, disks, anything. Nothing yet. And there was no mention of it anywhere else. *Our good old government at work, even now.*

Chapter Twelve

Marching Orders

As Emma walked to Don's, the swirling sun was setting through the trees, and birds were chirping, readying for their nightly lights-out, but even the birds seemed different, quieter. The air felt turgid and expectant, like the hush before a total solar eclipse, and the hum of the remaining working generators replaced absent traffic sounds from the nearby highway, except for periodic sirens. Emma waved solemnly to neighbors heading to Don's to get the Riot Act read to them from Mr. Clean Marine.

Not so clean after all, Emma thought, as she walked through the open door of Don's garage workshop to a giant back room that housed a full wall of firearms and a giant Army tank. Emma knew about the tank, because Don hauled it out every Memorial Day for the downtown parade, but she didn't know about the semi-nude Playboy-style pictures that festooned the walls of his workshop. She always suspected he was a "Playa," since he regularly complained about his distant wife, and liked to take long cycle trips on his Harley in macho regalia that was a cross between a Hell's Angel and a NASA astronaut.

She also caught him gazing appreciatively at her bottom as she turned away from him after an impromptu chat at the mailbox when he happened by in his white Ford 150. She was old meat though, and if fifty-something Don was going to play, it was likely with a woman who was still super-juicy. The cheesecake pictures attested to that.

He stood in the doorway of the ad-hoc conference room and gestured for neighbors to sit on an assortment of chairs arranged in front of a long table with a white board set up behind it. Another table held cans of soda, plates of cookies and bowls of chips, candy and pretzels. Like Emma and then some, Don was always prepared. "Help yourselves folks," he said grimly. "And take any leftovers with you. You'll need them." No one smiled.

Don reminded Emma of an upside-down isosceles triangle – his broad shoulders tapered into a slender waist and narrow hips, and his legs were slim under tight-fitting jeans. *If I met him in a bar, I would know he was a man on the prowl*, Emma thought. He moved with feral quickness, his light blue eyes darted as if on perpetual patrol, and his graying light brown hair was close cropped. He had high cheekbones and curvy lips almost always set in a wry purse, and when he spoke he barely opened his mouth in a sideways gesture, as if he meant to speak in perpetual sotto voce. Emma secretly dubbed him "Mr. Entre Nous (just between us)."

Don looked sideways at Emma and asked quizzically, "Where's the hubs?"

"Oh, he's exhausted from loading the trailer, so he's resting," Emma replied quietly. "I'm worried about him."

Don smiled slightly. "I'm sure you'll take good care of him."

Emma whispered, "We're in for it, aren't we?"

His face hardened. "Looks that way. We'll talk after everyone leaves. I know you've been in the trenches for a while."

Emma smiled gratefully, "Thanks. I need all the advice I can get."

Don scanned the assembled neighbors grimly and muttered, "Let's do this thing."

Don took his place behind the table and called the meeting to order. "OK folks. Have a seat. We've had a serious event, we're out of power and most communications, and may be for quite a while."

Fred Wehman, ex-union boss piped up, "How long?"

Dan frowned, "Could be weeks, could be months…" He paused grimly. "Even years."

A collective groan rose from the group. "I know, I know," he continued. "Until the condition of satellites and transformers can be assessed, we won't know for sure. The East Coast has a lot of power interconnectedness, so what happens here is also happening up and down major portions all along the line." Hands began to go up and neighbors spoke over each other. Don held his hand high in the air. "Look, you've got a lot of questions and concerns, so let me tell you what you need to know first, then we can get to questions."

A dark, heavy-set man in a turquoise jogging suit and heavy gold necklace boomed from the back of the room where he stood against the doorway, "What makes you the big expert?"

Don replied patiently, "Mario, you know I've been handling the nuts and bolts of a major Jersey town as a zoning official for years, but what you may not know is I've been communicating on my CB and ham radios with folks all over the country, in addition to using my military contacts. I've got a very good picture of where we are, and what we need to do. I hope you'll listen and take what I have to say to heart." Mario folded his arms and leaned impassively against the doorway.

I guess in Mario-speak that's a capitulation, thought Emma. *He's got to be the Mafia kingpin.*

Don wrote 'Anarchy' on the board in red marker. "This is what's coming. There is no power in the biggest American city just a few miles from here. As many of you already know, there are no working elevators, no traffic lights or streetlights, no heat and no air-conditioning, Gas stations will be out of gas in no time, and most grocery stores are already empty. Our supply chain is seriously disrupted, and may not be on track for a very long time, hampered by the fact that if a truck is making deliveries, it can be easily hijacked by black market folks looking to make a buck."

He paused briefly to let that sink in. The room had fallen silent. "Stores are being looted, hospitals will eventually run out of power, people are leaving in huge numbers by car, boat or on foot if they have to. Anything electrical that was running when the solar storm hit has been fried – that includes cars, planes, trains, you name it. There are already casualties, and there will be many, many more."

The air in the room grew heavy. Members of the group nodded grimly or looked nervously at each other, some held their loved ones' hands, others drew closer together. Low mumblings and whispers broke out in the group.

"You may be asking yourself, what can we do? Well, we can stay and pool our resources, or we can leave and try our luck in sparsely populated areas, if you have a destination in mind, and people you can hunker down

56

with. And speaking of resources, eventually money will need to be replaced by something more useful, so think of what you can barter for goods and services. Like what? Food, medicine, clothes, wood, something useful you're really good at, like cooking, doctoring, gardening. Some people might want gold or silver, but paper money or credit cards will very quickly be obsolete unless banks and online banking services reopen. Basically, we're the new pioneers. Let's look at it that way, if we can."

Attendees began talking audibly with each other, brainstorming. Don picked up a pool cue from against the wall and tapped it loudly against the board. The audience quieted, Mario smirked and shifted his position against the wall. "Folks, we'll have plenty of time for this afterward. Let's stay focused."

He wrote 'Protection' on the board. "Who here has guns?" He gestured to his wall of firearms. Police Chief Tom McMurphy raised his hand, along with Mario, Fred Wehman and Deputy Marshall Flynn who lived on the corner of the cul-de-sac that bordered a 14-acre wooded lot. Emma slowly raised her hand.

"Emma?" Don asked in surprise.

She replied apologetically, "Well, technically yes, I bought a shotgun, and shells, but I haven't actually used them yet. Y'know, be prepared and all."

Don smiled wryly. "OK, I guess that counts." *Thanks a lot, I love a little condescension with my doom.* Old Mrs. Daniels, a widow who lived alone in a modest cape on the lower edge of the cul-de-sac, raised her hand. Don was bemused.

"Agatha, really?"

Mrs. Daniels smiled, "Son, I learned to shoot on my father's farm. I can down a squirrel from a high tree, even with these old eyes."

Don smiled warmly and continued, "All right. Who is willing to stand guard? We'll have to work in shifts and position ourselves to cover at least eight locations around the cul-de-sac. And I'm going to position Sweet Betty," he gestured to the tank, "at the mouth of the drive."

"What are we protecting ourselves from?" asked Annie Mahoney, an old hippie sculptress who lived with her husband Martin in a sprawling ranch close to Don's house.

Don replied grimly, "Anyone who isn't us."

"What does that mean?" Annie asked plaintively, as Martin stood silently behind her and nodded.

"Annie, it means if they don't live here, and they try to break in, they get shot."

Annie shook her head, stood up and proclaimed, "I'm out. I help my neighbor – I don't shoot them."

She began to walk out, but Don called after her, "Annie, if you can't get with the program, you'll have to leave."

Annie turned, jutted her chin and replied rebelliously, "Try and make us. We pay taxes, we belong here. What happens on our property is our business."

Don responded gently, "I know how you feel, but I don't think you understand what happens to people when they're desperate. They'll do anything they have to do to survive. If we want to hunker down here, we have to establish a perimeter."

"Establish all you want," Annie replied angrily. "We'll have no part of it." She stormed out; the room was silent.

Mario piped up in deep tones, "I give Mr. and Mrs. Kumbaya a week."

Don smiled grimly, "If that." The room erupted in questions and exclamations. Don tapped the board again. "Listen guys, please let me finish, then we can talk."

He wrote 'Food & Water' on the board. "This is essential, of course. We'll have town water for a while, but eventually the pumps will run out of emergency power, and most likely there won't be personnel monitoring our water. I have a deep drilled well with a hand pump in the backyard, I can share that with you. Bring clean bottles and jars and fill up when the time comes."

"Now, don't tell me what food you have or don't have, but if you can get out and get to the grocery stores before they're completely cleaned out, do it. Buy as many non-perishable items as you can – soups, peanut butter, tuna fish, pasta, rice, mixes, like that. At some point the military will have food distribution points, depending on how long this lasts, but for your sake I hope you're stocked up."

Some members of the audience rolled their eyes, young Deputy Flynn said meekly, "Don, it's a lot. For most of us."

Don nodded grimly. "Do the best you can, if you have more than you need, find a neighbor who doesn't. We'll have to work together to get through this. Now..." He wrote 'Sanitation' on the board. "A messy business, I know. If this is a long dragged-out situation, eventually the sewer systems will stop running and we'll have to establish trenches for our waste, downstream of any potable water source. I know we have lots of little streams around here, but very soon people will be using that water for their own purposes if they can, so we can't use those water sources for waste." The room was deadly silent. "I know this is hard; we're all so used to our creature comforts, but in order to get through this, we have to be adaptable."

He looked at the grim faces looking back at him. "I wish I could sugarcoat it for you guys, but we could be in for a really long, tough haul. And one more thing."

He wrote 'Hypothermia and Heat Exposure.' "We're lucky this happened in late summer, not the middle of winter or the heat of mid-summer. You need to keep track of your body temperature as the weather changes. If we're still in this compromised energy state in late fall and winter, you'll need to figure out how to keep warm. If you have wood-burning fireplaces and access to firewood, great. If we have more hot days you need to go to the lowest part of your home to stay cool, and limit your activity. We can talk about that later when and if we need to. I think it's time for questions. Please raise your hands."

Emma raised her hand. "What are you hearing on CB radio? What are your military contacts saying? And why did this hit us so suddenly, why wasn't there early warning?"

Don smiled slightly. "Always the journalist, eh Emma? Even the experts at NOAA got caught with their pants down. What they saw a week ago was a predicted solar storm that literally grew massive in a matter of hours, and they don't know why, at least not yet. There are some areas that managed to shut down before the storm hit, but it's not a good idea to head out to find them, because people are protective of their resources, and you're bound to run into armed perimeters and very little help. I know, I wish it could be different. There may be Good Samaritans out there who will take you in, but you likely won't make it intact to find them. I'm sorry."

Chief McMurphy raised his hand.

"Tom?"

"Don, is there any idea how long it will take to recover the energy grid? Can you give me the best- and worst-case scenarios? We still have our patrol cars and gas supply, but our communications are seriously limited. It's hard to know who needs help, and what's happening. We're pretty hamstrung here."

Deputy Flynn nodded his head emphatically.

Don paused, sighed and continued, "Guys, I wish I had better news for you. Best case scenario, probably months. We need to use the military gas and oil stockpile to fuel necessary vehicles and repair energy infrastructures. Major transformers will be first, but satellites may be completely fried, so we will probably need to launch a lot more, but only after the solar waves have stopped. They're still going on."

Emma piped up again, "But I just don't get it. Why are these storms so intense? We've never seen them like this before, there have only been minor power disruptions in the past."

Don shook his head, "As I said, we don't know." He switched gears somewhat impatiently, "OK, there are already conspiracy theories floating around with survivalists, wackjobs and militia members that it's a "Deep State" thing. How they could have managed this is beyond my pay grade. If it's possible to amplify these things, look no farther than Russia, or China."

"Or aliens," Emma interjected.

Don folded his arms dismissively and intoned, "Whatever. We don't have time to go there."

The room was silent as the New Reality began to set in. Agatha Daniels raised her hand.

"Yes, Agatha?"

Agatha spoke forcefully. "I'm an old woman. My husband is gone, I live alone. I take a lot of medicine. What if I decide I don't want to live this way? How can I end it without too much pain? And don't feel sorry for me. I've led a good life, and I'd rather pass as painlessly as I can if I have to struggle to stay alive month after month."

Don replied solicitously, "Aggie, we don't want to lose you. Let's not think about that. We're going to do everything we can to keep you safe. Let's table this for now, but there are ways. Let's leave it there." Agatha nodded and patted the shoulder of Deputy Flynn, who looked stricken. It was his first month on the force, and his desire to help was in overdrive.

"Don't worry, sonny," she whispered to him. "This is new for all of us."

Don continued, "We need to set up our perimeter now. The reality is there are thousands, maybe hundreds of thousands of people heading out of the five boroughs as resources are stripped away and the new reality sets in. The suburbs are going to be their next resource, and as they get hungrier and more desperate, they aren't going to be polite. My CB and ham contacts are already reporting armed gangs, it's only a short matter of time before they get here, and by the time they do, their numbers will have increased. So, who is willing to stand guard?"

Mario Bonaventura stepped forward. "How many men you need?"

Don replied grimly, "How many you got?"

Mario joined him behind the table, angling to take over. "My men can stay in my house with their families, I can give you at least eight, with real guns." He gestured to Don's cache. "Not these popguns."

Don surveyed Mario up and down. "OK, Mario. You've got a deal. But no trigger-happy stuff, right? Warning shots first, OK?"

Mario smiled, "Sure, sure. We play nice, until we don't play nice."

This is getting real. Emma piped in, "But what about the military, the National Guard? Can't they be brought in to provide security?"

Don shook his head. "They are stretched thinner than they ever thought possible. Ex-military and law enforcement are being asked to

61

create their own safe zones in their own towns. Straight from General Osgood at CentCom."

Chief McMurphy stepped to Don's other side. "Deputy Flynn and I can do relief, depending on when we're off our shifts. But how can we stay in contact?

"Keep it low-tech" Don replied. "Walkie talkies, CB or ham radio. Some of your patrol cars may still have systems intact, if they weren't operating during solar waves, and if they're not running coms through cell towers." He paused and remarked ruefully, "I guess high-tech isn't always what it's cracked up to be. Tom, maybe the best thing to do is check in personally if all else fails. You can coordinate according to your schedules."

Mario sniffed, "Got no schedule. Make my own schedule."

Tom replied pointedly, "Nice work if you can get it. If memory serves, you had schedules in the joint."

Mario snorted. "I take care of them; they take care of me."

Don intervened. "OK, I know, times like this make for strange bedfellows, and there's some bad blood between you two, but we've got to be in this together."

Tom retorted, "I guess it would be a lot easier if I was on the take."

Mario rejoindered, "Boy Scouts finish last, Chiefie."

Agatha interjected, "OK boys, if you're done playing King of the Hill, we've got a lot of work to do, right Don?"

"Right! No time for old feuds, fellas," Don replied emphatically, then addressed the entire group. "Listen, in addition to an armed perimeter, we all have to be part of an active neighborhood watch. The savviest gangs know better than to march up the main drag to the cul-de-sac, though there'll be newbies who will try. They'll infiltrate through back yards and that strip of woods that runs all along the upper road behind my house and Deputy Flynn's place. The expression 'If you see something, say something' never meant more than it does now. And take an inventory of your food, eat as much of your perishable food in the next few weeks as you can, or give it to your neighbors. As soon as we set up our perimeter,

Mimosa Drive is a closed universe. Try and get some sleep folks. Tomorrow we begin."

Chapter Thirteen

Change of Plans

After the last neighbor left, Emma turned to Don. "Listen, I've got three cars and a U-Haul-style trailer loaded to the gills with food, water and supplies. We want to get to our mountain place as soon as we can. When do you think these gangs will start showing up?"

Don replied confidentially, "It's Mad Max out there. Some of them have gotten to Fort Lee and taken whatever they could, so it's only a matter of a day or two before they're here. There've already been a lot of casualties on both sides. Ex-military right-wingers, survivalists and self-styled militia folks make up one major group. Another is street gangs from the city, but so far they haven't banded together. My bet is they're going to do kind of a rival gangs thing. The good news - social media is down, so it's hard for them to add to their ranks at this point. The sooner you get out, the better. I'll probably head for my cabin in the mountains with Prince." Prince was Don's snow-white German Shepherd.

"Why don't you go now?" Emma asked.

Don replied slowly, "I guess it's a 'go down with the ship' thing. A lot of these people have nowhere else to go. Once we're overrun, and we most likely will be, I'm taking Prince and Sweet Betty to my cabin in the Catskills."

Emma's eyes widened. "Your *tank*? You're kidding! Wait, I thought they weren't allowed on the road, because they're too heavy?"

He shook his head. "I had her retrofitted with padded tracks so she won't damage the highways, and she's pretty impenetrable, unless someone ignites an IED under her. She's a little slow, tops out around 60 miles per hour if I gun her full out, but she'll get me there."

Emma shook her head in disbelief. "Wow. OK. Wait, but what about your wife?"

Don replied softly, "She's gone."

Emma gasped, "She's dead?"

He laughed ruefully. "No, she went off with a VP from her company. They're probably somewhere down the Shore by now."

"When?" Emma asked.

He replied, "Last year, last summer."

"Wow," Emma replied, shocked. "You really do play close to the vest, don't you? No wonder I haven't seen her in a while."

He smiled. "A man doesn't want this kinda stuff to get around."

Emma smiled back. "Afraid of the female swarm?"

"I like my privacy."

Don's CB radio crackled from a corner of the room, "Breaker, breaker, White Line Fever to PussyCat Wrangler, come in, come in." He sat in front of the transmitter and put on a pair of headphones with a microphone attached.

"PCW here White Line. Whatcha got?"

"Dude, they're heading North in a big hurry. Hitting groceries, liquor stores and pharmacies, looting houses, lots of guns, ammo, not enough to hit the big malls yet."

"How many?" Don asked urgently.

"Too many, man, too many. They had a plan. They know the cops are scattered with spotty coms, and they're horny for cars, they'll do just about anything for one, a lot of cars got fried with the shock waves."

"When will they hit the NY border?" asked Don.

"Tomorrow morning maybe, they just keep on comin'. Hunker down, man."

Don muttered quickly into the microphone "PCW out. Stay safe White Line. I'll be in touch." He removed his headphones and turned to Emma. "We're outta here."

Emma's eyes widened, "But, what about the perimeter, going down with the ship, and all that?"

He replied curtly, "No time, even if I can get Mario's boys here asap. Conditions are changing on the ground faster than I thought, and solar waves are winding down, so our engines won't be inactivated. We have to get out tonight."

"Tonight?" Emma exclaimed. "But I have freezers full of food!"

Don replied grimly, "Don't worry, it won't go to waste. Pack what you can in ice or coolers, I'm sure you have those, right?" Emma nodded, wide-eyed. "I'm going door to door to tell folks to hunker down somewhere safe, if they can find it. I'm sorry. Get ready to head out. Listen, my cabin at the Mason's Eddy exit is on the way to your place. Betty and I can escort you over an hour out, maybe by then you can make it. Is your gun loaded?"

Emma faltered, "Um, no. I don't know how."

Don snapped, "Well, read the instructions and figure it out!"

"All right, all right," Emma retorted. "Geez." She softened, "I really do appreciate this. I wish I could do something meaningful to thank you."

Don grabbed Emma's arm, turned her to him and said, "Just one kiss. That's all I want."

Emma startled. "I'm old enough to be your slightly older sister," she said playfully, then sobered. "I don't know how Earl would feel about this."

Don said gently, "Then don't tell him. I've never been a big fan of militant honesty."

Emma said coyly, "Just militant modes of transportation I guess." She took a deep breath. "When were you planning to collect on this debt?"

He smiled and pulled Emma to him. "No time like the present." And he planted a big, slightly wet, quite creditable kiss on Emma's surprised mouth. Not Earl level, she thought, but not bad.

She pulled back gently and said softly, "Well done, Marine. As you were."

He looked at Emma appreciatively. "You're really something, you know that?"

"So I've been told," Emma quipped. "What's our ETA?"

"Be ready to head out in one hour."

"God!" Emma rushed out of the room.

Chapter Fourteen

Exodus

Emma slammed the front door behind her and ran into the bedroom. Earl was watching an ancient VCR recording of a vintage Super Bowl game as he periodically tested his remote to see if any television stations were coming back. She panted, "Honey, we've got to go! In an hour! The maniacs are coming!"

Earl frowned and replied testily, "Where'd you hear that? Your Marine boyfriend?" Emma blanched; Earl always knew.

"Stop it, this is serious."

"So am I. I see the way he looks at you."

"He's a hornball, honey. He'd look that way at a paramecium if it had appropriate holes. He heard it from CB radio people, and his military connections. The hordes from the city are closing in, at this rate they'll be at the New York border by morning. We've got to get out. Don's going to escort us."

Earl's eyes widened. "Oh? On his macho man motorcycle? What 'hordes'? Disgruntled ultra libs from the Upper East Side looking for lattes and sympathy? Oooh, I'm scared."

Emma sat urgently next to Earl on the bed. "Please be serious for once in your life. It seems ultra-right militia types, survivalists, doomsday preppers, wackos and gang members are heading here in a big fat hurry…"

Earl interrupted, "How do you know?"

Emma took his hands. "Honey, if we don't get slaughtered on our way out, I'll explain it later. We've got to get it all together in a big hurry and get out of here. Please trust me. You've trusted me this far." She looked plaintively into his eyes.

He softened and kissed her. "Yes, your wavy gravy stuff has been very accurate." He sniffed the air around Emma. "And you smell like Paco Rabanne. Lover Boy's signature fragrance?"

"No, you idiot. I shook hands with Mario the Mafia Man and he was drenched in it. Stop it. I appreciate you still think I'm catnip to men, but we don't have time for this. We've got to get out of here. Work with me, please."

She jumped up and looked feverishly around the room. "Paintings, furniture, I wonder if they'll still be here when it's all over..." She ran down the hall and rapidly scanned room by room for anything useful and portable she might have forgotten. She shook her head and tears formed as she passed over heirlooms and mementos that could not be jammed into cars or the trailer. "It's stuff Emma, it's only important to you, get over it," she mumbled. She opened the refrigerator and surveyed the empty shelves and the half-empty bottles of ketchup, vinegar and Worcestershire sauce in the refrigerator door. "Nope, move on."

She ran down the basement stairs as Jed and Liza sat disconsolately on the sofa bed. "What's the matter? You heard, didn't you?"

Jed looked up blankly and Liza choked out between stifled tears, "We can't hear anything. We can't get on Facebook, Instagram, TikTok, nothing. Not even Apple TV. It's awful. And I'm sick of video games. All he wants to play is Call of Duty," she sobbed. Liza's darkly pretty face was streaked with mascara and eyeliner, and she had the petulant air of a beautiful woman used to getting her way.

Hoo boy. This one's going to be a picnic. "Dear," began Emma with slightly veiled impatience, "Satellites are down, you won't have the Internet for a while, at least not here. Jed, we have to leave. In," She looked at her watch, "Forty-five minutes."

Jed replied, shocked, "What? Why?"

"Oh, um, I don't know, because we're about to be descended upon by hordes of looters and marauders from the city?"

Jed regarded his mother with hooded, inscrutable eyes. "Mom. You're doing it again. Being all dramatic. Liza's sister Hannah is high up at NOAA – she said we had to get out of the city, not run away to the middle of nowhere."

Emma gritted her teeth and spoke in her best menacing tones, "Jed, for once in your life try not to treat me with the derision that made me leave your father. Don Melnick, ex-Marine, has been in touch via CB and ham radio with other operators in the area and with the military. Grids all along the coast and in much of the country are down, we don't know for how long. There are mercenaries taking advantage of the situation, and they could be in this area in a few hours. They're going to take anything that isn't nailed down, and they'll shoot you if you try and stop them. We are going. Now. You don't have to like it, but you are coming with me. It's the Wild Wild West on steroids, the world is seriously out of balance, and it's going to get worse."

Liza whined, "I want to be with my friends. I don't want to go."

Emma replied coldly, "Be my guest. Perhaps they're still in one piece."

Jed said defensively, "C'mon, Mom. Leave her alone. How many are there? How do you know they'll bother us?"

Emma replied curtly, "We're not going to stick around to find out. You've now got…" she checked her watch, "Forty-three minutes. Do what you have to do, go to the bathroom, have a snack, walk the dogs, but we are leaving. Now I have to go load the gun!"

In the garage Emma fumbled with a box of shotgun shells and picked up the very heavy rifle the gun shop guy said was "lightweight, for women."

"Maybe for Amazons," Emma muttered. "I'm going to throw my shoulder out if this thing has any kind of report, and I'm betting it does." She hastily reviewed the booklet that came with the gun, loaded three shells into it and briefly hoisted it to her shoulder. Jed came into the room as she lowered the rifle to the ground and winced at its weight.

"Mom, what are you doing? Do you have any idea how to shoot that?"

"No," Emma replied defensively, "But there's no time like the present."

Jed approached her and held out his hand. "Give it to me, I'll take care of it. I have another in the car, already loaded."

"Jed Campbell, I told you never to get a gun!"

Jed smiled darkly, "Aren't you glad I did now? And I know how to shoot it." He took the gun and ammunition from Emma and darted through the garage door to the cars.

Earl appeared, sweating and puffing as he lugged an overstuffed suitcase.

"Earl! What is in there? We already loaded the clothes you'll need."

Earl whined, "My Giants tapes, tapes of the kids, the pennies I've been saving, my Giants stuff from the Super Bowl, my photo albums."

Emma softened and climbed the stairs to him. "Honey, put it down. Sweetheart, we can't take it. There is literally not another inch of space in any of the cars, we can barely see over it to drive as it is."

Earl set his jaw. "I'm taking it. I'll tie it to the top of my car."

Emma sighed, "We really don't have time for this. Tie it with what?"

Earl pulled a clump of tangled bungee cords from a suitcase pocket. "These."

Emma sighed again, more gustily. "OK. Listen to me. I am not, I repeat, I am not going to do it. If you do it, the first puff of wind will blow it and the bungee cords off the car."

"Oh, come on," Earl replied impatiently.

"I don't have time for this. You figure it out." Emma stormed out of the room. *Giants, Giants, Giants. He has no idea how supremely unimportant any of this is now.* She stopped in her tracks, and wondered if she should pack snacks. "Dude, this isn't a soccer game," she muttered to herself. "Forget the frickin' snacks, there's food for later in the trailer. Besides, I don't want to have to pee or poop on the road."

A loud rumbling brought Emma to the living room picture window as Don's beloved Sweet Betty rolled ponderously to a stop in front of the house, its telescoping cannon protruding far in front of it. Don's white F-150 was hitched to the back of the tank, and Prince sat dutifully in the passenger seat. Emma opened one of the windows and shouted, "We're almost ready!"

Don shouted back, "I'm talking to Fred first, then we have to go!" He went to Fred Wehman's front door and Emma watched the two of them talk confidentially, arms folded, lit by the light of the half moon. Emma wondered if she would ever get used to no streetlights. For a moment she wondered what Times Square looked like now, without the garish spray of giant lighted billboards advertising Broadway shows, perfumes, clothing, and without the crush of gawkers and the blare of businesses and restaurants advertising their wares. Emma's girl, her city, overrun. Probably looted, dark and insane.

Emma, don't think about it.

Time to say goodbye to the house she and Earl lived in for over 25 years. The sprawling contemporary that was always perfect for big, rangy Earl but left Emma feeling lost as she ran back and forth between its large, sunny rooms. But it was home, and now, maybe for a brief time, maybe forever, it wasn't.

"Goodbye, old girl," she whispered, as she walked from room to room and touched the walls and doorways. "Thanks for the memories. I'm taking those with me, as they say." She locked the front door from the inside, then wondered if she should even bother. "Good, make it harder for the bastards to get in." She grabbed her purse, took a final look, and went down the basement stairs.

Don talked with Jed and Liza in the driveway as Earl glowered inside his car. As Emma approached she saw Agatha Daniels, old Mrs. Ciachi and Deputy Flynn and his young family walk into Fred Wehman's backyard as they dragged bags and suitcases, their dogs trailing behind them. "What's with the caravan?" she asked Don.

Don took her aside and whispered in his best sideways 'just between us' voice, "Fred has an underground shelter, large, fully equipped. He's a prepper. He invited older neighbors and those with children to stay until the first wave of looters passes by."

Emma replied, shocked, "What? Why didn't he tell me?"

Don smiled slightly. "He knows you have somewhere to go." Emma thought back to the numerous times Fred had workers in his backyard, often with excavating equipment, and Emma wondered what he was up to. She had contemplated creeping over the fence into his backyard at night to see what this major project was all about, but Fred's perimeter was guarded by surveillance cameras. "I've sent out the alarm, Mario's boys should be here any minute to protect those who are staying. We've got to go. Are you ready?"

"How do we do this?" Emma asked. "Do we go behind you or in front of you?"

Don called to Jed, "How much ammo you got?"

Jed smiled darkly, "Enough. I've got a semi-automatic with four high-capacity magazines." Emma gasped and her eyes widened.

"Good man," said Don curtly. "Jed, you bat cleanup from the rear, Earl can be behind me, and Emma, you're in front with the trailer. Here," he handed Emma a sheet of paper. "Directions to my place, it's on your regular route, Exit 39, Mason's Eddy, in case we get separated."

Emma exclaimed, "I want to go on record, Jed never grew up with gun toys, I have absolutely nothing to do with this. I told him to stop playing that damn Call of Duty video game…and why am *I* in front?"

Don interrupted impatiently, "Be glad your son didn't listen to you, and we don't have time for a debate on gun control and violent video games. You're in front because you'll have the most firepower covering you, and your supplies need to be protected." He looked tenderly at Liza, her terrified eyes wide. "I'm sorry dear, but you'll have to drive the tank, we need Jed for cover. You'll be safe in there. I have to man the guns up top."

Liza started to cry hysterically, "I can't drive a *tank*! I live in the city; I hardly even drive a *car*!"

Don replied urgently, "It's easy, you'll see. Just get down below and I'll show you how. You play video games?" Liza nodded mournfully and Don said with gentle assurance, "It's like Grand Theft Auto, just drive around the other cars and keep on the gas." He looked at Jed's concerned face. "It's the best place for her, trust me."

Liza sniffed as Don helped her into the tank and choked, "I can't do this, I want to go home!"

"You are going home, we're all going home. Prince will keep you company." He whistled for Prince, who jumped effortlessly to the ground from the open truck window and scampered to Don's side. Don pointed to the top of the tank and said "In!" Prince instantly leapt to the top of the turret and jumped inside.

"Wow," Emma exclaimed in admiration. "There's a job for him with Cirque du Soleil when this is over."

Don smiled wryly and disappeared into the tank as Emma, Jed, Sweet Betty and Earl waited, engines idling. A band of black stretch limos turned sharply past them up Mimosa Drive toward the upper cul-de-sac road, a few arms and swarthy faces appeared as windows opened. The arms brandished machine guns, the men cheered the tank with enthusiasm. Mario's boys had arrived.

I wonder how they'll feel when they find out Don's flown the coop.

Don reappeared from his tutorial with Liza wearing a military helmet and what looked like a bulletproof vest, and took his place at the turret as Sweet Betty's engine purred loudly.

Great. He's playing War, Little Miss Pussypants has inches of steel around her, and I'm the dried-up expendable old crone who gets to head this kamikaze parade. Well, so be it. I've had a good life. Better to go out with a bang than a whimper. Her stomach gurgled and she felt a pang in her solar plexus. *I'm not ready*, she thought.

Is anyone ever ready for this?

Don jumped down from the tank's turret holding a large plastic bag, and spoke with intensity as he gestured for everyone to open their windows. "Everybody, listen to me carefully. First, don't use turn signals, no point in other folks knowing where you're going. Second, and most important, you're going to see things that are going to shock you and upset you. Only pay full attention if someone is coming at us directly, otherwise, let it go. Keep your eyes moving, focus on present danger. A lot of cars will be scattered on the highways because their electronics were fried, we have to navigate around them. Any gas in their tanks has most likely already been siphoned off, but even if it hasn't, if we stop, we're toast. Whatever happens, do…not….stop. There will be people who will want your car, they will try to flag you down, but no matter how desperate and pathetic they look, you must not stop. I repeat, you must….not….stop. This is no time to be Good Samaritans."

"Now," he said as he opened the bag and began to distribute what looked like little radios to each car. "These are walkie-talkies so we can

73

communicate with each other, but don't, I repeat, don't use them unless you need to. Emma, if we hit any roadblocks, I'll be in touch with police and truckers to give you alternate routes. You'll see, we won't have time for chit chat. Just press this button down," he illustrated, "and release it after you've spoken. C'mon! Let's roll."

"Wait!" Emma exclaimed, and she pointed to Sweet Betty. "Is it/she loaded?"

Don smiled, "Three loaded machine guns on the turret, cannon packed and ready if necessary."

"Geez. Well, we really appreciate this, but since I'm in front of you, please don't blow my head off," Emma said worriedly.

Don replied with a chuckle, "I'll try not to. Your trailer will get it first." Emma widened her eyes, got inside the car and started the engine as she wondered if all this was overkill. *Maybe Don is just dying for war games. Well, too late now.*

Don softly muttered over his walkie talkie, "Move out." The caravan slowly pulled their vehicles into the moonlight and headed down Mimosa Drive. Emma scanned the sky briefly and was almost sure she saw several orbs shoot across the stars above her. *Probably shooting stars, but maybe not. A portent? Are they watching us?*

As they neared the bottom of Mimosa Drive and approached perpendicular Prospect Hill, Emma was struck by the absence of cars, except the occasional police or fire vehicle, sirens blaring. Everything was dark, even houses with their generators on full blast had their lights off. She wondered if people were peering at them from behind their window blinds. She reflexively locked her car doors and looked anxiously at Don and Sweet Betty in her rearview mirror. The tank blocked her view of Jed and Earl's cars, which increased her anxiety.

The convoy turned left onto Cedar Avenue and headed for Highway 29 North. Emma noticed windows in the Cedar Avenue mini mall were broken, people were running in and out of the drug store, arms full of supplies, and the pizza shop and dance supply store were similarly under attack. She heard a gunshot, crouched behind the wheel and vowed not to look as she stepped on the gas. So far, cumbersome Sweet Betty was keeping up.

She looked in her rearview mirror to see a crowd of teenagers running after their procession, so she gunned it across the overpass and swerved onto the highway. She looked behind her at the curving road and, yes, Earl's and Jed's cars were now barely visible behind Sweet Betty. She gazed upward. No orbs in sight.

We're on our own.

Chapter Fifteen

Highway to Hell

Dead cars. Everywhere. A jackknifed semi carrying snack foods from Little Maid was toppled on its side on the meridian, rear cargo door open as Emma approached Highway 29 North. A State Police car, lights flashing, was parked next to it, and the meridian was littered with open boxes and flying pieces of plastic wrap. A few teenagers ran from the scene, arms loaded with packages as a cop talked to a man sitting on the ground holding his head.

Probably the driver. Move on, Emma, don't stop.

The cop looked up in surprise at the tank, then waved distractedly and smiled briefly before returning to the victim. "Of course he knows Don," Emma mused. "Don knows everyone on the thin blue line. This might not be too bad if all we come across are teenagers looting snacks."

Emma maneuvered as quickly as she could around car after abandoned car, but she couldn't drive at top speed, or the trailer swerved dangerously. "Geez, great," she muttered. "Couldn't they at least push the cars off the road? This frickin' trailer is aerodynamically unstable." Sweet Betty was keeping pace, but Liza's driving skills left a lot to be desired, and the tank veered drunkenly around the dead cars. *Poor Prince is going to get seasick.* Emma's hands already felt cramped and sweaty from holding the steering wheel in a death grip.

This is a bad dream. And it's just beginning.

She always imagined her time on the "back nine" in amber-tinted terms, tending to her aging husband and gardens, focusing on her family, creative and home life, dying peacefully in her sleep in her nineties. During her last birthday celebration, Emma's older friend Sarah asked how she felt about growing older. She blithely responded "Oh, it's going to be beautiful, and poignant, like draining the last thick and gorgeous drops of honey from the jar. I plan to enjoy every minute of it."

Sarah had looked at her with haunted eyes from her arthritic world of pain, sighed and replied, "Emma, the secret to successful aging is learning how to deal effectively with loss." Emma didn't want to think about that. She replied she'd think about it when and if the time came.

That time had come. Emma stood to lose everything on this car-littered highway or what lay beyond, and she knew it. Never, even in her most fevered imaginings, could she ever have concocted a scenario like this.

She had it all planned, her life and its trajectory, without ever considering the conceit of believing she could control the myriad universes of other lives, global changes and challenges, or how they would inevitably collide with her unworldly, impractical and illogical beliefs. She believed she could successfully captain her little Good Ship Emma in these huge, choppy and predator-infested waters. After all, she had "the gift" of foresight, and even though she finally felt there was a reason for it, that maybe she had an advantage, foresight wasn't going to help her now. Now was all about careening metal, bullets, dumb luck and elusive orbs.

As she frantically zig-zagged her way along Highway 29, eyes wide, she scanned the terrain in front, to the side and behind her with increasing apprehension, but the biggest battle she was waging was with herself. She was slowly and inexorably realizing that now, right now, she was supremely unequipped to handle the crisis enveloping not only the nation, but the globe, and maybe beyond.

The only thing that propelled her forward was one pressing aim – to protect her family at all costs. That alone gave her the strength and conviction she needed to keep her right foot pressed squarely on the gas pedal. Thinking a few cartons of soup and peanut butter and a few books on eating bugs and living off the land were sufficient to stem this tsunami now seemed the height of naïve hubris. She knew her learning curve was beyond steep from this moment forward, but as her long-time friend Bess chuckled, "Emma, you love nothing better than a challenge."

"I'm going to make it," she said aloud. "We're going to make it. I won't have it any other way." She was answered by the loud hum of the tank behind her, as faint shouts came from the side of the road.

In her rearview mirror multiple vehicles approached rapidly in the faint light of dusk, and behind them a phalanx of large trucks, their headlights blazing through the approaching darkness. A woman appeared from the grassy roadside on the right. She held a wrapped child and waved her free arm as she tried to flag Emma down. Behind her was a man with a shotgun, followed by the shadowy forms of several more armed men. Emma waved her away and screamed "I can't, stop, go back!" but the woman ran in front of Emma's car and stopped cold, her hand held out in front of her. Emma swerved the car dangerously to avoid her; the trailer tilted precariously and almost collapsed.

As Emma stabilized her load, she looked feverishly in her rearview mirror and gaped as she watched the tank mow the woman and child down and Don shoot the men multiple times with his machine gun. "Wake up, wake up, I want to wake up!" she screamed, and broke into hot tears. She felt faint and nauseated, her hands were clammy and sweaty and threatened to slide off the steering wheel.

This. This was her life now, stripped of artifice or cheesy sitcom happy endings. Brute survival. Kill or be killed. Hot bile rose in her throat. She felt dizzy, grabbed a plastic bag in her purse and vomited into it as she tried to keep her eyes on the road. "No, no, no!" she cried, and babbled, "They would have killed you if they could, and not just you. Don, Jed, Liza, Earl. They would have killed all of us. It's not your fault. Forget about love thy neighbor, forget about turn the other cheek. I'm not that good, Lord and Angels, I'm not. I want to live."

The line of cars and trucks grew closer, and Emma muttered feverishly, "Friend or foe, friend or foe..." as a black SUV with tinted windows and a loaded rooftop appeared on her left. The front seat passenger, a bearded man with a grim expression, looked briefly at her and thrust a large pistol through the open window. Emma gasped, cringed, and waited for the bullet's impact. The man pointed forward with his gun as he sped past.

Emma shook her head and shouted, "What the hell do you think I'm doing? Going to the frickin' ball?" *Now, even now Emma, you're pushing back against male supremacy. Well, you need them now. You need them.*

A huge Mack truck pulled up on her right. The driver leaned out the window and brandished a semi-automatic rifle. He wore the telltale red cap of a Cain supporter, and gestured with his rifle and a thumbs up that he had Emma covered. *Thank God*, she thought, *he'll even protect a Subaru if he can keep the species going and working cars in the mix.*

Other loaded cars passed on her left, sometimes driving on the meridian to avoid dead vehicles. Giant trucks of all descriptions barreled past her on her right, sometimes crushing stalled cars, sometimes driving on the shoulder or the grass to avoid them. Emma realized it was a caravan. *Safety in numbers. Always remember that. Safety in numbers. Maybe we're going to make it.*

She, the tank and all their cars were sandwiched in between trucks on the right and armed refugees in their upscale SUVs on the left. In her rearview mirror she could see a jubilant Don wave his helmet in circles in the air and cheer on the caravan. "Stay with the pack," Emma urged herself. "Pedal to the metal." She gunned it to keep pace with the hurtling trucks and cars, and as they pulled away from suburban mini-malls and noise barriers erected in upscale neighborhoods and approached Interstate 80, the road became a little less littered with dead cars, and Emma relaxed.

For a moment.

"Oh shit. You've got to be kidding me!" Emma screamed as a horde of pickup trucks loaded to the rafters with rifle-toting marauders in combat fatigues and black ski masks barreled toward them driving the wrong way on the grassy meridian, lit by the headlights of oncoming cars. "Foe! Definitely foe! Holy shit! Don!" she screamed into the walkie-talkie.

Right on cue, a huge cannon blast split the ground open under one of the approaching pickup trucks and threw it into the air. Machine gun fire rained down on the pickup truck brigade, accompanied by the pop-pop shots of rifles and handguns from the SUVs and giant trucks. Emma glanced hurriedly into the cabin of a giant van next to her in the caravan, and saw the passenger hold the wheel as the driver opened fire on the attackers.

"I want out of this movie!" she screamed, and watched in her rearview mirror as the gangs were picked off one by one along the meridian.

Don's voice crackled over the walkie-talkie, "How's it hangin' in there Emma? Keeping it together? We're all still here, no worries."

Emma drew in a terrified, staggered breath and replied "Thank God. Sure, I'm fine. Piece of cake. Jed, Earl, come in, come in..."

Jed answered slowly, "I'm OK, Mom, just shaken up. Geez, this is nuts."

Earl piped up, "Is this the way it's going to be the whole trip? I don't think my heart can take this." *Wow, this must be bad. Earl never cops to frailty.*

"Holy shit, babe, are you all right?"

"Fine. Fine," he replied slowly. "I just want to get there."

Thank God for you and Sweet Betty, Don." Emma exclaimed. "I lost my lunch back there when you guys rolled over that poor woman. How did you get Liza to do it?"

Liza's sobbing voice crackled on the walkie-talkie, "I didn't do it, I didn't! I can't do this anymore, make it stop!"

Don responded gruffly, "I have some controls up top if I need to override. This is what they do, put women and children in front to stop us from opening fire. We'd be dead on the highway if I didn't."

Jed's voice broke in, "It's OK honey, it's OK. Keep it together, please baby."

Emma picked up the plastic vomit-filled bag, opened her window, winced and chucked it through an opening between trucks on the meridian. *And I always hated people who litter.*

Jed interjected, "Mom, I got three of them."

"Oh honey, that must have been so hard!" Emma gasped. *God, Jed. My Jed.* She felt like she was shaking herself awake from a nightmare.

"Not really. I have good aim," Jed laughed nervously.

Don broke in. "Folks, it should get a little easier on us as we get further away from civilization, but keep your eyes open for attacks from the woods or the road. We're still in it for the next 60 miles or so. At that point, when we get to the Mason's Eddy exit, you're on your own."

The convoy plowed safely past abandoned cars and the occasional interloper for the next 60 miles. Warning shots from the trucks and the tank seemed to subdue any threatened advances, and they drove into the night.

Chapter Sixteen

Truck Stop

The digital clock on Emma's Subaru read 10:32 as the exit sign loomed ahead. "Mason's Eddy, 1 mile, Exit 39." Just ahead on the right was a diner flanked by two vintage gas pumps. Candles glowed in the windows, and a sign over the door read "Mason's Eddy Diner." Several large trucks and SUVs from the caravan were parked in front, and Don's voice crackled over the walkie-talkie, "Folks, let's stop here. I know these folks, they've been prepping for years. Believe me, it's safe."

Emma heard the familiar sound of a generator as she pulled into the parking lot, opened her door and looked around furtively. Two armed men guarded the door of the diner, one gestured for Emma to enter. She waved at them and shouted, "I'm waiting for my family," and pointed to the off ramp as Sweet Betty pulled in, followed by Earl and Jed. Truckers in the parking lot cheered and whistled as Don smiled from the turret. "God, he loves this," Emma muttered to herself. "I've never liked macho man crap until tonight. They deserve it."

Don dismounted triumphantly and glad-handed his admirers as Liza emerged from the tank, tearstained and shell-shocked. Jed and Earl joined the group and helped Liza from the turret. "Pretty fancy driving there, girlie," Earl joked, as he jocularly patted Liza on the back.

She burst into tears and Jed held her comfortingly. "That…was the most… horrible… thing…I've ever…been…through…" she emoted through tearful shudders as Prince paced around her worriedly.

One of the red-hatted truck drivers standing next to Emma muttered in her ear, "She yers?"

Emma shook her head. "No. He is. She's his pregnant girlfriend."

"My condolences," he said with a slight smile. "Maybe you can toughen her up some. She's gonna need it."

Emma looked at him squarely. "And why is that my job? The elder crone imparting her wisdom to the young'uns?"

"It's your grandchild in there, isn't it?" he said gently.

Emma softened. "Yes. I haven't really been thinking much about that lately, what with the apocalypse and all."

Ben extended his hand. "I'm Ben Rhodes, dropped my load in D.C., on my way back home to Maine and the missus for the duration."

Emma shook his hand. "Emma Kaplan. I'm heading to Corinth, we have a cabin there, with my husband, Earl." She gestured to Earl. "My son is Jed, and that's Liza. The fellow with the tank is my neighbor Don Melnik, he's got a place here, so from here on in we're on our own."

"Yeah, Don and I are old friends. I can lead you a ways up the highway, but I'm going to sleep in my truck tonight. Think you can figure out a way to stay over and leave in the morning?"

"Will it be safe? I'm worried about being overrun."

Ben smiled, his blue eyes crinkled in his sunburned face. "Not here, darlin'. We're packin', and Connie inside the diner there has a perimeter set up. But it's up to you." He regarded her carefully. "Kaplan? Sounds Jewish."

Emma's eyes narrowed. "My husband. Problem? He packed his horns and tail for the trip."

Ben laughed heartily, "You're a touchy little snowflake, aren't you? Nah, no problem. We just don't see many of 'em 'round here."

"Well, this isn't exactly their natural habitat. The last time they were in the boonies they were being chased by Cossacks."

Ben smiled widely. "You're a funny one. My wife's feisty like you. You ever get up to Maine, look us up." He handed her a card that read "Ben's Long-Distance Hauling, Saco, Maine."

"Thanks," Emma replied slowly. "Will do. If we get out of this mess alive."

"Well," Ben replied, "That all depends on you and the luck of the draw. You look like you got the nerve for the long haul. Not so sure about little Missy there or your husband. He looks a bit worse for wear."

Earl looked pale and tired. Emma nodded. "You're right Ben, time to tend to the family. It was nice meeting you though, even under these circumstances. I can't thank you enough for helping us get through."

Ben waved as Emma headed for Earl and Jed. "No worries. Even though I'm pretty sure you voted for the other guy. Let me know if you plan to stay over. You can find me here in the morning, I'll be leaving around 8. I can take you as far as the 81 Junction, that's about sixty miles from here."

Emma waved back. "OK. Thanks so much." She joined Earl and put her arms around his waist. He looked at her coldly.

"Making new 'friends'?" he asked bitingly. "Slumming a bit aren't we, my dear, cozying up to red hats?"

Emma took her arm away from him and faced him squarely. "Earl Kaplan, if it wasn't for these 'red hats' we could be dead. They're not bad people, just, well, misinformed and tanked up on propaganda. We don't have time for this nonsense. This guy can help us get home safely, but we'll have to stay overnight."

Jed piped up, "No Mom! Let's keep going. The longer we wait, the worse it's going to get."

Don was listening to the conversation and stepped in. "Listen, it's safer for you to go at first light – at least you can see what's coming at you. My CB guys and the truckers tell me most of the gangs are still getting what they can Downstate for the next few days at least. We should be OK, we haven't seen anything the last 30 miles." A gunshot rang out close by. Don muttered, "Then again…."

A group of truckers gripped their rifles and semi-automatic weapons and took off toward the sound. As they reached the edge of the woods, two red-hats dragged a large dead male deer, antlers bobbing, and shouted "Hey Connie, venison stew and jerky time!"

Don relaxed. "I rest my case."

Emma looked at Earl imploringly. "Honey, it would be safer if we could have Ben, the trucker I was talking with, go with us tomorrow. He can take us to about 35 miles from the cabin. It's a good idea."

"Where are we going to sleep? There's no room in the cars." Earl said defensively. Don stepped in.

"You can stay at the cabin. I've got sleeping bags and an extra room."

"That's very kind of you. Isn't it, Earl?" Emma asked urgently.

"What about all the perishable food?" Earl was loath to spend the night under the same roof with Emma's Marine buddy. "It'll spoil."

"I'll see what I can put in the fridge, not much there right now, should be all right, unless you brought a side of beef," Don said lightly.

"Mostly yogurt and cheese in the cooler," Emma replied. "And some hummus. The rest is on dry ice."

Don smiled, "Sounds about right."

"Thanks Don, I love cultural stereotyping."

"If the shoe fits."

"I did bring beef, for the backward carnivores."

Jed stepped in, "OK, OK, we'll stay here, thank you Don. I'm freaking hungry, *I* could eat a deer at this point. I'm going in. Come on, honey." He put his arm around Liza and propelled her toward the diner.

"Sure," said Don. "Let's go."

Don held the door for Emma as two armed sentinels at the door high-fived him. He knew them by name. Earl followed behind grimly. Inside the diner, lighting was moody at best – a few lights and lots of candles illuminated the faces of the men and women seated at tables and booths. A lanky red-hatted man sat in a chair in a corner with an acoustic guitar, softly strumming, and the smell of grilling meat was strong, along with a slight smoky mist in the air.

I guess fans aren't included in the generator output, Emma thought. Several truckers and members of the van caravan cheered at Don, and a rosy, short, heavy-set woman scurried from behind the service counter to stand, arms akimbo, in front of him.

"I hear you brought your best girl Betty along. She serve you well on the trip?" she asked with mock seriousness.

Don smiled warmly, "Yep. Only woman I could ever trust, Connie."

Connie opened her arms, gave Don a big bear hug and scanned Emma and her family. "My money's always on you, Mr. Hot-Shot Marine. I knew you'd show up. And who have we here?"

Don gestured to Emma, "This is my neighbor Emma and her family. They're heading for their place in Corinth tomorrow. It's been a tough few hours for 'em, we had some skirmishes early on. Folks, this is Connie

85

Bratten, the best darn cook in the county. If she wasn't married already, I'd have nabbed her."

Connie looked up at Don and quipped, "And who's sayin' I'd hook up with a hound like you? I've got better sense."

Don clutched his heart in a mock heart attack as Connie waved him off and put an arm around Emma. "Honey, you look like you need a drink."

Emma startled. "You've got a bar here too?"

"Well, not so's you'd notice, but I've got whiskey behind the lunch counter that'll put hair on your chest."

"The whiskey part I like," Emma countered. "The hairy part not so much."

Connie laughed. "Like life, isn't it? How about you, Mr. Emma? And you young folks?"

Emma whispered softly into Connie's ear, "He's got heart problems, she's knocked up, and I can bet you dollars to donuts my son's probably aching to smoke a joint. But I could use a few stiff belts."

Earl was coming out of his discomfiture and approached Connie with his best charming, ingratiating smile. "I wouldn't say no to a diet coke, lovely lady."

Connie appraised Earl coolly. "Sure handsome. Anything else?" Earl put a friendly arm about her waist.

"Got any hamburgers back there, baby? And fries?"

Connie smiled, "Is this a diner? Does a bear shit in the woods? How do you like 'em?"

Early quipped, "Hamburgers, or bears? Medium well, and in the next county, in that order."

Connie whispered sexily, "Coming right up. You want lettuce, onion and tomato with that, big boy?" Earl gave her the thumbs up, she hurried behind the counter and yelled into the back kitchen, "Burn one, drag it through the garden and pin a rose on it!"

Emma watched the scene with mild amusement and whispered to Earl, "Another one bites the dust."

Earl looked at Emma wryly. "I'm keeping up with you. So far you're two to my one."

Emma scoffed. "Don't be ridiculous. I'm old enough to be their....I'm old enough," she tapered off guiltily, remembering the kiss with Don. "Besides, we're life and death here, all this la-dee-dah nonsense is superfluous."

Earl shook his head and tapped Emma on the tip of her nose. "First of all, my darling, you don't look your age and you know it, and secondly, remember your WWII research – when bombs fly, panties fly off and trousers fly open."

Emma smiled. "May I quote you? Very catchy."

Earl bowed with a flourish. "You have my permission, madame."

Emma hugged him. "I love you. Let's *eat*."

Chapter Seventeen

Last Chance Hotel

Emma had to admit, Connie was a kick-ass cook. No limp, canned green beans and flat, meager black hamburgers on stale buns at the Mason's Eddy Diner. Emma's fries, green beans and broiled half chicken were perfection, the fries were delicate and crispy without a hint of extra oil, the green beans held their bright green color and satisfying crunch, and the chicken, juicy and flavorful, could easily have been cut with a butter knife.

Emma yelled out to Connie as she bustled by their booth, arms full of food-laden plates, "Connie, I thought I was a good cook, but you put me to shame. You could cook in the finest restaurants in the city."

Connie stopped and mugged sexily, "And give up all this? Honey, I was in the city once, and that was once too many for me. All those people, all that noise, I couldn't wait to get out of there."

"Well," Emma replied, "I hope the folks around here appreciate you."

Connie smiled and yelled to the crowd, "Do y'all appreciate me?" Loud shouts, whistles and applause greeted her, she curtseyed slightly and whispered to Emma as she exited to the kitchen, "I rest my case."

Emma remarked to Earl, who was inhaling his hamburger and fries, "I wish I could stick around here for a while and learn at Connie's substantial knee."

Earl spoke with a muffled full mouth, "Honey, you're great. I love your cooking." Emma hugged him, which did not cause him to break stride. To Earl, food replaced female genitalia as his religion, and he was praying at the altar. "Do you think she has pie?" he asked hopefully.

Emma smiled, "I'm betting she does." She walked to the lunch counter and asked a painfully thin, young blonde waitress, "Is there any pie?"

The girl answered distractedly as she wiped the counter with a wet rag and pointed to a regiment of glass pastry domes that lined the back of the counter. "Yes ma'am, cherry, blueberry, lemon meringue and Dutch apple."

"One of each please," Emma smiled, and pointed to their table, "Over there." The girl nodded and flashed a mouthful of braces.

Don appeared next to Emma and said quietly to the girl, "Better make that to go Stacey. Emma, I'm heading out. You need to follow me to the cabin."

"At least this time I'll be behind you." She paused "If that's safe. I've got to admit, I'm nervous about what's lurking in the woods."

Don patted Emma's shoulder, "No worries. Connie's boys set up an ironclad perimeter. A flea couldn't get through."

"Well, that's a relief." Emma took the pastry box from the waitress and nodded her thank you. "If you're very good you may get a piece of this pie as a reward for everything you've done for us today."

Don smiled and whispered in Emma's ear, "I'm always good. And I don't ask for rewards, but I sure won't turn any down." Emma smiled enigmatically as she saw Earl observing her interaction with Don, smoke figuratively issuing from his ears.

"Gotta get the troops going – give me five minutes, OK?"

"You got it. I have to gas Betty up. I'll be outside."

Emma saluted good-naturedly and joined Earl at their booth. He glowered at her as she held up the pastry box. "Pie sir, as you requested."

Earl muttered, "Took you long enough."

Emma pulled back from him at arm's length, "Hey, I can't control who talks to me while I'm waiting to get *your* pie. Don is heading to his cabin, we need to follow him, we'll have pie when we get there." Earl slumped slightly. "OK now, don't pout. It's not pretty in someone over 70." Earl did not respond. "Come on honey, we have to go."

Earl replied sulkily, "I'm betting he doesn't have a king-sized bed. At least not for us."

Emma turned his downcast face to her with her hand on his chin. "Sweetheart, I know this is hard for you, it's hard for all of us, but you've got to try and get used to the idea that we're going to be roughing it for the foreseeable future. I know you like to go four-star all the way when you travel, and this is really alien to you, but you've got to try, for once in your life, to be flexible. Don is doing us a favor, he saved our asses, and tonight might be one of the most peaceful nights we're going to spend in a while."

She drew a deep, calming breath. "And speaking of alien things, I'm pretty sure I saw orbs over Mimosa Drive when we left, high up, and it's freaking me out. Please don't make me deal with all this on my own. I need to know you're with me."

Earl softened, took Emma's hand and kissed it. "Darling, I'm always with you. No matter what."

"Ditto my dear," Emma whispered, and kissed Earl lightly. "Let's round up the kids."

Don was outside in the moonlight filling several red gas cans from a rusty old pump as Jed helped him load the cans inside Sweet Betty.

"I'll leave my car here, see you in the Subaru." muttered Earl, loath to help.

"Hey Don," Emma yelled, "Can we get one of those? Actually, two? Just in case? I have one in the trailer, but it's buried. I know, I know, not a smart move."

Don waved and yelled back, "Sure, I'll put it on your tab!" He smiled slightly and continued loading as Emma got into the driver's seat.

Earl sat sullenly in the front passenger's seat. "Honey," Emma chided, "Please put on your seat belt." Earl buckled up as he continued to stare impassively straight ahead. *Great*, thought Emma. *He's doing his famous Cigar Store Indian act. What a baby.* She sighed loudly. "Really looking forward to tonight with you Mr. Sunshine. It should be tons of fun." Earl was unmoved. She gestured to Jed and Liza in their car behind the Subaru that they were moving out as Sweet Betty took the lead.

Emma started up the car, put on her brights and squinted in the darkness as Sweet Betty lumbered slowly up a dirt road just beyond the diner. "God, no streetlights, nothing," Emma marveled, and looked sideways at Earl. Crickets. Earl had left the building and was shacked up in Conjugal Paranoiaville. "Come on honey, snap out of it. Do we have to go through this now? I could really use your emotional support at this particular juncture, to quote Dubya's dad. You're with me no matter what, remember?"

Earl replied coldly, "I think maybe I'm in the way. All these men cozying up to you, you could have your pick."

Emma replied exasperatedly, "But I chose *you*. For almost thirty years, I chose only you. I know we can't make love anymore, and I'm painfully aware you rarely come near me beyond kissing because you can't, as you put it, 'deliver the goods' and it makes you sad, but I don't care. I've told you over and over it doesn't matter to me, but you don't believe me."

"Yes, I know," Earl replied sadly, "But maybe hard times call for hard men. Maybe you need something I can't give you anymore."

"Darling, you're killing me here. Extracurricular nookie is the last thing on my mind. All I'm thinking about is how to get us where we need to go in one healthy, intact piece, where to put our perishables overnight, and whether or not everyone will be comfortable. Can we please focus on that?"

Earl took a deep breath. "Yes. But I want you to know, if you need relief with one of these yoyos, even Mr. Marine, I'll understand. It's Last Chance Hotel baby, I'm no fool. If I could screw you silly tonight I would, because for all we know it could be our last. I married a hot little number, I'm proud of you. It's been on my mind, and I've said enough."

"Honey," she said solemnly as she tenderly held Earl's hand, "I appreciate that, and I love you more than you'll ever know. And I always will. You have been the only man I've wanted for almost thirty years. Now I've said enough.".

They held hands as Emma drove one-handed. The car was silent as it bounced and waved along the narrow dirt road, flanked by tall grasses and trees on either side and a thick grass meridian running down its center. Emma swore she could see bright eyes watch her from the forest, and at that moment they felt like judge and jury. She looked upward briefly at the clear night sky packed with stars. *How can it be so crazy and out of control down here and so quiet and peaceful up there?*

A clearing came into view a few miles up the dirt road. At its center was a neat little log cabin with a rustic covered porch complete with porch swing, and a wishing well to the right of the gravel driveway. A startled young deer darted in front of the Subaru and stopped briefly to blink confusedly at the bright headlights. Emma slammed on the brakes, thankful the cars were moving so slowly there was no impact, front or back. "So much for the welcome wagon," Emma muttered darkly.

At the front door Don held a bright halogen lantern as he looked for his keys. He withdrew a clutch of keys from his front pants pocket and went through them painstakingly until he found the right one. Emma, Earl, Jed and Liza lined up behind him, and Prince brought up the rear, tail wagging. Buddy and Shatzi nosed around the yard until Jed whistled for them to come to him.

"We'll have to use candles and flashlights," Don said "The grid's out almost everywhere, after all. I'm still not used to it."

"No worries," Emma said. "But what about the refrigerator? That's out too."

Don smiled. "You'd think so, wouldn't you? But no. Solar panels, just enough to run the fridge, well pump and hot water heater."

Emma laughed. "You really do come prepared, don't you?"

Don looked at Earl, hesitated and said calmly, "Old Boy Scouts never die."

Emma saluted and intoned, "Campfire Girls, Brownies, Girl Scouts and 4-H. Prepared and then some, reporting for duty, sir."

Don smiled, opened the door and held his high-powered halogen lantern high so everyone could survey the room. Emma was surprised by its warm, welcoming atmosphere, with its red-and-white checkered tablecloth on a long, rustic wooden dining table, lacy sheers in the windows, and whimsical touches. An oversized black ceramic cookie jar with splashes of large red bas-relief flowers sat on the galley kitchen counter, an enigmatic, graceful wooden cat sculpture graced the hearth, and tasteful botanical prints punctuated the walls.

"Wow Don," Emma exclaimed. "No cheesecake girlies? No mini Sherman tanks on the mantel?"

Don almost blushed, looked at his feet and in his patented sideways mumble intoned softly, "My wife. It's her doing. Haven't had a chance to put my signature on it yet."

Emma instantly felt chagrined. *Geez Emma, for a smart woman sometimes you don't engage your brain before putting your mouth in gear.* "Well," she replied too brightly, "I give it two big thumbs up!"

Jed sighed as he stood in the doorway, dropped two suitcases on the floor and asked plaintively, "Don, where are you putting us? We're really beat." He and Liza made a beeline for the floral print overstuffed sofa in front of the picture window and flopped wearily onto it.

"Jed, manners!" Emma exclaimed.

Don smiled. "Can you blame them? This has been a day for the record books. And I understand little Missy here has a bun in the oven." He gestured to the couch and said "You'll have to be in here – one of you can sleep on the couch. I have a sleeping bag for you....Jed?" He gestured to the floor, Jed nodded, Don nodded in agreement. "And Emma, you and Earl can sleep in my room, it's got a nice-sized bed Daddy Long Legs will appreciate."

"Oh, we can't take you out of your room!" Emma exclaimed.

"I'm used to the floor, I do a lot of camping, I'll bed down in the mud room with Prince, no worries," Don replied briskly. "Now let's get your hummus and other hippie food into the fridge, OK?"

Earl had been watching the scene carefully, and said slowly, "Thank you Don. Really. This means a lot to us, we're grateful."

Don approached Earl and put out his hand, Earl took it and gave it a slow shake. "What are neighbors for?" Don asked.

Emma smiled and hugged Earl. "And the bedroom is...?"

"Just down the hall on the right, bathroom right across from it." Don pointed as he turned on more halogen lamps and set them about the room. "I'll start a fire; it can get cold in the mountains at night. Make yourselves at home, and hit the hay early. Tomorrow's going to be a doozie for you folks." Earl grabbed their suitcases and headed for the bedroom. Emma stayed behind.

"He likes to unpack immediately and get organized. I leave him alone until he's done."

Jed fiddled with the dials of a radio on the mantel, but most stations were static. One was still on the air, a local country music station. "Don, do you think it needs new batteries?" Jed asked.

"Nope." Don replied. "They're brand new. I guess either most stations fried up in the solar waves or folks have more important things to do."

Jed turned up the volume as a country song finished with the plaintive line "Further on down the road, I'll be with you again." A somber deejay murmured in rich, deep tones, "Folks, this here's J.D. Cralls at WCTR 98.7 out of River Fork, here for you, and as long as we draw breath, no crazy city folks are going to bust us up. I'd like to see 'em try."

Jed muttered, "Just passing through, redneck turkey." He turned the volume down on the radio as a new country song began.

"Jed" Emma scolded gently. "Rednecks, as you put it, saved our asses today." Jed scowled.

Don walked past sleeping Liza on the couch and spoke confidentially to Jed. "Rednecks and refugees are pretty much all you're going to see from here on out, and if you give 'em half a chance you'll find they'll do a heck of a lot more for you than most city folks will. Around here, we do for each other." Jed hung his head and frowned; Don clapped him on the back. "Sorry man. I know this is hard for you, it's hard for all of us." He headed for the fridge. "You guys want a beer? A local brewer makes a pretty mean dark ale."

Jed nodded, Emma shook her head and laughed, "Don't want to mix Connie's whiskey with beer. I'm not that good." Don opened two beers, handed one to Jed and swigged deeply on the other.

"What are you going to do up here Don? All by yourself?" Jed took a swig and looked appreciatively at the bottle.

"Fella, I've been all by myself for years, in spirit. My wife Maria and I stayed together in name only for the kids, but they're on their own now, safe as far as I know. I asked 'em to come up here, maybe they will, maybe they won't. Maria took off with some pinstriped buttoned-down asshole from her office a year ago, haven't heard a peep from her since. It's Prince and me, and frankly that's the way I like it. I'll help out with the perimeter, and who knows what waits for me around the corner, after this mess is cleaned up."

"When will that be?" Jed asked urgently. "What am I supposed to do if Liza needs a doctor, or we run out of food? Earl isn't like you, he's not…handy, and he's old. It's me now, and Mom, we're the ones who'll have to carry most of the freight. I'm an ad man, not a mountain man, and it looks I'm going to be a father while the world falls apart." Emma moved toward Jed and patted his shoulder.

Don put his arm around Jed's other shoulder. "Jed, my man, you'd be surprised what you can do when you have to. Where you're going there'll be a lot of folks willing to school you in mountain and survival skills. And who knows, maybe you'll even like it. Just get there in one piece, get into the community, learn how to survive, and have hope for the future. It's going to be rough, really rough, and you'll see things you never dreamed of. You already know how to shoot, I saw that today, and I'm mighty grateful to you, because you had my back."

Jed choked up, looked toward the bedroom and whispered softly, "I wish you were coming with us."

"I'll be with you in spirit, and I hope we can meet up again when it's all over. You can do this man, you can."

"Jed can do anything," Emma declared emphatically as she began to unload food and find places for it in the refrigerator. Don took an afghan from the back of the couch and tucked it around Liza.

"I'll get your sleeping bag," he said to Jed, and disappeared into a back room.

Emma stopped what she was doing, went to Jed and hugged him. "Honey, I'm so glad we're together. I don't know how I would cope if I didn't know where you were."

Jed hugged her, then stood back and shook his head in disbelief. "I still keep hoping this is a bad dream."

"Well, it isn't," Emma replied. "I'm pretty sure I'm going to have a whopping case of PTSD when this is all over, but I'm going to do everything I can to keep all of us safe. I know you will, too. We *all* will, in our way."

Jed nodded. Don entered with a rolled sleeping bag and pillow, handed them to Jed and headed for the door. "It's not the Ritz, but it's clean and warm. I'm going to smoke on the porch for a while. 'Night all." The screen door closed gently behind him.

Emma stopped and exclaimed in a high voice. "Well. People come and go so quickly here. Isn't that what Alice in Wonderland said? We truly are through the looking glass now. Honey, I'm going to brush my teeth and go to bed. I hope you do the same."

Jed nodded as he unrolled the sleeping bag and set it on the floor next to Liza. "Soon, Mom, soon."

Emma smiled. "Just like the old days. My little night owl. Try and get some sleep, we're getting up early tomorrow. Ben's leaving around eight."

Jed sighed. "Maybe when I wake up it'll all be over, and we can go home." He and Emma looked at each other meaningfully. "And other fantasies. 'Night Mom." He kissed Emma on the cheek, she hugged him and headed for the bedroom.

Chapter Eighteen

Open and Closure

Three hours later Don was still on the porch. The light from his cigarette pierced the moonlight like a firefly as he rocked slowly back and forth on the porch swing. Emma appeared at the front screen door and peered out. She pulled her knitted shawl close around her flannel nightgown and opened the door tentatively. "Mind a little company? I can't sleep."

Don patted the space next to him on the swing and replied softly "Sure. I won't bite. The mosquitos might."

"You're not the only one who comes prepared, remember?" Emma responded. "I wiped myself down with heavy-duty repellent before I came out. I hate mosquitos, especially when they buzz right in your ear." She sat next to Don and peered out into the darkness. "It's the first time in my life I've dreaded sunrise," she said grimly as she stared into the night.

"Sure you don't want to set up housekeeping around here? It's about as safe as you can get."

"It crossed my mind," Emma said. "I guess if we can't get through, it's an option. But I love our place, we know people there, a lot of my family's near there. We have to try."

"I hear you," Don replied. "But strangers become friends pretty quick around here, especially when times get tough."

Emma turned to him and smiled. "I'm happy for you, you landed somewhere safe, where you won't be alone."

Don looked at her appraisingly. "You know, in the moonlight, without makeup, you look about 17, Miss Emma."

Emma bowed her head in mock appreciation. "And you, Mr. Melnick, are a silver-tongued devil."

Don smiled wickedly. "That's what they say." They looked at each other in silence, and Emma felt heat slowly growing in her body. Don said slowly, "You know, I always liked you. In a very special way. I like your gentle fire."

"And my ass, don't forget that. Caught you looking." Emma said slyly.

"Well, it's a monumental ass. I can't be the first who's said so." Emma nodded gently in reluctant assent. Another loaded, silent moment passed. Don moved closer to her, and she had an involuntary intake of breath. *It could happen now, Emma, ball in in your court. What are you going to do?* Earl was sleeping deeply, courtesy of the three sleeping pills he needed for sleep, and his melatonin gummy. *God, Earl.*

I can't, I can't do this to Earl. But…

Don took Emma's hand. She clasped it tightly, and they sat quietly for a few minutes. She didn't know what to say, but her mind was racing.

She moved to stand, still holding Don's hand. "I guess I better get back to bed," she said apologetically.

Don kept a tight hold on her hand, pulled her toward him and said "Please don't. Please stay with me. Maybe I'm wrong but I think we need each other right now." Emma paused, her mind rushing with a torrent of emotions – fear, longing, curiosity, desperation, pent-up desire. She sat next to him and looked down at her lap.

Don put his hand on Emma's cheek and gently turned her face to his. "We're grownups Emma, we know what's happening here. We know what might happen tomorrow. We went through something intense together today, it drew us closer to each other, and I'd be lying if I said I don't want to make love to you, because I do. But the last thing I ever want to do is anything you'll regret."

Emma took his hand and held it in her hands. "God. I…I don't know…what to say. It's been a really long season without rain, I haven't had a man inside me for almost 10 years. Maybe there are cobwebs in there, maybe it sewed itself shut. I'm not one of those juicy cheesecake cuties on your wall anymore, I've got mileage on me, and I smell like insect repellent. But inside, inside I'm still a teenager, maybe even younger. Inside I have no age. Maybe this is the last time I can ever have it, maybe I'll be a mashed-up body by the side of the road tomorrow."

Don shook his head forcefully. "Don't say that. Don't even think it. You're too tough to die – you just don't know it yet."

Emma looked upward at the sky filled with stars, her eyes teary, "I can't hurt Earl. But…he said he would understand if I….he loves me so much." She cried softly.

Don sat quietly. "Let's just sit here. That's enough." They sat in silence for a few minutes, Don periodically squeezed Emma's hand. Her mind raced with options. *Ball in your court Emma, now or never, maybe.* Emma looked up at him plaintively.

"I need you to kiss me again," she whispered. "Then I'll know."

Don held her gently and kissed her sweetly. She returned his kiss, and their exchange became more passionate as desire swelled. Emma began to caress Don's chest, he reached for her breast, and she gasped. "All right," she whispered. "Where, where do we go? And….I'm sorry to break the mood here, but…are you safe? You know, diseases? I don't want to be in the middle of nowhere with an STD."

Don looked at her with admiration and remarked passionately as their caresses continued, "You're really something, you know that? Only you would be this upfront. Yes, I'm clean as a whistle, I haven't had a woman in over a year, and I got tested for life insurance last month, the whole shebang. But what about you? I don't need any new babies at this point in my life."

Emma chuckled softly, "Oh honey, now that's flattering. Menopause, my man. The egg factory is closed."

Don smiled widely. "Well, m'dear, I see you've got a nice wooly shawl wrapped around you. If you're not averse to it, we can go out there, lay it on the soft ground and let nature take its course." He took Emma by the hand and led her past the clearing to a grassy spot under a large, spreading tree. He carefully unwrapped her from her shawl, like a Christmas gift, took his coat off, laid it on the ground and carefully smoothed the shawl over it. They slowly undressed in front of each other, Emma resisting the urge to fold their clothes in a neat pile. Rock Paper Scissors, Passion covers Neatness. Don's body was taut and smooth, Emma's soft and pliant.

They faced each other in the moonlight, no longer Don and Emma, but Man and Woman taken by desire, fear and longing, afraid of tomorrow, coveting every moment in the dark together. Don picked Emma up as if she were weightless, placed her on the shawl and whispered tenderly in her ear, "I'm going to make love to you." Emma moved to speak, he shushed her gently with his finger on her mouth. She allowed herself to feel completely vulnerable and open, opened her arms and welcomed him on top of her.

He looked down at her in wonder. "My God, you're beautiful," he marveled.

"Gravity," Emma said softly. "This is what I used to look like before it took over."

"In my eyes, this will be you forever," he said, and kissed her passionately as he entered her. She gasped at the pain, and he stopped.

"I was afraid of this," she said. "I'm like a nun down there now." He rolled off her and said gently "I think maybe you need a little more warmup."

"Yes," Emma quipped ruefully, "Like an old Chevy."

"No, never a Chevy," Don replied. "You are a vintage Jaguar, dear Emma, and I hope you'll let me start up your engine."

Don kissed her body, inch by inch, and as she began to writhe with desire he tenderly insinuated his fingers inside her. "There we go," he said appreciatively. "She sure feels ready now."

Emma gasped, "Oh yes. Please, please." He entered her, she moaned softly with pleasure, and as he gently moved on top of her she exploded into multiple orgasms and cried loudly into the night. He carefully put his hand on her mouth to keep others from hearing them, then climaxed silently inside her, gasping.

They lay in the moonlight, breathing hard, as light sweat covered their bodies. They stared into each other's eyes for several minutes as Emma shuddered with aftershocks. "Boy, when you come on, you really come on, don't you?" Don said admiringly.

"Well, it's been a long time, and you are one sexy beast,," Emma panted. "Thank you, really, thank you. I didn't know when Earl and I last made love that it was the final time. I always felt I needed closure, I wanted to be able to say, 'This is it' and mark it for history. Now I can do that, and what a way to go."

"Well, I wouldn't be so sure," Don said. "You've got a lot of life in you, and we don't know what's around the corner. Listen, you know where I am. If something changes, if you need me, I'm here."

Emma stroked his face tenderly. "Thank you. I would love to lay here and pillow talk all night, but Earl may get up to pee, and…I've got to go." She struggled to her feet, still giddy from their lovemaking, pulled on her nightgown, wrapped herself in her shawl, kissed him and wandered back to the cabin in the moonlight. Don watched her, lit a cigarette, and sat against the tree until little pink curls of sunrise began to appear in the East.

Chapter Nineteen

Wide and Deep

Emma's watch alarm went off at 6:30. For a moment she thought she was on Mimosa Drive, waking in their big soft bed, until the events of the previous day flooded over her like a tsunami, jumbled together like tide-swept flotsam. Orbs hurtling through the night sky, the woman and baby crushed by Sweet Betty, Connie and her "boys," the dead buck carried triumphantly from the woods, the ride in the dark to Don's cabin, Don's kisses. She quickly felt her vagina – it was still swollen and smelled like sex.

She jumped out of bed, ran to the bathroom and turned on the shower. *The shawl*, she thought. *It probably smells like sex too.* She ran to the bedroom, picked up the shawl and quickly draped it over the outside porch railing to air out. *Guilty, guilty, guilty*, she thought. *Am I going to tell Earl? How can I? He has radar, he'll guess. He knows me so well. Protect him, deny, at least for now. Today is going to be tough enough. God, remember when it all used to be so easy?* In a matter of a few weeks her former life seemed light years away.

When she emerged from the shower, hair wrapped in a towel, Don was in the kitchen making coffee as Prince wolfed down his food from a large dish on the kitchen floor. Jed and Liza were sound asleep in the open living space, but Buddy and Shatzi were starting to stir in their crates, alerted by the smell of Prince's food. Don and Emma stopped moving and stared at each other. Emma felt her vagina pulse with desire and thought, *Well, this isn't good. For the first time in 30 years another man is turning you on just by looking at him.*

Don blushed lightly and muttered a bashful, "Good morning."

Emma was still stationary, staring at him. "Good morning," she said, as if in a trance.

"Coffee?" Don asked uncomfortably.

"Um, sure," Emma said. Don took two mugs from a kitchen cabinet and poured coffee into them. Emma still didn't move. Don held up a mug to her and she startled, then approached him and moved to take it from his hand. They regarded each other silently.

After a long silence Don asked "Creamer? Sugar?" as he held onto the cup, letting his fingers touch hers.

"No....thanks." She accepted the cup and he dropped his hand. Glancing back toward the bedroom she whispered, "This isn't easy, is it?"

"Nope," he said laconically. "Nothing we can do about it...is there?"

"Nope," Emma said, in an unsuccessful attempt at levity. "Well," she added with false brightness, "We'll always have the shawl, the jacket, and the elm tree."

Don smiled wryly. "Magnolia, actually. Giant Tulip Tree. Lasts for years. Longer than we will." He looked at Jed and Liza, then at Emma and whispered, "You better get away from me or I'm going to take you right here on the kitchen counter."

Emma gasped and almost swooned. The bedroom door opened, Earl entered sleepily as he scratched his belly and adjusted his pajama pants. In that moment Emma was grateful Earl's mornings were semi-comatose in a sleeping-pill hangover. He asked blankly, "Bathroom free?"

"Yes, honey," Emma said quietly. "I'm all done in there."

"How much time do we have?" he asked.

Emma looked at the clock on the kitchen wall. "About an hour. Maybe we should go to Connie's for breakfast, yes?"

Earl smiled sleepily. "Yes ma'am," and went into the bathroom. Don grabbed Emma's arm and whisked her down the hall into the mudroom at the back of the cabin. Her towel fell off and her damp hair tumbled over her shoulders. He shut and locked the mud room door, looked at Emma with fierce intensity and picked her up. She wrapped her legs around him as he urgently unzipped his jeans and entered her, and they copulated like wild animals for what seemed like thirty seconds – *How could it take so little time?* Emma wondered, as her body took over and they climaxed together, panting softly.

103

"This is crazy," she whispered. "We've got to get out there." Don nodded, adjusted his pants and shook his head as if to wake himself. She shakily put the towel back on her head, kissed Don passionately, then opened the door. "Thanks, I think we have enough food, but your pantry is great," she said too brightly.

"Just thought I'd ask," replied Don lightly. Jed and Liza were stirring, Emma could hear the shower running. Safe. For the moment.

She whispered to Don, "We've got to keep it together. Earl has serious radar. And I feel like such a traitor right now."

"Bet it never felt so good," he said with a slight smile and glint in his eye. Emma looked at him openmouthed.

"Mr. Melnik, these are crazy times, I'm sure that's all this is, and you are a scalawag, sir," she whispered in a mock Southern belle voice.

"Sorry Miss Scarlett, your charms made me forget myself," Don muttered with his best Rhett Butler imitation, and managed a half smile. He sobered and looked at Emma tenderly.

"For years you were right around the corner, and who knew?" she said softly.

"I did," he said. She stared at him.

"Wonderful," she said darkly. "I need this like a hole in the head."

"Let's not talk about holes in heads, OK?" he said worriedly. "I wish I could go with you today."

"I think Ben will have us covered," she said. "God, I hope so." She smiled, "All….this…..has made me really hungry. We're going to Connie's. Better if you don't come along, if that's all right with you. Let's not push our luck."

Don nodded soberly. Emma felt the passion between them was a frisky puppy she was desperately and abortively trying to muzzle and sweep under the rug.

"Give it time – it will pass," Emma said.

"God, I hope not." Don replied.

"I know. My grandmother used to say that. But what did she know?" Don smiled. "You always make me laugh."

Jed sat up sleepily and nudged Liza, who whimpered. He looked around and saw Emma and Don. A look of understanding flashed on his face and he said, "Hi, you guys. Have a good night?"

Emma answered defensively, "Not at all. I had a really hard time sleeping."

"I bet," said Jed knowingly.

What am I, glowing or something? Emma wondered, and began to bustle around the room. She nudged Jed up and began to fold his sleeping bag, hurriedly handed the partially rolled bag and rumpled pillow to Don and collapsed in tears on the couch next to still-prone Liza. Jed stood next to her and petted her hair.

"It's OK, Mom, really. I know you, and I get it, it's OK. To me it was a foregone conclusion."

Emma looked up at him in wonder and said with open-mouthed awe, "Is there *anything* you *don't* know?"

Jed smiled. "Nope. Infuriating, isn't it?"

"What was a foregone thingie?" Liza asked sleepily, then convulsed and held her hand over her mouth. "Bathroom!" she screamed, and ran for the bathroom door.

"Earl's in there!" Emma shouted.

"Like I give a shit!" Liza bellowed, as she threw open the door and puking sounds were heard from the bathroom.

Earl ran out of the bathroom wrapped in a towel, his face half shaven and half covered in shaving cream. "Geez, what a way to start the day! God!" he exclaimed.

"She can't help it, Earl," Emma said with frustration, "It's morning sickness."

Earl stopped short. "Oh, right. I hope she doesn't get sick in the car." He looked closely at Emma. "You OK, honey? You look like you've been crying." He grabbed her in a bear hug and got shaving cream on her towel.

"Earl!" Emma exclaimed as she removed the towel and said to Don, "I'm sorry, I'll hang this in the bathroom, it's too wet to go in the hamper."

"No worries," Don said with a slight smile.

Earl followed Emma asking, "What's wrong, honey? I know something's wrong." They entered the bathroom to see Liza on the floor, head poised over the toilet.

"Sorry, Liza," Emma said apologetically, as she hung the towel over the shower curtain. She turned to Earl, grabbed his arm and propelled him out of the bathroom. "I'm stressed out!" she said emotionally. "The last 24 hours have been the most insane of my entire life, and we don't know what's ahead." Earl held her tenderly.

"Don't worry, honey. You've got the big guy to protect you." He stood back, grimaced like an ape and held his arms in the air in a mock body builder pose. This usually made Emma laugh, but she covered her face and erupted in fresh tears. "C'mon honey. We'll be all right. We'll figure it out," he crooned as he tried to hold her, but she evaded him.

"We have to get going, I'll be all right, I just want to get there." She shuddered in between her tears. "We have to pack up, I'm sure Don's had quite enough of us."

Don replied from the couch, "No, not nearly enough." Emma cried anew as she went into the bedroom.

Chapter Twenty

Tea and Sympathy

The diner was bustling as Earl, Emma, Jed and Liza entered and looked for a booth or a table. A tall, ruggedly handsome man approached them and introduced himself as Connie's husband, Wendell. "Sorry folks," he intoned in a deep bass. "You'll have to sit at the counter, tables are full up. You want a booth, you'll have to get here around 6 a.m." Emma recognized him as the Red-Hat who sat in the corner with his guitar the night before.

Wendell showed them to four stools at the lunch counter. Emma took him aside and asked, "How are you going to keep open, without supplies, propane, all that? This could go on a long time."

Wendell's leathery face creased in a smile, and his bright blue eyes twinkled. "Honey, we've been getting ready for the End Times for years. We've got stashes of food and fuel all over these hills, gardens, greenhouses, orchards, wells and streams full of water, woods full of meat, and enough guns and ammo to keep a small army out, rapture or no. I'm not worried. At times like this Christ and his Second Coming feel closer than ever, and I've got the best darn wife a man could ask for." He looked appreciatively at Connie as she yelled orders at harried cooks through the pass-thru to the kitchen and waitresses and busboys bustled back and forth.

"But," Emma paused, "How did you know?"

"Read your Good Book," he said soberly. "It's all in there. Sign of the Beast, Earth changes, all of it. We're as ready as anyone can be for the end of everything we know, and if we go down, we're going to go down swinging."

"I've been getting ready too, but my information came from a different source, something, well, a little more…"

"Wavy-gravy?" Wendell asked with a grin. "I figured you for one of those. But you know what they say, all roads lead to Rome." *I'm such a bigot. I thought these people didn't read anything beyond the Farm Report and the local Shopper.*

"That's what they say!" Emma replied brightly. "Thank you so much. I think we'll need our breakfast to go. Ben Rhodes is taking us about 60 miles up, we're heading to our place in Corinth."

"Pretty country," Wendell said appreciatively. "Truckers coming from there say it's still safe, but you'll have to pass through a bunch of perimeters."

Connie appeared behind the counter and said briskly, "So, what're y'all havin' this fine mornin'?" She wrote their orders down, gave Emma a wink and said confidentially, "Maybe you'd like to come on back and see how it's done around here, since your hubby says you're quite the cook."

Earl smiled. "She sure is, you should see her Thanksgivings. She starts cooking and freezing in September. Course after course, a table full of desserts. It's really something." He beamed and hugged Emma, who smiled weakly at him.

Connie laughed a big, hearty belly laugh. "Looks like I've got competition. Come on back, Emma, maybe you can teach me a thing or two."

She propelled Emma through a swinging door into the hot, hectic kitchen, handed the orders off to a cook, took a turn down a hall and gestured for Emma to come into the pantry. She shut the pantry door behind them, and Emma looked at her with confusion as they stood in front of high shelves loaded with giant cans of vegetables and fruit, and huge jugs of ketchup and mustard.

Connie took both Emma's hands, looked deeply into her eyes and said, "Honey, I got insomnia. Real bad. Guess in the end I don't need much sleep or somethin'. Anyhoo, I went out walkin' last night at oh, about 3:30 in the mornin' and heard what I thought was a polecat in heat, comin' from Don's place. I kinda figured he got another notch in that belt of his with your name on it." She looked intently at Emma. "I won't say nothin', I don't tell tales out of school, but darlin', if you did, well, I'm so sorry."

Emma's eyes welled up. "You can't be sorrier than I am. It's not possible." Connie hugged her as Emma convulsed in tears.

"Miss Emma, listen to me. I know Don, I've known him and his wife for a long, long time. There never were two people less suited to each other, but I guess early on that chemical thing was strong, he's loaded with it. She turned off to him and his extracurricular cuties after a while, and I think in his own way he loved her, because he kept at it even more, as if to get back at her for not lovin' him enough. There are plenty of young ladies around here still smartin' from bein' loved and left by Mr. Don Melnik." She pulled a tissue from her apron pocket and handed it to Emma, patting her shoulder gently.

"Anyhoo," she continued, "after his wife left him he stopped, that was oh, about a year ago. It's like he didn't have her to aggravate anymore, so he lost his taste for the hunt or somethin'. I've been in this business a long time, and I can read folks pretty well. I can see you and your husband love each other, but I can also see he's old and tired, and well, you're not. But the further away you get from Don, the better. He's lickin' his wounds right now, but he'll be back on the nookie train soon. Maybe last night was the start of it. Take it or leave it, I hope you don't mind me spoutin' off. You've got more than enough on your plate without givin' another thought to that hound. But I hope he gave you a good ride, I'm betting he did."

Emma smiled broadly through her tears and hugged Connie joyously. "Thank you so much, this is exactly what I needed to hear. You are a wonderful, caring, warm human being, and Don and everyone here at Mason's Eddy are so lucky to have you."

Connie smiled self-consciously. "Oh, now. I'm just doin' my best to do the Lord's work. Now you take your breakfast bags outside, they're on the house, and don't you even try to pay me. Ben's gassin' up, and you've got to get on the road. The Lord be with you." Connie gave Emma a playful spank and propelled her into the dining room.

In the parking lot Ben waved at them from the door of his semi, and yelled, "About ready?"

"Yes" Emma yelled back, "Just give us a few more minutes." She turned to Earl and asked "Did you take your final pee? And your morning meds?"

109

"Yes, Mommy," he falsettoed. "I'm a big boy now."

Emma hugged him gratefully, looked at him lovingly and said, "Then come away with me. The best is yet to be." They looked at each other and laughed. "Or not, but at least we'll be together."

Chapter Twenty-One

Perilous Perimeters

Just like Wendell said, the sixty miles from Mason's Eddy to the Highway 81 junction were uneventful. Nothing looked very different from earlier trips through the sparsely populated, scenic mountains to the junction where Interstate 80 kept heading west and 81 headed due north. Ben honked his horn and waved out his window as he continued west to Maine.

Emma was grateful, and hopeful. No marauders, no Mad Max style caravans – maybe if they stayed out of heavily populated areas they would be all right. Maybe everything would be all right. Earl kept pace behind her, followed by Jed and Liza, and for the moment, Emma finally relaxed. Maybe the nightmare was over, and she was hopeful her tryst in the moonlight with Don would soon become a murky memory, even though flashbacks of their couplings made her nether regions pulse. *Simmer down girl, more important things ahead…but I'll never look at a mudroom the same way again.*

Fifteen miles from their exit, Emma noticed armed men standing at each exit ramp they passed. *Not to worry*, thought Emma. *These are the perimeter checkpoints Ben mentioned.* Her walkie-talkie squawked. Earl said "Honey, what the fuck." Jed chimed in, "Yeah. What do we do?"

Emma responded calmly, "Ben said there would be perimeter checks, we have ID, it should be no problem. Get your identification out, everything you've got." She rummaged in her pocketbook on the front passenger seat and extracted her wallet. She added grimly, "Maybe best not to be holding a gun, Jed."

Jed answered slowly, "OK. Geez."

I'm going to have trouble with that one. Too much Call of Duty – he's trigger-happy.

At Exit 9 in the tiny hamlet of Freeland, 10 miles from the cabin, there was a heavily armed checkpoint at the entrance to the ramp. Several men and boys, some in camouflage gear, a few with war paint on their faces, many sporting extensive tattoos on their arms, bodies and faces, all carrying major firepower, were flagging cars to the side of the road. *No cops, no cop cars*, Emma thought. *These guys are definitely freelance. Shit.*

Earl radioed Emma and Jed on their walkie-talkies, "Let me handle this. Please."

"Jed, where are the guns?" Emma whispered worriedly into her receiver.

"Mom, I put them in the back. Remember, you told me no guns?"

"Since when do you listen to me?"

"Relax Mom, Earl's really good at this, and he's big and scary-looking."

"And old, with a bad ticker," Emma said anxiously.

"Mom, let him."

Earl intoned somberly, "Yes, Mom. Let me."

Emma softened. "All right." She rolled down her window to listen to the conversation Earl was preparing to have with a tall, portly man dressed in the requisite red hat, camo and combat boots, with flaming orange hair, masses of tattoos and several guns strapped to his body. He looked like he could be the ringleader of the gang.

"Hey there, good morning," Earl said heartily.

"Mornin'," the man replied curtly.

"I'm Earl, and you are…?"

"I'm curious, Earl. Real curious. What are you doin' here? And are these folks with you?"

"Well-sir, yes they are. We live here, in Corinth. Had a place there since aught six. Planned to retire up here from the Downstate in a few years, but it got moved up a bit, what with this crazy shit. I don't have to tell you." Emma was always impressed by how well Earl read the room, and how easily he could slip into whatever vernacular he felt would be most effective. When in Brooklyn or the Bronx he was a tough guy full of "deez" and "doze," and when in loftier Manhattan company he bordered on a British accent with just a hint of androgyny.

My chameleon, hard at work.

"Is that so? And why should I believe you? You know how many city people are tryin' to get in here? Let's just say we're buildin' a wall, and it's pretty hard to get past it."

"Well, my man, what kind of proof you need?"

"How about an ID with your address on it?" He sneered.

"Well now, that's going to be difficult, since our former Jersey address is on my driver's license." Earl paused, thinking hard, as the man put a hand on his holster. "You know Ben Conger? Up at the ski resort? He knows us. Maybe you could give him a ring."

"Now, I *could* do that, but the goddamn commies fried up all the satellites and my phone might as well be at the landfill!" he said angrily.

An older man in a red hat, flannel shirt and dungarees with a high-powered rifle strapped to his back walked up to the car and said gruffly, "I know 'em, Nate. Hey there, Earl." Emma recognized Dave Stafford, their handyman friend who lived in nearby Freeland, and had worked extensively on the cabin. Even though Emma and Earl knew Dave was a Red-Hat, they got past it by being regular human beings with each other, even though it took a few years before Dave would even entertain the idea that maybe, just maybe all the propaganda fed to him by State-run media might not actually be, well, as Emma tactfully put it, completely accurate all the time. Emma knew she was contributing to Dave's cognitive dissonance, so she tiptoed lightly around his defensive perimeter, but they were friends, and Dave and Earl enjoyed joking with each other.

Earl relaxed and smiled. "Dave, my man. Really good to see you. You see, Nate, we're the real deal."

Nate's eyes narrowed. "Don't know about that." He looked up abruptly and grabbed his rifle as a car exited the highway onto the ramp. Several checkpoint guards tried to flag the car down, but it wouldn't stop, instead it sped up.

"Hit the floor!" Nate yelled, and the entire group opened fire on the car. Emma ducked behind the steering wheel, she could hear Liza screaming and the dogs barking as the rear of the renegade car burst into flames in the middle of the off-ramp. A young male bolted from the driver's seat, followed by a large Golden Retriever. The boy, bleeding from

113

his face and left arm, was thrown to the ground on his stomach and his hands were quickly zip-tied as the dog barked and circled around the sentries.

Emma realized nowhere was going to be all right anymore.

The boy protested as one of the sentries put a foot on his back to hold him down, "Dude, my mother. She lives here, I've got to see her, she needs medicine. It's in the car, go check if you don't believe me."

"Cry me a river," the sentry growled, and redoubled his foot's pressure on the boy's back. *These goons are enjoying this way too much.*

Emma jumped out of her car and ran to Earl's car. Earl was shaken and gripped the steering wheel, all color drained from his face. She quickly took his pulse, it was racing erratically. She stared anxiously at Jed's car, he waved to her to signal they were OK.

Emma had officially reached her limit. The cumulative stress of the past several months of UFOs, crazy and unfortunately accurate psychics, books on eating worms and weeds, constant, relentless planning, stockpiling and worrying, frickin' solar apocalypse, opportunistic and ridiculously sexy neighbors, massive civil breakdown, a Sherman tank named Sweet Betty that readily crushed human flesh and blasted large trucks into the air, abandonment of her pampered life and her first foray into adultery (however sanctioned), and now these fucking Nazi pricks. Well, Sweet Jesus and all the fucking Saints, Gods and Spirits, enough was enough. Damn the fucking torpedoes.

"I've had just about enough of this macho shit!" she screamed. She ran up to Nate, grabbed a handful of his camo t-shirt, shoved her face into his, and unloaded. Earl and Jed knew better than to try and stop her, because when Emma had a Mad on, she was unstoppable. "Picture a mushroom cloud with blonde hair," Earl would say ruefully when Emma snapped, which was, thankfully, not very often.

"Look *Nate*, we don't deserve this shit. My husband, who is 73 with a bad heart, pays taxes here. We own a fucking home here, goddammit. We're neighbors. You treat neighbors this way? I grew up in Troyville, my parents were teachers. My son and his pregnant girlfriend and two dogs just want to fucking survive, like I'm sure all of you do. I understand you need to protect what you think is your 'territory' from what's coming, I truly do, but what the fuck Nate? Not everyone is trying to put one over on you. Some people are actually telling the truth. Maybe you need to consider that before threatening us with fucking guns or setting freaking cars on fire. Life's tough all over *Nate,* for all of us. Be a fucking human being."

Nate gaped openmouthed at Emma, scratched his head, looked at his crew, and chuckled. They followed suit. "Feisty little bugger, ain't she?" he said with amusement.

Dave chimed in, "She sure is. But they're good people Nate. Let 'em through."

Emma released her hold on Nate's collar and sent him a dirty look, then smiled slightly at Dave. "Dave Stafford, you're an angel in Levis. I always knew it."

Dave smiled slightly and looked at his feet. "I'll come by later, see if there's anything I can do to help," he said quietly.

"We would love that Dave. And I have a piece of pie with your name on it." Emma got back in her car and signaled to Earl and Jed to start up. Nate reluctantly signaled to a sentry further down the ramp to let them through. She gazed mournfully at the shackled boy, who was being shoved into the deck of a pickup truck, his dog left by the roadside.

One down, Emma thought. *How many more? Dave won't be there to save us next time. I wish we could go back for the dog, but we barely have enough dog food as it is.* She passed the sentry, a teenaged, freckled, red-headed boy in camo with a red bandana tied around his head. *I wouldn't be at all surprised if he's one of Nate's spawn* she thought, as she waved to him and he sneered back. *Just get us there,* she prayed, to whatever gods and ancestors were listening.

Chapter Twenty-Two

Confiscation

The next checkpoint was at the intersection of County Road 11 and Route 393, three miles to the cabin. It was inhabited by the same sullen, tattooed, red-hatted, heavily armed, camo-clad men and boys. Nate must have had some kind of relay system, because they were waved through. Emma relaxed her stiff, tense body just enough to release her death grip on the steering wheel, and she almost allowed herself to enjoy the climb up the steep road past rushing mountain streams, tall pines, Queen Anne's lace and Black-Eyed Susans that lined the curving, swooping road.

Earl broke in on the walkie-talkie, "Almost there darlin'. You did good."

"So did you, Zeke," she said. "I half expected you to have a chaw in your cheek and a blade of grass in your teeth when you were talking to that jerk."

"We aim to please," Earl said lightly.

"And you do, my dear. You surely do."

Jed interjected, "We really have to pee, Mom. And I've got to take a wicked crap."

Emma laughed lightly. "OK, OK, hold on honey, can you hold on a few more minutes?"

"Yeah. OK," Jed replied sullenly.

Another checkpoint loomed before the entrance to the cabin area. *Oh geez, will I have to sell my grandchild this time? Who do I have to blow to get to our fucking house?* Emma slowed down grimly as three swarthy, armed men in the ubiquitous red hats approached her. One stopped at her driver's side, the other two headed for Earl and Jed's cars. *Time for the fucking redneck inquisition, again. At least we have our stories straight, since they're all fucking TRUE.* She clenched her jaw and rolled down her window.

A young man with a red beard stuck his head inside the window and peered inside. *God, Nate must have been busy. Looks like a carbon copy of the big oaf.* "Good morning," Emma said darkly.

"Mornin'," he replied quietly. "What's in the trailer?"

"Oh, our life," Emma said ironically. "Just our life." The young man took off his hat briefly to swipe his hair back, and Emma recognized him as one of the men on the large riding mowers that traversed the sprawling resort lawns like rickety mechanical chariots. "I know you," she said. "Remember? Last summer you mowed under our tree, the maple with bird feeders hanging from it? You hit your head on one of them and knocked it down, and we came out to rehang it. You were really nice about it too, I was afraid maybe you got a concussion."

He looked at her quizzically, then nodded his head slowly. "Yep. That's right."

Emma smiled, going in for the win. "I'm Emma, my husband Earl, son Jed and his girlfriend are back there. We're going to stay at our cabin for the duration of whatever this is."

He did not provide his name, or respond, but stood still. She could see his wheels turning. He approached her window and whispered, "Listen, they're watching me. I gotta look in the trailer, and, well, if there's food in there, I gotta take it. And anything else we can use. I'm sorry."

Emma gasped, "What? What are we supposed to eat? You can't do that!"

He shushed her quietly, "If you don't let me, well, they said I can shoot you if you give me trouble, but if I don't, we can put you in the town jail, and that's no picnic. You gotta let me. Seriously. They'll tell you how rationing works when you get to the cabin. We're clearing it out right now."

Emma looked at him in wonder. "Clearing it out? What? Taking our furniture too?"

He pursed his lips and paused. "We left enough for you to use. Clearing out the people staying there. Nate radioed me from the highway you were comin'. Folks from local towns are setting up here, where they'll be protected, and the Boss has friends, family, kids staying in empty cabins. We're circling the wagons, getting ready, you know."

Emma did know. "The Boss?"

He nodded. "Yep. Mr. Conger."

Emma pursed her lips and nodded. *Of course. Ben Conger, that fucking criminal.*

He and his ditzy wife Kathy owned and ran the ski resort; they had for years. Every time they got in a financial bind, the resort would go bankrupt, they'd regroup, recruit a new generation of sucker investors, bilk the State for all they could, and move forward. *Like locusts. Of course they're running the show.* Conger cronies owned scattered log mansions high on the mountain overlooking the modest cabins below, which their very infrequent, supercilious mansion-dwellers dubbed "The Village." Emma sighed, and the two other Inquisitors joined the young man.

One of them gestured to the trailer, "Tell 'er to open the back."

The young man leaned into Emma's window and whispered, "My name's Andy. Take 'er easy."

Emma nodded soberly and replied softly, "Thank you, Andy." She got out of the car with her keys, glared sharply at the other two captors, shrugged her shoulders in surrender to Earl and Jed watching open-mouthed from their cars, and opened the back of the trailer. The three men started unloading it roughly as Earl and Jed vacated their cars in protest, but Emma waved them back and approached Earl's car as Jed joined them.

She shushed their loud objections quickly. "Stop it, do you want to get shot?" she whispered. "We have to let them take what they want. The frickin' Congers are running the show, and you know what that means, honey," she said to Earl urgently. "Jed, keep it down, really. We can't do anything about this. They say there's some kind of ration program, so it looks like we're going to eat. We've got to go along or we'll be dead or in hillbilly jail."

Jed said darkly, "This sucks, Mom. This really fucking sucks."

Emma touched his arm. "We've got to get to the cabin and strategize, get the lay of the land. You know how that works." She knew her mastermind son could relate. He nodded slowly. *Yes, figure out the route of march and how we can alter the tempo. Right Jed, give it time.* He relaxed and went back to his car.

Earl looked at her plaintively, "I'm hungry. Are they taking everything? Even the pie?"

Emma whispered conspiratorially, "It's on the passenger side floor in my car. Maybe these yahoos will miss it." Earl perked up slightly. Poor Earl. God, this is going to be really hard for him. *Thank God his suitcase full of booty is in his car, maybe they won't get to that.* Emma went back to her car and winced as she saw her cooler full of hummus, yogurt, eggs and cheese and her freezer bag full of Earl and Jed's beloved burgers, hot dogs and steaks spirited from the trailer into a nearby pickup truck, along with bag after bag of groceries, jugs of her carefully preserved water, more suitcases, furniture, almost everything.

Andy saw her expression and approached her. "If you want to open the suitcases and take out a few things, well, we'll let you, OK?"

Emma looked up at him and smiled wryly. "Thank you." She approached the pickup with its open cargo bed and pulled their suitcases forward. The young man watched as she took out articles of clothing and shoes, along with toiletries.

When she got to her jewelry box he put his hand out. "That we keep."

Emma's eyes welled up. "But, some of these are anniversary gifts, from my husband. Please? My kid's umbilical stump, for God's sake, at least let me take that."

He shook his head slowly. "Nope. Encourages private bartering. It stays. But OK, take your kid's thing." Emma set her jaw, wiped her eyes, opened the jewelry box and fished out the stump as she gazed mournfully at her diamond studs and delicate diamond filigree necklace with matching drop earrings. As she worked she waited for Andy to start conversing with his cronies, then quickly palmed the diamonds and shoved them in a pocket of Earl's pants.

She took her armfuls of clothes, toiletries and contraband and stuffed them onto her passenger seat. She felt layers were being stripped away from her, like an onion. What was going to be left? She was surprised they

119

didn't search her car too, but as she saw more vehicles arrive with trailers and packed trucks she understood. Go for the big stuff, and maybe, just maybe there's an element of decency there. Time will tell.

She gave Earl a thumbs up and mouthed the word, "Pie." He smiled and returned the gesture. They headed up a steep hill past scattered cabins to their new home Emma had already dubbed Holocaust Hotel.

Chapter Twenty-Three

Stripped Down

There it was, nestled between a few large maple trees. As the cars crunched onto the gravel drive, Emma noticed smoke coming from the chimney and winced at the procession of strangers walking up the macadam pathway to a rusty white truck that idled noisily. An impassive older woman sat in the passenger seat, glared at them briefly, frowned, and looked away.

The displaced family consisted of a rail-thin, deeply tanned father in the requisite flannel shirt and Levis, and yes, a rakish red Cain hat. A gently obese mom carried a pale little baby with bare feet, and a little girl with knotted, unkempt long blonde hair sucked her thumb and clung to her mother's dress. They carried a motley assortment of tote bags and loaded plastic garbage bags they dragged along the path. One of the garbage bags opened, and children's toys spilled out onto the ground. The little girl ran to a stuffed bear, picked it up and ran back to her mother as her father picked up the detritus, and the procession continued.

Once the family was ensconced in the truck, Emma got out of her car, signaled to Jed, Liza and Earl to come out, and they stood looking at the cabin. The two dogs, released from their bonds, joyfully romped and barked on the lawn, the truck screeched in protest on the gravel and sped away. "There it is," said Emma solemnly. "Home, for God knows how long." She set her shoulders and said resolutely, "Let's go in."

They walked single file down the pathway, and when they reached the front door, Emma stood poised with her key and stared at the missing lock on the door. It had been clumsily ripped out and replaced with a bit of screen taped over the hole. "How thoughtful," she said sarcastically. "We wouldn't want any bugs to get in, just squatters. Wonderful."

City-boy Earl, who always locked his car and worried about anything being left inside no matter where they were, was aghast. "We'll have to have it replaced," he said with conviction. "This way anyone can get in."

"That's the point," Emma said grimly. "Welcome to the New World."

Earl growled, "I'm going to talk to Ben Conger about this." His usually playful demeanor was replaced by what Emma called "The Gray Monster," a side of Earl that rarely emerged, but when it did, everyone knew to get out of his way. It was Earl's swarthy equivalent of Emma's blonde mushroom cloud.

"Down boy," Emma warned. "We've got to get the lay of the land here. Just because we pay a hefty HOA may have zero relevance now."

Earl scowled and took his cell phone out of his pocket to call Conger, dialed, realized there was no signal, and angrily stuffed the phone back in his pocket. Emma wondered how much longer he would keep hoping it would work after all these weeks.

"Open the door, dammit," he said gruffly. "Let's see what these redneck bandits have done to us."

"Honey, please calm down, let's just see what's what here." She worried his heart would go into overdrive, and vowed to keep him as calm as she could.

Emma gingerly opened the door and peered inside. She gasped at the empty walls, missing sofa, television, rocking chair and armchair, then walked in a trance to the dining room, now bereft of table and chairs. She ran upstairs and wailed at missing beds, dressers, paintings. Gone, all gone, even the mementos and photos on the mantel. Everything. In each corner were rolled up sleeping bags, pillows and a few blankets, clearly issued by the New Guard. *Screw calm, dammit.*

"Motherfuckers, motherfuckers!" she screamed, as she tumbled into the kitchen and feverishly opened cabinets and pulled open drawers. "Fucking motherfuckers! One saucepan, one frying pan, a few knives, spoons and forks, four glasses, four plates, one fucking spatula for God's sake!" she screamed. Earl tried to hold and calm her, but she was having none of it.

"They are going to be so, so sorry!" she exclaimed as she headed for the door and fought off Earl's attempts to subdue her. He finally corralled her next to the door and held her arms tightly. "I'm going to have bruises, you big galoot!" she screamed in his face. He blanched briefly but kept his hold on her. He knew she'd wriggle away if given any quarter.

"What are you going to do honey, huh?" he demanded forcefully, his face close to hers. "You can't fight these guys, they're armed to the teeth and hunting for bear, Emma and Earl-shaped bear."

Emma's eyes blazed and she forcefully wrested herself from Earl's grip. "I tell you what I'm *not* going to do, *honey*," she said disdainfully. "I'm sure as hell not going to lie down and play dead for these bastards. I'm going to figure these motherfuckers out and beat them at their own game. Just you wait."

Always the peacemaker to his fiery wife, Earl mumbled softly, "I'm sure you will."

Jed moved toward her. "Mom, he's not the enemy. He's on your side. So are we."

Emma softened slightly. Jed always knew how to set her off, and how to defuse her. "I'm sorry, OK? These bastards took away all my work, our haven, and left us like refugees desperate for handouts." She looked at crestfallen Earl, felt a pang in her chest, and squeezed his hand. "I'm sorry honey, there's no excuse for it, well, other than enormous *stress*. I mean, we've seen more death and destruction in the past two days than we've seen our whole lives. I'm kind of, well, on edge, to put it mildly." She looked searchingly into his downcast eyes and squeezed his hand. "Forgive me?"

Earl mumbled softly, "Always do." Emma hugged him and felt tears fill her eyes.

She took a deep breath and looked around the decimated kitchen. "At least we still have a refrigerator, a microwave and a stove, if we can get the generator going," she said grudgingly. "We're going to eat, I promise you." She paused and turned on a wall switch. A sconce glowed in the hallway. "Wait a minute. We have power. Why do we have power? Well, that's something, as long as it lasts."

"That's fine, honey, but there's nowhere to sit," Earl said plaintively, and Emma knew he had to have some level of comfort for his old, tired body.

"Oh geez," she said. "We'll have to figure something out." She walked to the back door to see if they left any lounge chairs on the deck. Nope, stripped, like everything else, then she remembered. "The storage space! In Troyville! We have extra chairs there, and lamps, and a few end tables. And blankets and pillows! We've got to go there. They can't get in without a padlock key, maybe they haven't gotten in yet."

Jed reminded her, "We need to unpack first, OK? See what we're dealing with, and where we're going to put things."

"You're right, as usual," Emma said, cheered by the idea of the storage space's booty. "Let's go." She paused and said grimly "Wait…the pantry." She slowly walked to the former coat closet off the dining room she converted to a pantry with the help of Dave Stafford, and stuffed it with shelf after shelf of canned and packaged foods. She opened the door slowly, the automatic light went on inside to reveal three cans of cream of mushroom soup and a package of ramen noodles. She slid down the wall next to the pantry in a heap and wept. All those months of stockpiling, no, not months, years. Emma refused to have a cabin with an empty larder, and now it was staring her blankly in the face, her work made moot and irrelevant by this ungodly purge.

Earl handed her one of his cloth handkerchiefs, still folded and unused. *Such an old gentleman* Emma thought tenderly through her tears. *My old-school guy. How am I going to take care of this tender, clueless man?* She smiled tearfully at him, wiped her eyes and blew her nose. "I'll give this back after I wash it," she said in an attempt at levity. "If the sons of bitches left us any laundry detergent. Will you go look in the utility room, Jed? I can't bear to do it right now."

Jed went down the hall and yelled out darkly, "Nope. Maybe we brought something we can use. I think we brought dishwashing liquid."

Liza piped up, "We did, the organic kind."

"Good" Emma said. "It looks like it's going to be organic and multi-use from now on. We still have water, don't we?" Earl went to the tap and turned it on. Clear water flowed from the spout.

"Yep," Earl said lightly. "Things are looking up."

"Don't say that," Emma said darkly. "I don't think we've reached Ultimate Down yet. Not by a long shot."

The front doorbell rang, which made everyone jump, partly because it was loud and unexpected, and because it lent an air of civility from the recent past that now seemed incongruous. "Hell, why don't they just walk in?" Emma quipped wryly. "There's no lock."

She opened the door to a young, chipper woman clad in jeans, t-shirt and a red hat. She wore a whistle around her neck, and carried a clipboard. She smiled artificially and chirped "Hi! I'm Ashley, with the Welcome Committee."

You mean the Nazi scourge, don't you?

Emma looked at her accusingly and said nothing.

"Um," Ashley said slowly, "May I come in?"

Emma paused and said through clenched teeth, "What happens if we don't let you?" Ashley blew her whistle, and a large red-haired goon emerged from a parked maroon Honda, dressed in the camo/gun/red-hat/tattooed uniform of the New World Order in Corinth, New York. *Jesus, they really do mean business, don't they? And what's with all the gingers? It's like a genetic going-out-of-business sale.*

Ashley smiled brightly and replied, "*That's* what happens. Nate Jr., this is the...." She looked at her clipboard, "Kaplan family. Kaplan family, Nate Jr."

Earl, Jed and Liza stood behind Emma and glared accusingly at the interlopers.

"Ashley, Nate Jr., let me ask you this," Earl began, as he stepped forward. Emma tried to shush him, but he continued. "We have legal rights here. Our belongings have been stolen; you have no right to do this. We can take action against you."

Nate Jr. sneered and brought his face next to Earl's. "Ever hear of Prominent Domain? We can do what we want if the sitcheashun says so." Emma feigned tears, turned her back to Nate Jr. and Ashley and buried her head in Earl's chest as she stifled her laughter.

Earl smiled slightly and continued, "Nate Jr., Nate Jr. is it? I believe we had the pleasure of meeting your Dad at the highway exit?"

"Yeah, what about it?" Nate glowered.

"I'm assuming you're not a lawyer, yes?"

Nate Jr. nodded, then shook his head slowly.

"Well, actually," Earl continued. "The phrase is Eminent Domain, and the efficacy of this argument could be determined in a court of law."

Emma burst into muffled laughter into Earl's chest, "I can't, I just can't. Honey, don't."

Nate Jr. jammed his oversized index finger into Earl's face. "Listen Mr. *Kaplan*, you money-grubbin', America-hatin' Jew bastard, the Boss says we gotta let you stay, and you should get down on your knees and thank him, 'cause if it was up to me you'd be pushin' up daisies at the landfill."

Earl carefully removed Nate Jr.'s digit from his face and smiled. Emma was shocked at his cool aplomb under fire, it was a side of him she rarely saw, and she gazed at him in wonder. "Honey," she whispered in his ear. "This troglodyte could pound you into the ground."

"Watch me," Earl whispered back, "I deal with guys like this in the city all the time." He set Emma behind him and put his arm around Nate Jr.'s shoulder. Nate Jr. shrugged, but didn't move away.

Wow, I forgot Earl can work his magic on men, women, missing links and various four-legged creatures.

"Colorful, very colorful, you certainly know how to paint pictures with words young man." Earl paused dramatically, stood back and surveyed a very confused Nate Jr. "Nate Jr., you're a big fella, and really strong. I bet I saw your little brother at one of the checkpoints coming in, a handsome red-haired young man in a red bandana?"

Nate Jr. nodded slowly. "That's Nate Jr. III, but we call him Peanut."

Earl laughed heartily and slapped Nate Jr. on the back. "Peanut. Perfect. I bet he can't wait to be as big as his big brother Nate Jr., right?"

Nate Jr. scoffed, "As if."

"Well Nate Jr.," Earl continued calmly. "We're really in a bind here. I'm an old man, you can see that, right?" Nate Jr. nodded. "My son-in-law and his girlfriend, who's expecting, by the way, can be very helpful, but there may be times when we'll really need a big, strong, smart guy like you to help us. I can make it worth your while, you know, we Jew bastards can do that, right?"

Nate Jr. snorted. "Yeah."

"Well, Nate Jr., I hope we can call on you to help us out, and you just let me know what you think your services are worth. Oh, and I have my gold, diamonds, silver and paper money squirreled away somewhere safe, along with the souls of multiple Christians, just kidding, off the premises, in case you're wondering, but here's a small down-payment." Earl pulled his wallet from his back pocket and extracted a $100 bill. "Will this be acceptable? Plenty more where that came from."

Emma could see the painfully slow wheels turning in Nate Jr.'s head as he took the bill and put it in his shirt pocket. "Well-sir," he replied slowly. "Could be, could be."

Earl smiled widely and shook Nate Jr.'s hand. "Good, good, now why don't you and the lovely Ashley come on in? And Ashley?"

"Yes, Mr. Kaplan?" she replied timorously, still confused by the scene.

"I'm sure there will be times when we will need someone with your expertise. I hope we can call on you as well."

"Um, I guess so," she said slowly.

"And probably best to keep this between us, right? Who knows, the Boss might want to take a cut." Ashley and Nate Jr. looked at each other, then back at Earl. "Well, you think about it, OK?" Earl gestured like a maître d for the two to enter the cabin. Ashley stopped and said, "Remember Junior, we have to look in the cars first?"

"Oh, yeah," Nate Jr. replied, then to Earl, "We have to look in your cars first."

Earl started peeling hundreds from his wallet and held them in his hand. "I'm sure you two have a big day ahead of you, what with all these new people showing up day and night with all their stuff. It's just personal items in the cars, a few snacks, one or two paltry bags of non-perishable food, kibble for the dogs, books, sheets, towels, mementos, bric a brac, that sort of thing. Nothing worth much."

Don't mention the guns. Right, the guns. They're starting to look really important now.

Earl asked, "What can you take with you and write down on your clipboard that will satisfy the Boss?"

Ashley and Nate Jr. stepped aside and held a hurried, whispered conference. They nodded in agreement, and approached Earl as Emma, Jed and Liza watched in astonishment.

Ashley said carefully as she looked at the money in Earl's hand. "Um, well," one bill was placed on her clipboard, "We can say that…" another bill went into Nate Jr.'s shirt pocket, "The guys at the Collective perimeter got it all, except for a few things we can't use…" Two more bills were distributed. Ashley and Nate Jr. smiled at each other, held another brief conference, then Ashley stepped in close to Earl and whispered, "Twenties are better, easier to spend, harder to track, and we wouldn't say no to silver or gold down the line."

Earl grinned and put his arm around Ashley's waist. "You got it, baby."

Ashley giggled self-consciously; Emma bristled slightly. *There he goes again. She's got that oh-so-familiar goofy gleam in her eye. Well, at least this time it's for a worthy cause.* "Thank you Mr. Kaplan, Mrs. Kaplan, we won't take up any more of your time."

As they turned toward the door, Earl asked, "How can we reach you? Texting is off the table these days."

Ashley thought briefly. "Put up the flag on your mailbox. We're always driving around checking things out," she said. "And the mail doesn't run these days."

"Won't that look suspicious?" Earl asked. Ashley thought, then Nate Jr. said, "Put a ribbon or something on that plant hook by the door, maybe something red, OK?"

Earl sent them a thumbs up. "Smart man. Sounds like a plan. Thanks guys." He waved at them as they drove away, then walked down the macadam pathway like a conquering hero. Emma gave him a bear hug and kiss, Jed and Liza followed suit.

"Geez, Earl," Jed exclaimed. "You're a playa'."

"Yes," Emma noted sourly. "Your aging pheromones hard at work." Earl pretended not to hear her.

128

"Don't let it get around," Earl said playfully to Jed. "Money talks, bullshit walks."

They began to unload their precious cargo from their cars while they looked furtively around them, since they had no way of knowing whether the woods or neighboring cabins had eyes, ears, and possibly guns.

Chapter Twenty-Four

Home Sweet (Collective) Home

Emma was grateful. She wasn't happy about it, but she couldn't help herself. "I should be furious with them," she told Earl as she unpacked. "But instead, like some weird Stockholm Syndrome, I'm grateful we at least have *some* of our stuff, since Earl bribed the great unwashed to overlook it. I just wish we had more food. All I brought in the cars were snacks and sodas, and a few bags of non-perishables and kitchen supplies. We only have enough snack bars, tuna, canned soup, spaghetti, GORP and chips for a few weeks at most. And what's this about gold and silver squirreled away somewhere?"

Earl replied from the makeshift seat Emma made for him on the floor against the wall, his back and legs bolstered by sleeping bags, as he read a Raymond Chandler novel. "Building a legend, my sweetheart. You know word will get around Earl Kaplan pays."

Emma stopped unpacking and looked at him approvingly. "Darling, I underestimated you. But how much largesse are we talking about here?"

Earl looked up briefly, then spoke as he continued to read. "I cleaned out the safe, of course, on our way out, and I'm counting on you to put our stash somewhere out of harm's way, because at some point you can bet these yahoos will start looking."

"Any ideas? I don't appreciate the onus being on me. Why can't you figure it out? Why does it always have to be me?"

Without looking up, he replied, "Because, my dear, you're so good at everything."

"Yes, and you're only very good at a few things, by design. So you can count on perfectionist me to do it." Earl kept reading with a slight smile. "Just a minute," she challenged. He looked up from his book, unperturbed.

"Yes?"

"Where, may I ask, is this 'stash' of yours, right now?"

Earl stretched luxuriously and began to unbutton his shirt.

"Earl!"

"Now, now…" He opened his shirt to reveal a triple money belt that extended from his abdomen to just below his nipples. "Here's $100,000 in $100 bills, plus $200,000 in gold and silver coins in the spare tire well of my car. I also have a considerable bankroll of hundreds in my pants, and my wallet. Oh, and this little number…," He pulled a small, bulging black velvet pouch from the money belt and jingled its contents. "Diamonds are a girl's best friend, after all."

Emma was open-mouthed, then countered, "Wait a minute. You agreed with the lovely Ashley to pay them in twenties."

Earl smiled lazily. "They'll take what I give them."

Jed had been listening from the loft, and descended the ladder to join Earl and Emma, as Liza and the dogs stuck their heads out between the loft slats. "That's why you asked me to store your spare in my car. You said you needed room for your vintage sports tapes."

Earl began to button his shirt and replied smugly, "I rest my case. But we have to find a safe place to stash this loot, since it looks like I'll be sleeping with this very uncomfortable thing around me if we don't. And who knows, my car may be commandeered by ravening hordes, so the coins have to go somewhere."

Emma and Jed's collective strategic gray matter began to sizzle and pop as they paced the cabin and stopped periodically to compare notes.

"We can't hide it anywhere people can see us going in and out, there are too many curious eyeballs around here," Emma postulated. "That eliminates under the deck, and if we put it in the crawlspace under the stairs, it's the first place they'll look."

Jed narrowed his eyes and scanned the space. "I brought my tools with me. I could cut a hole in the wall, put the stash behind it, then close it up."

Emma shook her head. "The Congers know every beam of these cabins – they built them. If they see a cutout on a wall they didn't make, no good. Even if it's in a closet. I don't trust these weasels." She stopped, looked around, put her finger to her mouth to hush Jed, and took a pad and pencil out of her pocketbook. She wrote, "For all we know this is like Russia, and they're listening. Make small talk."

Jed, airily, "How about we go to the storage unit and see what we can find? Earl can't sit on the floor forever."

"True, very true," Emma said, as they continued to look around. Jed held his finger in the air and ran up to the loft.

Jed descended with a hammer and screwdriver, and said loudly, "Mom, these nails are loose on the bannister," as he pulled a piece of molding from around the doorway. He took out the notepad and wrote, "See? Hollow. We can stash some of it in here." Emma nodded.

"Jed, can you come outside with me? I think we have some loose nails on the deck." They hurried outside and Emma whispered, "That's fine, the molding thing, and I think we should stash a little all over the place to throw them off the scent, but we have to put the lion's share of it somewhere else. Somewhere safe. I wish we could bury it, but we can't risk people seeing us dig it up."

Jed smiled triumphantly, and whispered, "Mom, where do people go to dig and plant where no one notices?"

Emma was nonplussed. "Um, on a farm?" Jed shook his head. "A ditch?" Jed shook his head. "Come on, what?"

Jed replied smugly, "At a cemetery. Isn't Great Grandma Murphy buried at the one in Haddonville? Don't you visit her there? You could get a good-looking bush or whatever you call it from the woods, plant it by her grave, and while you're at it, put the stash underneath. Hardly anyone ever goes to these cemeteries, so if you go there now and then to pay your respects and groom around the grave, no one will think it's weird and probably no one will even see you."

Emma thought a moment, patted Jed's shoulder and said, "You got your strategy from me, but you've made it a serious art form. Good plan."

Dave Stafford's shiny red pickup truck announced its arrival by crunching noisily on the gravel parking lot, and Emma sprinted to greet him. *I bet he wants pie.* "Dave!" she exclaimed. Dave smiled quietly and stood next to his truck.

"How you guys doin'?" he asked gently.

"Oh, great, just great," Emma replied with false brightness. "We love it when people threaten to kill us and steal our food and precious possessions. What the hell, Dave?"

"I know, I know," he said calmly. "But these folks are scared of being overrun and running out of things. It's about protection, you know."

Emma nodded. "I do. Protection is all I want for my family, and I'm sure all you want for yours. But the Congers are piling it on pretty heavy. It's like Nazis."

"Well, I don't work for them so much anymore, semi-retired, you know. They're in deep. They'll be no friend to you."

Emma gave Dave a light hug. "But you will be, right, Dave?" He nodded slightly. "Good. Can you do us a favor? Maybe we're being paranoid, but we're concerned the place might be bugged. Is there some way you can check it out?"

Dave thought briefly. "I don't know about that stuff, but my son does. He's working for Nate though…my nephew's a good kid, only 11, but he's a real electronics whiz, takes things apart, that kind of thing. I could bring him around. But I haven't heard about any bugging."

Emma was relieved. "Good, thank you so much. Would you like a piece of pie? We've got apple and blueberry."

Dave smiled and patted his stomach. "Oh no. Sarah's got me on a diet, high blood pressure and cholesterol stuff, you know, but thanks."

"You're a stronger man than I, Dave Stafford," Emma said affectionately. "Earl will make short work of it, you can bet on that."

"Anything else you need?" Dave asked solicitously.

"Well, decent food would be a start. How do we go about it?"

"Someone should be around to give you ration coupons – they've got a store all set up with food, furniture, everything…"

"I see," Emma said coldly. "They took our stuff so we can buy it back from them."

Dave looked at her sadly. "Something like that." Emma sighed and set her jaw.

"I so look forward to their visit." Emma replied with thick sarcasm. "Thanks, Dave."

"No problem," Dave waved, got back in his truck and drove away. Emma watched him soberly, her stomach growling with hunger.

"Power bar time," she whispered grimly. "Then off to the storage space."

Chapter Twenty-Five

Building Their Brand

As Emma and Jed approached the "Collective" Community checkpoint between Corinth and Haddonville, with part of Earl's stash hidden in the spare wheel well, they ran up against an unpleasant reality. Unless they had some kind of ID to get in and out, they were going to have to go through the Hillbilly Inquisition every time they needed to leave the perimeter.

The bustling downtown intersection of Corinth consisted of a dilapidated barn, an elementary school abandoned years earlier due to budget cuts, a welding shop in a Quonset hut and a tiny, moldy building with a sign reading "Corinth Historical Society" that looked like it hadn't been opened in decades.

As Emma and Jed approached "The Four Corners," the only intersection in town, there they were – three young, red-hatted, sullen sentries packing high-powered heat. Two slender, long-legged teenaged girls with braces sat on a crumbling fence, maybe girlfriends, maybe sisters, definitely spectators. The girls smiled expectantly as the car slowed down. An open barbecue grill blazed nearby, filled with a flaming fire. *Strange, grilling at the intersection? I don't see any tables, or food, and it's too hot today for a fire.*

The sentries flagged them down smugly and smiled conspiratorially at each other. *God, I hope they don't search the wheel well.* A surly teen signaled Emma to roll down her window.

"Where ya goin'?" he sneered. The girls giggled and whispered conspiratorially, the boy looked at them briefly, smirked and nodded his head.

I'm not telling them about the storage space, I'm not that dumb.

"Well," Emma began. "We plan to go to Haddonville, see if there are any stores open, and visit my grandmother's grave at the cemetery. We live here, we're the Kap-"

He interrupted. "Yeah, we know who you are." He jerked his head to his two compatriots and said, "More Jews." They chuckled, the girls giggled and booed. *Great, all these jerks need is more encouragement.*

Emma smiled nervously. "Well, word does get around. Since you know who we are, we should have no problem getting back in, right?"

He smiled broadly, clearly enjoying their predicament. "Well now, you'd think so, wouldn't you? But it ain't that easy. Not now. You need somethin' to show you live here."

"Oh, like a card?"

He leered and chuckled. "Nah, somethin' more permanent." More chuckles from the sentries and the pubescent peanut gallery.

Emma felt a pang in her solar plexus. Earlier her Spidey sense told her this trip was not a good idea, and here it was. *Gotta listen to that inner voice, Emma.* "I don't understand."

"Oh, you will." The boy headed for the grill and picked up what looked like a cast iron fireplace tool hanging from its handle. He approached the car and held the end of the tool up to Emma's face. "This marks you as part of the Collective, it's your ticket in and out of here. No brand, no go, unless you want to go to jail. Or worse. Up to you."

Emma felt dizzy, Jed was aghast. "You're kidding, right?" he said. "This is barbaric. We're not going to do it. Forget it."

The boy sneered. "Then turn around and go back home, 'cause you ain't goin' nowhere, unless you want some of this." He gestured to a smiling sentry who brandished a high-powered rifle in one hand and pointed to zip-ties hanging from his belt. The ringleader put his wrists together to mimic being handcuffed. "Barbaric enough for 'ya?"

"Yeah!" one of the girls yelled out. "How you like that, bitch?"

Emma's stomach knotted, she looked at Jed and said weakly, "Give us a minute, please?"

The boy pointed to a grassy, overgrown space next to the crumbling barn. "Sure, park and talk it out. We ain't goin' nowhere."

Emma pulled the car into the space and she and Jed stared at each other fearfully. "What are we going to do?" she whispered as they watched the boys posture with their guns and talk with the girls.

136

Jed's eyes darted back and forth. Emma knew that prodigious brain of his was sorting and sifting possibilities at lightning speed. "Mom, we have to do it, we have to. Later on, it will be evidence of crimes against humanity, if we get through this alive. Like the Holocaust, the numbers on the wrist, proof we were treated like animals."

"Well, I'm not thinking that far ahead," Emma replied anxiously. "We could get a wicked infection from that thing, not to mention a lot of pain. And where are they going to put it? It better not be our asses, like cows. I'm not dropping trow every time these goons want to check my pedigree."

"It's the only way we can make it out of here and get to the cemetery. And you want to go to the storage space in Troyville, and check out how your parents are doing. Maybe each zone does it now. God, this is awful." His eyes filled with tears. "They're going to do it to Liza too, maybe even the dogs."

"And Earl," Emma intoned grimly, and slumped back in her seat.

Jed squeezed Emma's hands tenderly. "Mom, we have to do it. It looks like a small thing, maybe it's no worse than a stove burn."

Emma shook her head. "Stove burns tend to heal, brands are forever. I don't know if I can do this, maybe we should think of another way to hide the money." She grew pensive. "But my parents, you're right, I am worried about them. I have no idea how they're doing, or even where they are at this point." She sat up rigidly. "OK. Let's do it. We have ice, bandages and antibiotic ointment back home – I can treat this. Come on."

Jed nodded grimly. They stepped out of the car and slowly approached the three boys. "OK," Emma said sadly. "We'll do it."

One of the boys stepped forward and said softly, "It's not so bad, see?" He turned his head and pointed under his right ear. A small brand consisting of a capital C with a smaller capital L attached to it, about the size of a quarter, blazed red and puffy under his ear. "It doesn't hurt anymore, not at all, just looks bad."

The ringleader pushed him back. "Shut up, Sean." He turned to Emma. "Who's first?"

Jed stepped forward. "I am."

"Jed!"

Jed took Emma aside and whispered, "Look, if it's really bad you don't have to do it. I'll go out and do what needs to be done alone."

"No way," Emma said forcefully, and she turned to the boy. "I'm going first. Jed, I'm your mother, you have to listen to me."

"Yeah," the boy taunted. "Listen to your Mommy." The sentries and girls laughed and repeated "Listen to your Mommy" in an ad-hoc chant.

Jed bristled, but stood still. *Later Jed, later you'll get yours, if I know anything about you.*

"C'mon," the boy said to Sean, "You hold 'er."

Sean stepped forward apologetically and held Emma's arms behind her as the boy turned her head roughly to one side and pushed her hair away from her right ear. "This is so's you'll always remember to listen when we tell you what's what." He leered into Emma's face.

Emma babbled nervously, "Can't you go easy on me, please? I don't suppose it would matter that I'm not Jewish, neither is my son, because you see, a child is only Jewish if the mother is, and though his name is Campbell, which doesn't even sound Jewish, his family name was changed on Ellis Island from Cantowicz to make things easier I guess, and because I'm not Jewish he basically isn't either, and I hope you get a chance to get to Ellis Island sometime, to see the Statue of Liberty, maybe get a slightly different point of view…"

The boy interrupted as he jerked Emma's head sharply, "No buyin' time. This won't take long." The third boy held the poker deeply in the flame, his hand covered in a thick glove. The ringleader put on a similar glove as Emma took several deep breaths and prepared herself for the worst. The third boy handed the poker to the ringleader, its brand glowing bright orange. Sean tightened his grip on Emma's hands and whispered into her ear, "It's OK, it's OK, it'll be over soon."

The girls started a slow chant of "Go….go….go" that increased in speed as the procedure accelerated.

"Shut up Sean! You want one on your other side?" Sean shook his head, the boy held Emma's head roughly and pressed the hot brand under her right ear. The pain was unbearable. Her flesh sizzled and smelled like

138

meat in a pan. The girls squealed with pleasure, Emma screamed as her entire head and neck felt like they were on fire. She felt herself sinking into a faint, and fell to the ground as the girls clapped and cheered. Jed ran to her, the boy pushed him away, and he and Sean laid a dizzy and moaning Emma on a dirty blanket they had spread on the ground.

"Happens all the time," the boy said gruffly, "Now you, Jew-boy. Let's see if you've got a pair of balls, or if you're like your pussy mother."

"Jed…" Emma whispered weakly and reached out her hand toward him.

Jed stood stiffly as the boys prepared him for the brand. "It's OK Mom. Come on, bring it," he said.

"Sure 'nuf capn', your wish is my command," the boy said with a smile. The girls began their chant that accelerated to a fever pitch as the boy pressed the hot poker roughly on Jed's neck. Jed yelled loudly and staggered briefly, then panted and wobbled as they released him. The girls whooped and hollered their approval, Jed sneered at them.

"Jest like a calf, right Glen?" the third boy sniggered. Jed half fell, half knelt next to Emma and held her hand. The boys and girls laughed.

Glen. I'll remember that name. And I'll never forget that face.

"What a touching sight," Glen scoffed. "Hurry up, get 'er outa here, we got work to do." He and the boys joined the girls in a series of high-fives.

"Mom, can you stand?" he urged gently. After a few seconds, she winced in pain and reached for her neck. Jed held her hand back. "I know it hurts Mom, but we've got to get out of here. Here, let me help you up."

Emma groaned as she struggled to her feet, and moved to touch Jed's neck. He flinched and pulled his head away, still holding onto her. "Oh Jed, your neck. Oh God. We've got to go home first; we've got to put something on these."

"Best not to do that," Sean warned. "Got to give your skin a chance to work around it. It's OK, it's clean, from the heat."

"I swear to fucking God, Sean, you've got to grow a pair. What a pussy!" Glen scolded. Wait 'til Pa hears about this. You won't be able to sit down for a week."

Emma turned briefly to Sean as Jed continued to hold her up. "Sean, I won't forget you. I hope you won't forget us."

They slid slowly into the car, Jed in the driver's seat, and drove through the checkpoint as Glen wrote their names on a clipboard. He shouted after them, "Better get back before dark, if you know what's good for ya'. Miss curfew, you don't get back in, and you're gonna be so, so sorry."

Chapter Twenty-Six

New Strategies

Emma cried softly as Jed careened down winding roads into the Haddonville valley. She looked mournfully out the window at waving fields of wildflowers – daisies, trefoil, buttercups and chicory, and lamented, "On my rides here I gloried in the wonders of nature, I was so happy, and now all I can think about is this horror, and when will it end?" She looked at Jed plaintively, "What did he mean, we're going to be sorry? I don't know how much more I can take today."

"I don't know Mom, they're total assholes, enjoying bossing the 'snowflakes' around. I want to know how to get this fucking thing off my neck."

Emma looked tearfully at the swollen, flaming-red circle under Jed's right ear. She wanted to move to touch it, to work some kind of healing magic on it, but she knew he only invited these things his way, in his time. She pulled the passenger side visor mirror down and turned her neck to see her lesion. It was red, puffy and glistening with serum. The pain seared through her neck, and she cried anew. "Earl is going to hate this thing, he's going to be so mad at me. God, we need ice."

"Why will he be mad at you? It's not your fault. You had to, or they would have gladly put you in jail, or shot you. These people are completely nuts. Goddamn asshole Cain and his idiot America First Koolaid drinkers."

"I'm hungry. Are you hungry? I know I shouldn't be – pain usually takes the hunger right out of me. Anyway, protein's good for healing. Want a bar?" She fished around in her pocketbook and pulled out a large Ziploc bag packed with a variety of "healthy" bars. Jed looked at it and wrinkled his nose.

"Yeah, I'm hungry, but not for that shit. Maybe there's a McDonald's, or a Burger King somewhere."

Emma looked at Jed in amazement as she unwrapped a protein bar and took a large bite out of it. "Are you kidding? Everything is shut down. We're at the mercy of these bastards, grocery stores were cleaned out weeks ago, the supply chain is practically nil. You're going to have to learn to eat whatever there is."

Jed replied gruffly, "I'm not there yet. I hope I never get there. I hope in a few weeks the grid is back up and running and I can find the most painful way to stick it to these creeps like they stuck it to us. Where are we going? I don't know how to get around this fucking place."

"Sorry, I forgot, you've only been here a few times. We're going to the cemetery to see if we can bury some of the money, but let's at least drive by the commercial district and see what's going on. Then we can head to Troyville."

As they approached the local golf course at the bottom of a steep, winding hill, Emma marveled at the panoramic expanse of rolling mountains and neat patchwork fields of corn, wheat and fallow plots, until the golf course came into view, with yet another checkpoint. Emma and Jed both gasped when they saw dozens of tents dotting the course, along with multiple campfires.

"What the…" said Jed in wonderment.

"Oh no," Emma gasped. "Maybe we should turn around."

"Let's see what these yahoos have to say. If they want to cut my balls off or scalp me, we'll turn around."

"Shit," Emma whispered, slunk down in her seat, swallowed her mouthful of protein bar and stuffed the rest in her pants pocket.

Three older men waited at the checkpoint this time, two sported the same red hats, guns, and tattoos; one wore a State Police uniform. This time all three of them surrounded the car, the trooper closest to Jed's side circled his hand and Jed dutifully rolled down his window.

"Where you goin' folks?"

Emma piped up, "We're at the ski resort in Corinth, we were just going into town to see if anything's open, and visit my grandmother's grave."

One of the red-hats grunted, "Got their marks, John."

"OK," John said in clipped tones. "You don't wanna do that. We can't be everywhere, and there are a lot of desperate people looking for whatever they can get, including your car. We can't protect you, so you need to stay in your Pod." *Oh, so that's what they're calling it, each district is a Pod.*

"We know," Emma said. "We came from Downstate, and we got here thanks to a lot of folks with guns. We thought we'd be safer here."

John softened his stance slightly. "Well, you're lucky you made it. Look, turn around, go back, and let the Congers take care of you. They've got a pretty good system set up there."

"Are you branding people too, in your 'pod'?" asked Jed accusingly as he pointed to his brand.

John's mouth tightened. "We haven't gotten to that point yet, but it might be the best way to keep track of who belongs here and who doesn't. It's a logistical nightmare. I'm sorry folks, this is the way it is right now. Go home, stay safe."

Emma held up her hand to stop Jed from moving. "One more thing, John" she said, using her best 'come-hither' voice as her neck wound throbbed. Jed looked at her sideways as if to say "C'mon Mom" but she persisted. "Why are there so many tents? Are these homeless people?"

"They are now," John replied, as he began to assess Emma more closely. "They're folks who live in remote areas who decided the protection of the Haddonville pod is better than anything they can do on their own. It's tough, especially when the weather turns cold. We're working on making space for them in warehouses and empty stores. Some are already there."

"Thank you for the information, John" Emma said with a smile. "John, I'm a reporter, and I don't have to tell you this is the story of the Century, right? The whole planet brought to its knees by Mother Nature and the awesome power of the sun. I wonder if I might talk briefly with some of these good people, maybe with my son and one of your men as protection?

Jed rolled his eyes, "Not now, Mom. We have other things to do," he said significantly.

"Oh, you're right. Well, are you on this checkpoint often, John? Maybe another day?"

John thought a few moments, "It's possible, I suppose. I'm sure these folks would like to talk. They're having a rough time."

"Good," Emma smiled beatifically at him. "We'll see you later then, good luck to you."

Jed and Emma waved as Jed made a U-turn and started back up the hill.

"Geez Mom, what was that? Don gave you taste and now you want more?"

"Oh, stop it, although…" Emma grew dreamy and thoughtful. "I'm a journalist, remember? I use various tactics to get information, and I want to find a way to write about this, all of it, because Mommy wants a Pulitzer, and if Mr. John State Trooper can help me with that, so be it. Besides, we don't know from one day to the next whether we're going to be here, or have our corpses shredded by raptors at the Montrose landfill." Jed was not amused.

"C'mon Mom, you're acting really stupid. You can write your post-apocalyptic memoir later. We have to figure out what to do next. Where do we hide the money? How can we find out about your parents? And I want to see if I can find Aaron, I can't stop thinking about him. Last I heard he was staying in Troyville with his girlfriend."

Emma sighed, winced, moved her hand to her neck, and replied resignedly, "I don't know. Mom and Dad are on my mind constantly, and Lynn, Carol, Joe and the kids. I wish we had carrier pigeons or something. Maybe someone at the damn Collective has a CB or ham radio." She set her aching jaw. "But now, today, I think it's time to keep our friends close and our enemies closer… It's… Conger time!" she said with sarcastic, mock glee in her best game show announcer voice.

Jed nodded solemnly in agreement. "You're reading my mind."

Emma smiled, "It's what I do." Jed looked at her sideways as they pulled into the parking lot outside the cabin.

"Probably a good idea to keep that to yourself for a while."

"Who knows? Maybe I can barter with psychic readings."

144

Jed looked at Emma skeptically. "Maybe. Geez Mom."

"C'mon, let's beard the Earl lion in his den. He's not going to like any of this, especially our new neck accessories."

As Emma's car crunched to a stop on the gravel parking area, Earl and Liza burst out of the cabin, followed by the dogs. "Crap," Emma said under her breath. "I wish we had scarves."

Earl ran to Emma's window and knocked on the glass, Emma reluctantly rolled the window down as she adjusted her hair to cover her brand mark. "Honey, you're back so soon! What happened?"

"It's a long, sad story," she said. "Can we go inside, please?"

"Of course, my darling, come on," Earl said solicitously, as he opened the passenger door. Emma stepped out and winced slightly as she put her pocketbook strap over her right shoulder. "What's wrong?"

"Let's just get inside first, OK?" Earl put his arm around her and they walked down the pathway as Jed and Liza stood next to the car and talked intimately. Liza reached her hand to Jed's neck and burst into tears. Jed held her comfortingly.

Inside the front door Earl gave Emma a huge bear hug and moved to kiss her neck. "Ow, ow, no, Earl, please don't!" Emma begged, and ran for the refrigerator.

"Honey, what's wrong?"

Emma opened the freezer and felt around inside the ice tray. "God dammit! No freaking ice?" She moved the lever over the ice tray that was in the shut-off position and slumped against the wall.

"Honey, what's going on?" Earl's concern was growing exponentially. He worriedly moved to comfort her, she waved him away, paused and looked at him wearily.

"OK. Now, I'd tell you to sit down, but we don't have any fucking *chairs*, so just lean on the counter, listen to me, and try, just try not to lose it, OK?"

Earl's face was furrowed into what Emma called "flapping birds" or alternately "monster furrow face." *He looks like a human Shar-Pei.* "OK," he said worriedly. Emma moved to him and took his hands.

"Honey," she said slowly, "We couldn't get to the cemetery or the storage space, we won't be able to go there for a very long time, probably until this is over. There was a checkpoint at the Four Corners, three goony teenagers in red-hat uniforms, guns, the whole thing, with a little girlie cheering section. It was like Hillbilly Lord of the Flies. They told us we couldn't leave until they, well, until they…." She slowly pulled her hair away from her neck to reveal the angry red brand under her ear.

"What the hell is that? Why did you let them? Why didn't you turn around and come home?" Earl's index finger was pointed accusingly at Emma. She grabbed it and pushed it away.

Emma responded angrily, "I knew it! I knew you'd blame me for allowing them to deface your little blonde shiksa wife. I did it because they said it was the only way to get out. I did it because we were going to try and hide the money, and see if we could find out about my parents. I did it for *you*, motherfucker, so you can stay here, read your stupid mystery novels and sit on your can! So, I'm deformed now, I no longer please the King, is that it? Fuck you!" She burst into tears. He tried to hold her, but she pushed him away and winced in pain.

Earl was upset, and chastened. "Honey, honey, no, I'm just so upset for you. Does it hurt a lot? Did they, did they do anything else to you?"

Emma blubbered, "If you mean did they feel me up or rape me or something, no, geez. I almost passed out, thank you, but Jed was there, they branded him too, and if you or Liza want to go anywhere outside our 'pod,' that's what they call it, you'll have to get one too, or go to jail or get shot, depending on how much you struggle. So put that in your pipe and smoke it! I want to go home, but this is all we have, this Nazi cattle camp!" She collapsed onto the floor. "I am so sick of crying, but if I don't, I think I'll lose my mind."

Earl knelt down with difficulty next to her, his knee thudded against the floor and he grimaced. "What can I do?"

Emma looked plaintively at him. "Ice would be great, do we dare ask anyone around here for it? Maybe we should just wait a few hours for the icemaker. Thank God it's still working."

Earl was grateful to change the subject, as he was chagrined and embarrassed by Emma's accusations. "What about a cold can of soda, will that help?" He moved to pick a can out of the refrigerator and handed it gently to Emma.

"I guess so," she said, and cringed as the cold can touched her wound. "For once I'm glad you drink this disgusting, chemical-and-sugar laden crap in these aluminum death cylinders…What are we going to do? We can't get to the storage space, we're going to have to go to their godawful Company Store and buy our stuff back, if it's still there. And what about the money? That's the main thing. We've got to figure out a way to hide it here. It's still got to be worth something."

She thought for a moment. "You know, I remember Owen's mom, she liked to squirrel money away all over the house. Her husband gave her a household allowance, but she only spent part of it and saved the rest in tons of different places. Toward the end she had tens of thousands stashed away in cookie tins and flour canisters."

Earl responded slowly, "They'll find it, won't they?"

Emma sat up, inspired. "Yes! But we'll let it get out we only have about fifty grand, so even if they find that amount, we can act really upset they found it all, and maybe they'll be stupid enough to believe us. I'm a good actor, and so are you."

Earl thought carefully. "I'll think about it."

"I know you don't want to lose a penny, I get it…oh shit, what if we're bugged? They heard everything. I'm such an idiot."

"Honey, do you really think we're bugged? They're not that sophisticated, and where are they going to hide it?"

"We'll find out soon enough, Dave is bringing his electronic-savvy nephew over soon. Shit. I hope Conger & Co. are as stupid as you think they are."

Jed and Liza came into the kitchen holding hands. Liza sniffed, wiped her nose on her sleeve and wailed, "I'm not going to let them brand me like an animal!" and burst into tears. Jed held her comfortingly as she sobbed. Emma tried to be sympathetic, but Liza's inability to grow a pair was very aggravating.

"Dear," she said coolly with veiled impatience. "As long as you stay on the resort and don't pass any checkpoints, maybe you'll avoid it. But if you have to get one, think of it as just another of your very decorative tattoos." Liza and Jed sported multiple black tattoos on their arms. Liza looked up and brightened slightly.

"I guess," she said, and shuddered gently. *God, this is going to be the mother of my grandchild. Well, so be it.*

Jed interrupted, "It's going to be dark soon. Let's finish unloading the cars and get something, anything to eat. I'll even eat one of your stupid bars if I have to."

Earl looked up plaintively from his crouched position on the kitchen floor and said reluctantly, "Can you give me a hand?" Jed, Emma and Liza helped Earl to his feet. They looked expectantly at Emma as she held the soda can to her neck. *My ball game, as usual. Batter up.*

"Let's have dinner," she said resignedly, and began rooting through the sparsely appointed pantry.

Chapter Twenty-Seven

Family Ties

Dinner was an ad-hoc mixture of whatever Emma could pull together: pasta with grated cheese topped with tuna and mayo, canned lentil soup and chocolate chip cookies. There was an unfortunate lack of greens, which pleased Jed, Liza and Earl and made Emma feel bereft.

"We've got to see what kind of meat we can get around here," she fretted. "These guys have to have their roast beast. They took all our meat and potatoes."

"Me too, I need roast beast," sulked Liza, as she picked at her tuna and let her bowl of soup grow cold. *Lovely. So grateful.*

"We do our best, dear. Maybe you'll adjust. My grandmother always used to say, hunger is the best appetizer. Who knows? Someday you may grow to love tuna fish and lentil soup," Emma declared with mock brightness. "And you've got another mouth to feed, yes? Who is going to help with the dishes?"

The dogs began barking wildly and rushed to the door. "Oh great," Emma muttered. "Perhaps it's the Grim Reaper, or Nate Jr. looking for more graft." As she approached the door, a paper slid under it. She picked up a one-page flyer with the heading, "Mandatory Collective meeting tomorrow, 8 a.m., Resort Ballroom, Second Floor. All new Collective members must attend." She opened the door to see who delivered it as a young, thin girl ran toward the next cabin, her arms full of papers and her hair streaming behind her. *They've got them all working, I see.*

She showed the flyer to Jed and intoned, "Collective meeting tomorrow morning with the big cheese. I hope we can get those elusive ration coupons everyone's talking about – what little food we have is going to run out in a few days. We have to scope out the players and get the lay of the land, then put our plans in motion."

Jed nodded. "What's this Conger guy like?"

"Big guy, kind of a human heat-seeking missile, if the heat is money and we're the targets. All he thinks about 24-7 is how to make more, any way he can, and how to work the system. He's a salesman, very aggressive, a steamroller. His wife Kathy is a real piece of work, a total ditz, but focused on doing her part to make their schemes work. Her thing is focusing on the family angle, and the church thing. They do a lot of family-friendly events, and she teaches Bible studies at the local church. As far as I'm concerned, it's all smoke and mirrors, but you know these evangelical types, some of them are really plugged into it. And of course they're big AF'ers, White America and President Cain, uber alles."

She performed a desultory Nazi salute, then paused thoughtfully. "Do we have any red hats? I think we'll have to go undercover as Cain supporters, but let's see what the climate is like tomorrow. I'm glad I took the 'Jail Cain' bumper sticker off my car."

Jed nodded his assent, yawned and headed for the loft ladder. "I'm beat, it's early, but I'm going to head off to bed." He gestured to Liza to follow and picked up Buddy to carry him up the ladder. "Oof boy, you're really heavy."

Liza picked up Shatzi and said brightly, "Maybe we could rig up a little basket over the stairs so Shatzi could go up and down without me carrying her?"

Jed smiled indulgently, set Buddy down, hugged Liza and kissed her cheek. "Cute. We could do that with snacks too. Mom, got any baskets, and rope?"

Emma replied wryly, "Um, no. They took all that. Maybe they'll have something at the Criminal Store tomorrow. But good thinking, Liza." She meant it, albeit grudgingly.

Liza looked at Emma in surprise. "Thanks," she said with a slight smile.

Emma found herself smiling back. *Maybe she's good for something after all.*

# # #

Morning, 6 a.m., their first morning in the Strange New World. Emma rubbed her eyes and grimaced as she rolled over on the hard floor. *This damn sleeping bag is thin as paper. I hate these people already. The pillows aren't much better.*

She vaguely remembered she had another episode of a recurring dream in which a golden orb tried to talk to her, and Lily Fortas's thin, sober face hovered nearby as the Mountain Man circled them like a deranged planet. Emma couldn't hear what the orb was saying, only static and a strange buzz. She tried to remember more, but like her other dreams and visions in the past few weeks, it faded within minutes.

Earl had a double layer of sleeping bags and two pillows, and in the past sleeping on the floor actually helped his twisted, tired back, but Emma girded herself for his morning reveille of blaring flatulence, catarrh-laced throat-clearing, and his inevitable inability to get up off the floor on his own. *I am not lifting 240 pounds by myself.* Emma staggered to her feet and whispered up the loft stairs. "Jed…..Jed!" *That boy can sleep through a nuclear blast.*

She gingerly climbed the ladder, paused at the top and smiled at Jed and Liza, wrapped in each other's arms as the two dogs curled around each other at their feet. They had opened two sleeping bags and zipped them together, Emma was loath to disturb the tableau, but business was business, Earl had to get up and use the bathroom, and they had to get to the meeting early, if possible, to case the scene.

She crawled to Jed and jiggled him back and forth vigorously. "Jed," she whispered sotto voce. He groaned slightly and kept sleeping. "Jed!" Liza's eye's popped open and she startled at Emma's face hovering over her.

"Um, what?" she said confusedly, then sat up abruptly, put her hand over her mouth and muttered "Bathroom, bathroom….no time" and turned and vomited into a large saucepan next to the sleeping bags. *Again, smart move.* Emma waited patiently and resisted the urge to rub Liza's back. Jed continued sleeping, the dogs rustled at the noise, and the unfortunate smell.

"I'm really sorry," Liza said as she wiped her mouth and sat back, the saucepan in her lap. "This morning barfie thingie is really brutal."

"No worries," Emma said, "I'm sorry you have to go through it. Want a mint, or a cracker or something?"

Liza perked up. "We have crackers?"

"Yeah, I think so. Those little oyster things Jed likes."

"That would be great…um, I'll come down." She poked Jed hard in the ribs, "Pookie. Pookie! We have to get up!"

Pookie?

Jed moaned and shifted slightly. Liza leaned over him and startled tickling him under his arm. "C'mon Pookster, wakey wakies!" Jed moaned and laughed, then curled into a defensive ball.

"OK, OK!" his eyes opened slightly "Mom…Mom…what are you doing here? What's wrong?"

"You have to help me with Earl, I know he won't be able to get up off the floor on his own, and I'm not busting a gut or a vertebra trying to lift him by myself."

Jed sat up lazily and muttered, "Give me a minute, OK?"

"Sure," Emma said, and she held out her hand for the saucepan. "Should I take that and flush it?"

Liza smiled apologetically. "Thanks! And those crackers sound really nice."

"You got it," Emma said.

As she descended the ladder, Shatzi and Buddy tried to lick her face. Liza chided, "Down boys and girls! Gramma does not like dog droolies on her face."

Gramma? Doesn't sound awful. Emma smiled to herself. *Maybe this won't be so bad, maybe we'll adjust.*

"I've got to come down; they have to be walked," Liza said. "Pookie, you have to carry Buddy."

"OK, OK," Jed groaned, and he carried Buddy down the ladder. "Maybe he could jump?"

"You want him to break a leg?" Lisa asked accusingly.

"…No?" Jed replied sarcastically.

"We'll figure it out," Emma said impatiently. "I have to pee, who's first? Mind if I go first, Pookie?"

Jed glared at Emma. "Nope. Nope. No Pookie, Mom. Go pee."

"Awww," Emma said with a smile. "And it's so cute." Jed waved her to the bathroom. Buddy and Shatzi circled impatiently by the door. Earl stirred on the floor, the dogs ran to him and pounced. Emma paused in the bathroom doorway and held the pot away from her face. *This should be interesting.*

"Hey!" Earl said sleepily, then passed gas noisily, which startled Shatzi, and she barked accusingly at Earl. Emma, Jed and Liza laughed, but Earl was chagrined. "Can't a guy wake up in peace around here?" he asked petulantly.

"Not around here," Emma said. "Welcome to the new world, babe. Jed, help me after I do this." She took care of the saucepan's contents and her own needs as quickly as she could. When she came back out, Earl had struggled to one elbow. He looked defensively at Jed. "I can do it, I can do it."

Emma smiled at him. "Sure you can honey, but it's much easier this way. Jed, take one ham hock, I'll take the other." They both took an arm and pulled Earl to a sitting position. A few more maneuvers, and he was up. "Thank you for the putrid cloud surrounding us, dear."

Earl scowled. "Bathroom, please?" he asked irritably. He sighed as Jed and Liza went outside with the dogs. "Kinda crowded around here," he said desultorily.

"We'll figure it out. C'mon honey, we've got the frickin' Nazi meeting in an hour. I'm hoping for food and furniture this morning. Bring money."

Earl shut the bathroom door with an evil smile. "Better be nice to me."

Emma smiled back. "Always." She yelled through the bathroom door. "What do you want for breakfast?"

"Won't they be serving at the meeting?"

Emma startled. "You're kidding, right?"

"Maybe."

"Let's assume they're not. This is not the Ramada. Or even Motel 6."

"Then I suppose bacon and eggs are out of the question."

"Unless you've got some in there, yes. You can have granola bars and rice milk," She surveyed the refrigerator. "Or granola and rice milk."

A brief pause, then a muttered "Granola and rice milk…Oy."

"Coming right up!" Emma chirped brightly, as she filled the saucepan with soapy water and took two bowls from a cabinet. "And don't 'oy' around these people. We're already concentration camp fodder because of your heritage. Boy, they really hate Jews around here."

Earl opened the bathroom door as he wiped his face with a towel. "Believe me, I know."

"But I'm sure you'll work your charms and your pocketbook on them, as always." Earl glanced meaningfully at her, went into the bedroom and pawed through his clothes piled in the suitcase next to his sleeping bag.

Jed and Liza came in breathlessly from outside. "Mom, it's awesome out there. The air is clean, and the sun is really strong and bright. We've been so used to Manhattan smog and dirt. Maybe this won't be so bad after all," he said hopefully.

Liza nodded in agreement. "Yeah Mom, it's so great! And the dogs really like it, all these places to run."

MOM? Hold the phone. Emma widened her eyes at Jed and mouthed, "Mom?" He shook his head and mouthed "Let it go." *Mother-in-law to be and Gramma, too much to process.*

"Breakfast?" she said to Jed. "Liza, your crackers are on the counter." Liza nodded and headed for the kitchen, followed by the dogs.

"Nah," Jed said. "I don't eat until later. Maybe we can get some actual real food this morning? We're still waiting for those ration coupons."

Liza poked Jed's shoulder. "Pookie, I have to pee, and maybe barf again. We'll meet them there, OK?"

Jed nodded and shrugged his shoulders. "OK. See you guys soon. This should be interesting."

"Yes," Emma replied skeptically. "If I know Conger, we'll get a whole song and dance along with our route of march. Be ready, it's his way or the highway."

Chapter Twenty-Eight

Meeting of the Minds

Signs with attached red balloons greeted Collective newbies and directed them to the Second Floor Ballroom as they filed through the main entrance of the Corinth Mountain Resort. A Conger brainchild for decades, Ben and Kathy finally found a way to finagle enough state and federal funding by presenting units in the proposed main building as at least 50% occupied, courtesy of their far-flung nefarious cronies.

"Can anyone say, 'money laundering'?" Emma had quipped ten years ago when news of resort ground-breaking circulated through the grapevine. But she had to give the Congers a grudging amount of credit for what they manifested in the middle of nowhere.

The main multi-storied building was impressive, with its rough-hewn log exterior and soaring lobby. An enormous floor-to-ceiling stone gas fireplace on perpetual burn graced the center of the lobby. "It's like a mini-Disney wilderness resort," Emma had marveled the first time she and Earl stepped inside. To the right, a large semi-circular Welcome desk, to the left, a commodious bar with a restaurant behind it. Down the hall to the right were administrative offices, a spa and banks of elevators. Today, the spa, bar and restaurant were closed, even the gas fireplace was dark, and one perennially chipper blonde clerk stood behind the Welcome desk, red hat firmly on her head. "Hi folks!" she said cheerily and pointed to the elevators.

Emma recognized elderly Dr. Spencer from a neighboring cabin as he stood in queue for the elevator. *He looks really tired, and even skinnier than I remember. I wonder if he had trouble getting here.* She tapped him on his shoulder, and he turned around with a light gasp, then relaxed when he saw Emma.

"Oh, Ellen my dear. Good to see you. And Fred." He smiled at Earl. They didn't bother to correct him, since they knew he was in accelerating stages of cognitive decline. But when it came to infectious diseases, his specialty, his mind was honed and clear.

"It's so good to see you, George," Emma said warmly, as she gently hugged his frail body. "How's Jenna?" His wife Jenna, a talented artist, was sidelined by her deteriorating spine and housebound for the most part, since getting her up and walking or into a car was a long, slow and painful procedure.

George's smile faded and he looked at his feet. "I lost her. On the way here. Maybe someday I'll tell you about it, but not here," he replied sadly. Emma grabbed his hands and squeezed them as she looked into his face. "George, oh George, I'm so sorry to hear this."

George's eyes filled with tears, "My girl, she was so brave."

The elevator doors opened. Emma and Earl guided George in and bookended him on the ride up as Emma held his hand. Emma didn't recognize most of the newbies, which wasn't unusual, since cabin part-timers kept to themselves, except for gregarious George and Jenna. They knew everyone, and had been coming to the mountain with their family for decades. When they got off the elevator Emma spied two more familiar faces exiting the adjacent elevator, Sam Schneider and Greta Sung, an unmarried couple who owned the cabin next to George. Their parents had been friends with George and Jenna since college, and their extended families had enjoyed cabin holidays together since the inception of the resort in the 1970s.

Sam, a successful Manhattan prosecutor and Greta, a corporate attorney with Thai ancestry, had been a couple for over 10 years, and George was freshly scandalized every time they told him they weren't married.

George whispered to Emma, "They're not married, you know."

Emma looked at George fondly, widened her eyes and replied indulgently, "You're kidding? Wow." George nodded solemnly. Sam and Greta smiled with relief at their familiar faces, and joined Emma, Earl and George in a closed circle off to the side of the elevators.

Greta nodded hello to Earl and Emma, folded her hands and stood silently beside Sam. Sam's dark brown eyes darted back and forth, and as

156

he spoke he continued to rapidly scan the newcomers. "We got here yesterday, You?"

Emma nodded. "It was no picnic."

Sam looked at her intently. "I bet. We took a lot of back roads in the middle of the night. I had to gun it past a lot of things I never thought were possible." He took Emma aside and whispered, "We brought George and Jenna with us. She had a heart attack on the way. I'll give you the details later."

Emma whispered back, "We took the highway with an armed caravan, another story for later. We can compare war wounds – come by when you can. Do you have Sirah with you?" Sirah was Sam and Greta's elegant beige whippet. Sam nodded. "Good, we have Jed and his girlfriend with us, they have a German Shepherd and a poodle. They'll be here in a few minutes, sans dogs. Maybe we can arrange a playdate."

Sam nodded and said curtly, "Let's go in." Emma always had the feeling Sam was not a fan of hers, especially when he learned of her esoteric leanings. This exchange with him was their friendliest to date. *Maybe disaster will open them up a bit. One can hope.*

The ballroom had a series of doorways flanked by armed, red-hatted sentries who stopped each entrant and wrote their name on a clipboard. Emma recognized Ashley at the entrance. The girl blanched and blushed when she saw Earl. Emma sighed wearily, and as they approached her, she couldn't take her eyes off Earl. *Geez, when does this primal sexual ooze wear off? He's probably 50 years her senior. Jack Nicholson, Warren Beatty, Sean Connery, Earl Kaplan. Lucky me, I guess.*

Ashley looked self-consciously at her clipboard and said shyly, "Um, Kaplan family, right? Aren't there four of you?"

Emma replied impatiently, anxious to get away from the Earl fan club. "Yes, my son and his girlfriend will be here soon. May we save them seats?"

"Oh sure, there'll be plenty of seats. You'll see. Go on in. Please visit the Welcome table first for your name tags and ration coupons."

"Thank you, dear," Earl said, as he patted Ashley's shoulder and flashed his multi-million dollar smile, courtesy of thousands of dollars in porcelain caps. Ashley practically swooned; Emma grabbed Earl's arm and propelled him into the room.

"C'mon honey. Plenty more unsuspecting prey in here, I would imagine."

Earl looked at Emma in mock innocence. "Oh, c'mon now. She's a nice kid. Besides, what's good for the goose is good for the gander, my lovely."

"Not now, dear. We can rehash this ancient argument later. I want those coupons." Earl joined Dr. Spencer, Sam and Greta in the seating section, and Emma approached the welcome table, a long series of folding tables set up against the wall, perpendicular to the ballroom stage. Several older women sat in folding chairs behind the tables, each with clipboards.

The ballroom was large and plain. It could have been a school gymnasium, with its polished wooden floors that smelled of shellac, and stack after stack of folding chairs against the wall. At one end of the room was a raised stage with several high-powered lighting instruments suspended above it. A large screen and podium were set up on the empty stage, and multiple rows of folding chairs were placed facing the stage.

Emma was chagrined but not surprised to see a huge portrait of The Orange Menace on the wall behind the screen. A few attendees were already seated and looking over documents given to them by the 'Welcome Ladies.' Emma noticed a table in the back of the room covered with electronic equipment where several red-hatted men were busy plugging in speakers and working various keyboards. *So, Conger likes his production numbers. This should be fun.*

Jed and Liza entered, Emma spotted them and gestured for them to join her at the Welcome table line. "Hey," Emma said. "Safe to leave the dogs alone? Think they might chew our sleeping bags to shreds?"

Jed and Liza looked at each other. "Um, I don't think so," Liza said doubtfully. "Shatzi hasn't chewed my shoes in months, and we left them toys."

Emma sighed. "So be it, I hate the damn sleeping bags anyway. Maybe we can get our beds back today."

"Next!" A bored gray-haired woman in a red hat, dungarees and a Tweetie Bird t-shirt gestured to them to come to her station. "Name?" she asked without looking up.

Emma adopted her most charming smile and said, "Good morning. Kaplan, Cabin 20 West. Love your t-shirt. Tweetie is my spirit animal."

The woman looked up and narrowed her eyes. "Uh huh…how many?"

"Four," Emma said cheerfully. "And two lovely dogs, Buddy and Shatzi."

The woman scanned them carefully. "All named Kaplan?"

"No, actually," Emma replied. "This is Jed Campbell, from my first marriage, and this is his girlfr..uh…partner Liza Lefkowitz. My husband Earl is over there." She pointed to Earl.

The woman's eyes narrowed further. "Kaplan, Campbell, Lefkowitz…" she wrote down on her clipboard.

Liza beamed and chirped, "Soon it will be five," and patted her belly. The woman sneered and said to the woman next to her, "Lefkowitz. Pregnant." The women looked at each other significantly, then both looked accusingly at Liza.

She was unfazed, looked at her inquisitors' name tags and asked innocently, "Mary, maybe you or Agnes could help me find a good obstetrician?"

Mary shook her head coldly. "Don't know any."

Agnes chimed, "Nope don't know any."

Liza smiled brightly and said, "Oh, sorry, it's past your time for that, isn't it?"

Emma stifled a smile and asked carefully, "We understand we can get food coupons here? That's what we were told at the door. Your guards took most of our food."

Mary looked coolly at Emma and replied curtly, "Our *Protectors* did what they had to do, for the good of all." Agnes nodded emphatically. Mary reached under the table and produced a metal lockbox, opened it with a key hanging around her neck and began shuffling what looked like raffle tickets. She began to deal them out like playing cards as she intoned, "Four dairy, four meat, four eggs, four bread, four vegetables." She looked at Emma with a twisted smile and handed her the coupons. "This should last you a week. It better."

Emma looked confusedly at the coupons. "What does this mean, four dairy, four meat…?"

Mary explained impatiently, "One serving for each per person per day for a week. You can see the coupon expires in one week. When you visit the Commissary they'll punch your coupons as you use them. Next."

She waved them away dismissively, but Emma stood her ground. "But, what about oil, butter, flour, sugar, pasta, fruit?"

Mary gestured for Emma to stand aside as she waved the next person forward. "You have to work that out with the Elders."

"Elders?" Emma asked incredulously.

Mary snapped, "Watch the presentation, they'll explain it. Next!"

The three stood to the side of the table, Emma whispered, "This is nuts. And speaking of nuts, how can we find some?" She looked at Liza appreciatively, "Nice move, past their time." She made a check mark in the air with her finger. "Chalk one up for Liza."

Liza smiled, phantom licked her index finger, touched it to her hip and made a sizzling sound with her lips. *I think I'm going to like this kid.* Emma laughed, but Jed was not amused.

"Mom," he said darkly, "This looks bad." Emma stopped giggling and looked anxiously at Jed. He had inherited her Spidey sense, and she knew better than to ignore it.

"What?" Emma whispered nervously. "What do you think? I mean, they're acting like power-mad assholes, but this can't last forever, the grids and satellites will come back online eventually, this is still America, after all. I think these yahoos are a temporary nuisance, and I'm pretty sure I'm going to lose weight, which isn't a bad thing in the end. My end, at least. You know what they say, you can never be too skinny or too compromised by bullshit authoritarian regimes." She laughed at her little joke, then realized she could be talking about the Holocaust. She smiled apologetically. "Oh God, sorry."

Jed looked at her and rolled his eyes. "Mom, come out of your bubble please. Maybe you think you're home free, except for that red blotch under your ear, and you're going to make everything home sweet home like you always do, and thank you for that, but this is just the beginning of something really, really bad."

Emma walked slowly to a folding chair in the last row and sat down next to Jed. She gestured for the others to follow, but Earl and Liza were kidding with each other, and Ashley had joined them. Emma glared at him and waved for him to join them. He nodded to her perfunctorily and continued to make the girls laugh. Jed grabbed Emma's arm and turned her to him.

"Get over it, Mom, it's Earl. Listen to me. Protectors? Elders? I'm telling you, if we don't bow down and play ball their way, this is going to be a 21st Century concentration camp. It already feels like the Warsaw Ghetto. They hate us because we're Jews, which makes it even worse. If anyone's going to get the short end of the baton, it's us. Rationing, no locks on the doors, branding, and this is just the beginning."

Emma sank into her chair. "But, I'm not Jewish, and therefore, technically you're not either. They're just not used to Jews around here. They probably don't have any. Earl will charm them out of it, like he did with Dave Stafford. You'll see."

"Mom, remember when that virus hit two years ago? And I told you it was going to go global, and kill millions of people? You didn't take me seriously then either."

"But, we have a vaccine now, it's under control, and soon we'll get the grid back." She became pensive. "Don did say it could take months, maybe even years to come all the way back. But look at us. We have power, Don said some places still have it, but they're scattered all over. Maybe we're among the lucky ones."

Jed took Emma's hands and looked intently into her eyes. "Focus Mom, listen to me. Remember what you always told me about 'the gift'? How frustrated you were when you were doing the readings that people didn't listen to you? You called it 'The Cassandra Complex'? Well, now you're not listening to me, even though you gave me the gift. Think about it."

161

Emma responded lightly. "OK honey, but I'm not getting those feelings about our future here. I think we're safe. Challenged, with a bunch of Cain-worshipping assholes, but safe. We own our cabin, we pay taxes. It's going to be all right."

Jed replied sadly, "Because that's what you desperately want to think. It's clouding you."

Emma squeezed Jed's hands. "Let's see what they have to say, OK? Let's see about getting food, and maybe furniture. Maybe we can get our beds back. It looks like they're about to start."

Kathy Conger was at the podium testing the microphone. "Testing, testing, one two three," she blared in a sharp, high voice. The microphone erupted with high-pitched feedback, Kathy stood back from the podium and laughingly held her hands over her ears. She tossed her uber-thick lion's mane of tastefully highlighted brown hair and pushed it back with a hand and wrist laden with bling. *Well fed, well-heeled, well fucked? I wonder. I bet that silk blouse cost a bundle.* A technician at the back table yelled out, "Just a minute! Workin' on it!" as he turned dials on various controls.

Earl and Liza were seated in the middle of the chair section, and waved Emma and Jed over. Sam, Greta and Dr. Spencer sat close by. Emma looked at Earl coldly and waved Jed into the seat next to Earl. Earl held up his hands as if to say 'what?' and Emma sat next to Dr. Spencer and looked straight ahead. *Every time we enter new territory he has to scope out the vulnerable females. Damn him and his fatal fucking charms. It never fucking ends. I'm sick of it.*

Emma sat back resignedly in her chair, Dr. Spencer looked at her with concern and squeezed her hand. "Are you all right, Mary dear?" he asked gently.

She nodded and smiled weakly, "I'm just tired, that's all. Thanks George." Earl looked over at them and noticed their handholding. Emma sent him a snide little smile. *The game goes on. Point, counterpoint baby.* Her smile disappeared when she remembered Don, and their couplings. *How do I categorize that in this game of cat and mouse? I don't think I can.*

162

Loud music blared over loudspeakers, President Cain's theme song vibrated through the air, a 'Presidential' version of "Electrifying" by Jim Johnston. Heavy metal guitar and drums blasted the airwaves as the voice rasped, "Can you smell, what the Cain, is cookin'!" From the rear ballroom doors emerged a battalion of red-hatted goons, armed to the teeth, beefy bare arms covered in tattoos, combat boots marching in time.

Kathy Conger exclaimed excitedly from the podium, "Welcome to the CMR Collective, where all are safe, and where the common good of our people is protected for all time! I'm very happy to introduce you to my husband, our hard-working Fearless Leader, Ben Conger!" She stood next to the podium and clapped enthusiastically, as two older red-hatted women at the foot of the stage encouraged the audience to clap. Most did, but with confusion and very little enthusiasm. Emma stared wide-eyed and open-mouthed at the burgeoning spectacle and looked in abject surprise at Earl, Jed and Liza. She glanced at Dr. Spencer, who had a slight smile on his face and looked out of it. Sam and Greta were impassive.

Behind the goons strode Ben Conger, a tall, imposing man with a stern, square jaw, flat-top buzz cut and deep, booming voice. He wore combat fatigues, and his shoulders sported military epaulets with three silver stars on each. Behind him were two marching lines of armed 'Protectors.' Emma recognized Nate, Nate Jr., Peanut, Andy, Sean and Glen among them. *Jesus, what kind of rabbit hole have we fallen into*?

The goons and Protectors took their places in straight lines behind Ben Conger, their hands clasped behind them, as he approached the podium. He held up his hand for the music to stop as Emma and Jed exchanged significant glances. "Holy shit," she mouthed, Jed nodded grimly and mouthed back, "Told you."

"Welcome, new and valued members of the Corinth Mountain Resort Collective. Many of you have been coming here for years, others have journeyed with your families from nearby towns with no protection, and we have welcomed you as our own." *Yeah, and smashed burning pokers on our necks.*

"We have established rules and guidelines for your safety, including ration coupons, and our Collective Commissary where you can secure food for your family. Down the hill from the Commissary you'll find our storage warehouse, run by our Church Elders, where you can buy furniture and other household items. But before we go into detail about that, we want to show you what it's like right now, out there, without protective perimeters, proper ID and reliable supply chains for food and medical supplies." Ben signaled to the back table, the screen lit up, lights dimmed in the ballroom and a spotlight was trained on Conger as he stood next to the screen with a remote.

"Fasten your jocks and pull up your socks," Emma whispered to Jed. "This is going to be off the hook."

Chapter Twenty-Nine

Achtung, Baby

Conger cleared his throat, squared his shoulders and clicked the remote. The screen read, "Troyville, September 1, 2017." A video with a soundtrack reminiscent of an Al Qaeda recruitment piece played, depicting scene after scene of food lines, dead bodies lying in town squares, crying children wandering alone in the street, and armed looters, interspersed with the names of multiple small towns in the area – Montrose, September 2, Lenders Mill, September 3, Foleyville, September 4. Emma recognized with horror the Troyville town square where several bodies lay, and knew she had to find some way to get to her elderly parents. If they were still alive.

The final town featured was, "Corinth Mountain Resort, our CMR Collective, today." A phalanx of heavily armed 'Protectors,' their surveillance extending to the top of the mountain, stood guard. Cows grazed on quiet green fields, farmers plowed their land, and women hung laundry on outside lines. A pie cooled on a windowsill as white sheer curtains billowed behind it. Another image of the protection line completed the video, and as the camera came in for a final closeup of a protector, he grinned, flashed a toothy smile, and brandished his high-capacity semi-automatic assault rifle.

Lights came back up in the ballroom, Conger surveyed the shocked faces in the audience and said quietly, "I know. It's a dangerous place outside our perimeter. We're doing everything we can to keep you, our people, safe, and we need your help, and your cooperation. When you arrived our Protectors began the process of consolidating our resources, and we'll continue to pool our assets for the Collective. We will also continue our Identification program." He gestured to his assembled troops behind him and bellowed ,"Face......left!" They turned their heads to the left in unison to reveal brand marks under their right ears. Ben turned his head to the left to reveal the same.

"We all need this permanent form of identification. All are mandated to receive this mark of honor, some of you already have. For those who have not, when you leave here our Welcome workers will direct you to our ID station. It's quick, any discomfort is temporary and can be easily alleviated, and will assure you are always welcome here, as long as you adhere to the rules. It will also alert Protectors from other pods, or districts, where you belong, should you wander. If by some chance you refuse our ID program, you will be escorted outside the perimeter with the rest of your family and belongings and left to fend for yourselves."

Dr. Spencer turned to Emma and whispered, "Gloria, what is this ID? Is it some kind of tattoo?"

Emma squeezed his hand and said softly, "Well, kind of, but they use heat." She lifted her hair and showed him her mark.

He gasped, and whispered, "My Jenna and I never thought something like that could happen here. I wish I'd gone with her." Tears formed in his eyes. "I don't want this."

"Let me talk with them. Maybe there's another way." He smiled tearfully and sat downcast; hands folded in his lap.

Emma raised her hand and stood up, Conger barked, "Questions later, please." She opened her mouth, thought better of it, and sat down. Dr. Spencer smiled gently and patted her hand.

Conger continued, "As I said, we can't guarantee your safety if you leave the perimeter, even with ID. If you stay within our boundaries, which lie between the Corinth Four Corners, the Tully Forest boundary, Palmer Road in Montrose and the highway 393 and County Road 11 intersection, you are protected. Curfew is nightfall, if you stay out past that, we can't guarantee your safety. Our Protectors shoot to kill." He paused briefly to let that sink in. "We have checkpoints at each location, and armed sentries stationed in shifts around the entire perimeter, on walkie-talkie and within sight of each other, day and night, 24-7."

"We have several major benefits many district pods don't. We have a built-in army of resort employees, many ex-military, myself included, and an independent energy system, in conjunction with Troyville and Haddonville. We have pooled our solar and wind farm resources into a sharing consortium, Spence's Dairy at the Four Corners is installing a methane plant using cow manure, and is working with other local dairies to get their systems online. We expect ours to be operational within a few months."

He stopped to take a long drink of water as the people in the audience stirred and murmured. He cleared his throat impatiently until the murmuring stopped. "We were lucky, we went off grid before the ejection clouds hit, thanks to scientists at the Troy University Observatory. A lot of folks weren't so lucky. Right now this energy is available at all times, but it might not always be the case, depending on wind and weather, so conserve, conserve, conserve. Use candles instead of lights, keep unnecessary appliances unplugged, and use wood burning for heat when you can – with hundreds of acres of forest, we have plenty of that. Gas for your cars is rationed and in very short supply, and it's unsafe to drive outside our borders, so best to stay put and stay out of your cars unless absolutely necessary."

He paused and scanned the audience. "Realize one thing, what we have here is special. There are going to be people who will try to bust in and take us over. We will deal with them without mercy. They will not be allowed in, and if they don't leave of their own volition, they will be eliminated." He stopped, smiled widely and looked back at his 'troops'. "Another thing we've got – we're on the mountain, we can see 'em comin'." The Protectors laughed amongst themselves. *They're as bad as Jed, maybe worse, it looks like they can't wait to bag their first interloper.*

"Now, one of the most important aspects of all our lives – food, and medicine. You may know the supply chain is broken, any food we have trucked in here comes with armed guards, and these brave folks go through a lot to bring food to your table. Our food needs to be local, as much as possible, and I'm talkin' back to pioneer times. We'll need to grind our own flour from our own wheat, corn and rye fields when our current supplies run out, use milk and meat from our local dairies, and if you don't hunt, you better learn, or have a good friend who does and is willing to share."

He paused to let that sink in. "We have some fishing resources in our district in the Towanda River, but it will soon be fished out. Our local farmers have laying hens and enough vegetable seed to get us through at least a season or two. Folks, it's going to be tight, and we're learning as we go. We have been able to have some foodstuffs flown in on small planes to a landing area we cleared in Fred Cutlass's corn field on Holler Road, these supplies are mostly government issue, the planes make weekly trips here, but we never know what they're going to bring. The same is true for medicine, we have a limited supply in our Collective Pharmacy, and we're doing our best using CB, ham radio and our military and corporate contacts to find out where essential medicines are being warehoused."

An elderly woman a few rows in front of Emma, raised her hand, but Conger waved her off impatiently. "We have limited food supplies outside our ration program, and you can pay for extras one of two ways – you can use paper money, jewelry, gold or silver coins, or you can work it off for the Collective in our kitchens, water treatment facility, lumber projects, fields or dairies. Any skills you have may be useful, for instance if you sew, knit, cook, are handy with a hammer, saw and nails, or if you're a medical professional, your value to the Collective is increased. Extras like furniture, clothes, etc., are first-come, first-served, and money talks." He paused and gestured to Kathy. "Before we open it up to questions, my wife has a few announcements."

Kathy grabbed the microphone from its stand and paced the stage as she brayed in a loud, strident voice, "Hi folks! Thank Jesus and the Good Lord Above, yes? Hallelujah! And my husband, of course, and thank the best President this great country has ever had, President Armand Cain!" Conger and his army cheered, some threw their hats in the air, than chanted "Cain, Cain, Cain….Cain, Cain, Cain!" Conger held up his hand, the men stopped abruptly and resumed their positions. Emma's eyes widened, she glanced sideways at Jed, who was whispering to Liza. Earl sat back in his chair, arms folded across his chest as he calmly assessed the scene.

"The Good Lord will get us through, you can count on that, right? OK folks, if your souls are hungry along with your bellies, we'll be holding church services here in the ballroom every Sunday at 10:00, and we're forming committees for our ladies, our teens and our little ones. Busy hands make light work, am I right? Put your faith in Jesus, and join us in prayer, you'll be glad you did!"

Kathy signaled to an older red-hat woman seated at a piano at the base of the stage. "Now, we're going to sing 'How Great Thou Art.' I'm sure most of you know it, but if you don't, just sing along as best you can." She motioned for the audience to stand. Most looked confused and mouthed along with Kathy and the Welcome Ladies as they sang fervently.

Emma stood slowly and rolled her eyes at Jed as she watched the audience and didn't even try to pretend she knew the words. Jed shook his head sharply at her and whispered, "Be cool."

Emma's brain worked overtime as she tried to absorb this information while reading between the lines. *Conger makes it all sound so, well, reasonable under the circumstances, and organized. We're all in this together, right? So why do I feel so uneasy?* She looked over at Jed. He shook his head grimly.

"OK," Conger said when the song finished with a flourish. "I'm opening it up to questions now." He pointed to Emma. "You had a question?"

Emma stood nervously, cleared her throat and spoke with a slight quiver, "Yes, um, well, the, uh…ID thing…for some folks it might be too much, like the elderly, small children and pets. Isn't there any other way?"

Conger replied curtly. "In a word, no." Several of his goons nodded their heads and sneered at Emma. "Unless you can come up with something better, and just as permanent, this is it. Next?"

Emma continued, "I have family in Troyville, including elderly parents. Your video showed trouble there. I can't reach them, and as you said, driving there is dangerous. How can I find out how they're doing?"

Conger paused, then replied gruffly, "We all have family we want to reach. It would require couriers with armed support going from town to town - it's too dangerous. You can try getting information through our Communication Center. Next, someone else, please?"

Emma sat down reluctantly, deflated and worried anew. The last she heard from Bonnie was on Facebook before emergency power went down. They were still in their apartment in Troyville and safe, and said they were planning to go to Carol and Joe's in Zion, but didn't know how they were going to transport Richard. Maybe they made it. And what about Lynn and the boys? They seemed light years away now. The last thing Lynn wrote to Emma on Facebook was they were going to try to get to Carol and Joe's, but did they get there, and if so, how? She vowed to visit the Communications tent after the meeting.

Her solar plexus ached. She patted Dr. Spencer's hand, then went to sit next to Earl, who was still contemplating the scene like the cat that swallowed the canary.

"What?" Emma whispered accusingly as Earl turned his head to her and smiled beatifically. "I can't believe you think this is amusing."

"What I think, my dear, is this is an opportunity."

"Always the businessman. OK, pray tell, oh Great Eyeglass Merchant, what kind of opportunity? Aren't you the least bit, oh, I don't know, *unnerved* at this Cain, God and Country-loving jingoistic spectacle?"

Earl put his finger to his lips to shush her. "Quiet, darling, I want to hear the questions." *Always the opportunist, looking for an opening, looking to make a buck, or a woman. Hey, you married him. OK, yes, so he got to me too, I'm a fool for love, OK?* Emma often held these running arguments with herself, especially about Earl, who continued to excite and perplex her after 30 years.

Most of the questions covered logistics, concerns about water safety, medication and food availability, and Conger answered each question succinctly, with only as much detail as he stated was available. No one challenged Conger's confiscation of their belongings, or asked about the Protectors' violent tactics, they were too cowed by the presence of high-powered weaponry, and the promise of protection from marauders outside the perimeter.

Populations under stress look to a strong man, and autocracy. Remember your history, Emma.

170

After the last question, Conger gestured to the Welcome ladies, who moved to the aisles, and stopped each person to check their neck for the Collective mark. Liza clung to Jed, and was loath to leave her seat, he kissed the top of her head and gently coaxed her to approach the Welcome lady and show her bare, pristine neck. The woman took Liza by the arm, Liza burst into tears and ran to Jed. Jed talked briefly with the woman, probably to tell her Liza was pregnant, but the woman shook her head and she and Jed shepherded Liza through a door to an outdoor patio where grills were blazing, staffed by armed Protectors.

Emma turned worriedly to Earl, "Should we go out there, for moral support?"

Earl replied grimly, "Well, sure, but I have to get one too, remember?"

"Oh, your hide is so thick, you probably won't even feel it. And if you do, you'll never let anyone know about it, Mr. Tough Guy."

"So kind, so kind."

"So loyal, so faithful. C'mon, maybe you can moo when they put their brand on you. That should crack them up."

Liza was already branded and crying in Jed's arms, he guided her to a table with bowls of ice and white terry washcloths. He wrapped several cubes of ice in a washcloth and applied it tenderly to Liza's wound, Emma marveled at how loving he could be, and for a moment her heart was gladdened. Earl stood in line for his time under the branding iron like he was waiting at the bank, and tried to engage people around him in light banter, but they weren't having it. When his turn came, he bent down obligingly, winced slightly when the iron sizzled his skin, then sauntered away with a slight smile and joined Emma.

"Well," she said approvingly. "I think you may be devoid of nerve endings. Would you like some ice?"

"I wouldn't say no," Earl replied, with a hint of urgency in his voice.

"Uh huh. I'll get it." She approached the table, wrapped ice in a cloth and motioned for Jed and Liza to join them. "Listen, Earl and Liza should go back to the cabin, there's antibiotic ointment and more ice there. Jed and I are going to scope out the Commissary and see if we can get some food, and maybe get some of our furniture back. Honey, money." She held out her hand. Earl sighed, handed her his ice cloth and fished several hundred dollar bills out of his wallet.

"Thanks. If I need more I'll let you know. 'Bye" She kissed him perfunctorily and turned away as they walked toward the cabin. "Let's shop," she said, and linked her arm with Jed's.

Earl wasn't ready to leave, he hadn't yet left his mark on the movers and shakers. Emma looked behind her on their way to the Commissary and saw Earl gladhanding Ben and Kathy. Jed turned and watched them. "Wow, didn't take him long, did it?"

Emma replied grimly, "He knows where his bread is buttered, and this man loves bread."

"I'm going to take Liza home, I'll meet you at the Commissary in a few," Jed said, and went to Liza, who mournfully held the ice-filled towel to her wound. They spoke briefly, Jed put his arm around her waist and guided her inside the building. Emma stood, arms on hips and tapped her foot as she watched Ben and Kathy explode with raucous laughter at something Earl said. She caught his eye, he nodded to her, shook hands again and waved goodbye as he approached Emma, a victorious smile on his face. Emma noticed Kathy watch him as he walked away. *She looks like she's going to have him for lunch. Wonderful. Here we go.*

Emma was torn between wanting Earl to use his wiles to benefit their family, and wanting him all to herself, even though she knew that was an impossibility. She also knew something intimately that other women instinctively felt about Earl. Not only was he teeming with some kind of magical male pheromone from every pore, he had, as Emma confided to a very few trusted friends, "the best dick East of the Mississippi."

Emma had plenty of experience with that particular part of male anatomy, and no matter width or length, no man's member compared with Earl's. Emma dubbed it "The Velvet Fog," preternaturally smooth, with an ineffable size and shape that insinuated into a woman with such ease and power that more than one of his lovers fainted at the intensity of the sensation. Earl walked like a man who was, as Emma liked to say "packin'", with an easy insouciance and confidence that telegraphed what lay between his thighs.

And here was that walk, and the look of a newly-conquered woman who knew what lay between those jean-clad thighs. The only thing that comforted Emma was this miraculous member no longer functioned, not for years, but only she and Earl knew it. *Look all you want honey, you're not going to be able to rouse that beast.*

"So," Emma said wryly. "You cracked up Der Fuhrer and Eva Braun. I'm dying to know what you said."

Earl smiled and spoke softly. "Oh, nothing much. I showed them my neck ornament and said, 'It's not a Jewish star, but it's darn good lookin'.' They loved it."

Emma shook her head in wonder. "Who wouldn't? You certainly have a million of 'em, don't you?"

Earl hugged her, but she didn't respond. "Yes, my darling, and all of them are for you, and for us." Emma knew in her heart he was right. "Stick with me, baby," he said in his best Bogart impression, "And you'll fart through silk."

"I'm going shopping," she said briskly. "You can come with me or not."

"Oh my dear, I'm coming with you. I want to see if they have a bakery. Oyster crackers and brown rice hockey pucks are not my thing, I want bread, bagels, butter, cream cheese, bring it on, baby!"

"I have to say, I love your optimism, and your fortitude after that hot poker," Emma replied darkly. "Well, let's see what's what."

Chapter Thirty

Food, Glorious Food?

They followed balloon-adorned signs to the newly-christened Commissary, previously a giant tent that housed weddings and other special events, a few yards away from the main building. Scores of folding tables ringed the perimeter inside the tent, and additional tables were set up in the center of the space, with aisles wide enough for shoppers two or three deep. At the far end of the space stood several large freezers and refrigerators monitored by Red-Hat Ladies, with armed guards evenly spaced between tables.

"It's not the A&P, that's for sure," Emma whispered.

"I'm going to find bread," Earl said urgently, and went on his carbohydrate mission.

"And meat, don't forget that!" Emma called after him, as she scanned table after table. Each table was more disappointing than the next. "What, did we get here too late?" Emma asked aloud. A few boxes of generic breakfast cereal, limp lettuce, soft, dented apples and baskets of junk food – potato chips, Fritos, cheese crackers, etc., were among the paltry offerings. "How am I supposed to get a week's worth of anything with this crap?" She muttered. "And where are the prices?"

A nearby woman intoned, "You'll get used to it. You can bicker with the wardens if you want something." She pointed to the back of the tent. "They've got the ration stuff in the back, under lock and key. These are the 'extras'," she said with a wry smile.

Emma scanned the woman. *She looks OK, long center-part hair, tie dye shirt, Birkenstocks, she may be one of us.* She held out her hand. "I'm Emma Kaplan, we're in a cabin in the West quadrant."

The woman smiled, "I'm Merry Goodman, like Merry Christmas. My partner Evan and I and our two kids are on the East side. When did you get here?"

"Yesterday, you?"

174

Merry thought, "It's been six days; it feels like more. We came from Manhattan. It got hairy pretty quickly – we had to get out. The cabin's our weekend place, mostly during ski season."

"My son's here from Manhattan with his girlfriend, they got out in a hurry too, and stayed with us in Jersey until it got too dangerous. Some indoctrination session, right?"

"I'd like to know who did their video. Evan and I are documentary filmmakers, but I suspect Ben Conger and Company won't be asking for our services." She lowered her voice. "We don't make propaganda films."

Emma gestured toward Earl, who was casing the tables with a scowl. "That's my husband Earl, looking for phantom bread. He's an eye doctor, I'm a writer. I'm glad to meet you, Merry. We haven't gotten to know many folks here."

"If he wants real bread, you're going to have to make it. I have sourdough starter that's been with me since college; I'm pretty good at the old kneading board. I can show you how."

Emma smiled ruefully, "Thank you so much. Now if only I can find some flour. What's your cabin number? Ours is 20 West. I've got to go see what I can cop before it's all gone."

"13 East. Come by any time. Seriously."

Emma waved to Merry as she joined an increasingly frustrated Earl. "Listen, honey, I doubt you're going to find any bread, but I just met someone who can help me make some, we need to find flour."

Earl looked at Emma desperately. "Can she make bagels?"

Emma hugged him comfortingly. "We'll see. Come on, we've got to get our rations in the back."

Earl tapped Emma's arm and looked behind her. "Wait, it looks like they're coming with more food." Several armed Protectors arrived carrying large cardboard boxes. A few of them stopped at the tables and dumped more aging produce and packaged crackers. The rest went to another tent behind the Commissary.

"Where are they going?" Emma asked, then turned to Earl. "OK, you grab whatever you think you can stomach, look for any kind of flour. I'll meet you outside. I'm going to see what these guys are up to. Here…" she handed him the ration coupons and pointed to the back tables. "The ration stuff is in the back, with the refrigerators. See if you can seduce a few post-menopausal crones into giving you the good stuff."

Earl grabbed Emma's arm. "Honey, I don't think that's a good idea. I know you love a good scoop, but these aren't UFOs, they're guys with guns, and if you were welcome back there, they would let you know."

"What? I'm just going outside for some air, that's all. There's no crime in that." She wandered studiously away, hands behind her back, as she perused the tables and slipped outside. Glancing back, she saw Earl shake his head and watch her worriedly.

Emma sauntered in front of the Commissary tent and slowly made her way along its grassy perimeter. A large, dark grey tent had been pitched behind the Commissary, and like its counterpart, it had floor-to-ceiling walls with closed, guarded entrance flaps. Emma waited at the back of the Commissary until guards at the entrance to the grey tent looked away from her position. She quickly hustled to the side of the tent and waited a few moments. The coast looked clear, so she knelt carefully, lifted a section of tent and peered inside. The space was also set up with folding tables, but festive lanterns hung from the rafters, along with strings of tiny white lights looped in festoons along the ceiling. The smell of cooking food reached her nostrils.

*Mmmm, roast chicken? I smell sauteed garlic…*At the far end of the tent stood men and women in white aprons and chef's hats, stirring large pots over commercial stoves. Syrupy Christian music issued from several strategically placed speakers, and a large group of well-dressed, smiling people carried glasses of wine and what looked like champagne as they munched and schmoozed. Emma recognized several log mansion owners in the crowd.

The tables were laden with baskets of bread, rolls and fruit, and other baskets held chocolates and specialty items, Emma was pretty sure she saw tins of caviar and plates of cold cuts, olives and cheese. A large oscillating fan whirred in front of the stoves and directed most of the cooking odors through an open flap at the back of the tent. *They thought of everything, didn't they? Don't rile the peons."*

Something nudged her knee, she gasped and looked up in surprise. Earl scowled, pulled her up and propelled her toward the Commissary. "Honey, you are asking for trouble. Come on."

Emma yanked her arm in protest. "But there's real food in there, real cooked food, bread, rolls, chocolate, even caviar!"

Earl stopped and looked at her. "Bread?" he asked hopefully. "Any butter?"

"I would imagine so, but it's clearly not for the rank and file. I saw George Brendell in there, you know, the guy with the herd of dogs who lives in that log mansion up the hill? The food is for Conger cronies, rich folks, not us."

Earl stopped, offended. "We're plenty rich."

"I'm sorry dear, we are not, not now. Most of our equity is in that monster house in Jersey, which is moot at this point. And we have never been second-or-third-vacation-mansion rich. Which is fine with me."

Earl set his jaw. "I want that food.

Emma grabbed his other arm. "Well, we're going to have to figure out a way. I think I have a plan. I see you're empty-handed, so I'm guessing you need me to pick our ration food. Let's get whatever scraps we can and go home. Come on."

Chapter Thirty-One

Hard Bargains

"How do they expect us to survive for one week on two hunks of generic cheese, one package each of hamburgers and hot dogs, a box of dried milk powder, one carton of eggs and two packages of dinner rolls? For four people? Earl can eat this himself in a week!" Emma exclaimed as she, Earl, Jed and Liza looked over the spoils. "And one head of wilted lettuce, a box of Hootie's oat clusters, four squishy apples and an ancient, oozing pineapple?"

Liza looked dispiritedly at the food laid out on the kitchen counter. "No mustard? No ketchup? I can't eat hot dogs and hamburgers without mustard and ketchup. And what brand of hot dogs are these? Murray's Wieners? Who is Murray?"

"He could be Jewish," Earl quipped dispiritedly as he surveyed the paltry offerings.

"Or the wieners could be made of Murray. Or worse. I'm still trying to figure out where these burgers came from, and whether they cluck, whinny or moo," Emma replied disconsolately as she flipped the frozen package of hamburgers back and forth. "There's absolutely no identification on this."

"Who cares? Just cook the shit out of it, let's have hamburgers for lunch," Earl snapped impatiently.

Emma stood back and glared at Earl. "Um, excuse me? Slave, make me food? Fine, fine, but you can only have one, these have to last all week, there are only eight of them, and twelve hot dogs. You do the math. And I'm telling you, tomorrow night it's going to be an omelet with a very thin layer of cheese. I've got to get to Merry's place and figure out how to make bread, I can see that. The red-hatted monsters took all our flour, and I'm dying to know what happened to our prime Delmonicos, crown lamb roast, London broil and organic chickens. Bastards, they took it all, and you can bet it didn't make it to the Commissary. Sons of bitches took it to the elite tent, you can bet on it. Jed, we have to figure out how to get in there."

"Can I have a hot dog?" Jed asked plaintively. "We can cut it in half and put it on one of these anemic rolls." He and Liza gazed mournfully at the sorry smorgasbord on the counter.

"That's it. They are not going to do this to us. OK, we'll have lunch, such as it is, I'm going to have lentil soup and crackers, there is no disaster on Earth that will induce me to eat hot dogs and hamburgers, lucky for you. And after that, we're going to put our heads together and figure this out."

# # #

Supremely dissatisfied after his one burger and the few remaining packaged chocolate chip cookies, Earl sulked in his makeshift throne on the floor. "That burger was flat as a pancake," he lamented. "You cooked it to death and it shrunk to the size of a silver dollar."

Emma burped loudly, as vestiges of lentil soup churned in her stomach like the Three Witches' cauldron in MacBeth. "I'm sorry, I should never eat when I'm upset. That Nazi song and dance is not a good pre-lunch appetizer. Earl, I don't know what to tell you. Burgers have to be cooked through, do you want to get E Coli poisoning? How about some crackers?"

He shook his head slowly and waved dismissively, "No, I don't want that." He paused. "What kind of crackers?"

Emma checked the pantry. "Brown rice, or stone-ground wheat," she intoned. "You know, you could stand up and look yourself." No response. "Do you want them or not?"

Earl muttered, "Not," and continued his sulk.

"Mom," Jed interjected from his prone position next to Liza and the dogs on the living room floor, "Did they have any dog food at the Commissary? Liza needed me, that's why I couldn't join you."

"Oh Geez," Emma stopped, winced and shook her head. "Jed, I'm so sorry, I forgot to look. I'm going back there in a few minutes to check out the warehouse for furniture. Why don't you come with me and we can look for kibble?" She looked over at Earl. "I suppose, Madam Mopester, you don't want to come with us?"

Earl looked up and muttered, "I'd better, your negotiating skills leave much to be desired, no offense."

"None taken, I know I suck at it. Good, maybe it will get you out of your funk, or maybe you can find some comely lass with bagels to assuage your misery." Earl glared at her silently. "OK, then let's go. Liza, are you coming?"

Liza looked up sadly, "No, I'm tired, I'll stay here. Can I have some crackers? I feel barfy again, I think it's the hot dog." Emma brought her a package of oyster crackers. "Thanks. See you guys later."

Jed kissed the top of her head and whispered, "I love you." She whispered, "I love you too."

The Commissary was almost picked clean, but they were able to find a giant bag of Prince Premium Dry Dog Food, a brand none of them had ever heard of, for the low, low price of $300.00. Earl snarled as he handed the bills to the armed cashier, and griped as soon as they got outside, "Robbers, criminals, gougers…" as Jed balanced the bag on top of his head and navigated down the wildflower-strewn grassy hill from the Commissary to the Warehouse.

Emma interrupted, "We're a captive audience, like Disney, but literally. Just be glad you've got a mega bankroll – you're going to need it." Emma wished she could enjoy the 360 degree panorama of mountains and low-hanging white clouds in the bright blue late-summer sky as they picked their way down the hill, but all she could think about was how to keep her family comfortable and safe. *Maslow's Ladder of Self-Actualization. We can only aspire to higher things when our lower needs are met. I guess college wasn't a total waste.*

The warehouse was a squatty concrete building with an aluminum roof, guarded at the entrance by a sullen armed teenager who briefly looked at their brands and waved them inside with his gun.

The interior was dark, lit only by scattered standing lamps and fluttering fluorescent lights suspended from the ceiling. It was packed with large pieces of furniture, some stacked on top of each other, some suspended from the ceiling, and tables loaded with smaller items. Jed dropped the bag of dog food and disappeared down a murky aisle. "Welcome to Conger's Funhouse," Emma muttered to Earl. "I half expect a zombie to jump out at me from behind that…what *is* that?" She approached a large, deep mahogany credenza with ornate carvings, briefly touched it, then recoiled. "Um, in a word, no. Unless we can buy a bunch of dishes to put in it. I want to see if they have our beds."

"It's a pretty big place," Earl said wearily, exhausted from his trek down the hill. He picked up the dog food. "I'll find a chair, guard the kibble and wait for you guys. Call me when it's time to negotiate."

"If you find a good chair, don't get out of it, we'll buy it," Emma said over her shoulder as she met Jed scouting the aisles. They found a section with bedding, and looked at the stacks of mattresses, headboards and box springs. "I wonder why there's so much here, I thought it would be slim pickins, like the Commissary," Emma wondered aloud.

"I think we'll find out when we ask the price," Jed said darkly.

Emma nodded. "I think you're right." She gasped and ran to a stack of bed frames. "Here it is! Our sleigh bed!" She smiled gleefully. "With our mattress and box spring still on it! Oh, you don't know how happy this makes me! I had a feeling it was going to be here." She ran to Earl, who was snoozing in an easy chair with the dog food on his lap. She shook his arm. "Honey, honey! They have our bed!"

His eyes fluttered open, he smiled slightly and replied lazily, "That's great. Wake me when it's time…" and fell back to sleep.

They found three floor lamps, a serviceable set of dishes, cups and silver, two end tables, a radio, a futon for Jed and Liza, an old wooden dining table and chairs, and two dog beds. Emma also unearthed usable pots and pans and kitchen utensils, and found several of her paintings and knickknacks, which she greeted and hugged like long-lost friends. She felt like it was Christmas, her birthday and her anniversary wrapped up in one, then realized ruefully she was happy to be forced to buy her own possessions back.

Boy, it doesn't take long, does it, to knuckle under?

She and Jed stacked everything but the bed on a large dolly and looked for someone to help them. "Wait, do you think we should take the credenza? It might come in handy, you know, for hiding things? Things?" she whispered meaningfully. Jed nodded slowly.

"Good idea," he whispered back. "False bottoms come to mind."

"Good, let's do it." Emma approached the armed kid in the doorway and asked, "We're ready to check out, can someone help us?"

The kid sighed and picked up his walkie-talkie, "Buyers. Come in Jeremy. Buyers." A voice rasped, "OK, we're on our way." The boy glanced at Emma and intoned, "Someone's comin.'"

Earl struggled to his feet and set the dog food next to the chair. He pointed to the chair and gestured to Emma across the room, "This is good, let's get this," he said loudly. He walked slowly around the warehouse, stopped stock still, and put his hands over his eyes. Confused, Emma ran to him.

"What's wrong honey? Are you feeling sick?"

Earl turned his face from her and walked into a corner. She followed him. "What is it honey?"

Earl shook with suppressed tears. "It just, it looks like…when they took their possessions, those warehouses full of mountains of shoes, and jewelry, and furniture…" He continued to shake, and tears flowed underneath his hands. Emma hugged him and petted his back. After a few minutes he wiped his eyes with his handkerchief, and tried to pull himself together. *It's finally getting to him, like water dripping on marble – eventually it gets through.*

"I know honey, I know. I'm so sorry, but we have nowhere else to go." She puffed up her chest and did her best Earl-as-macho-gorilla imitation as she put her arms in the air, grimaced and flexed her muscles. "Stick with me baby, and you'll fart through memory foam," she grunted. Earl laughed in spite of himself, hugged her tightly and whispered into her ear, "I love you so much, my darling."

She kissed him tenderly. "Me too, my sweetest. Let's go take these yahoos to the cleaners."

A skinny, leathery, deeply-tanned older man in the standard-issue red hat, plaid shirt and dungarees walked down an aisle, along with two young armed guards. Emma recognized Andy, from the final checkpoint, and smiled at him. He remained impassive. Earl walked up to the man and held out his hand, the man did not respond.

"Good afternoon, sir," Earl said cordially. The man nodded slightly. "Pleased to meet you, I'm Earl Kaplan. Are you the gentleman in charge of purchases?"

"Yeah. Whatcha want?"

Emma stepped in, "Well, all this on the dolly, that credenza over there, this chair, and…if you'll follow me…" she gestured for them to follow her to the bedding area. "This bedframe, box spring and mattress. It's ours, I'm so glad we found it."

The man replied laconically, "Three thousand dollars for the lot. That's a good price, take it or leave it."

Earl smiled coolly and said, "Sir, I don't know your name…"

The man replied coldly, "That's right."

"OK. Sir, I can see you've got a lot of inventory here. I'm a businessman myself.."

The man interrupted. "Know you are. You're a Jew, aintcha?"

Earl's patented smile faltered slightly, he gathered himself and replied calmly, "Yes, as a matter of fact I am. A Jew for Jesus by the way, and proud of it." *Oh, I see where he's going with this. Go Earl.*

The man's eyes flickered. "Never heard of that. All I know is there's too many Jews around here, city people." He scowled and glared at Earl.

"Well, my good man, it's like this. When a Jew is smart enough to realize Jesus was, in fact, the Messiah, and there's no need to wait around for him, because he's here, it's called being a Messianic Jew. Like the good book says in John 3:16, 'For God so loved the world that He gave His one and only Son, that everyone who believes in Him shall not perish but have eternal life.'"

The man was stunned, and looked at Earl for several seconds. "It's still three thousand dollars," he said tentatively.

Earl approached him and patted him genially on the shoulder, "Well-sir, that's just too rich for our blood. We were really hoping to get off those sleeping bags on the floor, and my son and his lady, who's expecting, would love a comfortable bed during her confinement, but I guess you're going to have to deal with a lot of inventory for a while. Too bad, I was more than willing to negotiate. Come on honey, Jed." Earl put his arm around Emma and gestured for Jed to follow him.

Emma whispered in his ear, "Earl! I want that bed!"

Earl whispered back, "Three…two…one…"

"Just a minute," the man said, and approached Earl.

Earl turned around and smiled. "Yes, sir? I wish I knew your name."

The man muttered reluctantly, "Ned. Ned Henderson."

Earl clapped Ned on the back. "Well Ned, what can you do for me?"

"All right. All right. Twenty-five hundred, and that's my final offer."

"Ned, my man, I wish I could, but I only came here with a thousand dollars, in hundreds, and swore I wasn't going to pay a penny more. You see, this furniture is used, really used, all this stuff is. A junk shop wouldn't be able to unload it for more than a couple hundred tops. When you drive off the lot with a new car, one minute it's worth one price, the next a whole lot less. It's like that. You're a smart guy, you're in charge here, I'm sure this isn't news to you. I certainly wouldn't want to offend you with what you feel is such a low offer, so we'll be on our way. Have a good day, Ned." Earl turned and started to walk away.

Jed followed, Emma skittered after him. "Earl!" she whispered, "You've taken it too far."

Earl put his arm around her and whispered, "Three….two…..one."

"Just a minute," Ned called after him.

Earl turned with a grin, "Ned, you're going to make me a happy man, aren't you?"

"Well, could be," Ned replied sourly. "All right. A thousand, but you hafta pay for delivery. That'll be another $250."

Earl smiled broadly, "And well worth it, Mr. Ned Henderson. You drive a hard bargain. I thank you, and my family thanks you." He extended his hand; Ned shook it reluctantly. "That's the way," Earl said jovially. "We're in Cabin 20 West, the $250 will be waiting for you boys when they get there." Earl opened his wallet, emptied it of $1000 in one-hundred-dollar bills and handed it to Ned as he splayed his wallet open to show its leather loneliness. "You cleaned me out, sir. You are one fine negotiator."

Ned grunted and took the money. "We'll be along in a little while." He gestured to the guards to follow him to the entrance, and shouted to them, "Bring the truck around!"

Emma hugged Earl as they walked up the hill, Earl slowed down, began to pant, and waved his arms to stop.

"Boy, you were right, money talks, bullshit walks," Emma said to Earl adoringly. "You big handsome negotiator you."

Earl answered grimly as he panted, hands on his knees, "Conger said Church Elders run the warehouse. I hit this Bible-thumper where he lives. They don't know who they're dealing with."

"But I do, and I'm so proud of you," Emma beamed. "I can't wait to sleep in our bed tonight! And we still have our sheets and pillowcases, thanks to you!"

He smiled and replied breathlessly, "And I've got another three grand in my back pocket. Rube." Emma felt her nether regions pulse with desire for this crafty, savvy, sexy man, even though she knew it would go unsatisfied.

They held hands and plodded up the hill to the cabin.

Chapter Thirty-Two

Hiding Places

By the time they arrived back at the cabin the truck was already there, idling, with Ned and two stone-faced Protectors in the front seat. Jed stood by the truck, helped unload the smaller items and carried them inside. Liza had gathered wildflowers on her walk with the dogs, and an artful spray of oxeye daisies, buttercups, ostrich ferns and purple scabiosa was on the kitchen counter inside an empty soda bottle. Liza held the dogs' collars and stood with them in a corner of the living room as they barked and jumped at the impassive delivery men.

Emma bustled from room to room and directed the men where to place the bed, chair and credenza. The futon was lugged to the loft for Jed and Liza, end tables and lamps were set beside the beds, and the credenza was placed against a wall next to the dining table. Earl handed Ned the delivery fee, he grunted, and the three men got in their rusty truck and puttered down the hill to the Main Building.

Emma began decoratively placing the new dishes and cups in the credenza's overhead glass cabinets, Jed arranged the sleeping bags and pillows into an ad hoc couch on the living room floor, and Earl's chair was placed near the fireplace.

"Very Zen," Emma said approvingly. "I'll go back tomorrow and see about a real sofa, and a few more things. Earl, you'll have to go with me."

"Oh joy," Earl said, as he sank with a grateful sigh into his chair. Emma pulled him out of the chair, bustled around it pensively and hit it periodically. "What in hell are you doing?" Earl whined.

Emma stopped squarely in front of him and put her hands on her hips. "Checking for bedbugs and cooties. You don't want that, do you? I know how much you hate bugs, Mr. City Boy." Earl scowled, sat, crossed his arms over his chest and wearily closed his eyes.

The doorbell rang and Emma hurried to it, "Geez, I hope they didn't decide they want more money." She opened it to find Dave Stafford and a young, thin boy wearing a New York Mets baseball cap turned sideways. "Hey, Dave! So nice to see you! And who have we here?"

Dave gestured for Emma to come outside, past the doorway, the boy followed. Dave said quietly, "This is my nephew, Tyson."

Emma bent down to Tyson, he looked at her shyly. "Are you the tech wizard nephew I've heard so much about?"

Tyson looked down and whispered, "I guess."

"Well, come on in. I'm betting Uncle Dave told you we were wondering if our place is bugged. Maybe we're crazy, you know, maybe we watch too many action movies, but he said, if anyone could find them, it would be you. And you know, if you do find them, even though it would be amazing, it's probably a good idea not to mention it to anyone, OK?"

Dave interjected laconically, "He knows the drill. He's a good kid. Go ahead Ty." He whispered to Emma, "Don't say anything about it when we get inside. Just in case."

Inside the cabin, Emma held her fingers to her lips to Earl to signify quiet as Tyson walked thoughtfully around the room, looked up and down, ran his hands along moldings and baseboards and searched inside the pantry.

As he headed for the credenza, Emma held up her hand and whispered into Dave's ear, "Oh, we just bought that, and all the furniture. I doubt there's anything in them." Dave shushed her and whispered, "Let him do his thing."

Tyson ran his hands along the bottom of the credenza and extracted a small device that looked like a button. He held up his index finger to indicate "number one." He took off his baseball cap and put the button inside, and self-consciously fixed his straight, mussed brown hair. He looked at Dave and mouthed "Ladder?" Dave nodded, went outside to his truck and brought in a stepladder. Tyson and Dave moved it next to the credenza and Tyson climbed to the highest rung and ran his hands along the top. Two more buttons, Tyson held up three fingers. As he went inch by inch over and under every piece of furniture he uncovered five more.

He emptied the contents of his cap onto the dining table and gestured for them go outside under a large maple tree.

"What do I do with them?" Emma whispered nervously.

"Well," Tyson replied slowly "You could drown 'em in the lake, I guess."

"But won't they get suspicious if they don't hear anything coming from our unit? Somebody must be monitoring these things."

Tyson looked questioningly at Dave; he shook his head. "I dunno. I guess maybe…do you have a radio?"

"Yes, I just got our old one back today," Emma said, confused.

"Well, you could leave one next to the radio, in an out of the way place no one goes, so they can still hear you a little maybe, but can't really make it out, and if you have to talk about private things, whisper, or go outside. Maybe that would work."

Emma nodded her head, hugged Dave and solemnly shook Tyson's hand. "Tyson, what can I do to repay you? As soon as I can find some flour and sugar I'll be making cookies, how's that?"

"No need," Dave replied, "He's a good kid, he doesn't like what's going on here anymore than I do."

Tyson piped up, "But cookies are nice."

Emma smiled and patted Tyson's back, "You got it, big guy."

Tyson smiled slightly and put his baseball cap back on. "C'mon Uncle Dave, you said we were going fishing."

"So I did," Dave replied jovially. "Well, let's go. Maybe we can get some stripers for dinner." They headed for the truck; Emma held up her hand.

"Dave? Uh, when you have time, would you mind showing me how to shoot my rifle? I figure maybe I'll need to know how to bring home the bacon, and my son will probably get impatient if he tries to teach me."

Dave smiled, "Sure. Tomorrow OK?"

"How about after breakfast, around 11?"

Dave gave her a thumbs-up. "See you then."

Emma went inside, picked up the bugs like they were loaded bombs, ran water in the bathroom sink and soaked all but one.

Liza stood behind her, puzzled. "What are you doing?" Emma turned and put her fingers to her lips. "Hey Liza, where's that radio? I think we need some music, or something. Have you found any stations?"

She left the working bug on the bathroom sink and hustled Liza to the living room. "Listen, the place was bugged" she whispered. Liza gasped. "I know, I know. We need to keep one bug working so they don't get suspicious, so we're going to put the bug in the bathroom, and keep the radio going next to it. If we're going to discuss anything about money, or other plans we don't want the Neo-Nazis to know about, we need to go outside or do it far away from the radio. I heard the radio playing in the loft, we need to borrow it. What stations did you find?"

Liza rolled her eyes and replied, "Nothing good. Two God and one Country music station, and they're not very clear. You can totally have it." She moved to the loft ladder and called up to Jed. "Pookie, can you give me the radio?"

"Why?" Jed yelled down, annoyed. "I kinda like this country stuff. Maybe I can write a country rap song."

"C'mon Pookie, just give it to me, OK? We need music down here. It's so boring." She winked at Emma and smiled. *I'm liking this kid better every day.*

"OK, OK," Jed replied reluctantly as he leaned down the stairs holding the radio. "Here."

Emma took it from him.

"Thanks, Pookie." She and Emma smiled conspiratorially and set up the system in the bathroom on a shelf. After a whispered conversation with Jed, Emma and Earl in the living room, they decided on the route of march for the cash, gold and silver. Most of the cash was inserted inside hollow doorway and floor moldings, and inside a secret bottom in one of Emma's backpacks, which was also serving as a repository for bullets and bear mace as part of their disaster "Go bags." At night they removed the hubcaps from all three cars and taped some of the gold and silver inside. The rest of the gold and silver was divided into plastic bags, and taped underneath the credenza so they could be easily ripped out and carried, if they had to get out in a hurry.

189

"It's the best we can do," Emma said wearily on Day Two of the Big Stash Caper, after the final hubcap was replaced at midnight. Earl still insisted on wearing his money belt with about $50,000 in cash tucked inside, and they agreed if Earl was searched, much should be made about their stash having been uncovered.

Let's hope that day never comes.

Chapter Thirty-Three

New Threats

"It's easy," Merry Goodman laughed, as Emma looked askance at the goopy, sticky dough dripping from her fingers. Merry expertly moved her dough back and forth on her kitchen's aged gold Formica countertop as Emma watched intently. It was "Bread Day" at Merry's cabin, and Emma was invited to come by for a tutorial on sourdough bread, with the understanding she would walk away with the fruits of her labors.

"I'm a pretty good baker," Emma declared defensively, "Except for bread. Maybe I don't have the patience. Pies, cakes, cookies, quick breads, muffins, I've got those down. But this, well, I'm not feeling it. I think this dough hates me."

"You need to listen to it, to feel it," Merry said, in between giggles at Emma's comical attempts at kneading. "Keep adding flour bit by bit until the dough becomes elastic, develops a life. It will tell you when it's ready to rise to its full potential."

"Sounds like, OK, I won't tell you what it sounds like," Emma said, which elicited fresh giggles from Merry. Merry's cabin was a cozy, happy place. Her two children Amity and Emmanuel played with building blocks on the floor, her partner Evan repaired a hole in the roof, and their Golden Retriever Blitz watched the children and occasionally tried to knock their creations down, which elicited good-natured laughter. "If I didn't know better, it doesn't seem like we're in the middle of a global disaster," Emma whispered to Merry.

"We've been lucky so far. Your home is a comfy place too, especially since you got that sofa yesterday," Merry replied.

"It probably cost ten times what it's worth, but it's going to be a real hangout for the family," Emma said softly. It reminded her of the floral overstuffed sofa at Don's cabin, which brought back a flood of tender and disconcerting memories.

Finally, Emma created a creditable loaf, and while the bread baked and filled the cabin with delicious smells, the two women sat outside on the deck with tea and homemade sugar cookies and told stories about their lives before the world turned upside down. Emma told Merry about her UFO encounters, and her recent sightings, and was thankful Merry took her experiences seriously. Merry and Evan had just finished editing their latest documentary about a battered woman's shelter, and her recounting of the horrors the women and children faced and escaped filled Emma with wonder and disgust. "How can people treat each other that way?" she asked angrily. "It reminds me of the pleasure those young goons got when they branded us at Four Corners."

Merry shook her head and replied gently, "Well, rage and power have a lot to do with it. Some days it was hard to get up and go to the editing room, but I know we can make a difference, a good difference."

Emma squeezed Merry's hand and said softly, "I know you can. You're good people. All of you. We need a lot more people like you." She leaned in, "Listen, if things go south here, where are you going to go?"

Merry pursed her lips and looked down into her lap. "We haven't really come up with a concrete plan. I guess we've been hoping this will be over soon."

Emma confided, "My sister Carol and her husband Joe have been living off the grid in the wilds of Zion for decades, they've got that lifestyle down, and a Sherpa would have trouble finding them. My family made a pact we would go there if we found ourselves without a safe place. I really hope you'll consider joining us, if the time comes."

Merry smiled gratefully, "That's sounds good. You've got a deal. Let's check the bread." Merry's loaves were smooth and uniform, Emma's lopsided, unevenly browned loaf was the black sheep of the bunch, but it had a decent hollow sound when tapped, and looked quite edible. Merry wrapped it in a tea towel, hugged Emma and waved as Emma walked back to her cabin. When she arrived at the parking area Dave's red truck was parked there, with Tyson in the front passenger seat of the cabin.

"Hi Tyson," Emma said cheerfully. "What's up?"

Tyson looked down and muttered, "Better ask Uncle Dave. He's inside."

Emma rushed down the macadam pathway and burst through the door. Dave, Jed, Liza and Earl were gathered around the sofa. Jed jumped up and ran to Emma.

"Mom, geez, I wish we had working phones, we didn't know where you were."

"I told Earl I was going to Merry's to make bread. Didn't he tell you?" She set the bread down in the kitchen and approached the group with trepidation.

Earl looked dazed, and replied quietly, "I didn't remember." Since the Exodus from New Jersey, Earl's memory was definitely on the wane, most likely from the stress of the transition, and the potential dangers they faced every day. He had been taking medication for what his neurologist called "Moderate Cognitive Impairment," not uncommon in his age group, but he ran out of pills, and hadn't found a way to replace them. As the days went by he had more and more episodes of what Emma called "blankness," where he stared into space and was difficult to engage, especially at night. *My wonderful, funny guy ... he's slowly disappearing.*

"What's going on?" Emma asked worriedly.

Dave replied gravely, "I was on my CB radio, and my contact in Granite Cove, about two days southwest of here on foot, he said they were overrun. It's not looking good. Eventually they're bound to come here."

"But, we have the perimeter, and all those guns! And we're way off the beaten path, not like Granite Cove. It's right off the Interstate."

Dave replied grimly, "They were locked, loaded and ready too. These raiders are armed to the teeth, and there are hundreds of them. It's going to be a battle, one we might not win. Conger wants to turn the resort into a fort, we're all supposed to go there first thing in the morning."

"But why are these raiders doing this? Why don't they just settle down somewhere, why do they keep going from town to town? And where's the military, and the police?"

"From what they're telling me, some of them stay and take over, they keep recruiting new folks and moving on, to consolidate resources.

193

Military and law enforcement are spread real thin, they're focusing on major infrastructure and big cities. We're on our own."

They sat in silence for several seconds, Dave stood up and headed for the door. "I've gotta go, we have to get ready to move in the morning. You better do the same."

Emma followed Dave outside and whispered, "Dave, do you know someone with the CB handle White Line Fever, or PussyCat Wrangler?"

Dave looked at her quizzically, "Yeah. Why?"

"Well, Wrangler has an army tank, I think we can use him, if he'll come. He's a friend of mine, he's at Mason's Eddy."

"For all we know, that's been overrun too," Dave said solemnly, "But I'll do what I can." Emma hugged him tightly and kissed him on the cheek, he bashfully looked at his feet, then sideways at Tyson, who was giggling in the truck with his hand over his mouth.

"I'm never going to hear the end of this," he said with a smile. He shook her hand gruffly and muttered, "Now, you folks take care of yourselves, whatever it takes."

"We will. Thank you so much Dave. We'll see you on the other side, for sure." Dave got in the truck, waved solemnly, and stirred up gravel as he sped away.

Chapter Thirty-Four

Choices

The family spent the afternoon and evening packing their bags and their cars with as much as they could, in preparation for the move to the Main Building. They decided to leave cash stashed in the moldings, since their fervent hope was the Raiders wouldn't have the smarts or time to find their hiding place. Even if they did, cash was becoming more and more superfluous as it became clearer and clearer the grid wasn't coming back anytime soon. Gold and silver coins were packed in small plastic bags and tucked into different nooks and crannies in suitcases and backpacks, along with their stashing places in the cars' hubcaps.

At dawn Emma ran to Merry's cabin and found them loading their car with supplies. She grabbed Merry's hands and whispered, "If we get separated, find Post House Road in Zion, it's a dirt road that goes on and on. Keep going until the road gets narrower and more covered by trees. Drive as far as you can, walk the rest of the way if you need to, past a large pond in a huge field on the right, and on the left, dug into a hill, is Joe and Carol's place. It's basically part of the hillside. OK?"

Merry swallowed hard, tears in her eyes. "OK. See you up at the Resort." They hugged, and Emma ran back to the cabin to find the cars almost completely packed, and the dogs seated in the back seat of Jed's car. Earl had the same dazed, out-of-it look when Emma first told him they had to leave their New Jersey home. *He can't take much more of this. Can he?* Emma hugged him and said gently, "Honey, do you have everything? Did we pack the gas cans?"

Earl nodded slowly, "Jed did. He has your gun too, you never did learn to shoot."

Emma nodded grimly, "That was supposed to be today. Maybe Jed can show me once we're settled in. No worries, I've got you. Why don't you get in the car, I'll check to see if we forgot anything."

She walked down the macadam path, the same path where she stopped in her tracks that night that seemed centuries ago, when the meteor winked out just above the mountaintop, fireflies flickered, and Emma felt oh-so-safe and part of a world that seemed to make at least a modicum of sense. A world that seemed to be moving forward to something better, kinder, smarter, a world with growing pains she was certain would subside into something richer and better over time, maybe even in her lifetime. Now here she was, back inside her dear little cabin, running her hands along walls and moldings, moldings now filled with hidden cash, saying goodbye again to a house that held a home, and a family, and not knowing what lay ahead.

"Goodbye," she said sadly. "I hope to see you again one day. I love you." As she closed the door she mused, "Not even a lock to slow the bastards down. I hate them. I fucking hate them."

When they arrived at the entrance to the Main Building they were met by Protectors and a series of orange cones set up to separate traffic and funnel it into different parking areas. Walkie talkies were in use between the three cars, and Earl rasped, "Leave this to me." Emma knew better than to protest. Even in his compromised state, Earl was still a charming force to be reckoned with. "Go for it, honey," Emma replied warmly.

He rolled down his window and recognized one of the Protectors as Ned Henderson. "Ned, my man! Nice to see you. We were hoping for a good spot in the back, and we're ready to make it worth your while."

Ned sneered, "Your paper ain't so good now, is it?"

Earl smiled broadly, "You couldn't be more right, what a smart fellow you are. Pesky stuff anyway, silver and gold are so much better, aren't they? He extracted a small plastic bag full of silver and gold coins from his glove compartment and put it in Ned's hands. "How's that?"

Ned looked around furtively, crammed the bag in his coat pocket and directed them to a covered parking area down the hill behind the Main Building. Other cars at the top of the hill beeped their horns in protest and tried to follow the three cars, but the Protectors shot their guns into the air to pacify them.

Emma radioed, "Money talks, bullshit walks, right?"

Earl replied calmly, "Indeed, my dear. Let's take these three spots, in case we have to get out of Dodge in a hurry." He parked at the end of a row and directed the other two cars to park behind him. As they unpacked what they needed for the night, they locked their cars, and said a little prayer they would still be there in the morning.

At the back entrance to the Main Building they were directed to the Second Floor Ballroom via the elevators or the stairs. Earl chose the elevator, and groaned as he dragged his suitcase into the long waiting line. Emma, Jed and Liza took the stairs with the dogs. "They better not put on another one of those song and dance numbers," Emma grumbled as the dogs scampered up the stairs. "I can't wait to see what paces they're going to put us through this time."

No chipper Welcome Committee greeted them at the entrance. Their brands were checked and they were hustled into the ballroom, which was set up with folding chairs from one end of the long room to the other.

"Hurry up, people!" shouted a Protector. "Sit wherever." Emma saved a seat for Earl, who appeared, ashen-faced, at a distant entrance. She stood up and waved. He found his way slowly to her as he dragged his suitcase behind him. *I bet it's packed with coins.*

The dogs sat under Liza and Jed's chairs, Liza sat uncomfortably. It had been a full month since the auroras first appeared, Liza's belly was starting to expand and her clothing was tight, since maternity wear was in short supply. Emma stood up to see if she could find Dr. Spencer, Merry, Sam or Greta, but the ballroom was packed, as worried people congregated in tight groups and conferred with each other. A few babies cried, children ran back and forth down the aisles. Emma recognized Amity and flagged her down as she giggled past her, chased by Emmanuel. "Amity honey, where's your Mom?" Amity stopped, thought for a moment, twirled her long brown hair and pointed to the back of the room. Emma spied Merry and tried to get her attention, but Merry was deep in conversation with an older woman Emma did not recognize.

The din in the room escalated until the walls and ceiling echoed, and was abruptly silenced by loud microphone feedback coming from the stage. "People, people, settle down!" boomed Ben Conger. Emma turned

197

around to see Ben in full military gear, including several holsters packed with firearms slung around his shoulders, waist and thighs. Behind him were Kathy and a battalion of Protectors, some with war paint, all armed to the teeth and deadly serious. Their numbers had increased since the initial indoctrination, Emma recognized a few farmers and shopkeepers in the area who had clearly been recruited. *God, it's Civil War.*

Conger spoke urgently, "Folks, it looks like we are in for a battle. We have scouts past our perimeter who haven't seen anything yet, but we're getting CB and ham reports that in a matter of hours, hundreds of rebels will be in our area. These people are ruthless, they will take everything they can, and will try to recruit you and turn our Collective into one of their outposts. If you don't cooperate, they will think nothing of shooting you." The crowd was silent, speechless.

He continued, "If you have a gun and know how to use it, please join us. The majority of our Protectors will be manning the perimeter, but if it is breached, we have other layers of coverage. If these fail, we will need to defend the Main Building, with snipers at windows, on the roof and around the building. Who's with us?" Many men in the audience stood, amidst the protests of their families. "Good. Please join us up here, my lieutenants will give you your assignments."

Jed stood up, Emma and Liza jumped up, grabbed him and tried to get him to sit. "Jed!" Emma whispered loudly, "This is no damn video game. No! I forbid it! You have a child on the way." Liza began to cry, sat down and cried loudly, her head in her hands.

Jed knelt in front of her and replied passionately, "I've got to, honey. I'm going to feel like a traitor if I don't."

Liza wailed, "I'm going to be a single mother if you do!"

Emma spoke into Jed's ear with gritted teeth, "I am not going to lose you. It's not necessary, we can get out of here, tonight, and drive to Zion. Please, Jed. Please don't!"

"Mom, I'm sorry. I love you. But I have to do this." Jed stood resolutely, strode up to the stage and joined the men. Emma and Liza held each other, and joined scores of other crying women and children as their fathers, brothers and husbands walked to the stage steps and joined the Protectors.

Conger continued, "Women, children, the elderly and those who refuse to fight for our safety will stay here in the ballroom. We have armed sentries at every entrance, and the metal doors can be locked if necessary. There are back exits through doors in the restrooms in the rear of the ballroom, if you have to escape. They lead directly outside. Men, please join me in the conference room." The Protectors and their recruits began to exit as their women and children wailed and ran at them, but ushers and Red Hat ladies held them back.

Kathy took the mike and tried to calm them. "Mothers, children, be proud of your men. They are doing this to protect you, and I believe with God's grace we're going to win, and turn these evildoers around. Be of good cheer, have faith in the Lord. Let's sing 'Amazing Grace.'" She gestured to one of the Red Hat ladies to go to the piano.

Emma stood up and strode purposefully to the foot of the stage. She addressed the recruits who were filing out of the ballroom. "Stop! Wait!" They turned and stopped, confused. She addressed them and the crowd. "Are you going to listen to this privileged bullshit artist?" Several Protectors moved to grab and subdue Emma, Kathy waved them back.

"Let her talk, boys. God is on our side." Kathy smirked.

"God has nothing to do with it." Emma retorted, as she shook off the Protectors. The room was silent.

"Go ahead," said Kathy smugly. "Go ahead. This is the woman who won't sing our songs, who married a Jew, and who fights and questions us at every turn. This Prodigal daughter is only here because of our fine Christian generosity."

Emma sneered. "Right. Sure. Come on people! The Congers could care less about any of us. I'm betting they've got a private plane or a helicopter just waiting to take their rich white asses somewhere safe, wherever that is, while the rest of us serve as cover. If we're going to be overrun, I say there's strength in numbers. I say, let's get in our cars and get the hell out of here. This place is a magnet for these marauders, it's got everything they want. We need to go far, far into the hinterlands, where we will at least have a chance to survive, where we can set up our own outpost, far from the highways. I know where we can go, where there are people who know how to live off the land, people who are real Christians." Kathy Conger was now fuming at the microphone. "Not fake hucksters like Ben and Kathy Conger. Who's with me?"

Kathy bellowed into the microphone, "Who's been taking care of you all along? Who brought you food, power, medicine, and a roof over your heads? We did, and we will fight to keep you safe from these murderous, ungodly occupiers. If you leave here now, you will have no protection. Not only will you be at the mercy of Godless rebels, but every town you enter will be full of desperate people who will do anything to get your car, your food, and yes, you. In ways you never imagined. Think I'm kidding? Go out there, go and find out. I guarantee you won't come out alive."

Emma faced her and countered passionately, "OK, OK, yes, thanks a lot. Thank you for stealing our possessions and making us buy them back from you. Thank you for disfiguring our bodies, destroying our privacy and bugging our cabins. Thank you for giving us rations that aren't much better than pig slop, while you and your rich buddies cozy up in the gray tent with music, chefs, caviar and champagne. Where are your rich pals now? I don't see any of them here. And I bet once this little get-together is over, you and your fascist husband will be blowing this pop stand to leave us to face this thing alone." She faced the audience. "Don't believe me? Hold them both here, hold them here until the raiders come. Make them fight, make them into cannon fodder like they're doing to us."

Several group members moved to restrain Kathy, but she broke away and exited behind the stage. "I rest my case. Good riddance." She yelled after Kathy's pursuers, "If you find a helicopter or plane on Holler Road, commandeer it and get people out of here. Come to Zion as far out on Post House Road as you can. We'll be there, and you'll be welcome."

She addressed the crowd. "Listen, there are hundreds of these rebels, and their numbers keep growing. I've counted no more than 50 Protectors. I can guarantee you, these raiders outnumber us, they outgun us, and they have no pity. You think this was bad? Wait until they get a hold of you. They'll either kill you outright if you're no use to them, or use you for slave labor and 'enjoyment.' I don't know about you, but my family and I are out of here, now, while there's still time. Anyone who wants to join us can meet us outside in the rear parking lot in half an hour. Jed?" She gestured to her son. "Believe me, you'll have plenty of opportunities to use your guns, but you'll be fighting for yourselves and your families. Come with us, now." Liza looked imploringly at Jed, and he reluctantly jumped down from the stage and joined them as the dogs circled and jumped on him.

"Mom, I'm only doing this because we're probably fucked either way, and if push comes to shove, I'd rather die with you guys."

Emma hugged him tearfully. "We're not going to die, dammit. I won't allow it." Liza hugged Jed and clung to him as they walked out of the ballroom which was erupting in jeers and loud confrontations. Emma whispered to Jed, "Is anyone else coming with us?" Jed looked behind him and shook his head.

"Motherfucking chickens," Emma muttered.

"Give them some time. Let's get ready to go," Jed replied grimly.

Chapter Thirty-Five

Exodus II

Jed and Earl groaned as they lifted Earl's suitcase into his car. Emma slapped the side of her head and exclaimed, "For God's sake, now that we're leaving for good, we've got to go back to the cabin, and bring everything we can, and I mean everything. Liza, you stay here with your car and the dogs, we'll take the two cars, hook up the trailer and grab whatever we can. Earl, please don't complain about your back or how tired you are, this is freaking life and death, please summon your inner gorilla, and let's go!"

Earl saluted stiffly and shouted, "Jawohl, Mein Commandant. Kathy and the Nazis are looking better every minute."

Emma snapped, "You're welcome to join them anytime, dearie. Perhaps Kathy will make you Court Jester."

Jed rolled his eyes. "C'mon you guys, we don't have time for the Drama King and Queen."

Emma continued, "Earl, sweetheart, I leave charm and bamboozling to you, please leave planning and execution to me. I've been working on my Zion scenario since we got here."

Earl muttered, "Far be it for me to question your intuition or your strategic skills."

"You got that right. And my intuition tells me we've got to get out of here within the hour, because these sons of bitches are coming. Come on!"

They barreled up the hill to the cabin, waved on by the Protectors. *Hmmm, I guess word of my speech got around.*

They rushed into the cabin, Jed began ripping money out of the moldings, Emma and Earl dragged the futon out of the loft, grabbed the sleeping bags and as many kitchen supplies as they could and crammed them into the trailer. "Goodbye again, old girl," Emma whispered as they hurtled down the hill to the back parking lot. A small caravan was waiting, including Sam, Greta, Dr. Spencer, Merry, Evan, their kids and dog, Dave Stafford, his wife Carolyn, their two sons Adam and John, nephew Tyson and his father Jacob. Dave was unloading the back of his truck and handed one semi-automatic rifle after another out to anyone who could hold them, along with magazines. "All right!" Jed exclaimed, and grabbed two rifles and several magazines.

Emma hugged Dave and his wife Carolyn, and heartily shook Adam, Jacob and John's hands. She bent down to Tyson and said, "Are you ready to rock and roll?"

Tyson looked at the ground and muttered, "They won't give me a rifle."

"You're our tech wizard," Emma said comfortingly. "You're going to be like E.T., and make an alien beacon out of a scrap heap, right?"

Tyson smiled slightly and said softly, "Yeah. I can do that."

Emma patted his shoulder. "Oh, I know you can. You're our secret weapon." She turned to Dave, "What made up your mind to come with us?"

Dave said quietly, "I can read tea leaves too. We're outta here. You're smart folks, but you can't shoot for a damn. You need us."

Emma hugged him, "As soon as we find a safe place, we'll have target practice, I promise."

Dave warned, "Don't wait too long."

"No worries," Emma said as she prepared to address the group. "God, I'm so glad you're here. OK, I've been thinking about how we can get out of here and avoid as much mayhem as possible. Sam, Evan, Dave, I can see you have sturdy vehicles that can go off-road, thank God we all have cars that can handle it. I'm a little worried about the trailer, but, OK, here's what I'm thinking. We have to stay off the highways, and all roads as much as possible except for back country roads, and even they will have their dangers. Lucky for you guys I've been riding my bike for years all around this area, specifically focused on the most remote back roads possible. We've got to go off-road almost immediately, go up the ski slopes and down the other side."

"What?" Earl exclaimed. "You're kidding!"

203

"I'm not. You can handle it. Yes, it's going to be really bumpy, and our suspensions are going to suffer, but if we stay on the main roads we're dead meat. It's the only way. Once we're over the top of the slope, I think if it looks safe those of us with very little gun knowledge should stop and get a shooting tutorial from Dave. We'll be past the protected perimeter at that point, we can let Protectors know any shooting sounds are coming from us. Who knows, maybe some of them will defect, but I'm not holding my breath. And as soon as it starts to get dark, which won't be long, we'll have to find a safe place to camp, it's too dangerous to travel at night."

Dave and Earl stood next to her and smiled admiringly.

I must be doing something right. Don't think Emma, just do.

Shouts came from the parking area in front of the Main Building, and Emma heard a familiar sound. There was no mistaking it. She gasped and exclaimed, "Guys, I think reinforcements are here. Hold on!" She ran up the hill to find Sweet Betty parked in front of the Main Building with Don and Prince in the turret. Behind him were several pickup trucks, Emma recognized Wendell and Connie Bratten, and several diners from Mason's Eddy.

She ran to the tank and yelled up at Don, "I'm so glad to see you! We're just getting out of here. What happened?"

Don yelled back, "We couldn't hold 'em off, we did get a bunch of 'em though, on the way out. I got your message from White Line. Where you headed?"

Emma pointed to the ski slopes, "There. We're going to Zion, out in the real boonies, with folks who've been roughing it for decades. We've got Troyville to contend with though, there's no getting around it. God, I'm glad to see you. Things are really looking up."

Don grinned, "You bet they are."

"Can Betty get up that hill?"

"She'll do anything I tell her to, honey."

Emma felt a familiar nether pang. Down girl. *Deal with the copulations, uh, complications later.* "We've got more people in the back, I'll bring them around." She shouted to the Protectors and others gaping at the tank. "If you want to join us, come now. We're outta here."

A motley ad hoc caravan formed behind Emma's trailer, Sweet Betty took up the rear, Dave and his boys' trucks were interspersed between Sam, Dr. Spencer and the Mason's Eddy contingent. They drove past the Protectors and orange cones in front of the Main Building. Ned Henderson and his boys grimly watched the procession, a few managed a wave. *They'll be joining us soon, bet on it.*

They crossed Route 393 and headed for the bottom of Alpha Crossing, the widest ski slope on the mountainside, punctuated by the main ski lift with cars wide enough to accommodate three skiers and their skis. The grass had grown waist-high since gas for the giant riding lawn mowers was in short supply, and Emma worried some vehicles may not be able to handle the steep slope that loomed in front of them.

Papery white moths and Monarch butterflies fluttered over tall grasses and multi-colored wildflowers as Emma put the Subaru in low gear, and gunned the gas pedal as the slope intensified. *So far so good, she's making it.* Emma checked her rearview mirror to see cars and trucks jostling over the bumpy terrain, keeping pace. She couldn't see Sweet Betty, but like the North Star, she knew she was there.

Midway up the slope she encountered a group of Protectors gathered next to a stand of trees to the left of the incline. One of them signaled for her to stop, she unrolled her window and shouted out "I can't, I don't know if I can get up this hill if I stop. We're going, please don't try and stop us." She recognized the man as Andy, the boy who mowed their lawn and hit his head on their bird feeder the summer before.

He jogged next to her as she drove and shouted, "We're going with you!"

Emma smiled gratefully and replied loudly "Well, a few of you can jump in my car, the rest can try your luck behind me." Andy gestured to the others, and he and two others opened her rear passenger door and jumped in.

"Mrs. Kaplan, this is Allan, and his brother Joe. Friends of mine. We hate the Congers, and we're no fools. We know what's comin', and figure maybe you're right. Maybe we have to go deep in country, and we figure you city folks could use a few more good guns."

Emma smiled at them in her rearview mirror and said gratefully, "Please, call me Emma. No time to stand on ceremony." They nodded and smiled at each other. The Subaru's engine was working hard, and Emma had to zigzag up the rest of the slope to give it a rest from the relentless climb, a trick she figured out when she encountered a particularly rough hill on her bike. "I hope you guys won't have to get out and push," she said apologetically.

"No worries" Andy said. "She'll make it."

"From your lips to God's ears," she yelled over the loud, struggling engine. They finally reached the summit, Emma looked behind her briefly and marveled at the expanse of distant hills dense with hundreds of acres of forest. "I've never been up here before. I don't ski and I'm afraid of heights, so the ski lift was out of the question."

"Funny," Andy shouted. "I didn't think you were afraid of much of anything."

Emma smiled ruefully. "Worry is my middle name. Maybe in this case it helps me plan our next moves. Whatever. We're here, and who knows what the hell comes next. I'm just glad you're here, we need you." She was finding it difficult to control the trailer on the way down the steep slope, she slowed to a crawl and pushed the brake pedal all the way to the floor.

Dave's truck pulled up beside her on her left, he rolled his right window down and shouted, "Having trouble? Need help?"

Emma shook her head, "No, but some of you may need to pass me until we level off." Dave touched his hand to his cap and passed her. Several trucks and cars followed suit until Emma found herself in front of Sweet Betty with Earl and Jed in front of her. Near the bottom of the slope, vehicles were parked haphazardly, and several members of the procession were out of their cars. *Waiting for me. Holy crap. I can't believe I'm the leader of this mad enterprise. I wonder how long this will last with all these Alpha males. Stop it Emma, be the Queen Bee. Be the Queen.*

She pulled behind Sam and Greta's car and parked. Sweet Betty pulled up next to her. As she got out of her car and gestured for everyone to join her in front of the parked vehicles, a helicopter came into view, whirring overhead. It passed over them and landed several hundred feet in front of them in a grassy field. "Great," she muttered to Andy. "Now what." Andy picked up his gun and gestured for Allan and Joe to follow suit.

"Come on, Emma. Let's see what they want." Several other Protectors grabbed their guns and followed behind them as they trotted to the helicopter. As they approached the slowly whirring and slowing blades, the door opened and two bodies were thrown face down onto the grass, their hands and feet bound with zip ties.

"Oh my God," gasped Emma. "Who are they? Are they alive?"

Nate Clark, the ringleader at the first checkpoint stepped out of the helicopter, war paint on his face, and answered, "Yeah, they're alive. Worth more alive than dead." He rolled them over to reveal Ben Conger and Kathy, mouths covered with tape, eyes wide and terrified as they struggled against their bonds. "They asked me to fly 'em out to the frickin' 'Hamptons', since I was a copter pilot in 'Nam, and I'd had just about enough."

He kicked Ben Conger in the groin which elicited muffled moans. "That's what you get, you sonofabitch. Didn't pay us for weeks, tried to run out on us. Now you're gonna pay. You're gonna pay big time."

Dave Stafford approached Nate, high-fived him and gave him a one-armed hug. "What's the plan, man?"

They turned to Emma, who realized she was still, indeed, the Queen. "Well," she said thoughtfully, "They're only worth something if we can get our hands on their booty, right?"

Earl and Jed stepped forward, ready to strategize and negotiate. Earl said slowly, "For most folks around here, the Congers' reputation precedes them. They have holdings, and most likely stashes of cash, and more. But we have to get them to talk. We might be able to trade them for safe passage if the need arises. They should fetch a hefty ransom." Jed nodded in agreement.

Nate chuckled and replied, "I was thinkin' maybe roast 'em on a spit."

Don stepped forward and said, "Listen, we've got a lot of trained guns, I'd like to be in charge of establishing our perimeter." Everyone looked at Emma.

Own it honey, you're the bitch in charge.

She yelled to the rest of the caravan, "Guys, this is Don, he's in charge of perimeter, so all you sharpshooters get your marching orders from him. Connie Bratten, you're in charge of getting the troops fed, everyone go to Connie with information on whatever foodstuffs you brought with you. Dr. Spencer, you're our medic, and Tyson, you're our tech expert. Anyone wants something taken apart, put together, repaired or constructed, go to this young man. Some of us might need firearm tutorials, we have so many gun-savvy folks in this group, so even though it's not necessary, it's still a good idea. If like me you've got a gun but don't really know how to use it, I'm sure one of these guys will be glad to help. Dave Stafford, you're in charge of shooting lessons. Listen, we need to keep going, there's a seasonal road at the bottom of the slope, we'll take that until we find a good place to make camp. Nate, we need you in the air during the day to provide cover, you'll need a couple of shooters with you. Now, what are we going to do with these two?"

She pointed to prone Ben and Kathy. "Does anyone have room for them?" Silence. Crickets. Emma looked at Nate. "Any ideas? Can they go back in the chopper?"

Nate snarled, "Let's tie 'em on top of those two cars." He pointed to Sam and Earl's cars. *Wow. That's brutal. But maybe they deserve it.*

"Um. OK, well, we need some bindings and strong folks to lift them. Volunteers?" All the Protectors stepped forward, eager to lord it over their former tormentors.

Earl emerged from the rear passenger seat of his car with a tangled mass of bungee cords. "Will these help?"

"Hell yes," Nate said, and gestured to Andy and Joe to help him hoist Ben onto the roof of Earl's car. Once he was face down on the roof they did the same with Kathy on Sam's car.

Earl began to industriously tie Ben down, and Emma interjected, "Um, can someone help Earl with that?"

Earl was testy, "I can do it dammit. Leave me be." The group stopped and stared, expecting a fight.

Emma shrugged, "It's your party, honey." *Worse that happens, Conger will fall off, but he probably won't die. Boy, Earl really hates not being the guy in charge, especially when the woman in charge is me. Men.*

Booty tied to cars, the caravan continued down the slope to the beginning of the rocky, bumpy seasonal road used by all-terrain vehicles and intrepid explorers in the summer, and snowmobiles in the winter months. The road extended for several miles, going was rough, and the caravan slowed to a crawl as the copter whirred overhead.

Emma used her walkie-talkie to contact Don at the rear of the caravan. "Don, I'm going to keep an eye out for marauders and look for a good place to make camp. I'll let you know if I see anything. Do we have any more walkie talkies? Over."

"Yeah, I gave one to Nate and distributed the rest to Dave, Sam and the boys. We're all on, no worries. Over."

"I had a feeling you did. Over." They were both careful to keep their communications all business, they knew Earl was listening. Emma didn't want to admit she couldn't wait to get Don alone in the dark again, but there it was.

Dave broke in, laughing. "Uh, guys, I think we have to stop for a minute. Looks like Conger is making like a shot buck."

"What?" Emma said, "OK, everybody stop. Over." To avoid a pileup, she looked in her rearview to make sure the message got through, stopped her car and sprinted to Earl's car. On the hood, hanging by a few stretched bungee cords, was Ben Conger, struggling and bug-eyed. Emma laughed in spite of herself at the sight, even though it was clear Earl was embarrassed at his public lack of bungee skills. Dave stood laughing next to Emma. "Dave, what do we do?"

Dave chuckled, "Well, no need to drag him back on top. We'll secure him to the hood, we need a little laugh right now." Dave and his sons adjusted the bungee cords around Ben's body, now sideways on the hood. "Wish we had some antlers, that would really make the day," Dave chortled, and the boys guffawed.

"Just a minute," Andy giggled, and ran into the woods.

"We don't have time for your shenanigans Andy," Dave yelled after him. He muttered to Emma, "He's the resident jokester."

Andy appeared a few minutes later holding two small branches. He took off his hat, put it on Conger's head, and stuffed the branches inside the hat's gaps near Conger's ears as Conger struggled and his eyes widened. Emma and several others laughed in spite of themselves, and Emma held up her hand. "OK, OK, it's funny, and frankly a little sad. Let's get going. Andy, you're too much."

Emma signaled for everyone to start up again, and they drove on a few more miles until they came to a clearing in the pines. Emma pulled in, the others followed and formed a ring around the perimeter of the clearing. *It's great, we're developing hive mind.*

Connie was already commandeering food, setting up tables and directing helpers where to start fires. Emma gave her a quick hug, Connie whispered in her ear, "I bet I know what you've got on your mind."

Emma smiled and whispered back, "I have no idea what you're talking about."

Dave and his boys pulled tents from the back of their pickups and began to set them up. A few Protectors gave shooting tutorials in the nearby woods, while Don directed the rest of the sharpshooters to form a perimeter in the surrounding pines and set up a sentinel schedule. Nate landed the helicopter noisily in the road and joined Don's group after he and a few Protectors tied the hostages to a tree.

Despite danger, approaching darkness and all it portended, Emma felt happy. Safe. Even though she knew it was fleeting, which made it even more precious. *Here they are Emma, those last rich drops of honey in the jar. Unexpected honey, unexpected jar.*

Earl stood silently in the middle of the industry, uncertain what to do. Emma approached him and gave him a warm hug. He did not respond and had that vacant look that was becoming all too familiar. "How are you honey? Why don't you sit in the car and rest? It's been a hard day. I'll let you know when dinner's ready."

Earl looked at her blankly, nodded and shuffled to his car. Emma watched him sadly. She caught Don watching them, shrugged her shoulders and joined Connie and the food brigade.

Chapter Thirty-Six

Fire Above, Fire Below

Generators whirred outside NOAA headquarters in Washington, D.C. as the building sat in darkness, lit only by a three-quarters moon. Inside, Hannah O'Malley, newly promoted Director of Operations, peered through an enormous telescope as Evan Holdset and Stuart Candler flanked her on either side. She squinted, rubbed her eyes, squinted again, then turned to Stuart and said huskily, "OK Stuart. I see it. What the hell *is* it?"

Stuart held the scope handles in both hands and gazed into the field of vision. "Um. Well. It's not a comet. Looks like an asteroid. A really big asteroid, probably knocked out of orbit from the Asteroid Belt."

"How big?" asked Evan nervously.

Stuart continued to peer into the telescope. "Well. A small planetoid. That's my guess. Its size is unusual for the Asteroid Belt, but if it came this far from the Kuiper Belt it must have been knocked out of orbit pretty hard by something."

Evan continued, "Aaaaand….do we know its trajectory?"

"Not yet," Stuart replied evenly. "We have so few coms from other observatories, but from what I'm seeing, and I'll know more in the next 36 hours, it could possibly, just possibly be headed this way."

"Jesus," Hannah exclaimed. "Come on. Really? What the fuck. Don't we have enough to deal with? Do I get on coms and call the asshole, or should I wait?"

Stuart thought a moment, then replied calmly, "Let's wait until tomorrow morning. No need to freak people out more than they already are, unless we have no choice."

"Well, I don't know about you," Evan said worriedly, "But I'm camping out here and watching that thing hour by hour until we have usable data."

"Right there with you," replied Hannah, and Stuart nodded in agreement.

# # #

After a fitful sleep, Hannah's eyes popped open and she reflexively reached for her cell phone, then realized if she wanted to know the time she'd have to consult her manual-wind watch. Five-thirty in the a.m., Day Two of the Monster Asteroid. She eased her way off the couch in her office, tossed her hair, ran her fingers over her teeth, and hurried to the Observatory where Stuart blearily tracked the asteroid's trajectory and took copious notes. Evan slept in a chair in front of his monitor.

"Talk to me," Hannah said grimly, as she pulled up a chair next to Stuart and poked Evan awake.

Stuart turned to her solemnly. "You want the good news or the bad news first?"

Hannah intoned, "You pick."

Stuart rotated to her in his chair. "OK, there's not much good news, except this thing, wherever it ends up, won't enter our orbit for the next two weeks. The bad news, it's on a beeline straight for Earth, and unless it encounters a mammoth obstacle, it's 90% certain it's gonna hit, and if it does, it's bye-bye baby. It's a planet killer." He slumped in his chair. "I wish I was wrong, but the numbers keep adding up. God, I fucking hate this."

They sat in silence for several seconds, then Hannah choked, "Can we get through to Griffith, or Kitt Peak? We need corroboration before we send out the alarm."

Stuart shook his head. "I've been trying, but radio sources aren't getting through."

"Shit. Are you sure?"

Stuart nodded grimly.

"Then we can't wait any longer, I've got to call the asshole. God, I hope they don't shoot the messenger."

Stuart said darkly, "Tell them 90% certainty, and we'll keep them apprised by the hour."

Hannah picked up the red landline to the White House, dialed and said urgently, "Hannah O'Malley, NOAA COO, highest priority urgency, must speak with POTUS." A pause of several seconds, then, "Good morning sir…yes, it's early, but I hear you don't need much sleep….yes, only great men need less than five hours….sir, we have a situation….Yes, I'd say it's incredible….yes….amazing would also be a good word…yes… yes…sir, maybe you might want to put your Chief of Staff on for details? You can come in for the big strokes, inform your adoring public, yes?"

She rolled her eyes and waited several seconds, "Yes, Mr. Kelly, thank you, Sir. Um, maybe you should sit down. Oh, you're on speaker. OK. Um, well, we have a very serious situation…oh, it is, trust me…may I finish? Thank you, Mr. President. A very large object is in a direct line to impact Earth in about two weeks. We've been tracking it overnight, we wish we could get confirmation from other observatories, but so far we can't get through. Current data indicates impact is about 90% certain…well, calculations indicate it is very large, we classify it as a planetoid, a small planet. About half the size of Pluto sir."

She pulled the receiver from her ear and grimaced as a flurry of shouted expletives issued from her phone. Stuart held his arms up in frustrated surrender, and Evan shook his head slowly.

"Yes, sir. I can answer that question. Well, um, it's a planet killer. If it hits, we're going to be a fireball, and we could be thrown off our orbit. It will be all over…no, nuking it won't do any good, it's too large….I wish I had better news…I don't know how you're going to get the message out, there are a few news outlets still running, that's the best way…yes, I know it's a lot to digest…I'm so sorry…yes…goodbye sir."

Hannah's eyes filled with tears, she sat at her desk and dissolved into deep sobs. "There are so many things I wanted to do, scale Everest, have a kid, take a rocket into Space, buy a log cabin in the woods. And I'll never see my sister, or her baby, ever. God. Oh God. Two weeks, two fucking weeks."

Stuart and Evan stood on either side of her, not sure what to do. Stuart patted her back, which elicited fresh sobs, then all three began to cry.

Chapter Thirty-Seven

Ignorance Is Bliss?

Night had fallen on the campsite, fires were burning brightly, and the waxing moon and stars added their illumination as Connie and her helpers washed the last of the pots and pans in a large soapy tub and dried them with dish towels. As usual, Connie had worked her magic on dried venison with cherry sauce, garden vegetables and home baked rolls. Members of the caravan prepared to bed down in tents, cars or the backs of flatbed trucks. Don and Prince were settled inside the tank, and Emma slowly walked the perimeter, heartened by the chirps from multiple sentinels' walkie-talkies and the soft strum of Wendell Bratten's guitar.

Earl had cleared away part of the trunk and back seat of his car, lowered the back seat, and was uncomfortably tucked into a sleeping bag. Emma opened the door, peeked inside and offered solicitously, "Honey, there's more room in the tents, or in the back of one of the trucks."

"Bugs," Earl said dully. "I'll be fine."

Emma squeezed inside and snuggled next to Earl. "My city boy, still afraid of bugs. Maybe I can sleep here with you?" she asked gently.

Earl softened slightly and replied "Sweetheart, you know I can't sleep with anyone, not even you, right up against me."

Emma kissed his forehead gently. "I know."

After a short silence, Earl mumbled, "Besides, you have things to do, don't you?"

Emma looked at him in surprise. "Most everything's done. It's close to bedtime. I'm just trying to figure out where to sleep."

Earl turned away from her and muttered, "I think you know where to go... Do I have to continue?"

Emma hesitated, then said resolutely, "Yes, please do."

"Are you sure?" Earl asked accusingly.

"What do you mean?" Emma asked, and her heart jumped in her chest. *What did he know, and when did he know it?*

"I may be old, and I may be losing it, but I'm not stupid, and I've been around the block more times than I can count. I know you got your jollies with Mr. Clean Marine back in Mason's Eddy. The perfume of love is unmistakable, it was all over you that morning. I gave you permission, I understand your needs maybe better than anyone, and I love you more than I've ever loved any woman in my life. I thought your little tryst was the end of it, but no, you had to summon your lover to you again. He must be good. Maybe better than me."

Emma hesitated, should she admit it? Should she deny it? What was best for Earl? She decided, as usual, honesty was best. She held Earl's sad face in her hands. "Honey, nobody, absolutely nobody will ever be better, or even close to you. I've told you that for almost 30 years, and it's as true today as it was in the early days. You still take my breath away, and I love you more than I've loved any man. You know that." She hesitated, then forged ahead. "I don't love Don. He filled a physical need, something primal, that's all. I'm sorry. But you did say…"

Earl interrupted harshly, "I know what I said. But you can't expect me to be happy about it."

"Of course I don't. And I didn't want to tell you. But here it is. Now what? What do you want me to do?"

Earl looked at her pointedly. "What do *you* want to do?"

Emma looked down, hesitated, and replied softly, "I want both of you." She looked at him plaintively. "Honey, can I keep him?"

"Jesus Emma, he's not a puppy."

"I need it, especially now, and I wish I could have it with you, but I can't. You haven't treated me like a sexual being for years, beyond those nuclear kisses of yours that drive me wild. What do you expect me to do? I'm flesh and blood, and desire, and frustration. And time may not be on anyone's side."

Earl turned his face away from her. "Do what you want. I'm not going anywhere."

Emma sat quietly and contemplated her next move. She pulsed with desire for Don and deep love for Earl, she needed release, but she also knew it would be almost impossible to have Don in the current environment. Someone was sure to see or hear them, and that would undermine her position. She rarely thought about how she was perceived by others, but she recognized that as the leader of this band of upstarts, she needed to set an example. She settled into the front passenger seat, closed her eyes, and slept.

# # #

Dawn was breaking at camp. Connie stoked the campfire under a cast-iron grating that held a huge frying pan packed with sizzling bacon, another fire held a similar pan loaded with freeze-dried scrambled eggs. The fragrance of fresh coffee filled the air, and members of the caravan began to emerge from their various cocoons. "How are we coming with those biscuits?" she hollered at Merry, who was making baking powder pan biscuits over a third fire.

"Just about there!" Merry shouted back cheerily. Emma wandered the campground as she rubbed her sore neck from sleeping in the front seat. Earl was still asleep, and Emma sorted through her weary brain for today's marching orders. *We should be able to get to Zion by tonight, if we don't run into too much trouble.*

Nate approached her and mumbled intimately, "The Congers are bitching. They want to talk to you. I tell you, I'm ready to line 'em up and shoot 'em right now. She won't eat the food, he's threatening us with lawsuits and other stuff, and she must have a mouse bladder the number of times she's had to pee. I'm not going to be their nursemaid much longer, I tell you that."

Emma set her shoulders, sighed and said, "OK. Where are they?"

Nate pointed to a tree along the perimeter where they sat, tied to its trunk, looking profoundly disgruntled. Emma couldn't resist a slight smile at their discomfiture, then approached them with brisk efficiency as Nate followed behind her. "So" she said curtly, "I understand you want to talk with me."

"You are going to be so, so sorry," Kathy screamed. "You are going to be in a world of pain!"

Emma smiled wryly and replied, "It wasn't me who hog-tied you and brought you here. That privilege belongs to the employees you wronged. Did I incite a rebellion against you? Yes. Were you trying to escape? Yes. Did you lie to everyone, as is your wont? Yes. I believe what is currently happening to you is called Karma."

Nate nodded his head. "Damn straight."

Conger bellowed, "Generals are rarely in the field of battle. They need to be outside the battle theatre, for strategic purposes. We were looking for a better vantage point."

Nate approached Conger with an upraised fist and stopped just short of punching him. "I suppose that vantage point was in the fucking Hamptons? You're a fucking liar right to the end, aren't you, you sonofabitch?"

Emma continued, "None of us are thrilled with the accommodations, especially you, I would imagine, since you don't have freedom of movement and have to be spoon fed and taken to the toilet under guard. Not a lot of fun. You need to get used to the idea that you have become commodities for trade, not unlike the way you treated all of us. What you can do for us is a lot more important than what we can do for you. You've had your time in the catbird seat. It's our turn."

Nate took her aside and whispered in her ear, "Sorry I lost it there. Maybe tone it down a bit? If their cronies find us, we could be in a world of hurt."

Emma nodded, and whispered back, "Who saw you hogtie them?

Ned muttered, "Just my boys, they helped me."

Emma smiled. "I think we're good." She addressed the Congers, "We're going to be on the road soon, and we'll play it by ear in terms of what's going to happen to you. As far as I'm concerned, you're not welcome where we're going, and Nate doesn't seem inclined to take you to your desired destination, so you're going to have to learn to deal with ambiguity."

As she turned and started to walk away, Ben Conger boomed "Lady, you're in shit deeper than you ever imagined."

Emma turned, smiled, and replied, "It started as soon as your goons branded me. And I won't forget that. Neither will they." She gestured to the group who had gathered to hear their exchange. Many of them applauded. Ben and Kathy sneered and struggled against their bonds. As they walked away, Emma whispered to Nate, "I almost peed my pants. They are fucking terrifying."

Nate responded, "I knew you were a feisty bugger at the exit ramp, don't let those sons of bitches get to you. All they had was money, and jobs for us, and none of that means a darn anymore."

Emma stopped walking, turned to Nate and replied in her best Bogart imitation, "Nate, I think this is the beginning of a beautiful friendship."

Nate grinned and said, "Hot damn. Casablanca. One of my favorites."

Emma grinned back. "Me too, go figure." They high-fived and Emma headed for Earl's car. Earl was sitting, dazed, on the front passenger seat with the door open, holding his head. Emma hurried to him.

"Honey, are you all right?" He looked up at her in confusion.

"I forgot where we were. I'm OK, just, kinda…fuzzy, or something."

Emma felt his pulse, it was weak and fast. "You need to hydrate." She rummaged through several grocery bags in the car and came up with a warm bottle of Gatorade. "We don't have ice, of course, but drink this."

Earl opened the cap and winced as he swigged the warm, sweet drink. "Don't send my compliments to the chef."

Emma relaxed. *He's making jokes; he's all right.* "Speaking of the chef, Connie's got eggs, bacon and biscuits with your name all over them. Want me to bring you some?" Earl's eyes widened as he drank, and he nodded emphatically.

Emma got in line for food, Don stepped behind her and whispered in her ear, "I waited for you last night." Emma continued facing forward and said, all business, "Yes, we need to talk about that. Let's set up a time to talk before we hit the road." She smiled at Merry as she took two biscuits and a helping of eggs.

Don chuckled. "Got it. How about Sweet Betty after breakfast? I've been thinking about all kinds of logistics."

"Sounds good," Emma said briskly, and her groin ached in spite of herself. *God, it's like a dick, even after all this time it has a mind of its own. Down girl.*

She filled a plate for Earl, steadfastly avoided Don's gaze, returned to the car, handed the plate to Earl and sat in the passenger seat to eat her breakfast. Earl looked sideways at her, munched on a piece of bacon and said quietly, "It's OK honey. It's OK. I know you love me." Emma's eyes filled with tears, and she set her plate down in her lap.

"I hate myself right now. And I hate her," she pointed to her groin. "She's making my life miserable."

"Well, she made mine heavenly for many years. I would hate to see her go to waste."

Emma kissed him tenderly. "You are way too good to me."

"You deserve it," he said. "Maybe you'll pretend it's me."

"You have no idea how many times my electronic friends took me to fantasyland where it was all you, all the time. It's always been you. But since this madness started, it's like she wants to take it all in, like there's very little time left. It's weird." She stopped, almost sniffed the air, her eyes dimmed, and she felt herself melt into 'The Ethers', where past, present and future are simultaneous. "Just a minute." She sat quietly, felt the disruption in the Earth's rhythms, and said, "Something's coming. Something really, really bad."

"You're kidding. Sweetheart, I think you're going backward in time. That something bad already happened, and it's still happening."

"No. No. This is something else, something dark and huge and horrible. God, what *is* this?

"Probably Cain taking a shit." Earl quipped.

"I'm serious honey. Something's coming in…" she sat quietly and tried to decode the images. "This is the same thing that happened the night before 9-11. Remember? I was up until 3 in the morning with these images, fire, screaming, clouds of confetti, and the words 'Juggernaut. Nothing will ever be the same.' I couldn't identify it, I only knew it was coming, and a few hours later the towers got hit. Now all I'm seeing is darkness and fire and destruction, but I don't know what it is."

"This is not exactly light breakfast conversation," Earl said darkly. "Come on honey, maybe you're wrong."

"This frequency is never wrong. Believe me, I wish to God it was." She handed her plate to Earl and got out of the car. "Here, I'm betting you can finish mine. I have to go for a walk, maybe find some water, some kind of stream, water always seems to help. We're going to be leaving soon, honey, better get everything together. Today's going to be a doozie."

She walked, almost trancelike, past Don waiting by Sweet Betty, into the woods as she waved perimeter guards away and walked through underbrush, drawn like a divining rod to a small, gurgling stream. She knelt next to it, cupped her hands in the water and splashed her face, then looked at her reflection in a tiny pond.

There she was, Emma Kaplan, Mountain Woman, her fantasy on the Gorge Trail three thousand years ago. "What's happening?" she asked the stream, the trees and the air. "What is it?" She gazed in supplication at the sky, and above her circled three golden orbs. "Are you real?" she asked in wonder, "Or am I losing it?"

Her inner ear received a shimmering message "We are here for you. When the time is right, you will know."

"Oh great," she responded. "Like I need more uncertainty right now." The orbs swirled upward in a spiral formation and vanished in seconds. Emma heard rustling leaves behind her, and turned to see Don walking toward her. She held up her hand, her open palm faced him. "I'm sorry," she said apologetically. "I have a lot going on right now."

Don grabbed her, pulled her to him and kissed her passionately. "We have a lot going on right now. You and me, and you know it," he whispered into her ear.

She pulled away and confronted him. "Listen, Loverboy, I'm not one of your little cuties. You've already got my notch on your belt, it's time to move along and find another horny female. I've never been one for waiting in line for a man, and I'm not going to start now. We had something special, but that night has come and gone. A lot of people are depending on me, maybe what I need doesn't matter."

Don shot back, "Listen, Hot Stuff, I haven't been able to get you out of my mind since that night at Mason's Eddy, and I'm betting dollars to donuts you haven't either. Tell me I'm wrong."

Emma hesitated, then muttered, "You're not wrong. But I hate myself for it. I love my husband, and he loves me."

"But he can't give you what I can, and you're nobody's little cutie. Why do you think I came all this way when I got the message from White Line? I couldn't wait to see you again. You make me smile, and you make me hotter than I've been in years. So there. Put that in your pipe and smoke it, honey."

"I have to get back," she said curtly, and walked past him. He grabbed her arm, she pulled it away, then he picked her up and carried her, struggling, deeper into the woods, and set her down next to a giant spruce. "Are you done with the macho man thing?" she demanded. "Very entertaining. I have to get back, and so do you."

"Not yet we don't," he said gruffly, and kissed her deeply. She pushed her hands against him, he held her harder, and finally she gave in to the feelings she'd been holding in for weeks, her desire for this man, this man who matched her power for power, stroke for stroke. She stripped off her jeans, he unzipped and away they went against the spruce tree until they were satisfied, and panted softly in each other's grasp.

"Damn you," she whispered.

"Damn you back," he retorted, as he turned away and zipped his pants. "I should have remembered, good fences make good neighbors."

"We'll figure this out later, if there is a later," she said darkly. "I'm not feeling good about the future, but that's another story. We have work to do."

Chapter Thirty-Eight

Mouth of Hell, Mountain of Peace

Fires were doused, and trucks and cars were almost fully packed and ready when Emma and Don reached the campground. Connie sent Emma a knowing look, and Emma figured it wouldn't be long before the grapevine buzzed with news of their couplings. *Maybe she can keep a secret. We'll soon find out.* Jed and Liza ran up to her with the dogs.

"Mom, what's the deal?" Jed asked impatiently. *Why is it always up to me?*

"Give me a minute," she replied curtly. "I'll talk to everyone before we start out." She yelled out, "Don, Nate, Dave, everybody, we need to talk about the next leg. Everybody gather in a circle, OK?" Connie and Wendell herded members into a circle, Don, Dave and Nate joined Emma in the center. "OK guys," Emma said as she scanned the group. "God, it's so good to be on this challenging journey with you. I am so grateful to all of you for your dedication, hard work and determination. Today is probably going to be one of the hardest days of our lives. We have to go through Troyville to get to Zion, there's no way around it. I'm as certain as I can be it's overrun by looters and others desperate for resources. We have numbers and firepower on the ground and above on our side, and my hope is there will be no bloodshed."

She turned to Nate, "Nate, is the copter fueled and ready?"

Nate nodded assuredly. "Yep, so far our stockpile is holding out. It'll get us where we need to go."

Emma nodded. "OK, I think we need to take a couple of sharpshooters on board and check out the danger zones before we set out. We have several miles to go on the seasonal road, so while you're navigating that, and Don, I'd like you to spearhead that caravan, we're going to be your advance scouts. Sound good?" Don, Nate and Dave nodded in agreement. "Awesome. When you reach the end of the road, stay safe and wait for us to join you. OK, let's get ready to roll."

Nate beckoned to Andy and Nate Jr. to join him with their assault rifles, and they sprinted to the helicopter. Emma whispered to Nate, "I'm not a good flyer, I like my feet on the ground."

Nate smiled and responded, "Darlin', you're safer in the air with me than you've ever been. I've seen it all."

Emma turned and ran to Earl, hugged him tightly and kissed him passionately. "I love you. I will always love you. I'll see you soon honey." She tried to ignore Don's stricken face as she trotted to the waiting copter and climbed on board.

Earl yelled after her, "I love you. Be careful my sweetheart!"

"Strap in back there," Nate advised, as Nate Jr. buckled himself into the co-pilot's seat and Andy took the seat next to Emma. "Let's head out." He started the engine, onlookers scattered on the ground as the whirring blades stirred up clouds of dust.

Andy reached behind him, brought out two assault rifles and handed one each to Nate Jr. and Emma.

Emma's eyes widened, "Um. I haven't learned how to handle one of these yet, just a regular hunting rifle."

"No time like the present," said Andy. "You right-handed?" Emma nodded, wide-eyed. "OK, now, it's loaded and ready to fire. All you have to do is use your left hand to grab the forestock as close as you can and put the butt end against your shoulder until it feels comfy." Emma lifted the rifle to her shoulder and groaned at its weight. "No worries, when you're shooting, your adrenaline will be pumping, and it will feel light as a feather. Now, tilt your head so your right eye is looking straight down the top of the barrel…yeah, like that, and the butt stock should be right up against your right cheek…good. OK, now look down at your front sight, that round thing at the end of the barrel. The sight should be at 6 o'clock over your target. When you've got your target clearly in your sight, just squeeze the trigger slowly, don't do what we call 'drag wood', don't slide it along the side, pull it straight back. And if you want to fire multiple rounds, just keep pulling that trigger as fast as you can. When you need another magazine, I'll load it for you."

Emma protested, "No, thanks, I want you to show me how."

Andy sighed and smiled slightly. "When things get going, if they do, there won't be time for you to do it unless it's a reflex. You might want to be like those women in Alien or Terminator or something, and maybe someday, right? But trust me, you need to let me do it."

Nate interjected from the pilot's seat, "The boy knows what he's talking about. Once we're on the ground at our destination, you can practice."

Geez, I'm not a child. "Thank you," said Emma. "I'll do my best." She picked up the rifle and practiced as best she could in the cramped space. "How do I open the window?" She asked. The men laughed.

Nate chuckled. "We open the doors and hang out the side. Like in 'Nam. You'll have room." Emma sat back, overwhelmed. As the rooftops of Troyville's biggest mall came into view, Emma realized with a start, maybe she could find out about her parents.

"Guys, is it at all possible we could hover over my parents' apartment in town and see what's going on down there?"

Nate frowned, "That's asking a lot, lady. Let's see if we get any fire before we try that."

"OK, thank you so much. They're on Court Street, right across from the park." She squints as the hills of Troyville Community College came into view. "Can we go down a little closer?" She asked. "I can't believe what I'm seeing." The campus football field was ablaze with several giant fires, and writhing bodies were dancing around the flames. As the helicopter drew closer, they heard what sounded like drumbeats in a hypnotic rhythm.

Emma gazed into the fires, and could just make out giant poles stretched across them, with what looked like large roasting animals being turned manually by people on either side. "Does anyone have binoculars?" she asked urgently. Andy handed her a pair from his backpack. She peered into the sights and adjusted the lenses. "Oh my God," she gasped. "Those aren't cows, or deer. Those are people." She sat back in her seat as if punched and dazedly handed the binoculars back to Andy, who quickly used them to look at the scene.

"Jesus Mary and Joseph," he intoned. "I never thought I'd ever see anything like that in this country."

Nate quipped darkly, "I wonder if they taste like chicken."

"Look out!" Andy yelled, "Go higher, quick!" Emma looked out the window to see several people with guns pointed at the copter.

"No worries," Nate said. "Hold on!" He moved the helicopter side to side as he rapidly ascended. Emma heard a few small pops against the copter's side. "Fuckin' bastards," Nate growled.

"Did they get anything important? Emma asked anxiously as she looked out the window and the figures disappeared behind a cloud.

"Nah," Nate replied offhandedly. "You'd know if they did."

Emma said grimly, "I don't think I want to know what's going on at my parents' place. The Communication Center couldn't tell me anything. It looks like total mayhem down there."

"The Communication Center was a crock," Nate replied. "Wait 'til we get to Zion. Maybe you can find something out there."

"God," Emma said, and she sat back resignedly in her seat. "I keep hoping I'll wake up from this nightmare. Ever since the Northern Lights, it's been totally insane."

Andy replied gently, "I think they call it the New Normal." The men nodded solemnly, and the inside of the helicopter grew quiet.

Nate broke the silence. "Let's do a quick pass over Route 31, where all the stores and fast food joints are. I'm betting we can bypass the college and follow the stream around downtown, then through the fields and over small side roads most of the way to Zion."

Emma broke in, "I was thinking the same thing. The commercial areas are probably close to a ghost town by now, but who knows? There may be people living there."

Nate replied grimly, "We're probably going to run into serious shit, one way or the other, but this way it might be a little less shit. Let's go back. Don't want to waste fuel."

They rode in silence back to the bottom of the service road, several miles outside Troyville, where the caravan was waiting for them.

"Do we tell them about the barbecue?" Emma asked worriedly.

"Nah" said Nate. "No need to add more worry, right?"

Emma nodded solemnly. "Right." *Maybe I'll tell Jed and Earl about it when we get to Zion.*

Nate set the helicopter down in a grassy lot next to the service road outlet, where Earl, Don and Sam were waiting for them with long faces. "Oh Geez, something's wrong," Emma fretted. She jumped out of the helicopter, ducked underneath the whirring blades and coughed from swirling clouds of dust. She approached Earl with trepidation. "What is it? You look like somebody died."

Earl put his arms around Emma, hugged her and began to sob. "Honey, oh honey."

"What? What? Where's Jed? Is he all right?"

Don stepped forward. "I was talking to White Line on the CB. He heard from CentCom. There's a giant asteroid, he called it a planetoid, heading for Earth, they're pretty sure it's going to hit in under two weeks, and it's going to destroy everything. That's all we've got. That's all any of us has got. I'm sorry, I'm sorry for all of us."

Emma grew dizzy, and stumbled, Earl caught her and set her on the ground. *Damn, damn that frequency, it wasn't wrong. It's all going to be over soon. Oh God, what's the point of all of this? What do we do now?* "I'm all right, does anyone have any water? Holy shit, are you sure?" she asked Don plaintively.

He nodded. "It's pretty definite, close to 100%."

Emma grew pensive. "Well, we were due for another extinction event, and I can't say we don't deserve it, the way we've been treating each other and the planet."

Don snapped, "Oh come on, we don't have time for your wavy gravy stuff today."

"Oh, as if your macho man Mr. Cool thing is going to save us."

"OK, enough," said Nate, and he turned to Emma. "What do you want to do?"

Emma thought deeply. "I need to get to Zion to see my family, but you guys might be better off going back to camp and waiting it out there. Or come with us, it's up to you. The situation on the ground has definitely changed. And you might as well let the Congers loose, nothing much matters about them now. Nate, can you take us? Earl, Jed, Liza and the dogs?"

Connie stepped forward and said tearfully, "Honey, we've been talkin', all of us, and we want to go with you. You're family now, and if it's going to be all over soon, well, we want to be together, come hell or high water. We'll take our chances with you all on the road."

Emma burst into tears and hugged Connie tightly. She whispered in her ear, "If we had more time, I know you'd be my BFF."

Connie whispered back, "Already there, honey." They hugged again, wiped their eyes and Emma went to hug Jed and Liza, who were standing mournfully next to their dogs watching the tableau.

"Mom," Jed said mournfully, "Mom, maybe they're wrong. They're almost always wrong about the weather. Maybe it will hit the moon or something and get thrown off course. I'm not giving up yet."

"No, neither am I," Emma said as she hugged him, then Liza, and petted the circling dogs. "God, I love you so much." She patted Liza's belly. "And I love you too, tiny thing." She dissolved in tears again, and all three of them hugged. Earl walked tearfully to them and joined in the group hug. Don stood on the outside and watched sadly, Emma caught his eye and mouthed "I'm sorry." He mouthed back "It's OK." Connie went to Don and put her arm around his waist and her head on his shoulder, Wendell joined her on Don's other side.

As if on cue, the rest of the caravan joined them in a giant group hug, with tears and occasionally even laughter. Emma went from person to person, to Sam, Greta, Dr. Spencer, Merry, Evan and the kids, Dave, his family, dear little Tyson who was trying to be so brave, Nate, Nate Jr., Andy, Joe, all the Protectors. All together, all reaching a new level of awareness and understanding, knowing their time on this hurtling rock was short, and oh so sweet.

"OK," Emma said shakily as she addressed the group. "Let's get ready to hit the road. We'll be right with you providing cover, don't shoot unless you have to, and stay safe. With luck we should get there before nightfall."

Chapter Thirty-Nine

The Game Changer

"Nate, do you have a bullhorn, or something I can use to amplify my voice?" Emma asked, as she, Nate, Nate Jr. and Andy prepared to board the helicopter for their last lap before Zion, and caravan members quickly broke camp.

"Didn't we use one at my football games, Dad?" asked Nate Jr.

"Yep," Nate replied casually, then puffed out his chest proudly. "But you won't need it. Got a long-range Sonix audio system, like the one we had in 'Nam. You know, like that part in Apocalypse Now, with the music."

"Yes," Emma replied dreamily. "One of my favorites. Wagner's Ride of the Valkyries."

"Whatever," Nate said. "You can use that. They can hear it fine over the prop sounds."

"Awesome," Emma said, and turned to Nate. "I'm going to tell folks below what's happening, a lot of them probably don't know. I'm going to tell them to lay down their arms and stop hurting each other. Maybe it will work."

Nate shook his head. "You don't know how they're going to react. Maybe it's better to keep 'em in the dark."

Emma pursed her lips, "Wouldn't you want to know? Wouldn't you want the chance to hold your loved ones close and enjoy every last minute together? I know I would."

Nate was pensive. "You could be right. OK, you're on. We'll have to put white flags on her, maybe they won't open fire. This could be a lot more trouble than it's worth."

Emma shook her head, "I need to do this. My final act as a diehard do-gooder."

Nate smiled appreciatively, "You're somethin', you know that?"

Emma patted his arm and whispered, "Don't let it get around."

Don dragged Ben and Kathy Conger, newly released and resisting his grasp, to Emma and Nate. "These folks want to go with you, they want to be dropped off in town at the compound of a friend."

Nate's eyes narrowed. "Whereabouts? You know I'm going to have to tie you up and strap you to the seat, right?"

Ben Conger boomed, "In the Heights, on Bambury Road."

"No can do," Nate replied, shaking his head. "I can take you close to the Troyville campus. You'll like it there. They've got barbecue going day and night, and I swear I heard them dancing and singing gospel tunes when we flew over. Right up your alley, Missus. I'm betting there'll be good Christians there who can take you where you need to go." Emma's eyes widened slightly as Nate figuratively signed Ben and Kathy's death warrants.

Ben and Kathy conferred quietly, then nodded their heads in agreement. "All right," Ben said, "But you're going to be sorry, brother. When this is all over."

Kathy nodded emphatically, looked skyward and raised her hands, "Judgement Day's around the bend for you, Nathan Clark, just wait and see. There's a place in hell for traitors and liars."

"Don't they know what's comin'?" Nate whispered to Don.

Don shook his head, "Nope. I had 'em tied up at the perimeter, it'll be news to them."

Nate smiled widely. "Good. Somethin' to talk about after we get their mouths taped up. I've had enough of their jawin'. Emma, stay here until I do this little errand, why it's the least I could do for my old bosses now, isn't it? C'mon Andy, Don, help me with 'em."

Boy, I'm glad I'm on his side of the fence. Emma nodded innocently, "Yes, it should be very illuminating." She almost felt a pang thinking about their fate. Almost.

Don, Andy, Nate and Nate Jr. hogtied the protesting Congers, taped their mouths and shoved them into the helicopter. Andy went along with Nate, both carried assault weapons and had grenades strapped to their belts. "See you in a bit." Nate waved to Emma. "Be ready to go."

Emma called after them, "Gotcha. Be safe." Nate saluted, he and Andy boarded the helicopter and lifted off. Emma looked at Don, neither one knew what to say. "It's a lot." She said softly. "I still can't believe it."

"None of us can," Don replied. "Everyone expects a happy ending, everyone expects to be saved. Let them think that way for a while. I know one thing for sure, we're all going to appreciate every moment we're still here. And for what it's worth, I'm glad I'm spending these last days with you, any way we can." Emma looked at him sadly. "I know, family comes first. But now, this is my family, these folks from Mason's Eddy, you, your kids, all of them. My kids never showed up, my wife's gone. I belong here. No worries."

Emma held his hand briefly, then let go when she saw Earl watching them. "Thank you, really. I couldn't have done any of this without you and your help. I hope you know that."

"Let's not Kumbaya just yet," Don cautioned. "We're heading into dangerous territory."

Emma nodded ominously. "The Congers don't know it yet, but they're going to be next on the menu. Nate's dropping them at Cannibal Corners. We really can't go anywhere near that campus, those kids have taken Wilding to a whole new level." Don was taken aback; Emma was unaccustomed to seeing him express anything but Man in Control. "I don't know what's gotten into me these days. I guess revenge really is sweet."

Don shook his head in disbelief. Earl approached them and said sarcastically, "May I cut in? I'd like to talk with my wife." Don nodded and walked over to Connie and Wendell, who were packing up the last of the food they brought out for snacks while the caravan was waiting. "Planning your next tryst?" Earl asked archly.

Emma pursed her lips. "For your information, I was telling him about students roasting people on a spit on the campus football field. That's where Nate is taking the Congers. Trysts are the last thing on my mind right now. Frankly, my mind is pretty close to being blown, or at least short-circuited. The only thing keeping me sane right now is knowing I'll be spending these last days with my family."

Earl softened, and encircled Emma in his arms. "Oh honey, you had to see that? My poor baby."

Emma allowed herself to melt into his arms, and for a blessed moment she imagined they were back in their New Jersey home, getting up together in the morning, kissing each other before Earl went to work. She looked into his eyes and whispered, "Who would ever imagine we'd be here, in this place, waiting for the end of the World."

Earl nuzzled her neck, kissed her softly and said, "I'm glad we're going together. It was hard for me to imagine one of us without the other."

Emma cried softly against Earl's chest. *My tough, tender guy, right to the end.* Don had been watching them, he turned and walked to Sweet Betty, whistled for Prince and climbed inside.

The campers readied themselves for the last leg of their journey, clustering in small groups next to their vehicles, craving connection, hugging, crying, some laughing, as they waited for Nate to return. Earl and Emma stood with their arms around each other next to Jed and Liza as the dogs circled around them. In the distance they could see the helicopter approach from the South, its engine sounded loud and uneven, and there was smoke issuing from it. It landed in a cloud of smoke, Nate opened the door and yelled, "We need a doctor, now!" He carried Andy in his arms like a child, Andy's head gushed blood from his temple and his eyes were rolled back.

Emma screamed "Where's Doctor Spencer? Doc? Where are you?"

She heard a thin voice from a distance, "Here, I'm coming" and Doctor Spencer picked his way gingerly to the helicopter. Andy lay on a blanket on the ground, Connie pressed a dishtowel against his forehead and tried to stop the bleeding. Doctor Spencer knelt beside Andy, felt for a pulse and yelled, "Andy, Andy, can you hear me? Andy?" He addressed Nate, "He's not breathing, his pulse is very weak, there's not much I can do for him. I'm so sorry."

Nate said tearfully, "Those little bastards shot him as we were dropping the Congers out, we got away, but they hit the engine. Andy said he was glad he was going, he didn't want to see the end of everything he loved." Tears welled up in his eyes and he turned away.

Dr. Spencer felt for a pulse, shook his head and closed Andy's eyes with his fingers. "He's gone." A wail rose from the group, Emma cried in Earl's arms, and beseeched Nate, "Did they shoot the Congers?"

Nate nodded. "Oh yeah. They're toast. Or maybe barbecue is a better word. But I got a chance to tell them what was coming before they went to the Great Beyond. They didn't end well, that's for sure. Sons of bitches…listen, does anyone have a shovel? We have to bury Andy before we go, or take him with us and bury him in Zion. And I need help with this engine."

Emma declared, "He's got to come to Zion with us. He's just got to."

Tyson stepped forward and said "I can help you. I'm really good with engines."

Nate smiled down at him. "I bet you are little buddy, but this ain't no Matchbox car."

Tyson replied firmly, "It looks like you've got a reciprocating gas engine, but until I look inside I won't know if the fuel line, compressor or something else got hit. My guess is the fuel line. If that's the case I can fix it without looking for substitute parts."

Nate bent over in a bow, and swept his hand from Tyson to the helicopter. "Well then, be my guest, my man."

Tyson smiled and yelled sideways to Dave, "Uncle Dave, can you bring me a ladder?"

Nate spoke confidentially to Emma, "While he's doing that, we need to figure out where to put Andy. I can make room in the back of my truck, move some things around. I hate to think of him jiggling around back there, but it can't be helped."

Several Protectors grimly lifted Andy as others cleared a spot in Nate's flatbed, Connie brought blankets to cushion him, and three Protectors sat in the back around him, assault rifles at their side.

Emma approached Tyson, whose upper half was submerged inside the helicopter's engine as Dave held his ladder steady. "How are we coming, Tyson? Did you find the problem?" She asked.

Tyson straightened up and said matter-of-factly, "Yep. They punctured the fuel line. I put fireproof tape on it, it should work fine now." He

233

jumped down and rubbed his hands on his pants to wipe off as much grease and dirt as he could.

Emma hugged him, which embarrassed him, and he looked sheepishly down at the ground. "Oh, sorry" she said, stood back and shook his hand. "I don't know what we would do without you Tyson, really. You've come to our aid when it really mattered, and today is no different." Tyson smiled slightly, touched the cap of his hat, then helped Dave fold the ladder and put it in his truck.

"We'll be ready to take off in a few minutes," Nate said to Emma. "I got more gas from Don, he said his CB contacts tell him the raiders are almost at the Collective. We've got to head out as soon as we can."

Emma circulated among the group to make sure the caravan was ready. A few stragglers were still loading their vehicles, but by and large the group was in synch. Most faces were grim, some were tear-streaked. Emma climbed onto Sweet Betty's turret and gestured for everyone to listen.

"Folks, I still can't believe we're here, and I can't believe what's ahead for us, but there's no one I'd rather go into this frightening new territory with than all of you. We're going to stay off road as much as we can and follow Turner Creek around the outskirts of Troyville, this way maybe we can avoid taking much fire. Dave, Don, have you coordinated our cover plans?"

Dave yelled out, "Ready. We got our marching orders. I know the way, Don's gonna bring up the rear."

A few people chuckled. *I guess word got around. Well, so be it.* "Good. Nate, Nate Jr. and I will cover from the air, and I'm going to try and talk some sense into these folks and let them know what's coming. Are we ready?"

A loud roar issued from the crowd, and Emma's eyes teared as she realized it sounded like the primal roar that bounced and echoed from Manhattan's skyscrapers as she and hundreds of thousands of outraged Americans protested the Inauguration of The Orange Menace two years prior. A century ago. She wiped her eyes, blew kisses to Jed, Earl and Liza, and she, Nate and Nate Jr. climbed into the helicopter, now decorated with three makeshift white flags attached to tree branches. "Here we go," she said grimly, as she strapped into her seat. Nate had covered the bloody seats from Andy's fatal wound with several towels, and the floor of the helicopter was stained with blood. Emma swallowed hard and asked grimly, "Will the branches hold in the wind?"

"Ironwood" Nate replied gruffly. "Indians used it, for strength. They'll hold." He handed her a microphone and pointed to a small instrument panel next to her seat. "When you want to talk, push that switch there. And talk loud."

They lifted off, and hovered over the first several trucks in the caravan, Dave's truck was in the lead. He led them over the highway into flat grassland that bordered Turner Creek, a meandering stream that curved around the perimeter of Troyville, crossed under an overpass that led to the commercial district, then continued through woodlands for several miles until it intersected a small country road in Zion. Emma was relieved they were going to avoid the Troyville campus, and she allowed herself a moment to imagine Kathy rotating on a spit, a ship's carved brown figurehead, sizzling over an open firepit. She shuddered briefly, shocked not only by the image, but her ability to conjure it.

She was surprised to see empty grassland, no campsites, no cars, no one on foot. "It's deserted," she commented to Nate.

"Don't be so sure," he said grimly. "It's too darn quiet for me." As if on cue, three young men popped out of the underbrush, rifles in hand. Emma grabbed her microphone, flipped the switch and yelled as loudly as she could as Nate put the copter into a hover over the men.

"Stop! We come in peace, but we have many shooters in our group. You don't want to go out this way, do you? In several days it will all be over, for all of us. There is a giant asteroid heading straight for Earth, a planet killer. We only have a few special days left on this precious space, let's please not spend it killing each other. If you don't believe us, find someone who has contact with the outside, with law enforcement or the military. They'll confirm it. Come with us. We're going to Zion, we're going to go out together. We have food, and caring people. Please, spread the word. Come to the end of Post House Road in Zion, join us for the Last Days."

The young men stood open-mouthed, and Emma waved Nate forward. "Well" he said with a slight smile, "You can talk the legs off a table, lady. Good on 'ya. Not what I expected."

"Maybe they'll join us" Emma replied hopefully, as her shaking hand set the microphone on the control panel. "Let's hope there's not much more of this." Nate nodded grimly. Shots were heard behind them, Nate doubled back and hovered over the caravan as the three young men were splayed on the ground. Emma watched Dave and Adam drag them out of the caravan's path, and she shook her head softly. "Why?" she asked.

"In their blood I guess. They hoped they could get something, I don't know. None of it ever made much sense to me." He looked at Emma squarely. "Can we stop the Kumbaya now? Let's get where we're goin'."

Emma sat pensively. "Maybe my do-gooder days are coming to an end."

"Nah, but right now they're damned inconvenient. You've done enough good for one day. Let's concentrate on getting there in one piece."

Emma smiled, pulled her iPhone out of her pocket and said triumphantly, "Nate, my man. I can't get a signal on this thing anymore, but my handy dandy solar charger has given me access to a little traveling music. Maybe this will keep them away." She scrolled through her considerable classical music collection, found what she was looking for, and asked, "How do I put this through the system?

Nate grunted. "Just plug in that input there. This better not be any of your drippy snowflake stuff."

Emma grinned. "Nah. This you'll like. Trust me." She plugged the phone in, flipped the switch and turned the volume on high, as The Ride of the Valkyries blasted from the sound system.

Nate broke into a broad smile. "Now *that's* what I'm talkin' 'bout! Yeah!" He bobbed up and down in delight.

"Thought so," Emma said. "Let's do this thing." She looked down to see several members of the caravan cheer as they brandished their weapons.

"Missy, if I wasn't a married man, I'd kiss you into next Sunday. Sorry, Son."

"No worries Pop." Nate Jr. intoned laconically.

"Honey, if I wasn't a married woman with a side man, I'd do the same."

Nate guffawed and slapped his knee, Nate Jr. chuckled softly.

"Damn, you're fun, lady." Nate said laughingly, then grew quiet. "Too bad we didn't know each other sooner. Too bad."

Emma patted his knee. "We know each other now, that's enough." He nodded soberly, they continued in silence as Wagner blasted into the grasslands, and startled deer scattered beneath them.

Chapter Forty

The Promised Land

Maybe it was the Wagner, or maybe word of the asteroid had gotten out, but the Turner Creek grasslands yielded only stampeding deer and circling birds. As they approached the Troyville Mall, Emma and Nate Jr. surveyed the scene with binoculars and were surprised by well-appointed camps dotting the parking lot, with large grills and designer firepits outside large, new-looking tents and gazebos. Several inhabitants lounging on cushy outdoor furniture looked up in surprise at the helicopter and began waving.

"Of course," Emma exclaimed. "They got all this stuff from the Mall."

"Nice work if you can get it," Nate Jr. grumbled.

"I just hope there isn't an outdoor store with guns here." Emma said worriedly.

"Looks pretty peaceful to me," Nate Jr. observed. "Maybe our shooters and tank are keeping them well-behaved."

Emma turned the music down as multiple people on the ground gestured for them to set down in the parking lot. "Is this an ambush?" she asked Nate.

"Could be. Maybe you should talk to them with that." He pointed to the microphone.

"Good idea," Emma replied, and picked up the microphone. "Hello. We're passing through, are well-protected, and don't want any trouble. Have you heard? About what's coming?" Several people waved their arms and jumped up and down. "OK, listen. We're not stopping, we're going to Zion to wait it out together. You're welcome to join us. Follow us now, if you can, or come to Post House Road in Zion, go to the end, past where the road ends, past the pond, and you'll find us." The waving continued, Emma sighed and looked at Nate. "It looks like word is getting around. So far so good."

238

"Don't expect much," Nate Jr. intoned. "They look pretty comfy right here."

"I had to extend the invitation. Humankind is about to become extinct, I feel like we need to be together, I'm not sure why, but I feel it really strongly."

"OK," Nate said dismissively. "We're going back in the woods now, still following the stream. I've got to go higher to keep out of the trees." They hovered over the caravan as they made their way slowly above the treetops. The air was turgid, and the sky still held vestiges of Aurora Borealis from the solar mass ejections, a constant reminder life had forever changed.

"I thought this would be harder," Emma said to Nate. "It feels like a lot of folks are giving up, waiting for the end. I always thought we'd go out with a bang, not a whimper."

"I'm sure we'll start partying pretty hard, and praying pretty hard, once we get where we're goin'," Nate ruminated. "I know I'm going to be going at my Missus and hitting the JD big time, I'm betting it'll be the same for a lot of us." He looked significantly at Emma. "And that's all right."

"When bombs fly, panties fly off and trousers fly open," Emma said softly.

"Huh?" Nate asked quizzically.

"Something Earl said to me a hundred years ago." She stopped short and looked below. "I know this spot, the road is near the creek, we're getting really close. Can we get back on the road? In just a few clicks we'll be at Post House Road."

"Clicks?" Nate said approvingly.

"War movies," Emma replied proudly.

"Yeah, get on the horn and tell 'em."

Emma picked up her walkie talkie, "Guys, we're going on the road now. We're almost there. Stay sharp, I know you will. Over."

Dave crackled over the walkie-talkie, "Not soon enough. My suspension is shot."

"Sorry Dave. But we've been pretty safe so far. Over."

"Yep," Dave replied grimly. "Hear that everybody? Head for the road. Over."

Various affirmative replies came from Earl, Jed, Adam and Don.

Emma took a deep breath. "Here we go." They veered away from the tree line and hovered over the narrow country road. It was deserted, and abandoned trucks and cars were moved to the side, which made travel easy for the caravan. "It's like they're paving the way for us," Emma mused. "I keep expecting rifle-toting maniacs to pop out at us from the woods, like when we were heading up the highway to Corinth. Where is everybody?"

"Probably hunkered down, trying to make the most of things. Word probably got out, even way out here," Nate said quietly. "What a thing this is. What a thing." He sounded like he was finally allowing himself to feel the gravity of what was ahead.

"There it is," Emma pointed excitedly. "Post House Road. Turn left here." Nate hovered the copter over the intersection as the caravan caught up with them. "We should be able to find plenty of places to set down, once we get to their encampment."

Post House Road was unpaved, and clouds of dust followed the caravan as they climbed the hilly road for several miles. They passed abandoned trailers and singlewides close to the roadside, overgrown with weeds and tall grasses. At the top of the hill on the right was a large man-made, spring-fed pond. Several cows grazed peacefully around it, beyond them a flock of sheep and several miniature horses. "Leave it to Carol and Joe to have a menagerie," Emma said approvingly. "It's like they knew what was coming years ago….maybe they did…there it is!" She pointed excitedly to a series of mounds poking up from a large hill on the left a quarter mile ahead. "Holy crap. Hobbitville, for God's sake. They told me their plans for this years ago, and they really did it."

"I heard about that," Nate Jr. said. "A friend of mine told me about these Hobbit houses in the boonies around Zion. I thought he was kidding."

Emma gazed in wonder at the series of neat little doorways with gardens on top of the mounds and around front entryways. "Let's set down over there." She gestured to a flat area next to a large vegetable garden. She got on the microphone and shouted "We come in peace, it's me, Emma, Carol's sister. Don't shoot, OK?" Several people poked their heads out of the doorways, a few popped up from behind trees and bushes, rifles in hand.

"They must have seen us coming," Emma said to Nate. "But I know them. They're peace lovers, first and foremost. Thank God."

Nate shook his head as he took in the scene. "Never seen anything like it, right son?" Nate Jr. nodded in agreement, mouth agape. They set the helicopter down in tall grasses, and Emma unbuckled quickly and darted underneath the whirring blades, anxious to see her family. *Amazing what blood and apocalypse can do, isn't it Emma?* Bonnie appeared in a doorway. She and Emma burst into tears and ran to each other.

For the first time Emma could remember, Bonnie hugged her hard, with unbridled feeling. In the past she held her children like they were Faberge eggs; Emma was shocked and moved by Bonnie's depth of expression.

"My girl, my girl, I thought you were dead, and here you are, you're here, and…" she looked at the caravan with wonder, "So many people, my goodness." She smiled confusedly through her tears.

Emma kissed Bonnie's wet cheeks and petted her face. "Ma, I know we both have stories to tell, but right now we need to get the lay of the land and figure out where everyone's going. Can you show us around? Where's Dad, and Carol? Is Lynn here? I brought Jed, and Earl, of course, and Jed's girlfriend, and…" She looked at the smiling caravan members who gathered around them. "Some amazing, wonderful people."

Bonnie's face fell. "Dad's gone. And Joe, and Carol hasn't been out of bed since. Lynn's here, with the kids, and the nieces and nephews. We've got quite a crew, you'll be amazed what they're doing here."

Emma's eyes filled with fresh tears. "I'm so sorry Ma, I hope it wasn't too painful for Dad and Joe. I wish we could sit and talk, but I've got to get these people situated, then you and I can sit down and tell each other about our adventures and travails."

241

Bonnie smiled slightly. "You and Lynn always were the ones in charge, like your father. Let me get Lynn, she's been overseeing things here for weeks." Bonnie opened one of the round hobbit-house doors and disappeared inside. Screams of joy were heard, the door flew open, and Lynn burst into the front garden. She was even thinner than usual, but her face had the glow of a woman running on an engine fueled by love and indefatigable determination.

"My God! My God!" she exclaimed as she and Emma hugged joyously and laughed through their tears. "And Earl, and Jed, and, wow, you brought a lot of people along, didn't you? Amazing!" She moved to hug Earl and Jed, and smiled widely at the assembled group. "You have no idea how happy I am to see you, alive, all of you!" Lynn stopped, grew quiet, and drew Emma aside. "Do you know? About, the asteroid?"

Emma nodded solemnly. "Yeah, I know. We all know. We wanted to be here, together, to see it through."

"I still can't believe it, can you?" Emma shook her head and Lynn took her hand. "I can't help it, I know you think I'm a Pollyanna, but I just can't believe in less than two weeks it will all be gone, we'll all be gone."

"I feel the same," Emma replied. "Maybe we're just not able to process something this big."

"Maybe," Lynn said, without conviction. "We've got to get these folks settled. How many are you?"

"Gosh, I don't know the exact count. A few dozen at least, and a tank, as you can see, and a helicopter, and a lot of lovely armed folks. Without them we wouldn't have made it."

Lynn looked down the hill, "Looks like a lot more than a few dozen…" Emma twirled around and gasped as a throng of people trudge up the hill.

"When we flew over Troyville I invited folks camped at the mall to join us. I feel strongly we need to be together, in the same place, as much as possible. One of my spidey things." Lynn nodded knowingly. "I hope we won't have any trouble, and I hope we can feed and house everyone."

Emma turned to Don, Jed, Earl and her mother, "Guys, Lynn is going to show me around so I can figure out our next moves. Please take care of introductions, and Don, please take some guys with you and check out the

242

newcomers. Any trouble, we'll have to figure out where to put them." Don saluted with a grin. Earl shot him a dirty look, then put one arm around Jed and the other around Bonnie, gathered Caravan members and started going door to door as Zionites slowly approached them.

Lynn looked approvingly at Emma, hugged her and whispered, "Tarzana on the Vine, my intrepid sister. Looks like you're firing on all cylinders. And what's that guy's name? Don? He's a cutie."

Emma smiled and whispered back, "Hands off lady, he's mine." Lynn's eyes widened. "And before you get all judgey, Earl has given his blessing. You know about the enforced celibacy thing. But there are a lot of fellas hankering for female companionship, if that's your thing. But that's for later. Show me, show me everything."

"OK," Lynn said firmly. "Get ready."

Chapter Forty-One

Hobbit Land

Lynn took her hand and led her toward a Hobbit house. "Here are my digs. Everyone's place is pretty much the same on the outside, but inside we can trick it out any way we want." She gestured to a small oval doorway made of oak hung on rustic iron hinges. The door squeaked as it swung open, and Emma peered inside and squinted into the darkness.

"Nothing is going to fall on my head or run under my feet, right? No snakes, mice, or rats for starters?"

Lynn smiled. "Can't guarantee no mice, but no, no rats or snakes. Wait a minute…" She picked up a small square device with a crank leaning against the doorway and cranked enthusiastically. "It's a solar light, hold on…" After several rotations the device emitted a soft glow. "It should last about half an hour." They entered the tiny space, Lynn gestured widely with one hand as she held the light over her head. "Here it is. Home until, well, until." Emma had expected the walls to be made of sod, and was surprised to find the interior space entirely enclosed by small terracotta brick walls and a stretched waterproof tarpaulin ceiling held up by crisscrossed metal poles. A tiny table and two chairs sat against one wall, several rolled sleeping bags and pillows were piled neatly against the wall on the opposite side.

"Wow. I thought it was going to smell murky in here, but this feels quite dry."

Lynn nodded proudly. "Joe and the boys learned from Joe's friend Moe. He builds these for a living. They stay cool in the summer and warm in the winter, and look, isn't my fireplace cute?" She gestured to a small woodstove on a brick hearth; a few embers smoldered in its base. "At nightfall I make a fire, mostly for light, if I want to read. Our dog Kayla sleeps by the fire, she's out marauding right now, probably terrorizing squirrels, and the kids have their own place next door. Carol and Joe's old place, Carol's in with Mom now, this is technically Cal's place."

"Cal?" Emma asked quizzically. Lynn chuckled.

"You'll meet him later. I can't wait for that."

Emma's nose wrinkled. "Your boyfriend?"

Lynn snorted. "Not likely. You'll see. C'mon, I'll show you the gardens, and the critters." They stepped outside, Emma blinked into the sunlight. "I feel like I'm coming out of a molehill."

"You get used to it," Lynn replied briskly, then stopped in her tracks and her eyes filled with tears. "No, you won't have time…oh God. This can't be happening." She began to cry softly.

Emma hugged her and whispered, "Where's my rose-colored glasses girl? Maybe they're wrong, maybe it will graze us and just give us a hard time."

Lynn looked tearfully at her. "Do you really believe that? What does your spidey sense tell you? I've trusted it since we were little." Emma sighed and looked meaningfully at Lynn. "Say no more. Come on, dear sister."

She led Emma past a row of mound homes, and gestured to a large fenced garden on a gentle slope with tiered raised beds, bursting with berry bushes, fruit trees and vegetables. Dozens of chickens clucked and picked their way in between the beds, and Lynn gestured to a small outbuilding with a hand pump behind it. "That's the coop, to keep out foxes and hawks. The chickens usually just hide underneath plants when predators show up, but we have lost quite a few. Past the coop is our well pump, it's really deep, through layers of rock, and the water's really pure, but it takes some elbow grease." She took Emma past the coop to an open field dotted with crosses and large stones. "I guess I don't have to tell you what this is."

Emma replied hoarsely, "Hallowed ground? Or final resting places for folks who didn't play nicely in the sandbox?"

Lynn replied grimly, "A little of both. We've had our rocky times, believe me. But not anymore. I want to show you Dad's grave, and Joe's." They solemnly approached a rough-hewn headstone with 'Richard Shaw, beloved husband, father, grandfather. Lover of Truth' carved on its face.

Emma stood soberly and asked quietly, "Was it bad?"

Lynn nodded her head. "He was in a lot of pain, and wanted to go. I think his body just gave up. Bonnie and I were with him at the end. His last words were 'turn off the television,' and of course there wasn't one. He was hallucinating toward the end, talking to the air, maybe connecting with the other side. He asked about you several times."

Emma's eyes watered. "I wish he had opened up to me. We spent our time circling each other like feral cats."

Lynn looked at her appraisingly. "Too much alike. I think he was a little afraid of you. We all were."

Emma shook her head. "I still don't get that. But maybe none of it matters now."

Lynn hugged her. "What matters now is we're together, like little Hobbits, at the end of all things."

Emma smiled, "God, Lord of the Rings. Well, you've got the Hobbit houses, and instead of ravening armies, we've got a fireball. Maybe giant eagles will rescue us in the end and take us to the Promised Land."

Lynn smiled slightly. "Maybe. Come on, I want to show you Joe." They walked a few paces to another stone carved with "Joe Morrissey, God-loving husband and father. Gone too soon."

"How did it happen?" Emma asked.

"Heart attack," Lynn replied grimly. "He was digging a garden bed and boom. Gone in a matter of minutes. Carol hasn't been out of bed since, and that was over two months ago, before the grids went down. I wish I could be buried next to Rob back in Minnesota, that was my plan… God, so much has changed in such a short time."

"And the others?" Emma asked, pointing to the dozens of wooden crosses and smaller stones.

"Mostly folks who wanted to cause trouble, a few too sickly to save. We tried confining the troublemakers, some of them came around, but some wanted to do us harm. I don't want to go into details, I'm still processing it."

"OK," Emma replied softly. "We'd better get back and see what's going on up there at the ad hoc meet and greet." She pointed up the hill to the mound homes where crowds were congregating. "But before we do, a delicate question…where do we, you know, relieve ourselves? "

Lynn smiled and pointed to a series of upright rectangular wooden shelters down the hill from the gardens. "Our Dew Drop Inn facility, we rotate who gets the lovely job of dealing with the chemical toilets. We keep it downwind for our comfort, and downstream from the aquifer that feeds the well. You can also go into the woods over there" she pointed to the mountainous pine forest at the base of the clearing. "You'll need to take a shovel so you can bury it."

Emma replied grimly, "I guess there won't be a lot of time to get used to that either. God."

Lynn nodded solemnly. "Life out of balance. I think the Hopi call it Koyannisqatsi. Maybe after all this our dear Mother Earth will find her balance again."

Emma replied quietly "I've never felt smaller."

"We can wax philosophical later next to the fire, if you like, but you've got a lot of people waiting for you, and I think the natives may be getting restless."

Shouts were ringing out from up the hill, and someone was speaking into a bullhorn. Emma and Lynn raced up the hill to find Don doing his best to calm the crowd. "People, people, I know we've got a lot to deal with, and that's an understatement, but we'll figure it all out. Try and keep it together."

A woman pointed to Emma and piped up, "She said we would be safe here, and taken care of. I'm so hungry, I haven't eaten anything for three days, and my kids are sick."

A strong woman's voice boomed from the front of a Hobbit house. "What do you need? Ask and you shall receive." The crowd turned around to see a much thinner Carol leaning on her cane, eyes blazing. "Our gardens are full of food, we have a root cellar, chickens, eggs, milk cows and goats, woods full of game, a trout stream, fresh water, and I'm a pretty darn good medicine woman. All we need is a little organization, right, Emma?"

Emma slowly approached Carol and asked quietly, "May I hug you, or will it hurt?"

Carol smiled, opened her free arm and said, "Bring it." They hugged tearfully, Emma turned to the crowd. Don handed her the bullhorn.

"Folks, this is my sister Carol Morrissey, she and these lovely Zion residents want to help us through this challenging time. Connie Bratten here," she gestured to Connie, "is our Master Chef, anyone with foodstuffs or cooking chops, please see Connie. Folks with hunting skills, see Don here, or Dave over there, and organize a hunting party. If you're thirsty, bring containers just past the gardens over there and use the hand pump for fresh water. And please bring any vehicles to that level field" she pointed to large open grassland to the left of the residences above the pond and grazing animals. "We need to set up camp, gather firewood, Wendell, will you spearhead that?"

Wendell ambled up to Emma and nodded to the crowd "Sure will. Come on folks." He led the group to the open field, the original caravan members followed with their vehicles, and Don and Prince got into Sweet Betty and followed behind.

Carol limped to Emma and whispered into her ear, "No footprints in the sand." Emma looked at her quizzically. "We don't have guideposts for what is about to happen. This is virgin ground."

Emma nodded emphatically, "Got that right." She paused, then took Carol's hand and said quietly, "It's so good to see you. I...know we haven't been close, but..."

Carol interrupted. "We're sisters, and I love you. Enough said. I've got to go lie down for a bit, I'm betting I'll be called upon for my herbal mixtures before you know it."

Emma followed her as she gingerly limped inside her structure, "I'm so sorry about Joe. He was a good guy." Carol didn't respond. "I'm sorry, I know you're mourning. It must be like losing an arm."

"More like losing half my body, and my soul," Carol said softly as she eased onto her bed. "If it wasn't for God and the boys, I would have packed it in, it's been hard. Really hard."

Emma tucked her in. "Rest, rest now. I think I know someone who can help you with medicines." Emma went outside and called out "Merry, Merry Goodman, can you hear me?"

A voice came from down the hill, "I'm here. You need me?"

"Yes!" Emma yelled. "When you have a minute." She spoke to Carol through the open door. "Merry Goodman is a good friend, and knows a lot about natural medicine. Once she and her partner Evan get squared away with their kids, I'm sure she can help you."

Merry appeared breathlessly next to Emma. "What's up, fearless leader?"

Emma hugged Merry. "I'm betting you have a lot in common with my sister here when it comes to natural living, and healing. When you're settled, can you help with doctoring needs?"

Merry smiled, "Sure can, give me a little while, and I'll be back. Nice to meet you!" She waved at Carol. Carol waved back weakly.

Emma turned to Carol. "There you go." She called after Merry who was scampering down the hill, "Thanks so much, Merry, I'll be down soon to help everyone set up."

Carol rested back into her bed with a soft sigh. "How is it all going to end? Will we burn up immediately, or languish for days as nuclear winter sets in and everything dies?"

Emma replied slowly, "It all depends on where it hits, I guess."

Carol sighed. "The boys have been excavating a deep shelter where they hope a lot of us can wait it out. I don't know...all I do know is I want to be buried next to Joe." She gave Emma a significant look. "I've been praying, asking if I'll be forgiven if I go early, so I can be buried with him. God is against suicide, but maybe these are special enough circumstances."

Emma sat next to Carol and grasped her hand. Carol winced in pain and gently withdrew her hand. "God, it really hurts, doesn't it?" Emma asked solicitously.

Carol smiled slightly. "Sometimes the boys ask me what doesn't hurt, and I say, 'the tip of my nose.' Weed used to help with the pain, but it's not touching it now, and we grow some really good stuff. It's been so much worse since Joe went. My body is mourning him along with my heart and soul. I know he was eccentric, and self-absorbed at times, but we became two parts of a larger entity over the years, I honestly can't stand being without him. I can't." She cried gently, Emma looked on helplessly.

"Do the boys know you're thinking about this?"

Carol nodded slowly. "They do. They're against it, of course, but they know once I've set my mind to a thing…"

Emma interrupted. "No more needs to be said. You are a determined bugger. Always were. But how would you do it?"

Carol looked suspiciously at Emma, "This is between us, right?" Emma nodded reluctantly, since she wanted to sic Lynn on Carol to talk her out of it. As if reading Emma's mind, Carol said, "Lynn knows too. But no one else. Lynn and the boys have sworn not to tell Mom, or anyone else. I have foxglove plants, a.k.a. digitalis, and other toxic herbal substances I made into something along with belladonna, atropine, you know, that will put me to sleep, then slowly stop my heart. It won't hurt."

Emma replied through her tears, "Promise me, promise me you won't do this without letting us know, OK? Give us a chance to say goodbye. I wish you'd reconsider."

Carol smiled weakly. "I've been dealing with pain for so long, Joe's gone, and I've had a full life and much love along with struggles. I'm ready. Really. And when the time comes there might be others who would rather go peacefully." Emma shook her head, the thought of group suicide had not entered her mind.

Merry appeared at the doorway carrying a box of various vials and plastic bags full of dried herbs. "I'm here, ready to rock and roll!"

Emma dried her eyes and hugged Merry. "You're our ray of sunshine, you truly are. Ladies, I leave you to it. How's it going out there?"

Merry smiled and sighed. "Well, factions are being formed. I guess that's to be expected. From what I can gather, the teens and 20's are already planning a 'hook up tent,' since they don't have to worry about pregnancy or STDs at this point, the Evangelicals are making their own camp and readying for what they're sure will be The Rapture, so they're a happy bunch. The atheists and agnostics are wavering between gloom and doom and bugging Don to get on the CB to get updates, since everyone still hopes the experts are wrong and this thing will miss us, the hunters have promised a barbecue tonight, probably deer, maybe rabbit, and a group of survivalists headed by Carol's sons and their friends are working on a deep shelter, hoping to wait it out."

Carol quipped, "If it misses us there are going to be a bunch of young folks with baby bellies and crabs, or worse."

Emma shook her head. "This is what happens when groups of disparate people get together. Kinda like that reality show 'Survivor,' except they won't have a lot of time to form alliances and figuratively stab other contestants in the back, at least I hope not. Gotta get down there, ladies. Carry on." She waved, blew a kiss to them both and headed down the hill where encampments were forming.

Chapter Forty-Two

Mountain Man Redux

Night was falling as campsite fires blazed, and the aroma of roasting chicken filled the air. Connie had gotten permission from the Zionite Chicken Wrangler to slaughter several aging capons that now rotated on wooden spits suspended over a long trench fire, along with several skinned rabbits caught by Don, Dave, Nate and his boys. Merry and Connie manned cast-iron skillets full of biscuits and vegetables, running children wove around seated campers, and Wendell, Jed and Carol's musical sons jammed on their guitars and harmonicas.

Chatter rose from several camping areas, there was an air of expectancy, and a high-pitched sense that the group wanted to absorb as much as they could out of every moment. The major topic of conversation was the planetoid, and whether or not it was really, truly coming.

"It's the end days, I'm sure of it," Wendell declared, and several campers nodded. "Revelation, it's coming, but you know what that means, don't you?" No one answered, the campers grew silent.

Connie piped up, "The Judgment. He's coming back. Some say the dead will rise, and we'll all be taken up into the air, the Rapture, you know? Others say we'll fall under crumbling mountains or get burned up in Holy Fire, and our souls will be judged."

A young man stepped forward, "That's a great story, but that's all it is. We die, we die. That's all. I've done my research, Virgin Births, rising from the dead after three days, these stories way predate Christ. Sorry guys."

Wendell and Connie bristled, looked at each other and relaxed. Connie said quietly, "Well, we're going to find out soon enough, aren't we? I'm sticking with my faith. You can believe whatever you want to, son."

The young man grew pensive. "I wish I had the comfort of believing we'll be saved by some miraculous, otherworldly force. All I see coming is fire, darkness and pain, and none of it makes much sense to me. Why do we learn so much, and grow and become wise, only to die in the end? Maybe we just pass bits of ourselves on, maybe that's all there is."

Connie approached him and held his hand. "None of us know what lies beyond. But I know a little bit about science, and I know once something has been created, its energy can never be destroyed, just turned into something else. What's that word Wendell?"

Wendell smiled slightly, "Transmuted. Kinda like butterflies from caterpillars. Our souls can't die, young fella. You can take that to the bank."

The young man sat next to the fire. "Maybe," he replied, and poked at the fire with a stick.

A deep voice intoned from the darkness outside the campfires. "It's coming. The Great Migration upward is coming, and we're all invited." An unnaturally tall, rail-thin man stepped into the firelight. He had piercing pale blue eyes, long matted brown locks and a fuzzy dark brown beard past his navel. His clothes were soiled and tattered, and he wore knotted rags for shoes. The group grew silent, and several men bristled, standing on alert and muttering amongst themselves. Emma was sitting by the fire with Lynn and gasped as she recognized him. She stood and approached the stranger slowly as the men moved toward them.

"It's you…it's you!" She held up her hand to the advancing men. "Wait a minute guys…" She turned toward the tall man. "I was walking in the Glen on the high trail. You popped out of the grass and scared me. Do you remember?"

The man's eyes narrowed as he scanned her. "The woman who threatened to kick my balls? Hard to forget. I got as far away from you as I could…and we meet again."

Nate piped up, "Smart man. She's a pistol." The group relaxed, and laughed.

Emma grew defensive. "Well, you did pop up out of nowhere, and you're…well…quite a sight to behold."

The man bowed dramatically, "My apologies, dear lady. I was in a deep meditative state, and almost no one walks up there."

Lynn stepped next to the scruffy stranger. "Folks, this is Cal. Calvin McCafferty. He's…well, he's hard to categorize, he's our resident guru, seer and King Solomon. He saw the changes coming before anyone else did. Cal, this is my sister Emma."

Emma's eyes narrowed. She sensed the possibility Cal was a con man, as Carol and her neighbors were babes in the woods and easy prey for a con man talking about the End of the World. Nevertheless, she approached Cal and held out her hand. *He looks like a raggedy Rasputin.* They shook hands and gazed intently into each other's eyes while Lynn looked on approvingly.

Cal nodded to Emma and sat by the fire next to Bruiser while Lynn took Emma aside. "He's for real Emma, truly. He's got the gift, like you. I was wondering how you two might or might not get along. I can already see you're suspicious."

Emma remarked caustically, "Well, if he'd popped up out of nowhere and grunted at you, you might not be so kindly disposed. What did he mean, the Great Migration upward? Who is he, the second coming of Moses or something? Where are his Commandment tablets? Has he spoken to any burning bushes lately? I just don't want to see you guys taken in and sold a bill of goods."

Lynn shook her head emphatically. "It's not like that. You know me, I've got my own brand of radar, and I've spent time with this guy. He knew the asteroid was coming before the news came out, he saw it in a dream. And he talks about bodies floating into white light, being taken up into the air. He says we'll be saved. He's kept us sane, he really has."

Emma's eyes widened. "Bodies floating into white light?" She sat with a thud on a nearby log and put her head in her hands.

Lynn sat next to her solicitously. "What's wrong? Are you all right?"

Emma raised her head and gazed upward. "I had a dream, just before the Reunion. I was floating into intense hot white light, there were bodies floating upward with me, so many, and I couldn't find Earl, or Jed. It was horrifying, one of 'those' dreams, you know? The technicolor ones that stick with me forever."

Lynn took Emma's hands. "You see? You're both on the same wavelength. I knew it. Maybe you can help each other. Maybe you can help clarify what's coming, if it's real, wishful thinking, or our souls rising into Heaven."

"Give me a minute," Emma responded huskily. "It's a lot. Maybe, just maybe, is it possible, we're going to get out of this alive? It's too much to process, but hell, I'm hanging onto it. Gotta talk to this guy." She stood up resolutely and approached Cal by the fire. Don and Earl hurried to stand on either side of her.

Cal looked up coolly and quipped, "I see there are gargoyles at your gate, Emma. But we don't need them, do we?"

Emma responded briskly, "Maybe not. We'll see. But I'd like to have a private conversation." She hugged Earl and squeezed Don's hand. "I'll be all right. Don't worry." She and Cal walked side by side from the campfire into the moonlight as the others watched, then went back to their conversations.

They were silent for several minutes as they walked, until they reached a bluff overlooking the encampment. Cal raised his arms skyward, closed his eyes and began chanting, "Om Mani Padme Hum" over and over as Emma watched him carefully. Without opening his eyes, he whispered to her, "Join me. It's stronger if we both do it. It's the Mantra of Compassion."

She reluctantly joined him, and after several minutes of chanting her body began to vibrate vigorously. "Don't be afraid," he assured her. "We're resonating with the Universe. It's going to talk to us."

He touched Emma's solar plexus and a warm light entered her body. She felt she might swoon, and muttered, "I have to lie down."

"Do what you have to do," he replied, as he continued chanting. She lay down in tall, soft grasses, gazed at the massive array of stars overhead, and wondered what in the world was coming next with this ragtag Disciple. He had the same kind of physical pull Earl had, but on a much higher vibrational level. *Why am I always drawn to these charismatic human energy converters?*

He stopped chanting after several more minutes and sat cross-legged next to her. "Not to burst your bubble or anything," Emma said softly. "But you don't think you're the Second Coming or anything, do you?"

Cal chuckled. "Not likely. I used to be a carpet salesman, not a carpenter. An atheist and a meth addict. I guess you could say I had my Saul of Tarsus moment on my own private road to Damascus about a year ago. And all this happened. This energy, this knowing. It goes through me..."

Emma interrupted, "But you're the receiver, the conduit, you condense, convert and transmit it, but you don't create it. You're a human crystal. I know."

Cal looked at her intently. "I know you do. Lynn's told me a lot about you. You've been at this a lot longer than I have. I think I have this so I can help people through the changes."

Emma sat up and asked urgently, "But what changes? What does it all mean? We need answers, and we need them in a big hurry. Literally, the fate of the world and all those people down there depends on what happens next."

Cal replied evenly, "The orbs. You've seen them, so have I. They're the key, I'm sure of it."

"But we can't fit even one person on one of those things. And maybe they're high-tech military drones, maybe they're ours."

"They've been scouting and reporting back for thousands of years. Look for the orbs. You've seen them very recently, haven't you? Just a few days ago? By the water?"

Emma looked at Cal in wonder. "I guess I should ask how you know, but..."

Cal interrupted, "But you don't have to, right?"

Emma responded lightly, "If we get through this, there's a psychic in Ocala, Florida I think you should meet."

"Lily Fortas?" Cal asked off-handedly, then grinned.

"Jesus on a crutch, you know her?"

"Better sit down, oh, you're already sitting. She's my mother. She remarried Aaron Fortas after she divorced my Dad, Brian McCafferty."

"What? Wait a minute…you're the meth-addicted son who came to Jesus?" She tapped her forehead, "Yes! She told me your name was Cal."

Cal nodded. "I think I had to hit rock-bottom before I could rise, but I got the gift from her. I chose to ignore it until it wouldn't let me. No amount of drugs could blunt the dreams, and the knowing. It haunted me, until I embraced it. Until I saw its value."

Emma sat back, stunned. "Boy, six-degrees of separation on steroids."

"It's called synchronicity. You know about that. It's all coming together."

"So, what do we do?"

"Look for signs, get ready, have faith. Try to convince the others not to give up and descend into hedonism and despair. Some of us are going to survive, I don't know how or where, maybe even here, I'm not that good. But I know something is coming. Something that will change the end of the world into the beginning of something so new, we can't even give it a name."

Emma sat pensively. "I don't know what to think. If it wasn't for you seeing the same white light I did and knowing about the orbs, I don't know if I'd believe you."

Cal stood up. "Let's get back. I'm betting your men are worrying I'm having my way with you."

Emma laughed, "Not unless you have a shower and a change of wardrobe. I do have my standards."

Cal chuckled. "I think you've got enough on your plate already."

Emma smiled up at him. "Got that right."

They walked silently back to the campsites in the moonlight.

Chapter Forty-Three

Shelter From the Storm

In a hollowed-out, massive Pennsylvania mountain, grim-faced Intelligence and Logistics personnel were very busy doing what they'd been doing for years, but this time it wasn't a drill. They were readying a giant labyrinthine chain of top-secret underground bunkers for residence by top government, finance and science & tech movers and shakers. Other giant bunkers created during the Cold War and continually updated over the decades were being readied across the country and in Europe, China and Russia. This one, Raven Rock near Waynesboro, PA, was where Hannah O'Malley and the NOAA crew and their families were preparing to, with luck, live through the approaching firestorm. A full moon glowed brightly in the East, and the approach was brightly lighted by scores of towering solar stadium lights.

As Hannah approached the mammoth, thick concrete opening to the complex in her purple Toyota Celica along with a slow, serpentine convoy of other invited VIPs, her aged, scruffy Irish Wolfhound Max emitted deep woofs from the back seat, joined by soprano yips from her feisty Cairn Terrier Sisu. "Quiet guys! Make nice or they won't let you in!" As if on cue, both dogs quieted. The car was packed to the roof with suitcases, tote bags and ice chests, with Hannah's mountain bike mounted on top. Her mother June sat in the passenger seat, her teenaged brother Colin was sandwiched between the dogs.

"Your bike?" her mother June asked quizzically as they loaded the car. "When do you plan to use that?"

"Ma," Hannah answered impatiently, "You should see the corridors, it's a giant maze, and I've got to get exercise or I'll lose my shit. Just be glad you guys are coming with me, OK? Be glad I got my PhD in Meteorology and Climate Studies from Penn State, and be super glad we're the first ones who reported the planetoid to POTUS. We get carte blanche, baby."

Colin muttered from the back seat, "I guess I won't be getting WiFi down there."

"Guess again," Hannah crowed. "They've got everything, their grid is up, they launched a ton of Coms satellites so we can monitor this thing and its aftermath, and they even have a game room. Be of good cheer, bro."

Colin's face brightened, then grew sullen, "Yeah, but who am I going to talk to?"

Hannah assured him, "You'll meet people. Lots of NOAA folks are bringing their kids. OK, we're going in." Hannah was waved forward by two military guards who gestured for her to roll down her window. Hannah picked up her identification card from around her neck and showed it to a guard. "Hannah O'Malley, NOAA Director of Operations. My mother June, brother Colin and my two dogs." The other guard checked his clipboard, marked them off, nodded, tapped his helmet with two fingers to sentries by the bunker opening, and the guards moved to the next car.

June lamented tearfully, "Liza should be here. Are you still trying to reach her?"

"Yes Mom, we're using all possible contacts. She was last tracked at a ski resort in Upstate New York, but it's been overrun. Believe me, I'm trying as hard as I can. I want her here too, and the baby."

June wiped her eyes, "What's the young man's name again? John?"

"Jed," Hannah replied tersely. "I haven't met him. Yet." Their car was waved by a sentry into the bunker entryway. "Here we go, our tax dollars at work," Hannah said expectantly.

The car drove through the massive, thick open metal doors and began a long, steep decline into the bowels of the mountain. As they reached multiple openings, they were waved through various passages by armed MPs until they reached a large elevator door. A guard checked Hannah's ID, then pushed a button to open the elevator for Hannah's car.

"Stop!" the guard yelled as Hannah began to steer the car into the opening. "That bike's gotta come down."

"Oh geez," Hannah muttered. "Guess they didn't think of everything." She yelled to the guard "Just a minute!" She put the car in park and she and the guard took the bike down. "Colin?" she yelled to her brother. "Come out here and hold the bike while we go down."

Colin grumbled, got out of the car and sullenly held the bike next to the car as Hannah got back in the car, and the elevator descended floor after floor, until a ding signaled Level 23, their destination – home for the next who knew how many years.

The door opened to reveal a wide corridor flanked by multiple doors to dozens of residences, all NOAA personnel and their families. Several adults and children milled around in the hallway as military personnel bustled from room to room. Next to the elevator were marked spots for cars, Hannah parked, got out and sniffed the air. "I figured since we seem to be in steerage, it might not smell so great down here, but it's not bad. Pretty clean, actually."

A cheerful middle-aged blonde Captain approached her and chirped, "Triple-purified, along with the water. It'll smell pretty down here for years. You are?"

"Hannah O'Malley and family. We're pretty bagged, where are we?"

"I'm Captain Maggie, I'll be getting you settled in…" she checked Hannah's ID against the names on her clipboard, "Suite 23G, follow me." She led them down the corridor, Hannah waved through an open doorway to Stuart Candler and his wife Susan, who waved back solemnly from their living space as Colin followed grimly along with June.

"Here we are…" Captain Maggie used a key to open a metal door to a small, plain, cream-colored room with a galley kitchen, sofa and a few chairs. She pointed to a narrow hall. "Down there is the bathroom and two bedrooms, two of you will have to share, and here…" she said, pulling down a table from its attachment to the wall, "is your dining table. Cupboards up here, cooking pots, pans and utensils, your silverware drawer, and your mini fridge. We don't encourage much cooking in the residences, the mess hall is where you'll be taking most of your meals, but there is a Commissary where you can get whatever you need. As far as the dogs and their toileting requirements, there are pee pee pads, poopie bags and cleaning supplies in the bathroom linen closet, and the trash chute is just down the hall. Well, I'll let you get settled, but Ms. O'Malley, you and your colleagues are needed up on Level 13, the monitoring station, as soon as possible."

"Hey Mom, Colin, can you start to unload the car? Thanks." They exited into the hall as Hannah touched Captain Maggie's arm and asked, "If I can reach my sister and her partner, can they stay on this floor?"

She stared pointedly at Hannah. "Partner? Male or female?"

"Male. Why?"

She replied briskly, "Only if they're married."

Hannah sighed. "Oh Geez. C'mon, really?"

Maggie replied firmly. "Really. Anything else?"

Hannah lowered her voice and looked around her furtively. "What are the chances we're going to survive impact? Or is that above your pay grade?"

Captain Maggie smiled brightly, "We may get a little banged up, but top brass seems to think we'll make it."

"Thanks," Hannah said grimly. Maggie saluted, smiled and exited.

Hannah sat on the sofa and held her head in her hands.

# # #

Hours later, Max's large, wet nose nudged Hannah's sleeping face as he whimpered, and Sisu's toenails clicked rhythmically on the tile floor as she tried in vain to jump on Hannah's bed. Max began to systematically lick each quadrant of Hannah's face as she sputtered awake and turned her face into her pillow.

"Maxie, c'mon! Hell, what time is it?" She felt around in the semi-darkness for her watch and blinked at its lighted dial. "Six a.m. Jesus, dude." Max looked at her plaintively and Sisu yipped loudly. "Shhhh, Sisu, crap, you'll wake everybody. Stop!" Hannah sat up in bed, fluffed her hair and vigorously rubbed her face and eyes. "OK, OK, I know what you've gotta do. Remember the drill?" Hannah set down doggie pads, put on her no-nonsense fish-eye face, and the dogs complied.

"Good babies, good babies!" she crowed, as she scooped up the pads and opened the door to the corridor. "Be right back. Stay." The dogs waited, noses pointed toward the door, until she came back from the garbage chute. As the dogs gobbled down their breakfast reward, Hannah sat wearily on her bed and checked her messages. The intercom next to the exit door blared "Hannah to Surveillance Floor asap. Out." She mumbled to the dogs, "You're on your own guys," threw on her shoes and hurried toward the door.

NOAA's underground monitoring facility was humming with activity as Hannah rushed off the elevator. Evan and Stuart manned computers and tracked ETOAJ43, the Agency's name for the planetoid, translated as Extra Terrestrial Object Alpha Juliet 43, the 43rd object of its size plotted by the Agency since its inception. "I guess this makes us Romeo, and it won't end well," Hannah grumbled as she dug a Mars bar out of her pocket. "Stewie, what's going on with Satellite coms?"

Stewart looked up grimly and replied quietly, "At her present trajectory she's 6 days out from an evening impact in the Pacific Atoll, the Marshall Islands. Ground Zero looks to be the island of Kwajalein, but she's wobbling a bit. Not enough to count."

Hannah glared at him, "Do you have to call it 'she'? C'mon man."

Stewart replied calmly without looking up, "More important things, more important things…"

Hannah sighed and began to calculate, "So, Japan, Indonesia, Australia, toast immediately. Next, Europe, Africa, then us. It's coming in from the East, so impacts here will be within one, two days?"

Evan replied, "My calculations indicate it hits on Sunday, October 14th and we get it Monday night, around 10, give or take."

Hannah mumbled, "No wonder I always hated Mondays. Send the timetable to the top, I don't have the stomach to talk to that sonofabitch."

Chapter Forty-Four

Signs

Emma couldn't sleep that night, and slipped out of Lynn's place as Earl snored in his sleeping bag. Lynn and Kayla slept cuddled together next to the fire and Cal slept on top of the mound wrapped in a moth-eaten blanket. Jed, Liza and the dogs slept inside their SUV near the mound. The campgrounds were silent, save occasional sounds of pleasure from the 'hook up' tent. Emma wasn't headed for Don's open arms, she wasn't even sure he was available, since several young ladies gravitated to him around the campfire. None of that mattered now – all she wanted was answers, and time, more time.

She walked past the chicken coop and pump, into the makeshift graveyard. She stood briefly next to Andy's newly dug and covered resting place, then sat next to Richard's grave. "Hi Dad," she said softly. "Fancy meeting you here. Bet you never thought you'd be buried in the boonies just before the End of the World." She stopped and thought for a moment. "This is nice. I actually feel I can talk to you. Maybe now that you're on the other side, you've softened a bit. Dad, if you're hovering around here to be near Mom, and I'm betting you are, maybe you know more than we do. Maybe you can send us a sign, something to let us know the other side isn't so bad, in case we join you there in a few days." She turned to Joe's headstone. "Joe, this goes for you too. We need our ancestors and departed loved ones in our corner now, more than we ever did before."

She hugged her knees, and tucked her nightgown and shawl around her as she peered into the sky, half expecting to see a distant, blazing fireball move inexorably through the stars. A red fox paused at the forest opening nearby and sniffed the air, then bolted back into the trees. An owl hooted from an adjacent pine, and Emma startled as she spotted a misty cloud form beneath the owl's perch and slowly assume an amorphous human shape.

"Dad? Joe? Who are you?" Goosebumps rose on her arms, and her hair stood up at the back of her neck. The figure pointed upward, and slowly vanished. Emma looked skyward as a group of orbs in regimented formation moved slowly across the sky. Occasionally one of them would emit a flare, and adjacent orbs flashed in response. "Holy crap…holy crap." Emma stood up and watched as they headed for Lake Macanaw and disappeared.

"Jesus," Emma muttered, and sprinted toward the mound. As she approached, Cal stood legs akimbo on top of the mound, arms outstretched, head thrown back in an ecstatic state as he howled and exalted with sounds Emma never heard issue from any human being. People burst from their sleeping places, exclaiming and confused, gathered around the mound and grew silent as Cal continued his exaltations for several more minutes.

Don appeared at Emma's side and muttered, "What the fuck," in her ear. She was surprised to find herself glaring back at him like a jealous girlfriend, even in the face of these extraordinary happenings. "What?" he whispered.

She hissed, "Did you leave her, or them, back in the tank, or maybe you were sampling the offerings at the hook-up tent?"

He looked at her in disbelief and growled, "You've got a lot of nerve, lady. A lot of nerve."

"We don't have time for this, I'm sorry I started it. Do what you want to do, I have no rights over that. I apologize. And I don't want to know, OK?"

Don nodded. Emma sadly squeezed his hand. *I need this like a hole in the head.*

Cal's vocalizations slowed into a rhythmic hum, and the group began to pepper him with questions. He waved them away, jumped down from atop the mound and approached Emma joyously. "Did you see them? She nodded slowly, eyes wide. "They're coming. One hundred percent. Maybe they can stop it, I don't know, but they're here, and they're going to save us. Can you feel it?"

Emma said softly, "I think so."

Don shook his head as clamoring campers shouted questions. "It's a lot to hang your hat on, these 'feelings.'"

Cal stood quietly in front of Don. "Faith, man. You gotta believe, otherwise, what do you have?" Don stood silently, unable to answer.

Emma took Cal aside and gestured for the campers to give them room. "What do we do? How do we prepare? And do you think they'll come for all of us, or what?"

Cal smiled slightly. "I think we need to go with the flow and let it unfold."

Emma took a deep breath and replied, "OK, while you're flowing, I'm going to pack."

Cal put his hand on her shoulder. "I wouldn't expect anything less. Go for it. Spread the good word." He disappeared into the excited crowd, and led them like a shepherd back to their campsites.

Emma walked toward Lynn's place and Don took her arm. "Emma...Emma. Are you buying this?"

Emma faced him urgently. "I don't like the alternative. I don't want to entertain the idea I'm going to be a slab of sizzling jerky or cowering in a muddy shelter in just over a week. Maybe he's right. I'm holding out hope, and I'm going to prepare as well as I can for something I know absolutely nothing about."

Don replied tersely, "Suit yourself. I'm not buying it."

Emma turned and walked back into Lynn's shelter, Don shook his head and climbed into Sweet Betty.

# # #

Emma lay next to Earl in early morning light that insinuated through cracks in the round front door. For a brief moment when she awoke she thought they were back in their bed in New Jersey, then in the cabin, until finally she landed on the dirt floor of Cal's mound home, and stared at the tarpaulin ceiling. *Carol was certainly right, there are no footprints in the sand for this condition, past is in no way prologue.* She watched Earl's slow, regular breathing and her brain felt oddly empty. She couldn't remember a time when her thoughts were so quiet, so still. *Maybe it's because there's no way to plan for what's coming, I have no receptors for this.*

On cue, Earl started to rustle inside his sleeping bag, and Emma waited for the inevitable gas emissions that signaled her lovely beast was awake. His morning intestinal reveille began, and Emma couldn't stop herself from laughing. She felt tender – every moment needed to be cherished and held close to her heart. Everything, and everyone was precious now. *God, I'm becoming such a sap. It's all right, it's kind of like knowing you're going to die soon; everything is amplified. Hell, maybe I am going to die soon, and maybe I'm wasting my time listening to Cal's ramblings.*

Earl and Emma whispered to each other. "Hi, honey," Emma crooned.

Earl looked at her with glistening eyes and replied sweetly, "Good morning, my darling. Did you sleep all right?"

"Surprisingly, yes, this floor agrees with me. Must be my Neanderthal roots."

Earl reached from inside his sleeping bag and stroked Emma's face. "You know what we'd be doing now, don't you, if I was…"

Emma said softly, "I know."

"Well, Mr. Marine is ready to take care of that. And it's OK, if that's what you want."

"And you can go to the hook-up tent and watch, or thrill some of the more mature ladies with your charms. I don't know about you, but all I want right now is to be with you."

Earl smiled broadly. "Me too, honey-pie."

"Good." Emma snuggled down into her sleeping bag and she and Earl held hands and smiled at each other.

Jed knocked on the door and called out, "You guys decent in there?"

Emma got up, opened the door gently and whispered, "As decent as we're going to be. Lynn's still sleeping. You know her, she could sleep through a nuclear blast…oh, sorry. What's up, honey?" She wrapped herself in a shawl and stepped outside. Jed's face was pale and worried.

"I think Liza's maybe having a miscarriage or something. She's bleeding a little, and has cramps. What do I do?"

"Oh God, I don't know. She has to rest, and try to relax. I'm going to wake Carol, she might have something for her. Come with me."

They hurried to Carol's mound and Emma opened the door carefully and whispered into the darkness, "Carol? Carol? Can you wake up please? We need you." There was no answer, Carol was another deep sleeper. Emma crept into the semi-darkness and gently jiggled Carol's shoulder. Carol's eyes opened slightly, and she mumbled, "What? Is it coming now?"

"No, no, but we think maybe Liza might be having a miscarriage. What do we do?"

Carol's eyes widened as she struggled to wake up. "Um, raspberry leaf tea I think, and maybe some chamomile and lavender essence. But you know, the baby will do what it's going to do, we can't go to a hospital."

"Tell me where it is, I'll get it." Carol directed Emma to her herb cupboard as Jed ran to his car. After she located the items, she caught up with Jed. Cal spotted them, climbed out of his blanket and approached with concern.

"What's going on? Can I help?"

Jed replied worriedly "I don't know. Our baby might be in trouble."

Cal ran ahead of them toward Jed's car, Jed sprinted protectively next to him. "You've got to trust me, man," Cal said urgently.

"Why should I? Maybe I don't go for all your wavy-gravy medicine man shit. This is my kid – you do anything to make this worse, you won't see another day."

Cal looked at Jed kindly. "I hear you, I promise, I'm here to help."

Liza was crying inside the car, holding her belly, and her eyes widened fearfully as Cal approached her. "Keep him away from me!" she screamed, and covered herself in a blanket.

"How far along is she?" he asked Jed.

"Around four months," Jed replied huskily. "Sweetie, he says he can help, and Mom's got some kind of tea to make for you. He won't hurt you, I promise." He whispered in Cal's ear, "Will you?"

267

Cal shook his head and slowly opened the car door. "Liza, I'm not going to hurt you, I swear, but I need you to lie down. Please. Then you can have some tea after."

"Please honey, please," Jed begged. "We need to try anything to stop it."

Liza lay back tearfully on the floor of the SUV, her body shuddered with sobs, and Cal knelt carefully next to her. He waved his hands slowly above her body, then settled them above her belly. "I'm not even going to touch you, don't worry" he said, as his hands hovered above her pelvis. Liza began to relax, and her eyes closed. Cal began to hum softly, and a white light emitted between his hands and Liza's belly. Jed and Emma gasped, Cal stopped humming and whispered to them, "It's coming in, whatever happens now, is meant to be."

Liza fell asleep, and Cal continued for several more minutes, then shook his hands skyward, stood up and said, "She may be all right now. The baby is still alive, I could feel that."

Jed confided, "My Mom used to do that, take my headaches away, that sort of thing. Thank you." He shook Cal's hand and smiled at Emma.

Emma smiled back in relief. "When she wakes up, I'll give her the tea. And make sure to put these essential oils on her pulse points." She handed him two small vials.

"I will Mom," he replied warmly, and hugged her.

"I'll be back soon," she said, "I have to see how everything's going at the campsites. I'm hoping maybe Don has some information about the thing. I don't even know what to call it. The Beast – I think that works."

"Mom, do you really think we're going to be saved? It sounds totally way out to me, but of course I want it to be true, we all do."

Emma smiled wryly. "Well, the *Deus ex machina* is a great device. Maybe it exists in real life too."

Chapter Forty-Five

More Choices

Emma knelt next to Liza, who was camped inside Carol's mound house on a sleeping bag. Jed sat at the foot of the sleeping bag as Emma moved her hands slowly above Liza's belly and Carol slept. "Any better? How are the cramps?" Emma asked urgently.

Liza responded tentatively, "Better, I think. Not much bleeding now, just a few spots."

Jed and Emma relaxed noticeably.

"Liza, would you consider having Doc Spencer check you out?" Emma asked carefully. "He won't do an internal unless you say OK, we wouldn't want to stir anything up, but he's got his medical bag, he can listen to the baby, take your blood pressure, all that."

Liza looked expectantly at Jed, he nodded. "OK, I guess so. OK." She began to cry softly. "It's not like it matters anyway, right? We're all going to go soon, maybe it's better if the baby doesn't live." Jed moved to sit behind Liza, cradled her head and upper body on his lap and stroked her hair.

"I don't know about that dear, I really don't," Emma replied hopefully. "I have no idea what's coming next, I know it's hard to take Cal seriously, I mean, he's pretty weird, but I have to say, he's been on target so far."

Liza smiled slightly. "That would be awesome, wouldn't it, Pookie?" Jed nodded and hugged her.

Emma stood up and headed for the door, "I'm going for Doc, I'll be back soon." She stepped into the sunlight. It was Thursday, October 9th, a sunny morning, and the campgrounds buzzed with activity, especially up the hill near the bluff, where Carol's boys, Nate and his sons, Dave & Co., Wendell and several other men from the encampment hauled soil and rocks in buckets out of a large opening in the hill. Emma puffed up the hill and stopped Wendell. "Seen Doc Spencer?" she asked. "How's it going?"

Wendell's leathery face crinkled into a smile, "It's pretty amazing down there, these folks found an old cave, might have been some kind of mine back in the day, or a hideout, but it's deep and sturdy. We might decide to give it a try when the time comes, but we're still counting on the Rapture."

"How many can it take?" Emma asked.

"Oh, probably around 50, but it's pretty primitive. I don't figure folks will be too happy in there for very long. But it's better than nothing. Last I saw the Doc he was talking to Connie by the cooking tent."

"Thanks," Emma replied cheerily as she headed down the hill. Doctor Spencer sat on a folding lawn chair drinking coffee, and smiled as Emma approached him.

"Hello Shirley," he said warmly. "Want some coffee?"

"Thank you Doc, no, but I could use a favor."

"Sure" he said, and leaned forward with interest. "Anything to oblige."

"My son's partner Liza…"

Doctor Spencer interrupted. "A sweet little thing, but why don't they get married? I don't know what's wrong with young folks today, partners and upsy downsy sexual activities…"

Emma interrupted gently, "Yes, I know, it's a different world…Doc, can you take a look at her? She's in her second trimester and has been bleeding and cramping."

Doctor Spencer's brow furrowed, "Oh my. Well, you know that's not my specialty, but I'll do what I can, dear. Where is she?"

"Follow me, she's staying with my sister," and Emma walked slowly along with Doctor Spencer as he picked his way across the encampment.

At Carol's, Doc Spencer listened intently with his stethoscope pressed against Liza's belly and used his watch as a timer. "It's a strong little heartbeat, and if you believe in old wives and their tales, it's about 178 beats per minute. They say a slightly faster heartbeat means it's a girl." He took the stethoscope away from Liza's belly and looked at her intently. "Dear, I would need to take a look inside to see if your cervix might be dilating prematurely, which might explain your spotting and cramping. Would you be willing to have me do that?"

270

Liza looked anxiously at Jed. "Pookie, what should I do?"

Jed looked uncertainly at his mother, then to Doc Spencer. "I don't know. Can anything be done if that's what's happening?"

Doc Spencer answered slowly, "Well, I can take a few stitches in it to close it, but when she's ready to give birth they'll have to be removed. There is some pain involved, I can give you morphine for pain at this point in your pregnancy. It's up to you."

Liza answered tremulously, "We should look. We should."

Doc stood up, set his shoulders and turned to Emma. "Gloria, I need more light. I have a tool that can be used as a speculum, and you need to get water boiling for sterilization. I'll be back in a few minutes, I have to go visit the privy." He exited slowly.

Jed turned to Emma anxiously, "Mom, he doesn't even know your name, how can we expect him to know what he's doing."

Emma held Jed's hand firmly, "Honey, the doctor part of his brain is working fine, it often happens that way with older people. They remember everything from long ago, including how to do their jobs, but can't remember what they did five minutes ago." Jed relaxed slightly, and they bustled about the woodstove as they prepared for the potential procedure.

Chapter Forty-Six

Best Laid Plans

"Nukes?" Hannah exclaimed. "Somebody talk to that fool, now!" She muttered angrily as iron-jawed Three-Star General Gordon Osgood stood impassively in front of her. "We told that asshole nuking this thing is like using a peashooter on a charging rhino. It's not going to fucking work! Shit! And it's going to create massive clouds of fallout. Tell him no!"

Osgood answered evenly, "Miss, it's an order from the President."

"And I know the rules – you don't have to do it if you think it's wrong for the country," Hannah replied belligerently."

He shifted uncomfortably. "I'm not completely convinced it *is* wrong."

"Oh God. Come on! You know what he said. 'Why do we have nukes if we don't use them?' It's so fucking obvious. This moron thinks this move will make him look good to whatever followers he has left after the rest of the world fucking burns to a crisp. Don't do it, I'm begging you."

"The fallout will be above the stratosphere," Osgood replied, straightening his shoulders. "Most of it will not filter back down to Earth."

"Is that the talking point? Is that what they teach you in General school? I happen to know it will result in radioactive rain, among other things. Remember, I'm the one with the Climate Ph.D.?" Osgood was impassive. Hannah shrugged her shoulders and muttered, "Go ahead, do your thing. You don't need my permission."

"I thought you should know. We launch at 0800 on the 14th. Our plan is to knock it from its trajectory. It would behoove you to pray for this initiative to be successful."

Hannah smiled wickedly. "I look forward to it. As I'm sure, do you." Osgood turned and walked from the monitoring station as NOAA personnel watched silently. Hannah put her head in her hands as multiple alarms blared through the complex. "What, what?" she exclaimed in frustration.

Evan ran to her, shook her and shouted, "Look! Look at the monitors!"

The bunker's NOAA Monitoring Facility exploded into activity as Hannah and her colleagues breathlessly track hundreds of radar pings on their screens. "What the hell!" Hannah bellowed, as military brass conferred urgently in small groups and Evan and Stuart shouted orders to colleagues manning dozens of monitors.

"We don't know who or what they are," Stuart yelled at General Osgood, who was demanding answers. "And no, sir, I seriously doubt they're Russian or Chinese, since they can change locations by miles in *seconds*. Unless you know something I don't, none of us has that kind of technology."

"They're clustering," Evan shouted. "They're clustering around nuclear silos. All of them. Holy shit."

Hannah laughed maniacally. "Jesus Christ on a crutch, they're going to keep the asshole from launching. Whoever they are, I think I love them!"

General Osgood turned to several officers nearby, "Get as many launch facilities as you can on the horn. Get the status of their payloads. Now!" The officers scurried to their monitors and grabbed their cell phones. "Dammit. Get me the President." Hannah picked up a red phone against a wall, pushed a button and handed the phone to General Osgood.

"Osgood for Commander in Chief. Highest priority. I don't care what he's doing, get him…yes sir…good evening sir…I'm sorry sir, but this is crucial…I'm sure they won't mind waiting for you…yes, I can understand you wanting to get as much pus…companionship as you can at this juncture…I'm on 23 in NOAA headquarters. Unidentified objects are congregating around all our nuclear launch facilities…OK, *your* nuclear launch facilities…I'm working to ascertain that sir…very well, I will contact you…all right, I will contact your Chief of Staff when I have answers for you…as you were…uh…sir." General Osgood hung up the phone, cleared his throat and looked almost sheepish.

Hannah smiled at him and whispered, "I know you think he's an asshole too, sir, and it's OK." He bristled, then allowed a slight smile to curl his lips as an officer approached him breathlessly.

"Sir, General sir, as far as we can tell our missiles have been disabled…somehow. We're trying to get them back online."

"Well try harder, dammit!" Osgood shouted.

Hannah approached him carefully and said confidentially, "Sir, as I tried to explain before, along with your engineers, nuking this thing will do nothing to stop it. It's way too big for any number of nukes to have any influence on its trajectory, and it's only going to make our atmosphere more uninhabitable. I'm much more interested in whether these visitors can get us off this powder keg. Aren't you?"

He growled, "I'm interested in carrying out my orders, not hobnobbing with God knows what. Keep tracking them!" He turned on his heel and marched out of the room.

Chapter Forty-Seven

Battle Lines

At the encampment, rifts were intensifying between believers in an imminent Rapture event and frustrated atheists, humanists and skeptics who saw Cal's pronouncements as nothing more than wishful thinking. Heading the opposing factions were Wendell Bratten and Don Melnick, at serious loggerheads with each other as they tried to maintain open dialogue amid the ever-increasing clamor from their respective ideological groups. Thursday night, just days before Armageddon Eve, they gathered around a large campfire to have what Wendell called, "a powwow."

"OK, then tell me why you're helping with the underground bunker if you think we're going to be swept up into the air by Jesus," Don challenged Wendell.

"There's nothing wrong with preparing. We don't know how many will be taken, we don't know if this thing is going to knock everything and everyone out, and maybe it won't. Maybe after a time folks can come back out, rebuild, start again. I hope he takes me, but if he doesn't, we should prepare."

"That's right," Connie interjected. "We're not Jehovah's Witnesses or anything, but who knows who's going to be saved."

"This is ridiculous, I'm sorry, but it is. You're living on false hope and fairy stories," a young man blurted from the gathering crowd.

Nate Jr. stepped forward and said, "Spoke like a little woke snowflake. What the hell do you know about faith, bro'?" Don moved next to Nate Jr. and put his hand on his shoulder.

"OK," Don said. "We're not going to agree, and no one knows what's going to happen next. What we do know is this thing is coming in four days, and we need to try to shelter in place as best we can. The mound homes might actually provide some protection, depending on which way the wind is blowing, but the underground bunker would be better. The cavern is deep, and we've put in a lot of supplies. It's not going to be easy, and not all of us can get in there, so we need to have a lottery."

Outcries rose from the crowd, and people spoke on top of each other until no one could be understood. Don raised his hand high and shouted, "We can get 50 people in there tops, that's a lot of us, but 28 will have to hunker down in the mounds. Maybe it would be best if believers stayed above ground. Or, we could write our names on a piece of paper. Wendell, you could oversee that, put them in a hat, and Connie, you could draw from it."

"That's not fair!" a woman yelled from the crowd. "The older people shouldn't get in, you should take young people, women, children, and strong men."

Wendell interjected, "Right now, Doc Spencer is taking care of a pregnant woman, and every older person I know, myself included, has a lot of wisdom to bring to the table. No one is going to be excluded, right Don?" Don nodded in assent. "See, we agree. And if you've got young kids, they go with you. Let's go."

Connie brought a notebook from her car and started tearing paper into strips.

# # #

Liza lay sleepily in Carol's mound home, still drowsy from Doc Spencer's morphine shot as Carol slept in her bed. Jed whispered to Emma, "He said morphine was OK. God this is nuts. Why are we even worrying about any of this now? What's the point?"

Emma whispered back, "Well, her cervix is repaired, and she has to take it easy from now on, until, well, until whatever happens, happens. I need to step outside for a while, sorry, I have to clear my head. Stay with her." She hugged Jed and checked to see where Earl was. She spotted him talking to Wendell and Connie at the encampment, she waved to him and gestured she was going for a walk. He waved and nodded, and Emma headed for the woods. She felt her head would explode, her life was so far afield from the status quo she cherished she no longer recognized herself, and thought maybe she could commune with the ethers in the woods for some kind of clarity, some kind of sign about what was to come.

But you already got a sign Emma, remember? Why don't you trust it? The orbs. Pay attention to them.

She heard quick footsteps crackle the underbrush behind her, she turned quickly as Don sprinted toward her in the moonlight, and she waved him away. "I appreciate it man, really, but I'm not in the mood right now."

Don stopped abruptly and replied, "Nope, not this time lady, not that I wouldn't like to. I just heard from my contact at CentCom."

Emma's eyes widened, "What? What's happening?"

Don replied grimly, "They're going to try and nuke it. The morning of the impact. They're going to throw the arsenal at it."

"Could it work?"

Don shook his head. "Not likely. They're hoping it might knock it off its path, but experts I've talked to say it can't work. There isn't time to land and drill into it, so it'll probably be a bunch of toxic fireworks. They say it's going to hit in the Pacific that night, and we won't feel the brunt until the next morning. The nuke stuff complicates things."

"How?"

"Well, if your buddy's Rapture thing happens, you could be going into a shitload of radiation. And there's another thing."

"Geez, what? Elvis is coming back on a flaming Ferrari?"

Don smiled slightly. "Even at the end of the world, you make me smile, lady. No." He pulled her to him and spoke in a soft whisper. "Listen. I've got a message for Liza from CentCom."

Emma looked at Don in disbelief. "Liza? From CentCom? What? Why?"

"Her sister at NOAA's been looking for her. She's in an underground bunker in Pennsylvania and wants Liza and Jed to come there, at 1 a.m. Only military and government family members are allowed in, and they can bring the dogs. If they wait any longer it won't be safe to fly."

Emma stared openmouthed at Don. "What? Tomorrow?! Will they be safe there?"

277

Don replied calmly "A hell of a lot safer than they will be here. Listen, there's a spot for me too, General Osgood was my commanding officer. White Line's going, he sent me the message over the CB." He paused, "Another thing, they have to get married before they go."

Emma gasped. "What? Why?"

"You know the military. By the book. You're only family if you're married. Know anyone who can perform the ceremony on the QT?"

Emma thought. "Carol got ordained years ago, along with her husband Joe. She can do it. But how can they prove it?"

"Draw something up, have her put her credentials on it," Don replied impatiently. "But get going." He took a breath and swallowed. "Come with me. I'll tell them you're my wife. I miss you. There, I said it." Emma stared at him, moments passed. He looked at his feet and mumbled. "I guess you're not going to respond to my invitation."

Emma thought carefully, and answered slowly. "You've always come through for me, and I will never forget it. But no, I can't go with you. Earl needs me, and if Jed, Liza and that little baby can be safe, that's what I want."

Don pursed his lips. "Fine, OK. I understand. You've got to tell them right now, they're sending a transport jet with copters to pick up military folks in the area. I'm meeting a copter at the bottom of Post House Road at 1 a.m. sharp. And you've got to keep it quiet, lots of folks will want to jump on board, but they can't."

Emma shook her head slowly. "Boy, this is a lot. Married, then gone. Wow. So much for Mother of the Groom."

Don smiled ruefully. "I don't suppose we could have one more for the road? It might cheer you up, and it would mean a lot to me. Wouldn't you like to go out with a bang? Or several bangs, if only we had the time? I sure would. With someone who means something to me. The moonlight, the stars, like that night at Mason's Eddy."

Emma hugged him, and replied gently, "Not tonight Josephine. I've got to break the news to them. But thank you, really." She turned and hurried up the hill as Don watched her sadly. She tentatively opened the door to Carol's shelter. The room was dark, a few tiny embers glowed in the woodstove.

"Jed? Liza?" she whispered.

Jed sat up from their sleeping bag and shushed her gently. "Liza's sleeping. What?"

"Come outside with me, now" Emma urged softly.

Jed rubbed his eyes, got up slowly and whispered, "No more bad news, OK Mom?"

"No, not this time. Good news, very good news." Emma looked around carefully and gestured for Jed to join her away from the mound. She spoke softly. "Jed, you know Liza's sister is with NOAA, right?" Jed nodded, confused. "Well, she got through to Don's CB friend, and she and Liza's Mom and brother are in a deep military bunker in Pennsylvania. If anything is safe on this Earth, this would be it. Hannah's family and pets are allowed in, so she wants to send a copter for you, Liza and the dogs. Tomorrow at 1 a.m."

Jed shook his head slowly. "No...uh uh, not going to happen."

Honey, you've got to go. For Liza and the baby." She swallowed painfully and tears welled in her eyes. "And for me."

"So you're coming too?" Jed asked urgently. Emma shook her head slowly. "Then I'm not going. I'm staying with you. C'mon, Mom." Jed began to cry, and turned away from Emma. She moved to hug him, resting her head on his shoulder.

"Honey, I love you so, so much. You know that. And I have only wanted the best for you, your whole life. This is what's best, for you to be safe with Liza and your little baby." She paused. "And there's another thing..."

Jed rolled his eyes. "Geez, what?"

"Well, you're only considered family if you're married."

Jed threw his hands in the air and yelled, "What the fuck!"

"Shhh," Emma admonished. "You'll wake Liza, and this must be kept quiet. It's the rule. Carol can do it. I know this is a lot, but please, do it for me. You have to be at the bottom of Post House Road tomorrow at one in the morning. You've got to hurry and not tell anyone. Don's going too, he'll be with you, but no one else can go. Please honey."

Jed turned angrily to Emma. "I can't take much more of this crap. Everything's happening too fast, first we were going to burn up in a firestorm, then this lunatic dude says we're going to be miraculously saved by God knows what, and now we have to get married and go on a helicopter to some buttoned-up asshole military installation, away from everything and everyone that matters to me."

Emma looked fondly at Jed. "Not everyone. Not everything. You're a man now, you have a baby on the way, and this is your life now. Your life! You have a chance to live, to watch your child grow, at least a chance! I'll always be with you, as long as you can remember everything we've shared together, and I will always, always love you more than anyone or anything in my life. Please, honey."

Jed's shoulders slumped. He hugged Emma sadly and replied, "OK. OK. Just let me get my head together a little. Wait for me out here, please? I've got to talk to Liza."

Emma sat on a log outside the mound, put her elbows on her knees and her head in her hands.

Jed emerged 15 minutes later and gestured to Emma. "Mom, Carol's going to do it now, and you can be our witness. It's the only way to keep it quiet. You know how Earl is, he forgets things and might say something. This is the way to do it. Besides, Liza's recovering."

Emma looked up expectantly and shook herself out of her reverie. "Great. Let's go!" She scrambled to her feet and ran to Carol's door.

Chapter Forty-Eight

They Do

When Emma entered Carol's shelter Liza was sitting propped with pillows against the brick wall next to the woodstove, dazed and bleary-eyed from the morphine.

"So we're getting married now?" she asked confusedly. "Do I have to stand up?"

"No, honey," Emma crooned. "You just have to say I do."

"And I'm going to see Hannah?"

"Yes, tomorrow."

"And I'm not dreaming?"

"No, sweetheart."

Jed stood next to the door and bit his lip. Emma approached him gently.

"A little nervous, honey?"

"Oh, just a little," he muttered sarcastically. "Since I never thought I'd have to go through this archaic exercise."

"Oh come on," Emma said encouragingly. "You must have a little romance in your soul."

Jed replied sourly, "Not last time I looked."

"Think of it this way," Emma replied, "The baby will have your name, if you want it to. Believe me, it makes things a lot easier if you're married, legally speaking."

"Mom!" Jed exploded. "Do you understand that bullshit like law and judges and well, basically everything have no meaning now? The earth is going to freaking be on fire! I would never in a million years join the military, and now I'll be living with them! Maybe for years!"

Emma replied evenly. "Yes. And you'll be alive. And maybe, just maybe your prodigious strategic skills can be used to make things better, to make things work. And you'll have Liza, and your child, and a freaking life! Be grateful. Please."

Carol painfully maneuvered herself into a sitting position, put on her reading glasses and picked up a small leather-bound book. "If you guys are ready, I am."

"Wait!" Liza said sleepily. "Flowers. I want flowers." She looked plaintively at Emma. "Can you bring me some flowers?"

"Oh for heaven's sake," Emma whispered under her breath, then softened at Liza's childlike expression. "Of course. Every bride needs flowers. Give me a few minutes." She went outside and looked furtively around for flowers, found a hillside with goldenrod, asters and Queen Anne's lace, grabbed a handful of each and tied them together at the base with a few long grasses. She reentered the shelter.

"Voila! Flowers for the bride! And wait…" she plucked a few white asters from the bouquet and place them in Liza's hair. "Now you're ready."

Liza held the bouquet unsteadily and touched her hair. "I'm a bride," she mumbled with a lopsided smile.

Carol looked tenderly at the scene. "Jed, please join Liza, I guess on the floor."

Jed knelt next to Liza, held her hand and gulped loudly.

"Pookie, you're not going to barf, are you?" Liza asked solicitiously.

"No honey. No. I'm OK. Let's do this," he replied quietly.

Carol began. "We are gathered here to join this man and this woman in holy matrimony, an occasion filled with hopes, dreams and excitement." Carol paused. "A lot of excitement." She continued. "They are ready to spend the rest of their lives together, building new memories as partners for life." She turned to Jed and Liza.

"Do you, Jed Campbell, take Liza Lefkowitz to be your wife. To love, honor and cherish through all of life's ups and downs, from this day forward?"

Jed paused, then said quietly. "I do."

"And do you, Liza Lefkowitz, take Jed Campbell to be your husband, to love, honor and cherish though all of life's ups and downs, from this day forward?"

Liza smiled broadly and answered loudly, "I do!"

"Wonderful. By the power vested in me by the State of New York, I pronounce you husband and wife. You may kiss."

Jed and Liza looked at each other, smiled, and kissed deeply.

Emma and Carol erupted in tears, and the dogs rushed to them with concern. Jed and Liza laughed and hugged each other, and for a very brief moment, Emma experienced a moment of pure happiness.

"Thank you," she whispered to the air. "Thank you for all of it."

Jed turned to Carol and said dryly, "Well, there won't be much of a wedding night, but thank you, Aunt Carol. Really."

Carol replied warmly, "I'm so happy I could be part of it, as unorthodox as all of this is. I'm going back to sleep now." She lay down, nestled against her pillow and picked up a piece of paper from her nightstand. "Here's your Marriage Certificate Jed. Put it someplace safe." Jed nodded soberly, took the paper, folded it and put in in a zippered pocket in his backpack.

"I'm tired too, Pookie. Thank you everybody. Night night," Liza said sleepily, as she curled up in her sleeping bag, clutching her little bouquet of wildflowers.

Emma and Jed looked at each other and laughed. While Liza slept, Emma and Jed prepared for their journey to the bunker.

"Now Jed, you guys need to leave no later than midnight, and walk very slowly down the road. Wait a minute. There's gas in Earl's car, I can drive you, then I can wait with you. Is that all right? Liza shouldn't be doing any walking now anyway."

"Sure Mom" Jed said evenly. "Just try not to get too emotional, OK? I know how you are."

Liza stirred in her sleeping bag, opened her eyes and asked sleepily, "Pookie, should we bring dog food?"

"God I don't know. Hannah has dogs, I bet she has some."

"I can't believe I'll see Hannah tonight. I haven't seen her since she graduated and went to DC. This is all so weird." She turned to Emma, "Mom, I wish you were coming."

Emma replied too brightly, "Well I can't, and that's the end of it. But I'll be thinking of you. If there's some way you can get a message to me that you made it, please do."

At 12:30 they quietly crept outside, climbed carefully into Earl's car, released the brake and glided slowly down Post House Road until they were far enough away to start the engine. Don was waiting at the bottom of the hill with a shadowy figure. As they drew closer, Emma recognized her as one of the girls at the "hookup tent." She muffled a disgusted snort, stopped the car and put it in park.

"Well, here we are!" she said brightly, and shot a dirty look at Don.

"Be cool, Mom," Jed whispered in her ear. "This is the last time we're going to see each other. Focus on that."

Emma replied tearfully, "What am I going to do without you to set me straight? You're like the Emma Whisperer."

"It's on you now, Mom. You can do it."

They looked at each other lovingly and hugged. They could hear the sound of an approaching helicopter, and saw lights flashing in the sky. Don approached them.

"It's coming from the East. I'm going to signal it." He took a powerful flashlight from his backpack and flashed it into the sky. The helicopter drew nearer and landed in the road. Wind from the rotors threw dust in the air as Don approached it expertly, head down. A man in green military gear and a helmet got out of the copter and conferred with Don, then approached Liza.

"Good evening ma'am, I'm Raymond Specter, gunner First Class, and I would like to escort you to the copter. I understand you're expecting, and I'm here to help you."

"Wait!" Liza said, and turned to Emma. "Mom" she said softly, "Mom, if the baby's a girl, I'm going to call her Emma. And if it's a boy, I don't know, maybe Emmett?"

Emma hugged Liza and cried, "I'll be right there with you, I swear I will. I will always be with you, all of you." She turned to Don's girlfriend. "Well, maybe not you."

"OK," Don said crisply. "We've got to go."

"Mom!" Jed said, and bear hugged Emma. "Mom, I love you. I love you so much, and I know I never said it enough. You've been the best Mom to me, and I hope I can be as good a Dad to whoever it is in there. Oh God, this is so hard."

"I know honey. I know. But you've got to go. I'll tell everyone about this tomorrow, and all I want now is for you to be all right, to live on. Please do that, for me. I will love you forever."

Don sent Emma a salute, and shepherded Jed, his hookup girl and Liza into the copter. Emma stood alone in moonlight and watched them lift off. Jed and Liza waved tearfully from the window and disappeared into the night sky. She opened the car door and slumped into the driver's seat, looked at the stars and screamed, "Why? Why??"

Chapter Forty-Nine

Eyes on the Sky

Saturday, October 13th arrived with unwelcome visitors. Scores of flaming meteors broke away from the planetoid and began pelting Earth, harbingers of the approaching killer. Several of them plummeted into the encampment as campers screamed and ran for shelter. Wendell and several men furiously pumped well water into whatever receptacles they could find to douse the flames. The chicken coop was on fire, along with Nate Sr.'s truck, and flames dotted the pasture. Panic became the order of the day, as everyone scanned the sky anxiously for signs of the next wave. As the morning wore on, the meteors began to let up, and campers prepared for the arrival of The Beast.

A lottery had been held the previous evening around a large campfire. Nate, Nate Jr., Lynn, Bonnie, Dave Stafford, Doc Spencer, Merry Goodman and her family were picked. Carol, Emma, Earl, Wendell and Connie were not selected.

"It's OK," Emma said lightly. "Maybe my son and his family can carry on. I'm ready. I'm ready for whatever comes, and I'm glad to be spending these last moments with people I have grown to love and respect." Those selected solemnly began to gather their belongings and trudge up the hill to the bunker.

Wendell and Emma climbed into Sweet Betty and monitored the CB for any news of the upcoming nuke attack, and Wendell chuckled as he told Emma, "You know, that scalawag took Ashley with him, you know, that pretty young thing with the…you know…the…"

"Large rack?" Emma asked mischievously. "Yeah, I know. He said he could bring a plus one and pass her off as his wife, cradle robber. I fully expected him to revert to form." Wendell looked pointedly at Emma and didn't respond. They smiled at each other. "I'm sorry I couldn't tell anyone about Jed and Liza. In Don's defense, he got the message to me, and at least they have a chance to be safe."

Wendell nodded knowingly, put on headphones and dialed as he read Don's CB contact book. "I'm glad I know how to work one of these things,"

"Look for White Line Fever," Emma advised. "He can tell you the frequency for Don's Cent Com contact."

Wendell turned dials past static and urgent chatter until he found White Line's frequency. "What should I call myself? I haven't had a handle in a long time, my CB gathered dust in our basement."

"Hell, I don't know…how about Country Picker? Maybe it's taken."

"Sounds good, I'll try it. Country Picker to White Line Fever, come in White Line…PussyCat Wrangler's a friend of mine…come in White Line…"

A muted voice crackled over static. "White Line here, Picker…I don't have much time. Going underground real soon."

"Heard anything from Cent Com? About the nukes?"

"Just that they're launching tomorrow morning, 0800. The whole shebang. Seems a little dicey though, there seems to be some problems with the silos. We're going underground now, I'll tell Wrangler you said hey. Lord help us all. Take cover man, hold your people close."

"Thanks White Line, Country Picker out." Wendell looked solemnly at Emma, they sat in silence. A scream rose from the mound homes, Emma and Wendell climbed out of the tank and rushed up the hill. Bonnie and Lynn were crying, screaming and holding each other.

Carol. It's Carol. Emma felt a sharp pang in her solar plexus, and reached out to hold her mother and sister. "She's gone, she's gone!" Bonnie sobbed, and Lynn shrieked as Kayla anxiously twined around her legs.

"I should have stayed with her," Lynn wept. "Maybe I could have stopped her."

Emma hugged her sister and whispered softly, "When could we ever stop her from doing what she wanted? She wanted this, to be buried next to Joe, she told me even if we're somehow saved, she doesn't want to leave her home, or Joe. She made her choice. Wendell, would you go to the bunker and get the boys? Tell them what happened. I want to see her."

Emma gently opened the door to Carol's home, lit a candle by the doorway and slowly approached Carol's bed. Carol lay face up, arms folded across her chest. Emma touched her peaceful face, it was already cold, and she was ashen gray. "There, darling. You're free." She whispered. "You're with Dad, and Joe, and Papa Jack, you don't have to see any more suffering, or feel any more pain."

Carol's sons burst crying into the room, Bruiser leading the pack. He fell on his knees next to her, put his hand on her cheek and wept loudly. Aaron and his brothers gathered around Carol's bed.

Emma felt she was intruding, softly closed the door and stood outside. Several campers heard the news and began to gather outside Carol's door. Earl walked slowly to Emma and hugged her warmly. She burst into tears and buried her head in his chest. "I wish we were closer…I wish a lot of things. But at least I can help her rest in peace next to her husband." She turned to the assembled group. "Would some of you mind taking a break from what you're doing for a little while and help dig Carol's grave next to her husband?"

"I'll get shovels, when you can, ask the boys how they want to handle it. You know, how they want to put her to rest." Wendell ran up the hill with several campers, Emma turned tearfully to Earl.

"She was so…cold. God, she was all alone when she went."

Earl replied softly, "Because she wanted it that way. You know how private she was."

Emma nodded. The door to Carol's home opened, Aaron stepped out and said calmly, "We found a note, she said she wants us to play her and Dad's wedding songs, then put her in the ground."

# # #

As Carol, shrouded in white sheets, was lowered into the ground by several men, Carol's sons played songs from her wedding to Joe on their guitars as Bonnie and Lynn surrounded Carol's body with wild purple and white frost asters. Bonnie, Lynn and Emma turned away from the grave and held each other as the first clods of earth fell on the carefully shrouded body.

After soil was mounded on Carol's grave, the mourners slowly went back to their tasks – some continued to bring their belongings to the bunker, others sat on top of the mounds and stared at the sky, or brought supplies into the mound homes. Emma and Earl sat on the grassy top of Cal's mound home and held hands. Connie approached and yelled up, "Big barbecue tonight, any meat that hasn't been jerkified is going to be cooked up." She smiled, hands on her hips.

Emma replied, "You sure look happy for a woman looking the End of the World straight in the face."

Connie beamed, "Faith, darlin'. Keeps me on the bright side." She waved and continued to make her rounds, announcing the evening's plans.

Emma nestled next to Earl. "I feel like I can't get close enough to you," she whispered. "I wish I could climb inside you. I want to roll up in a fetal ball."

Earl kissed her forehead and whispered, "Go for it, darlin'. I love you so."

"I've got our backpacks ready in case we have to get out of Dodge in a hurry, and everything else is inside Cal's place. Where is he, anyway? Have you seen him?"

"Last I saw him was last night. After dinner he disappeared. I figure he'll be back, he's probably communing with something out there."

Shouts came from Sweet Betty, Emma ran down the hill as Wendell climbed out of the tank with Nate and Nate Jr. "What? What?" she exclaimed anxiously.

"Disks, flying disks, White Line says they're everywhere, do you see any?" Nate yelled as he ran up the hill scanning the sky.

Emma looked upward, so far no orbs, no disks. "What does Cent Com say, Wendell? Are they responding at all?"

"It's nuts," Wendell said grimly. "No one knows what to make of it."

"Did he say how big they are?"

"Yep, pretty big. A light aluminum color, lights all around the edge, really quiet, they're showing up everywhere."

"Holy shit. Holy shit," Emma whispered. "It's happening. What…what do we do?"

Wendell frowned. "Not like any Rapture I ever heard of, flying disks. Next thing they'll be saying Jesus was an alien."

Emma took Wendell's hands and stared intently into his eyes. "Maybe he was, Wendell, maybe he was. I mean, walking on water? Reviving the dead? Ascending into the heavens after rising on the third day? Sounds extraterrestrial to me. If they're coming for us, I'm going. I hope you are, too."

Wendell crossed his arms across his chest. "I'm waiting on the Lord, not bug-eyed critters in flying disks."

Night fell as the campers anxiously scanned the skies for any sign of disks or orbs, but there were only blinking stars and a sliver moon. A few meteors plummeted toward the horizon, most fizzled before they made impact. Barely anyone had the stomach for Connie's barbecue as they stood vigil.

"I'm going inside," Emma yawned to Lynn as she yanked Earl toward Cal's mound home. "Are you going to the bunker?"

Lynn replied soberly, "I want to be with you. Can I stay with you guys tonight?"

Emma hugged Lynn tearfully, "You have to ask? We'll have a little watch party."

Lynn shook her head softly. "I don't know what to think, or how to feel."

Emma nodded. "It's almost more than I can bear. Frankly, I want to fall asleep and wake up, or not, when it's all over. I don't know if I'm scared, excited, exhausted, or something I can't define."

"I get it, honey. We've all been running and working and roughing it for what seems like forever. We're burned out, and now this. It makes fried grids and auroras look like a day in the park. Go to sleep. I'll be in soon."

Chapter Fifty

They're Here

Campers gathered in groups around campfires, some slept, some lay on the ground and stared at the sky as periodic small meteors lit up the sky over distant mountains. Even the hook-up tent lost its luster as campers young and old clamored for solace and meaningful connection.

Suddenly the night sky began to brighten, and to the wonder and amazement of the encampment, a large silver disk ringed by glowing gold lights descended rapidly from seemingly out of nowhere, and hovered silently just above the ground in the open field next to what was left of the chicken coop. Screams and hollers issued from the campers as they rushed to get close to the disk, but were pushed back by its brightness and heat, and had to shield their eyes. As they gaped in wonder at the spectacle, a small opening appeared in the bottom of the craft, and two figures drifted to the ground.

To everyone's shock, Cal was first to appear, still dressed in rags, with a beatific smile on his face, followed by a beautiful blonde woman with unusual features – a very large head, enormous pale blue eyes, very fine white-blonde hair and a small, delicate body. She glowed with an unearthly light, and glided rather than walked as Cal directed her to his mound home.

They didn't speak, but seemed to commune silently, and the woman entered the mound. Emma, Earl and Lynn lay sleeping on the floor, Lynn's dog Kayla began to woof. The woman silenced her with a raised hand, and gently touched Emma's face. Emma opened her eyes slowly and gasped at the glowing countenance above her. "I'm dreaming, I'm dreaming, I'm dreaming," she muttered, and the woman smiled fondly down at her. Emma sat abruptly upright and shook her head vigorously. "I must be dreaming, come on!" She jiggled Earl, then Lynn, but they remained asleep, to her surprise, and Kayla sat and stared silently at the two women.

"Who are you?" Emma whispered loudly.

The woman answered silently, telepathically, her words entered Emma's ears as a soft, gentle female voice as she continued to smile kindly at Emma. "I am Leila. I am a Rescuer, and I am your daughter, Sky Woman. I was taken up from your womb many years ago, the night of the loud lights and noises. Remember?"

Emma sat back in shock and answered slowly. "Yes..."

"I have come for you, we have come for all of you, all who wish to come with us, but we must leave now. Your beautiful Earth is going to be badly wounded for a long time, then she will heal, and be beautiful again."

"But how? Why?" Emma blurted. "Did your people do this to us?"

Leila smiled sadly. "No. You did this to yourselves. We did amplify the sun's emissions, as cruel as it sounds, to separate those who could not survive from those who can learn how to live in a whole different way, and so many of you passed the test. We knew the object was coming, we knew it was time for Earth to begin again, and we did nothing to stop it. It is the way it has always been."

Emma stared at Leila in awe. "Always?"

The silent, beautiful voice continued, "You are but one of many generations of Earth dwellers who lived and thrived for millennia, only to start again from the beginning, time after time. But it is time for you to leave. I know you have many questions, and we will answer them for you, but we must leave now, for the object will begin to emit more and more fiery projectiles, and it will not be safe for us to navigate through so many of them. Please, gather your people, bring them to the field, and say goodbye to your dear Mother Earth. I will awaken your loved ones now. Please hurry."

Leila passed her hand over the sleeping figures and glided out of the door. Emma shook herself as if from a dream as Earl and Lynn began to stir and Emma went from sleeping bag to sleeping bag and jostled them awake. "We've got to go now!" she yelled. "They're here!"

"What?" Lynn exclaimed. "Who's here!"

"The...I don't know, them!" Emma blurted. "One of them just visited me. She said we have to go now, more meteorites are coming, we've got to get out! Earl, come on!" She and Lynn dragged half-awake, protesting Earl upright as Kayla barked. Emma laughed in spite of herself, and shook with fear and excitement.

They stumbled outside and gaped at three large disks that hovered above the open field. Cal was the Pied Piper of the encampment as he emptied the bunker of all its inhabitants and guided campers to the field. Wendell and Connie stopped and refused to go further, but Leila approached them and began to speak, but this time, her voice was heard by everyone present.

"Even though in your book your Jesus says it is a wicked and adulterous generation that demands a sign, I will give you one. You need to come with us, for your Rapture is here." She glided to the cemetery and stood in the middle of the graves. She raised her arms, her glow increased, and dozens of shimmering bodies appeared, the dead resurrected, as they slowly began to take more solid form.

Carol, Joe and Richard stood, transfigured. Emma began to run to them, but Leila held up her hand. "You must not disturb them, for they are going to the Creator. You will join them when your time comes. No soul will remain here on Earth – all will be redeemed and sent to their Creator. Now, dear believers, come with us, because you see, Jesus was indeed, one of us."

Wendell and Connie followed Leila as if in a trance, and the entire encampment stood expectantly, laden with their belongings, eyes averted from the brilliant light, underneath the glowing disks. As if on cue, the disks rose slightly in the air, and large openings appeared in their undersides. Brilliant, searing white light covered the campers, and one by one they rose into the air. Emma realized with a gasp that her dream, her dream of bodies rising into intense, hot white light was now a reality. She rose, blinded by the light, seared within and without, and as she struggled against a force so much stronger than herself, struggled to reach for Earl, Bonnie, Lynn, and all her beloved friends, she began to relax and flow into the light. She knew that now, and in a world and reality none of them had ever known before, they would be together.

Chapter Fifty-One

The End, and the Beginning

Emma, Earl, Bonnie, Lynn, Connie and Leila stood in front of a massive window in a Mother Ship the size of a small city. Leila told them that the silver disks, filled with refugees from across the globe, had emptied their inhabitants into scores of Mother Ships circling the Earth. The Rescuers wanted their new charges to see the impact on their beloved planet. Closure, they said, was important in moving forward.

Emma stood with her loved ones and watched tearfully as the planetoid struck the Earth's surface, and the shock of the impact caused even the enormous ship to shudder. Screams and cries echoed against the walls of the Mother Ship as fire ripped across Earth's landscape, along with shock waves that rippled with supersonic speed from country to country. Leila held Emma's hand comfortingly.

"Your lives will go on. We are going to a very special place, a planet very much like Earth, but much more, shall we say, civilized? We have had much more time to learn how to live together in peace, and we hope we can teach you and your future generations how to do the same. One day, your seed will return to Earth, and maybe this time, it truly will be a Paradise."

"From your lips to God's ear," Emma replied grimly as she watched Earth burn.

"Yes" Leila answered softly. "Yes. And we have something for you, to make your transition easier." Leila gestured to an opening doorway as Jed and Liza entered the room.

Emma screamed and ran to Jed. They hugged and cried and exclaimed jubilantly as Earl and Liza joined them. "Come," Emma said urgently as she wiped her tears. "Come to the window. Look at her. She's on fire."

They stood, arms around each other, and watched soberly as light from Earth's conflagration played on their faces. Leila glided next to Emma.

Emma looked around her, at all the shocked, sad faces, and spoke softly. "We're together. For whatever comes next. I'm grateful, for all of it. And I love you all so much."

The Mother Ship slowly pulled away, until all Emma and her family could see ahead was a dark night full of bright stars.

The End

Art by Jeannine McLaughlin

Epilogue

On the Air

(The following is an actual transcript of a radio show the author appeared on shortly after her sighting.)

Renfrew Show Transcript

Announcer: The views and opinions expressed by the guests, callers and host of this and all Renfrew network radio programs do not necessarily reflect or agree with those of the network, its commercial sponsors, its radio station affiliates, or Internet broadcast platforms.

In these controversial times, we believe The First Amendment and freedom of the press are absolutely essential to the survival of our nation. Thank you. And now, enjoy the program.

(Urgent, otherworldly SFX)

Jeff: Hi, here we are, and we are on the doorstep of another weekend, the middle of the month of July, already half gone folks, half gone! Amazing. August just around the corner, hope you have a good weekend, wherever you are, and hopefully you're not being inundated with flood waters or roasted to death, broiled as it were in West Texas and some of the plains states, its...uh...it's extreme. Glad to have you along this evening, we have three fascinating hours for you, we'll start our things off tonight with Peter Davenport, our friend and colleague of so many years.

We have many things going on the skies above this country, and other countries, but especially the Northern Hemisphere and North America. The reports are really remarkable, it's almost as if we have entered some kind of a new 'stage' of visitation. There are obviously more than one or two intelligent groups of intelligent life forms visiting this planet. This may represent a third or a fourth or a twentieth, for all that matters. It's most commonly represented by what they call 'orange fireballs' or 'fireballs.' These are strange things, and they are clearly under some kind of intelligent control. What that is is anybody's guess. Hello Peter, welcome back.

Peter: Good Evening Jeff, thank you, it's always nice to be back, and thank you very much for making time available on this very important subject, and making it available on such short notice, I really appreciate it. I've been trying to call this...as you know...I've been trying to call this phenomenon to the attention of the American people for now about a year.

Jeff: Yeah...yeah...

Peter: We've done several programs on this.

Jeff: Yep.

Peter: ...And I'm having a hard time gaining traction anywhere but on the Jeff Renfrew radio program, so I am indebted to you and particularly grateful for your willingness to make some airtime available so we can bring this information to a large group of people.

Jeff: Well it's my honor and pleasure, and I want to say one thing. You mentioned gaining traction. I honestly don't think it matters much anymore what radio program or show you're on, I don't think that the...I just don't think that the issue is tractionable with an awful lot of people now, for some reason. They just kind of yawn and look the other way. This is an enormously important question. We are being visited by intelligent life, that's obvious, probably for as long as the current regime of the sentient species called Human Beings has been around, and maybe prior incarnations of that too. But, yeah, this is a weird thing, and it's new, so let's proceed. We have at least one special guest, and if you would, we have e. k. on the line, and go right ahead.

Peter: We'll have to change the schedule a little bit. I'm particularly indebted to our first guest, e. k., with whom I spoke for the first time just an hour ago Jeff, and she very considerately consented to come on the program, and when I was unable to get our first guest on his telephone at about 6:15 tonight, she consented to a second stipulation that she come on in the first half of the hour, so we start indebted to this woman in New Jersey tonight...let's set it up here for e. k. Just last night I got a very, very interesting report from an anonymous source about a sighting just two nights ago, so this is very fresh information.

Jeff: Uh..hmmm...

Peter: Two nights ago in Watkins Glen, a woman was driving back to New Jersey from Upstate New York and saw a very, very unusual object. And since I have not been really privy to this report for very long, what I would like to do is just allow her to tell her own story and describe just what it was she saw just about twenty...forty-eight hours ago in Watkins Glen, New York. Why don't we go right to her?

e. k.: (nervously) OK....is it my cue?

Peter: (laughs) Your cue.

e. k.: All right. Good evening gentlemen. All right, I'll just start my story, and you stop me anytime you have a question or if I'm running on too long, but...um...I was traveling from Watkins Glen, New York, I was actually on my way to Virgil, New York, not quite New Jersey yet, at about 9:40 p.m. on Wednesday evening, July 13th, and..uh..when I arrived at the intersection of Routes 91 and 224, 91goes straight and 224 curves to the right, I saw a large, unusually bright, low-lying yellow light in the sky. Um...since I had no frame of reference for what it might be, it caught my attention, so I went straight ahead on 224 to find a good vantage point. I stopped my car and looked at the object.

It was round, totally still and glowed a yellowish white. It was hovering about, I'd say, three telephone lengths above the ground and must have been at least 10 feet in diameter, maybe more. It looked like the ball that drops in Times Square on New Year's Eve, it seemed faceted. So I watched it, just hovering there, for at least a minute, it was completely motionless, then it started to move, slowly to the right toward Route 79, and as it moved, it pulsated, and as it accelerated, it pulsated faster, it was still this golden color. And at this point, needless to say, I was extremely excited. I jumped in my car, I called my son. His phone was off, so I called my sister and yelled "UFO! UFO!" And general bedlam ensued after that as I drove on Route 91 and tried to track the object, my phone kept going in and out of service, my sister and son were frantically calling me over and over as they jumped into a van with two of my nephews and raced off to find me.

The object ascended very smoothly and swiftly into the sky, it was amazing how quickly it got very, very high, and to my complete surprise it met up with three objects that looked pretty much the same. They were slightly different colors at times, it's almost like they were changing colors from amber to red to white...um...they looked like twinkling stars, they were that far up, but they were moving in these strange patterns, and then three more joined them up high, and I stopped my car again, because I couldn't believe what I was seeing, to watch them, and I saw another low moving, low round object on the horizon, it was at about the same height the other one was before, but it was farther away from me, on the left. It started moving toward me, then it ascended very quickly to meet the others, and I jumped back in my car, because they were moving quite far away at that point and I was startled to not see them. And I continued to follow them, so excited I almost hit a deer, and then up ahead I saw someone screeching out of their driveway in their car, and then they moved back in again, and I thought 'Huh, I wonder if they're seeing the same thing I'm seeing.'

By that time I met up with my sister, my son, and my nephews in Ithaca, I had finally gotten that far. We scanned the skies, we couldn't see them anymore, just the regular flight patterns of planes, and uh...that's it. That's what I saw.

Peter and Jeff: Wow.

Peter: When I spoke with you just a little bit ago, e. k., I knew immediately that you were going to be an excellent guest on this program.

e. k.: (flattered) Thank you.

Peter: You're very well spoken, you described very, very clearly so others can understand what it was you saw. You've done a marvelous job, really, and I'm terribly grateful to you. This is…it sounds to me as though you may have seen some of these objects that Jeff and I have been talking about for probably a year now.

e. k.: (incredulous) Really. Wow.

Peter: And you've described them extremely well. When you saw the first object, you described it as large, but if you were to have put it right next to a full moon, I think the moon a few nights ago was almost full, how big would the object have been?

e. k.: Oh, I see, uh huh…I remember the moon that night. I'd say that this object was about a fifth of the size of the moon, it was quite large.

Peter: The question we always struggle with, e. k., Jeff and I have talked about this many, many times, is whether the object could have been, in your opinion, could have been some kind of pyrotechnic that had been released at a celebration, a so-called Chinese lantern. Is that a possibility at all?

e. k.: No. Not at all. No.

Peter: Why would you say that?

e. k.: It was too…it was controlled. It had a purpose. It wasn't just floating around. It was like something inside it was moving it or it was being directed by something else. It had an intelligence to it.

Jeff: (urgently) Peter, can you hear me now?

Peter: Yes, I can.

Jeff: We had a massive power failure at my end, and we tried a couple of different lines. I was able to hear. Hello, e. k.

e. k.: Hi.

Jeff: I was able to hear most of e. k.'s absolutely exquisite description of...I've never heard a smoother description and a more intelligent, articulate description of something that is mind-boggling than I've just heard from e. k.

Peter: Yep.

e. k.: Well, thank you.

Jeff: So I want to commend you for that, e. k. May I ask just generally, what kind of work do you do? You're so articulate, we don't run across that kind of...that level of explanation.

e. k.: Actually, I'm a writer. I was a copywriter and journalist, and now I'm a script writer.

Jeff: OK, very good. Now, if I could go back, not many journalists around, Peter, they stick out like a sore thumb when you run into them...

Peter: You can spot 'em from a mile away, can't you? (Peter and e. k. laugh)

Jeff: e. k., when you first saw the object, and this is where I came back in after the power went out, it was about three telephone poles in height, you said.

e. k.: It was about three telephone poles in length above the ground.

Jeff: OK. Where were you standing, or where were you when you first acquired view of this object?

e. k.: I was heading down the road toward this intersection, and it was just past the intersection in the sky, I'd say...oh gosh...no more than one hundred yards past the intersection.

Jeff: OK. And what time of day was it? Was it day or evening?

e. k.: It was 9:40 at night.

Jeff: All right. So it's dark.

e. k.: Mhmm.

Jeff: So, this object. If you were to hold something in your hand while you're in the car the first time you saw the object, what would it be? A penny, a nickel, a quarter, an egg, an orange, a grapefruit, what would it be?

e. k.: Umm...

Jeff: At arms' distance.

e. k.: OK, I would say it would be...I don't know if it would be an egg, it would definitely be bigger than a quarter and smaller than an egg, like a...what would that be...

Peter: A silver dollar?

e. k.: (after a pause) Yes. Maybe a little bigger than that.

Peter: Held at arms' length, that's bigger than a full moon of course.

e. k.: Well, the moon was huge that night, it wasn't bigger than the moon, the moon was really big that night.

Jeff: Hmm. So, you saw the object, would you describe the luminescence of it as uniform, was it flickering at all, was there any texture in the light?

e. k.: Yes. There was texture in the light, it wasn't like a light bulb. It had different gradations, it almost seemed faceted, and almost seemed like there were bits of it that flared, almost like it was burning.

Jeff: Was it giving off any kind of sparks, or glow, a projected glow off its radius?

e. k.: Yes, it almost seemed like the sun, you know, where the sun would have these little flares, and things? It sort of had some flare to it.

Jeff: Wow. Wow. That would probably fall into the category of fireball to some people, when you don't get a perfectly defined edge on something and it does emit light or an irregular luminescence, people do tend to describe that as a fireball, so that's very interesting.

e. k.: But when it moved, it pulsated, when it moved these flares would pulsate and when it moved faster they would pulsate faster, it almost seemed like it was prismatic and faceted in some way. I don't know if that was the propulsion, I don't know, I was just trying to figure it out. I was looking at...what is this thing?

Jeff: I'm amazed at your determination to track it, obviously without any overt fear, obviously this tremendous burning journalist's desire to find out the truth.

e. k.: (brightly) That's me. Gotta find out what's at the bottom of things, that's my thing.

Jeff: Good job.

e. k.: (laughs) Thank you.

Peter: Can you liken the color, e. k., to anything that people are familiar with? You mentioned that it was...uh...a yellowish, can you compare it to anything that people are familiar with?

e. k.: Umm...boy that's a tough one...almost as if you make a fire, you know, a wood fire, and that yellow kind of glow in the middle of it, not the orange, when it's not so hot, or the orange part's the hot part, I can't remember, but you know, like a yellow, glowing fire, that's what it was like. That kind of color.

Jeff: You also said, e. k., that it was clearly under intelligent operation of some kind...

e. k.: It seemed to me to be, I mean, it hovered, it was completely still, and then it started to move very slowly, and then it just very smoothly accelerated and it pulsated more and more as it accelerated.

Jeff: The concept of something doing that and then rendezvousing with other objects is obviously intelligent.

e. k.: I know! And when I watched them higher up I noticed occasionally a couple of them seemed more amber and when they moved rapidly they set off kind of like a flare, almost like an orange tail, like a fume almost, it was very, very strange.

Peter: mhmm, mhmm...Have you ever seen a UFO before, e. k.?

e. k.: I have to admit, I did see one in the 80's on the Northern Parkway on Long Island, and it was completely different. And I was sure when I got home from that ride that it would be all over the news, and there was nothing. I couldn't believe it.

Jeff: Yeah, that's so frustrating, especially for someone with a background like yours...

e. k.: It was enormous, it must have been the size of a football field. It was huge.

Jeff: There you go. Well, if you haven't figured it out by now, in the UK they call it a D Notice, that means you don't cover certain stories, the government decides what the media can cover.

e. k.: Really?

Jeff: Over here we don't have D Notice but we have a de facto understanding on the basis of editors in all the basic media that the issues are just not covered. There might be a story that sneaks in, but there's no follow-up, and as we know from the O'Hare airport sighting, a broad daylight disc hovering over one of the actual boarding terminals at O'Hare...

e. k.: Really? When was that?

Jeff: Well, nothing was done about it until Peter Davenport raised Cain with the Chicago press, and finally somebody there, a transportation writer, took it on.

e. k.: Wow.

Peter: After I had to, I had to force him to look into it. You asked when that was, e. k., it was Election Night in 2006, the first Tuesday of November 2006. Jeff, the first broad coverage of this occurred on this program, Jeff and I did a program and broke the news, and the Chicago Tribune for six weeks refused to cover it, finally they did, and they forgot to mention who had broken the story initially. That was Jeff Renfrew together with me, on his program.

Jeff: You know, it's interesting, e. k., that Peter mentions that, because you've heard certainly of the Phoenix lights…

e. k.: Yes, I have heard of that.

Jeff: Yeah, the same thing happened there, the case was ignored Peter, for how many months before they finally decided to cover it in the media? Three months?

Peter: Just over 10 weeks Jeff. It occurred on the 15th of March as you well know, and the first national article appeared on Wednesday, the 18th of June, 1997.

e. k.: Well you mentioned that these fireballs have been seen in many different places over the past two years, is that what you told me?

Peter: Just one year.

e. k.: One year? OK.

Peter: It started about the 18th of June, 2015, just over a year ago. Jeff and I have been talking about this phenomenon ever since. He's been kind enough to make radio time and airtime available so his listeners can know what's really going on as opposed to what the government apparently wants us to know or not know is going on. It's a very strange phenomenon, but when we find a witness like you, e. k., who's so eloquent, so willing to come forward, so willing to come on a radio program, it's like stumbling upon a 10-ounce gold nugget.

e. k.: Oh, I'm so glad I could be of help, I just hope that you guys can figure out what this is. Could it possibly be a military operation?

Jeff: Highly unlikely, I would say.

Peter: I'd invite e. k. to, at her convenience, to go to our website, ufocenter.com, and look at the hundreds and hundreds of reports of red, orange, yellow, amber and gold fireballs that have been reported to our center over the last roughly 13 months. It's astonishing that it's not getting coverage.

e. k.: I'm wondering if it might be some kind of government thing, some new technology like a probe?

Jeff: I don't think so. This phenomenon is so sophisticated and has more than we can count in terms of configurations, forms, habits, profiles, sightings, it's all over the map, it's not one or two things seen over and over again, this is an incredible phenomenon over the years. What you saw earlier in your life, the large object is a perfect case in point there. We have to pause for just a minute, e. k., could you wait around for us to come right back, I have a few more questions for you.

e. k.: Oh, OK.

Jeff: Stand by, Peter and I will be right back after this.

(Urgent otherworldly music)

Jeff: OK, we're back, and I hope my phone line is holding up. We had a couple of lightning strikes. Do you hear me all right e. k.?

e. k.: Yes, I hear you fine.

Jeff: Well good, Peter, I'm sure you can hear me if e. k. can, so...

Peter: Yep, you sound fine Jeff.

Jeff: The question I have, a couple of them please, the issue of the objects accelerating upward quickly is very common, but what I'm really interested in is they got to a height where they took on the appearance to you, the general appearance of stars, even though they were probably moving in anomalous directions.

e. k.: Yes.

Jeff: They still looked like stars.

e. k.: Yes.

Jeff: And many people who watch the night sky report stars moving, in not just a single trajectory, east/west, west/east, whatever it might be, a typical satellite trajectory or something. They move all over the sky, if you watch for them. I assume that from now on when you look up, you will look at these star-like objects, perhaps a little differently, in some cases.

e. k.: Oh, absolutely.

Peter: How many did you see at one time, e. k.? What was the largest number you saw?

e. k.: Eight. I saw eight.

Peter: Eight. Were they all the same color? And were they maneuvering relative to one another, or were they in a fixed, unwavering configuration?

e. k.: They were moving very oddly, um...it didn't seem to have much structure to it. It wasn't like they were in a formation of any kind, they did seem to be sort of, this is going to sound strange, but it almost looked like they were playing, like they were almost, like doing a star dance or something, I mean they were just kind of wandering around in the sky, it was almost as if they were chatting. It was the strangest thing to watch. There was this kind of orange flare that came off of one, some of them were more amber colored, some were gold, and some were almost white. It was really, the strangest thing I've ever seen.

Jeff: With respect to the others that you were talking to who were obviously involved with this, how many total are you aware of who saw these objects that night?

e. k.: My sister, my son and my two nephews. They were in a van behind me by about, oh I don't know, 20 minutes or so because they had to get themselves together and get out on the road.

Jeff: Since that event, what has the tenor of the conversations been between you all? What did you come up with as a group?

e. k.: Well, the first thing that happened was that my sister started researching UFOs and found that a lot of these round glowing objects have been seen, and she sent me a lot of links to it. She seemed very very, she's very interested in it, and her son as well, my nephew was very interested, and we've been talking online about it, but I have to admit, I wanted to mention it on Facebook but I thought, Oh, I wonder if anyone's going to believe me, you know, it's such a, it sounds so crazy, but it happened.

Jeff: Well, first of all, you contacted the right man, Peter, and the National UFO Reporting Center. But secondly, I think ultimately we need to kind of suspend the idea of gee, do we really worry, or do we not worry about what people think? You know, just report what you saw, that's it. They can take it or leave it. You can put that caveat in there, this is what I saw, take it or leave it. But I think getting these reports out there in any fashion is very important to do, and what you've done tonight, coming on here and sharing this with us, has not only brought an excellent description of an eyewitness encounter of something that is obviously not normal, but you've encouraged other people to do it as well. To that end you are also to be commended, and we thank you very, very much for that.

e. k.: Well, thank you. It was my pleasure.

Peter: And for the benefit of our listeners tonight, Jeff and e. k., I'd like to point out that what you described, e. k. is one of hundreds, perhaps by now thousands, of similar reports that are posted to our website, the National UFO Reporting Center website, ufocenter.com. And if people want to see what's really going on, thanks to Jeff Renfrew, and allowing us to bring this subject to the public forum, I invite people to go to our website and just start scrolling down through the many, many similar reports that we have received over the, actually, it's been over the last month, but it goes back to June of 2015.

Jeff: It's a treasury of information, and e. k., thank you very much, I guess my last quick question…

e. k.: Sure.

Jeff: Do you want to see it again?

e. k.: (chuckles) Well, yeah, I do, but I'm just a little concerned about what or who they might be, you know, what's their purpose for being here.

Jeff: I think the logical deduction to make in lieu of what you've described here, is if these, whatever they are, had hostile intentions, I think you would have known it.

e. k.: You think? They're not just gathering data for some further...

Jeff: Who knows? Maybe one of those was some kind of intelligent individuated being in and of itself. Maybe these kinds of beings are life forms. No one knows, I think the door is open.

e. k.: That's true. Right. Absolutely. You're right, you're right.

Peter: With regard to the government question, e. k., you posed that rhetorically earlier on, could it be a government project. That's an explanation that people frequently default to because if it's not from this planet then it has to be the government, but I don't think it is. If the government had a very, very sophisticated program like this, they would probably not be testing it over Watkins Glen.

e. k.: (chuckles) True.

Peter: Jeff and I are going to be, later on, talking about a sighting that occurred in Flint, Michigan on the evening of the fourth of July. A gentleman had a sighting very similar to yours except the object was red, it was a disk, a distinct disk-shaped object with very sharp edges to it, and it drifted towards him slowly, hovered over him for about five minutes and suddenly accelerated like a marble coming out of a slingshot. I don't think these are government sponsored programs, and even if they were, they wouldn't be tested over our heads, I don't think.

Jeff: I totally, totally concur – e. k., thank you so much for staying up and sharing, your, so well-described experience.

e. k.: Thank you, it was my pleasure. Have a good evening.

Peter: Boy, I wish all our guests were like that, Jeff.

Jeff: Yeah, but that's not to take away from anyone's ability to describe what they saw. When people are describing the indescribable, it becomes a matter of emotion, intellect, and all kinds of factors. People are in shock, and so we're more than grateful for anyone from any walk of life to contact Peter and file a report and maybe even come on the program. It just so happens that once in a while we get a professional journalist to describe something. You hear that immediately, and it's just so unusual, we don't get that very often.

Peter: Yep.

# # #

www.ingramcontent.com/pod-product-compliance
Lightning Source LLC
Chambersburg PA
CBHW072104020726
47501CB00003B/701